When the Universe Called

*To Don
I hope you enjoy this story. Looking forward to reading your story one day! Maggie D.*

Maggie Denhearn

Copyright © 2015 Maggie Denhearn.

All rights reserved. No part of this book may be used or reproduced by any means, graphic, electronic, or mechanical, including photocopying, recording, taping or by any information storage retrieval system without the written permission of the author except in the case of brief quotations embodied in critical articles and reviews.

Balboa Press books may be ordered through booksellers or by contacting:

Balboa Press
A Division of Hay House
1663 Liberty Drive
Bloomington, IN 47403
www.balboapress.com
1 (877) 407-4847

Because of the dynamic nature of the Internet, any web addresses or links contained in this book may have changed since publication and may no longer be valid. The views expressed in this work are solely those of the author and do not necessarily reflect the views of the publisher, and the publisher hereby disclaims any responsibility for them.

The author of this book does not dispense medical advice or prescribe the use of any technique as a form of treatment for physical, emotional, or medical problems without the advice of a physician, either directly or indirectly. The intent of the author is only to offer information of a general nature to help you in your quest for emotional and spiritual well-being. In the event you use any of the information in this book for yourself, which is your constitutional right, the author and the publisher assume no responsibility for your actions.

Any people depicted in stock imagery provided by Thinkstock are models, and such images are being used for illustrative purposes only.
Certain stock imagery © Thinkstock.

Print information available on the last page.

ISBN: 978-1-5043-3971-1 (sc)
ISBN: 978-1-5043-3973-5 (hc)
ISBN: 978-1-5043-3972-8 (e)

Library of Congress Control Number: 2015913984

Balboa Press rev. date: 10/28/2015

In loving memory of Dondi.

"Without asking, you will receive no answer"
—Esther and Jerry Hicks

ACKNOWLEDGEMENTS

While *When the Universe Called* is a work of fiction, I would like to acknowledge the inspiration I drew from various writers:

Esther and Jerry Hicks — *The Law of Attraction*

Pam Grout — *E^2 Squared*

Bruce Lipton — *The Biology of Belief*

I would also like to thank everyone at Balboa Press for their kindness in helping me navigate my first tentative steps into the world of publishing. And most deeply I would like to thank:

- All my dear friends, near and far, old and new, for all your help and support. If you thought I was crazy starting this book, you were kind enough not to say so. Melanie, Barry, Sharon, Jan, and Arthur for reading the whole or excerpts of my first draft and for helping me on my way, and Dave for helping me choose a title. A special thank you to Carol for all the time you spent giving me detailed feedback on *all* my drafts. Your comments and enthusiasm were invaluable.

- Phyllis, for opening my mind to a whole new way of seeing the world.

- My local writers' group, WIP Qualicum, for helping me get this far, for the fun and support of the writing retreats, and the inspiration of seasoned writers.

- My local running group the WoBs, for teaching me Canadian English, and for keeping my feet on the ground (and sometimes other parts of me too).

- My family, as always, who have kept me well fed and motivated and believed in me.
- And my little dog, Wilbur, for reminding me that the most important moment is right now and that sometimes chasing a butterfly is the most important thing to do.

PROLOGUE

MONDAY NIGHT, AUGUST 5, 1963

Anja saw Frost's gun pointing directly at her, a cigarette dangling casually between the index and middle fingers of his free hand. She had always wondered why he smoked with his left hand, when he was right-handed. Now she knew why. She averted her eyes, focusing all her attention instead on her bright red shoes—the softness of the ribbons, the comfort of the leather. The first time she wore them, their sparkles caught in the rays of sunlight as she moved, making her want to dance along the street. She wasn't dancing now. And the pale moonlight wasn't catching the sparkles. Her soft brown hair had fallen forward, brushing her flushed cheek, like his hand used to do, a tender gesture now a distant memory as she heard him cock the trigger. They were down a dingy back alley behind one of the jazz clubs where he used to hold her in his arms as they swayed to the music, lost in a lovers' embrace. The night was humid, and the smell of car grease and rotting trash made her want to retch, but she daren't move. The tension in her body was starting to hurt as she tried to remain perfectly still. The distant lament of a saxophone drifted along the cool night air. She could smell his cigarettes—Gauloises. She knew the minute she looked up it would all be over for her. Images of the intimate moments they had shared flashed through her mind as though she were watching a movie in fast-forward, touch by touch, all points leading here. Anja knew her life was about to be extinguished, and she didn't feel ready. It was pointless begging for her life; she knew too much, had found out who Frost truly was. And somehow he had discovered her betrayal.

xi

She took one last look at her shoes, took a deep breath, and slowly raised her limpid green eyes. She stared defiantly at him and down the barrel of his gun. Tears were streaming down Frost's face. She had never seen him cry before. His face looked crumpled, older. He took a long drag on his cigarette; a haze of smoke blurred his face as he exhaled.

"I loved you," he whispered and pulled the trigger.

CHAPTER 1

Early Monday evening, April 14, 2014

It was in the way she made him a cup of tea that Maria suddenly realized that her husband, Luke, and Charlotte were having an affair. It wasn't anything tangible that she could put her finger on or that would make sense if she tried to explain it to anyone else. He and Charlotte were work colleagues, so it was conceivable she would know how Luke took his tea. But it wasn't that. It was something in her manner, the familiarity with which she went about a task so mundane that most of us would barely notice the ritual. Yet Maria did. It was her job as director of communications for Mayor Andy McDowell to notice human behavior, the minute details that would give him the edge over his opponents. The slightest flicker in the eye or change of expression could reveal a lie or a weakness. She could read people. And it was something in Charlotte's coy smile and the way, with her head slightly tilted downward, she glanced up at Luke, her face ever so lightly flushed, that gave them away. Luke in turn smiled with his eyes as he took the cup from her with the same look of affection that he used to give Maria, but which she hadn't experienced for a good while now. Like a memory resurfacing from long ago, that look reminded her of how long that affection had been missing between her and her husband.

At that moment it all became crystal clear to Maria. The late night phone calls, the going out at all times of the evening—it could only mean one thing. Luke had been behaving oddly for months. How had this not occurred to her before now? Maria had stopped asking him where he was going and what he was up to. Inquiring inevitably led to conflict neither of them were any good at navigating. She had assumed he was preoccupied with work and had been too caught up in her own to give it further consideration. He had never been forthcoming about his job, so the fact he hadn't been confiding in her about it when something was up did not seem any different than usual. The evidence before her of having completely misjudged the situation was now irrefutable. The realization that he had been cheating on her came like a swift blow to her stomach, and she had to stop herself from bending forward and gasping. Numbness overtook her, her whole body losing sensation. She nearly dropped her cup of tea, no longer able to feel it in her fingers. Very slowly placing the cup on the countertop, she used both hands to steady herself on the kitchen sideboard. The sudden rage she felt was a paralyzing force. In her mind she was shouting and screaming at them both, hurling the tea across the room and sending a wind of fury whirling around the kitchen. But she was unable to move.

Maria began to scan her memory for other signs in their marital life that were more profound, more indicative of infidelity, but she could honestly say, at least at the level of her conscious mind, that she had not until that moment even conceived of the idea that Luke might be unfaithful. Indeed, if someone had asked her about anything that might possibly jeopardize their relationship, she had always thought that an affair would be the least likely for either of them. Yet how could she have been so blind? She had been so convinced that it was just worries at work that were causing him to be distant that she'd not stopped to entertain other possibilities. Now she reflected, his edginess seemed to have started around the same time the car started appearing. Always parked in the shadows a little way down the street, it was black or dark blue, one of those cars designed to be inconspicuous. The windows were tinted, so it was impossible to see who was in it. She wasn't quite sure what had prompted her to notice it, but it would appear at the most peculiar times. It didn't belong to a neighbor. She'd checked. Maria had taken to surreptitiously looking out of the bedroom window every now and then when she was home to see if it was there. She'd mentioned it to Luke one time, but he had dismissed her concerns about their being watched, had told her she was being paranoid. Had Charlotte been spying on them? Was she stalking him? Maria had never actually seen Luke get into the car. It wasn't

When the Universe Called

for want of peering out of the window when he went out on some pretext or other. It had to be her. Maria felt queasy and like a complete and utter fool. She, who prided herself on her ability to evaluate other people, could not even read her own husband. The jarring sound of a metal spoon dropping onto the stone kitchen floor jolted her out of her thoughts, and she glanced quickly at Luke and Charlotte. No tender looks were being exchanged, no furtive smiles, and yet, there it was, an unmistakable connection. It was as though they had a neon sign above their heads flashing *We're Having Sex.*

Luke glanced across at her. "Are you okay, Maria? You look really flushed." He bent down, picked up the errant spoon, and put it into the sink. Maria noticed how his hand shook as he did so.

"No. Yes, I'm fine. I er … I … er … just … I just remembered I've forgotten to do something. I'd better write myself a note so I don't forget again." She couldn't look him in the eye, look either of them in the eye. She felt her cheeks burning even though she suddenly felt cold and shivery. She busied herself with finding her phone and made a big deal of seeming to write herself a note. It was hard to stop her hands from shaking, and there was no feeling in her fingers as she tried to type. All she could think was, *He mustn't know I've found out. He mustn't know I've found out.* She wasn't sure why. She wasn't in control. She wanted Charlotte out of her house, away from her husband, but her intuition was telling her to hold off, to wait before confronting him, either of them. Her friend Brina was always telling her to trust her intuition.

She should talk to Brina. That was it. Brina would know what to do. Oh Lord, what if she already knew? What if her running group, the WOECs all knew? The embarrassment! A wave of mortification spread over her. Luke glanced over at her then carried on talking with Charlotte as they moved into the living room.

Maria lingered on in the kitchen, trying to look as though she was busy with something, anything. Placing the palm of her hand on her chest, she felt her heart pounding. Sensation was returning to her body in patches in a way that made her feel like her body didn't quite belong to her. Usually the ever-changing scene from her kitchen window would soothe her, but today it provided little comfort. Breathing deeply, she looked out at the ocean, only twenty meters away. The wind was whipping up the water, the

Maggie Denhearn

whitecaps hurling themselves onto the shoreline. Leaden sky merged with slate water so that it was impossible to see the horizon. Beyond the ocean line, the imposing range of coastal mountains was invisible, hiding behind a somber shroud, the desolation of an impending April storm desperate yet unable to break. She caught sight of an eagle swooping down to the dark ocean, plucking out a poor, defenseless gull that had been floating, trying to find its supper among the fish. She saw the gull struggle in the eagle's talons and could hear the distant screeching, to which the eagle seemed ambivalent as it soared up into the gray evening sky. How quickly life as you knew it could be over.

She walked over to the mirror above the kitchen dresser, strategically placed to reflect the light from the window back into the room, an optical illusion to make the kitchen seem bigger. She stared at her reflection; a middle-aged woman stared back. Maria almost didn't recognize herself. Her cheeks were crimson, and a single tear had escaped her right eye, slightly smudging her mascara. She had a startled look in her eyes that she'd never seen before. Every day she got closer to looking like her mother. One of her greatest fears was the invisibility that would inevitably come with age. And now she felt invisible to Luke. She had woken up to a nightmare. Only now that her life with Luke was in danger did she realize how much she had been missing him and how good they had once been together.

A painful thought flashed through Maria's brain. Had she made this happen? Brina had been teaching her about *manifestation*. She said that thoughts have power; that if you focus intently on something or think about it a lot, it can grow and eventually *manifest*, become reality. What if, by giving attention to her fear that she would one day be invisible, she'd accidentally made that fear come true? No, she refused to believe that. Wasn't manifesting about creating what you did want rather than the opposite? As she pushed the idea aside, the fury swirling around inside her was making her chest feel tight and compressed, ready to burst. Grabbing her cup, she slammed it down onto the kitchen floor. The sound of smashing crockery reverberated around the room. Tiny shards of pottery scooted across the floor as though they had suddenly been released from captivity. Luke hurried back into the kitchen, a look of alarm on his face.

When the Universe Called

"What the …? Are you okay?" For a brief moment Maria wondered if she'd been imagining all of this, wondering if she was going crazy like her now-demented father. Luke eyed her with a look of nervousness. "What happened?"

"I … My hands must have been greasy from the hand cream. The cup just slipped." She could tell from his look that he didn't quite believe her, but he said nothing and started picking up the pieces. Watching him, she felt more tears fighting their way to the surface, but she fought them back. This was not the time to show any weakness, not while Charlotte was anywhere near.

"It's okay. I'll make more tea." Maria turned away, knowing she wouldn't have the strength to keep up this charade if she met Luke's gaze. He finished clearing up the pieces and silently went back into the living room.

*   *   *   .*

"What was all that about?" Charlotte fidgeted on the sofa.

"Nothing. Maria just dropped something." Luke studied his fingernails and kept an eye on the open door between the living room and the kitchen, watching to see if Maria would reappear.

"I'm telling you she knows—something at least!" Charlotte seemed to choke on the words, as she whispered across at him.

"I don't think so." Luke pretended not to be worried, but he was; very, but not just about his wife. There were details about him Charlotte did not yet know, details Maria did not even know. It was safer for both of them that way. Luke tried to sound casual. "I can't see how she could have found out about us. She'd have said something if she had."

For all that, Luke knew his wife well enough to know that her behavior was out of character and that something was up. Was it possible Maria had found out what he had been hiding all these years? It seemed unlikely, and yet … He felt himself blanche at the thought.

Charlotte looked at him but remained silent. He couldn't interpret her expression, and it was disconcerting. Usually he was good at reading people, but he hadn't yet managed to quite figure her out even though he'd known her for quite a few months. She had a way of arching her eyebrows

Maggie Denhearn

that seemed to indicate she was about to ask a question, yet she wouldn't ask anything. She would just stare with those pale blue eyes that were like looking into the depths of a lake—deep and bottomless and with a whole life buried beneath that probably few people would ever see. He wasn't used to women who were quite so circumspect. Her head was tilted to one side, her hair falling down her back, her lips pursed as though she were holding something back. She seemed agitated this evening.

"What's up, anyway? You seem nervous."

She paused perceptibly before she responded, and she glanced away briefly before she did so. "What do you think? It's coming here! Why did you have to get me to drop off the papers here of all places? And with Maria home too." She was lying, he could tell. That wasn't why she was nervous. For now he decided not to push her. He was growing fond of Charlotte but certainly didn't completely trust her. He realized he had already let his guard down with her too much. He would have to be more vigilant. Now was not the time to let his feelings cloud his judgment.

"I couldn't wait. There's vital information I need to take to the conference tomorrow." It was his turn to look away. He'd been collecting information about the Consortium, and he had new evidence about its corruption he needed to share with Brina before he left for the mainland in the morning. He was careful enough to write everything down in his own code, just in case anyone else did take a look at the papers. It was careless of him to forget them at the office, though. It had been the lesser of two evils, having Charlotte stop by to bring them to him and risk her reading them, risk her seeing Maria. He was jittery, and it was causing him to make mistakes he couldn't afford.

*   *   *   *

As she waited for the kettle to come to a boil, Maria stared at herself again in the mirror. Time seemed cruel to her. That expensive face cream she had bought three months ago didn't seem to be having much effect on winding back the years. She still had good hair, though—a sleek, glossy brown, thanks to her gifted stylist, cut into a long, sophisticated bob. Short enough to look tidy and elegant when down, long enough to tie back when

When the Universe Called

she was running. Smudged mascara notwithstanding, you could cover a multitude of sins with clever coloring and contouring of face powder and blusher, although apparently not enough to stop a husband from straying after a younger woman. She pulled a compact out of the top drawer of the dresser and began to touch up her face. It wouldn't do to show any vulnerability, let her mask slip, even if she didn't know who was underneath it anymore.

Maria listened to the buzz of their conversation through the open door, unable to quite make out what they were saying. Did they think she was stupid? Did they really think she couldn't see what was going on? Did Luke think so little of Maria that he would bring Charlotte home with him? She felt her fists clenching. Her thoughts started to turn murderous. He needed to feel the pain she was feeling. He needed to have every inch of his being hurting the way she was hurting.

Managing to unclench her hands, she switched the kettle back on to ensure the water would be properly boiled. Emptying out the cold, soggy tea bags from the teapot into the compost bin, she took three more bags out of the tea caddy and put them on the sideboard, ready to be added to the pot, after it had been properly warmed, of course. Holding on to the mundane, the normal, felt like the only lifeline. Making tea was a ritual instilled in her by her English mother. There was a right way to do it, and that was the Yorkshire way. Anything else was just, well, it wasn't tea. Vanna, who had recently joined her local running group, was the only one who didn't roll her eyes at her tea making habits, but then she was British. Maria could do with some brandy in hers. If she'd had cyanide, she was sure she'd have put it in Luke and Charlotte's. Being jilted for a younger woman was such an embarrassing cliché.

Another fear that seemed to have been plaguing her more of late had now come true. That jarring thought popped into her head again: Had she made this happen? Had her thoughts and fears created this situation? And was everyone laughing at her behind her back? Or worse, pitying her?

The insistent whistle of the kettle finally broke into her thoughts, steam billowing into the air. She swirled a little hot water in the teapot, poured it down the sink, added the tea bags to the pot, and then filled it to the brim with boiling water. She put the ridiculous pink tea cozy her aunt had knitted for her over the pot and put it on a tray to take back into the living room.

Maggie Denhearn

She took out some clean mugs from the cupboard and put them on the tray, poured some milk into an equally ridiculous pink cow-shaped milk jug that her other aunt had given her, and put that on the tray too. She regarded the tray—very Martha Stewart. Luke and Charlotte would never suspect that she knew their secret. She could do this. If she knew how to maintain her composure with Mayor McDowell and all his maneuvering, she could do this.

Maria took another deep breath and carried the tray into the living room, each step requiring immense effort. She felt like she had a huge elastic band holding her legs together. Her courteous "we have guests" smile was fixed firmly back in place. It did not escape her notice that their conversation stopped as she walked in. Charlotte blushed. Luke cleared his throat, taking a sudden and intense interest in the pattern on the rug. They both seemed tense. She poured fresh tea and had to concentrate on not pouring it all over the coffee table. As they all politely sat there, she felt like she was in some kind of parallel universe. Why didn't she just come out and confront them both? Or at the very least, make her excuses and leave? Why was she putting herself through this torture? She wanted to observe them, gather more evidence.

Random thoughts ebbed and flowed through her mind as she nibbled another chocolate digestive. She'd lost track of how many she'd eaten, and she was usually particular about how much she consumed. She'd been on a diet for a couple of months now and had lost so much weight that even her wedding ring was loose. With each mouthful she tried to stifle any rogue emotion that might disturb her cool demeanor, yet each bite tasted like dust.

"You seem distracted." Luke's words were a slap across her forehead.

"What?" She couldn't help blushing. Although she was loath to admit it, she felt shamed, not just angry and hurt.

"You're distracted." Maria noticed Luke's upper lip curl, always a sign he was irritated.

"I'd better go," said Charlotte, getting up and placing her mug on the coffee table. Luke coughed. Maria looked up at Charlotte.

"Sorry, I'm just … what were you saying? I'm sorry. I'm being rude." Maria knew she was overcompensating, but now that she had feigned ignorance of their liaison, she wasn't quite sure how to stop. Forcing herself to smile was making her cheeks hurt. She relaxed her face muscles. Charlotte hovered for a few moments, perceptibly embarrassed and as though she was not entirely sure what to do, then finally sat down again. Maria glanced from one to the other, trying to decipher their expressions. There was that familiarity again. Her head felt fuzzy, stuffed with cotton balls.

"Here, have another cookie." Maria thrust the plate of cookies that was on the coffee table in Charlotte's direction. Charlotte hesitated and looked up at her, then took one of the digestives, quickly averting her eyes. Maria stared at her. Charlotte's eyes were a liquid faded blue color and her skin pallid, almost translucent. Did she ever see the sun? She was thin and unpresupposing, her hair thin and lank, a dull, mousy brown color. She was so young. Maria wondered what Luke saw in her. Was it just youth which had turned his head? She was bland, so nondescript, the kind of person you don't notice standing next to you. Realizing she had been staring intently at her, Maria tried to make conversation.

"So, how are things with you?" The question hung in the air like some embarrassing smell. Charlotte paused before responding,

"Well, you know, same old." Maria continued to scrutinize Charlotte, watching her pale lips as she spoke, noticing how the young woman couldn't look at her. That had to be a sign of guilt. Charlotte was evidently trying to be polite, but it was clearly an effort for her. Maria caught Luke glancing over at the clock as though he was waiting for something. He was up to something. They both were.

Maria laughed uncomfortably. She forced herself to smile, noticing how Charlotte was fiddling with her hair and scrunching her toes in and out. At least she had the decency to feel uncomfortable. Maria had met her at one of Luke's office Christmas parties, but Charlotte had never actually been back to their house, as far as she knew anyway. Perhaps she was here often, in her kitchen, making Luke tea. Quite why Charlotte was dropping off those papers for Luke at his home on this particular day when she was around, Maria wasn't sure. Perhaps they'd thought she wouldn't be here. Her stomach churned. Had he been using their marital bed when she was out? The thought of the two of them sharing the same intimacy that she used to have with him, brought on a wave of nausea. Taking deep breaths, she focused on maintaining her "interested" face, while she heard Charlotte in

Maggie Denhearn

the background of her thoughts, now telling a supposedly funny story. The desire to slap her welled up inside her. Instead, Maria bit her lip as though she were thinking about what Charlotte was saying. She saw Luke smile and smiled too. Charlotte must have got to the punch line.

"How funny!" Maria forced a laugh and tried to look as though she knew what they found amusing. Charlotte continued with more details and Luke nodded. He was avoiding looking at Maria; she could tell.

"Sorry, but I have some reports that I really need to get on with." Maria needed to escape. Keeping up the pretense was too hard. Feigning interest at cocktail parties and pretending she liked her boss the mayor were easy. Pretending she hadn't just discovered her husband was cheating on her was not. If she didn't leave now, she would end up doing them all bodily harm. She heard Luke sigh. She no longer understood him. It was as though they had started speaking different languages. He was a stranger to her, and she was in a bizarre land; a land where one minute she had been trundling along, barely looking up, the next she'd tripped over a great big tree root and had slammed down, abruptly seeing her life and him for the first time in a long while.

Sitting behind her desk in her home office, Maria breathed in deeply and closed her eyes, fighting back the urge to cry. Hurt, anger, disappointment, fear, confusion, all of the above surged up and down within her like her own tumultuous ocean. As much as anything she was furious with herself for being so naïve. She was not that woman, the woman about whom the community gossips while to her face giving tea and sympathy without ever revealing why. She could hear Brina's voice in her head reminding her to breathe, breathe deeply. Focusing on that was the only thing she could think of to do to stop herself from disintegrating.

Brina. Brina must know about Luke and Charlotte. She had to know. Brina owned the Kavama, the local coffee shop, and knew everything that was going on at Eagle Cove. How could her friend not tell her? Maria could still faintly hear Luke and Charlotte as they continued chatting away. She wanted to scream, but there was no sound left inside her. She was stalled. Angry as she was with her, Brina was the only person Maria could turn to. Picking up her cell phone, she was about to start typing her a text message when her phone started to ring.

When the Universe Called

"Maria, you have to come, and you have to come now!"

Maria cleared her throat, which was hoarse and dry. "Kali, what's wrong? Are you okay?" Something in Kali's voice sounded peculiar. Kali was the mayor's wife. If she was calling in such a state, this could not be good.

"I can't tell you on the phone. Just ... please, I really need you. You have to come!" Kali started to wail, and Maria could barely make out the directions she proceeded to give her.

"Stay there. I'll be with you as soon as I can." Maria slipped her phone into her pocket, grabbed her purse and keys, and left the house without bothering to say goodbye. No doubt she would have to clear up another of the mayor's indiscretions. It wasn't the first time that Kali had called her to sort out Andy after a drinking binge or getting into an altercation with another politician. Mayor Andy McDowell was known for being something of a hothead, a characteristic that so far Maria had managed to use to his advantage in his campaigns. She was glad for the excuse to leave the house, to escape for a while the weight of her husband's deception. As she pulled out of the driveway, she noticed the dark car parked again at a distance down the street.

*   *   *   *

"Luke, seriously, she knows something." Charlotte seemed like she was about to burst when they heard the front door slam and the crunch of tires on gravel as Maria drove away.

Luke didn't respond, replaying the last few minutes in his head.

"I bet ... you know, I think she thinks we're having an affair." Charlotte blushed as she said this.

Luke almost spat out his tea then tried to regain his composure as he managed to stop himself from choking. What a thought! "You're imagining things. You need to calm down. We'll just have to be more careful, that's all."

"Calm down? *Calm down?* You're the one that asked me to come round here!" Her tone was indignant.

"I'm sorry, poor choice of words. I know this is hard, but I can't tell her now, not yet. You need to give me more time. Finding out you're my daughter isn't exactly going to go down well I'm afraid."

Maggie Denhearn

Luke took another sip of his tea and avoided looking at her. Charlotte was too young to understand what it would do to Maria, knowing he had a child of his own, when they had spent so many years trying to have a family together. He couldn't bring himself to tell her. It seemed too unfair. He also wasn't too keen to examine the feelings of guilt that he was struggling to keep in a separate compartment of his head so that he could avoid thinking about them.

He glanced at the clock again. He'd expected a call from his brother by now. This wasn't a good sign. He had this feeling in his gut that he was trying to ignore but that wouldn't go away. The Consortium was on to him. That had to be the only explanation possible for the car that had been watching him for weeks. Had they found out about what his brother had been up to, about all the research Noah had been doing on them? If they had, it would be only a matter of time before they found out about what Luke had been up to, and Brina.

Dread was filling his stomach like a growing ball of steel wire. This morning when he'd got up and looked in the mirror to start shaving, he had felt old. It was the first time. He knew logically that by today's standards, he wasn't. He was forty-five. Wasn't that the new thirty-something? The last few months he'd done his best to ignore the gray encroaching on his temples and making its way through the rest of his hair like someone was sprinkling silver threads over his head. The sands of time flow in only one direction. He wasn't sure why he had a greater sense lately of his own mortality. Maybe it was being around Charlotte—young, fresh, not going gray. Or more likely, it was the lurking presence of the Consortium. With everything he was finding out about their illegal activities, he realized his time was running out. And he feared his brother's already had.

Friday afternoon, August 2, 1963

"The answer is blowin' in the wind ... How many years can a mountain exist ..."

Anja sang to herself as she wandered around the laboratory, tidying up supplies and putting equipment back where it should be. She liked this part of the day. Everyone else would leave early to catch the remains of the summer day, but she would stay behind, just an hour or so, to have some quiet time to

When the Universe Called

think. She had been an intern for almost a year now at Frost Pharma Health, or FPH, as everyone who worked there called it. Anja brushed her long, auburn hair out of her eyes, her loose ponytail hanging over her left shoulder. As she gathered up in one hand some files left on Frost's desk, she picked up his coffee cup and tutted. John Frost—her boss and the company founder—was always leaving his dirty cup for someone (her) to clean up. Moving it over to one of the lab sinks where she could wash it, the bottom file of the pile she was carrying slipped out of her hands and fell all over the floor. She just managed to keep hold of all the others and dropped them on to the side bench, then bent down to pick up the loose paper that had flown in all directions. She caught sight of the drug name highlighted in red on one of the papers: FERISIT. That was strange. She'd put that file away already. She knew she had because she'd been reading it that afternoon and had been amazed and impressed that this new drug for anxiety and depression had so quickly received FDA approval to go to market. It was a real coup for the company and was the reason that the following evening there was going to be a celebratory dinner for everyone involved. Although she hadn't actually been involved with any of the work on FERISIT, she was invited anyway. Frost's wife did not like to attend company events, so Frost had invited Anja instead. She wasn't sure that was such a good idea. They were supposed to be keeping their affair secret, and she wasn't convinced she would be able to hide her feelings for him quite so easily out of the lab. But he wasn't the kind of man you said no to. Sorting through the papers and trying to get them back into some kind of order, it struck her as odd that this file was out again. Frost couldn't have been looking at it that afternoon because he'd been out of the office since before lunch, yet it was in his pile of work on his desk. No one other than Anja and Frost's secretary Gina ever went near his desk. As she scanned the papers to make sure she was putting them back in the right order, a sickly feeling began washing over her.

"Oh my God!" She looked up, all of a sudden scared that someone could see and hear her. She was alone. Anja's heart began to race. Shoving the papers back into the file as quickly as she could, she crammed them into her satchel. She paused, thinking. Rifling through the filing cabinet, she pulled out a blue file and stuffed that also into her satchel, then hurried out of the lab.

CHAPTER 2

EARLY MONDAY EVENING, APRIL 14, 2014

"Well at least we have a great love life." Kali tried not to choke on her coffee when she heard Andy speaking on the phone. Was he referring to them or was he sleeping with someone else? It wouldn't be the first time. He seemed to think she didn't know about some of his extracurricular activities, but she was all too well aware of them. His inflated ego as mayor of Eagle Cove was such that he thought he could do whatever he wanted and with impunity. And of course he had Maria to clean up after his more obvious indiscretions.

Kali just managed to stop herself from dropping the travel mug she had in her hand and from snort-laughing, almost saying out loud, "Really? You have to be kidding!" She'd just walked through the front door and had accidentally caught him mid-conversation. Andy hadn't noticed her come in, his six foot five frame filling the hallway as he boomed to whoever was on the other end of the line. Mayor Andy McDowell was so used to speaking in public that he often forgot how thunderous his voice could be. He had no concept of an inside voice. She wondered who he was speaking to but decided she didn't care. They were both keeping up the pretense of a happy and harmonious marriage as though nothing was wrong. She'd at least had a lot of practice. She knew how much it meant to Andy to be reelected mayor of Eagle Cove, and even she had to admit that waiting until after the local mayoral election to go their separate ways would be better. She didn't fancy any negative publicity and the media hounds sniffing round. The *Ocean*

When the Universe Called

Waves Gazette wasn't known for being kind and sympathetic, and any hint of marital disharmony surrounding the illustrious mayor would be food for the newspaper piranhas. His occasional drunken fling with random women was only briefly ever alluded to in the press, but she knew it would never do if *she* were suspected of being unfaithful. He had a charisma that seemed to charm the media. At one time it had her too. She was no longer particularly fond of her husband, but she didn't want him to lose the election, either. He had a mean streak that she rarely saw, but the few times she did had warned her to tread extremely carefully.

Getting married had seemed like such a gift at the time, an opportunity to be normal. Gaining a PhD by the age of twenty-one wasn't all it was cracked up to be. Even at the university where she now worked, most people thought she was a freak and avoided her unless they had a problem with their computer security software. Not Andy. He wasn't intimidated by her genius. He wasn't intimidated by anything.

It didn't occur to her until much later on in their marriage that she wasn't actually in love with him and that she never had been. When she finally got around to telling Andy she was leaving, his hurt manhood and fears for his career had been more his concern than a bruised heart, as she suspected it would be. It was his heart that she'd been missing, and that was why she needed to leave.

Kicking off her shoes and hanging her jacket on the banister, she wandered absentmindedly into the living room. The memory of the last time they'd made love came to mind when she caught sight of a photo on the wall of them on holiday in Mexico. That last time was less than a week before she woke up one morning and decided that she just couldn't stay married to him any longer. She supposed it must have been on her mind for a while. She couldn't imagine that she would actually just wake up one day and say she wanted a divorce while she poured the coffee and crunched her toast. The feelings must have been bubbling away long before.

She had been feeling bored and tried not to yawn as he reached over to her. There were so many other things that she could be getting on with. Kali stifled a sigh as she and Andy went through the motions, the mechanical lovemaking of those who no longer see each other. She knew exactly what they both would do, gesture by gesture, move by move. He was in another

15

Maggie Denhearn

world, and she felt like she was having some kind of out-of-body experience, staring down at herself, neither of them present in the experience.

She was only thirty, and already she felt like she was going numb. Would it have been different if she'd married a man closer to her own age? The ten-year age gap had started to feel like a gigantic chasm between them. It was an odd sensation, feeling like you're in a relationship on your own.

Andy had rolled over and started snoring, but Kali hadn't been able to stop her mind from whirring round and round. She wanted to stop thinking and to start feeling. She wanted to feel that rush she had felt when she and Andy first met, not the apathy of the somnambulant relationship they were now in.

While Andy continued to snore, Kali started to make her exit plan. It's never easy ending a relationship, but this was one that could potentially be particularly hard to extricate herself from. She didn't want to admit to herself how much she was actually frightened of what he might do. That said, he was so caught up in his own self-importance and his political career at the moment, she was tempted to just leave and see if he actually noticed. They had been married for seven years. Now that the door to their marriage was finally closing in her head, she wouldn't be able to open it again.

When Kali met Noah, the door between her and Andy truly slammed shut and the one to Noah flung open. She hadn't intended to start having an affair with him. It had just happened. Kali knew that sounded pathetic, like an excuse, but it was true. Maybe her subconscious mind had been looking for alternatives when her conscious mind wasn't looking. If what Brina claimed was actually true, that thoughts could create reality, then perhaps she had attracted Noah into her life without realizing where her thoughts were going. The illicit nature of her affair with him had added a certain intoxicating frisson to her life, an excitement that she had definitely been hankering after. For a while they had been exchanging glances at the university where they both worked and it had crossed her mind more than once that she wouldn't say no if he asked her out. Everyone knew Mayor Andy McDowell. Noah knew she was married, and so she just figured it wouldn't happen, despite her increasing longing and her vivid daydreams about him.

When the Universe Called

One day in January, something changed, something subtle in the way Noah glanced over at her during a meeting—an invitation. She smiled a yes. Without exchanging a word, they left the university together at the end of the day, and she followed him to his car. He opened the car door for her and she got in. As he climbed in the other side, he looked across at her and grinned.

"Shall we?"

"Sure."

They drove for about twenty minutes out of Eagle Cove to a motel. During the whole drive, they remained silent. They pulled up and she remained in the car while he checked in. The room was basic but clean and surprisingly not sleazy. He locked the door behind them.

"So."

"I want to take a shower," she said, smiling deliberately, coyly.

As she entered the bathroom and reached up to switch on the shower, he grabbed her gently, pulling her to him, searching out the nape of her neck with his mouth. Her hair was still up, wound in a loose knot at the back of her head. He pulled at the clip and let her blonde hair wash over him like a silken scarf. She remembered how he sighed deeply, as she leaned into him, gently guiding him where she wanted him to go with the sway of her body. She had been longing for this for a very long time.

That was the first time. One morning, after their affair had been going on for a couple of months, she couldn't hold back telling Andy she wanted to end their marriage. It had been something about the smug way he was eating his toast and fiddling with his cuff links that just made her snap and blurt it out.

"Is there someone else?" He looked her straight in the eye. She looked straight back, trying not to show how afraid she suddenly felt of him.

"Of course not. It's not that." As he glared at her, she turned to buttering her toast for the second time, trying to keep her hands steady. She didn't know whether she was a good liar or not. Sneaking around wasn't the same as telling out-and-out lies. Andy was away so much that most of the time she could come and go as she pleased. And truly, Noah wasn't the reason she'd finally decided to leave.

Maggie Denhearn

"Are you sure? I'm coming up to reelection. This can't come out now. Why are you telling me now?" He looked peeved rather than hurt. She had expected him to shout, to wave his hands, to pound his fists on the table. Instead he poured himself more coffee and opened the newspaper.

"Andy, just leave it. I'm not going to do anything before the election, I promise. I just can't do this anymore." She waved her hand around the breakfast table. "I'm moving into the spare room."

"I'll move. I'm away a lot anyway." And that had been that—another marriage snuffed out like a candle in one single motion.

* * * *

"Good day?"

"Yes. You?" Kali slumped down into an armchair and picked up a magazine from the coffee table. She couldn't look at Andy. She hadn't expected him to be home just yet, and her skin was still warm from being in bed with Noah. She felt Noah's touch on her cheek, his lips caressing her neck. Being with him gave her that heady feeling of being slightly and pleasantly intoxicated. Her skin was still tingling all over. She felt herself blush and glanced over to Andy to see if he had noticed, but he was now lounging on the sofa and had already picked up the remote control and was flicking through the TV channels. Their usual evening routine was beginning. Somehow since her revelation that she was planning on leaving, they had managed to settle into an existence more akin to an elderly couple who have been together all their lives and have long since slipped from rancor to indifference.

Flinching as Andy switched to the sports channel and turned up the volume, always too loud for her, she felt her phone buzz in her pocket. Casually, she glanced at the screen—a text message from Noah: "I have an idea." They had been interrupted earlier that afternoon when Noah received a phone call he insisted he needed to answer, just as they had been about to make love again. He'd promised her he would call her later. This was sooner. She got up.

"Want a beer?" Andy grunted. Kali took that as a yes. Heading into the kitchen, she started to text Noah back.

"Enlighten me."

18

When the Universe Called

"Meet me at the trail in twenty minutes."

"Why?"

"Want something a bit different?"

"That depends."

"See you there." She knew he had her figured out and that she wouldn't be able to resist. Getting a beer out of the fridge, she sidled as casually as she could back into the living room. She put the opened beer bottle on the table next to Andy.

"I'm just heading out for a bit." Picking up the bottle, her husband didn't look away from the TV screen. Kali didn't wait for a response.

*　　*　　*　　*

Andy pretended to be engrossed in the television until he heard Kali slam the front door. He gave her a few more minutes to make sure she wasn't coming back, then muted the volume and picked up his phone.

"Hi, it's me. Kali has just gone out. I'm pretty sure she's meeting Noah. ... Yes, yes. I'll let you know if I find out anything more."

He clicked off his phone and threw it down on the sofa, turning up the volume again and continuing to watch the hockey. He wasn't paying real attention, his mind whirring. At first he was livid when he'd found out his wife was having an affair. He'd been about to confront her about it when Bailey got in touch. Alexis Bailey was a powerful woman, even in her retirement from being police commissioner of British Columbia. When she offered to help him with his political career, he of course jumped at the chance. He had no intention of staying in Eagle Cove all his life. He had aspirations beyond such an insignificant community and far beyond Vancouver Island. A contact like Bailey was exactly what he needed. While it had initially seemed strange that Bailey should be so interested in Kali's lover, that she had in fact been the one to tell Andy about his wife's affair, he liked the idea of killing two birds with one stone—furthering his career and getting back at his wife. All Bailey wanted was any information he could find about Noah. Andy was happy to oblige. And he'd been in politics long enough to know it was never wise to ask too many questions about the

19

Maggie Denhearn

motivations of people like Bailey. In truth, he didn't care, so long as Bailey followed through on her offer to get him into the Consortium.

* * * *

Kali felt a shudder of excitement as she pulled up at the trail entrance. It was a five-minute walk from Noah's place and where they had come a few times, later in the evening, when it was unlikely anyone would be around.

"Nice evening don't you think?" He grinned at her mischievously. He had a boyish air that could be completely disarming.

"What? Dark and stormy?" This was Kali's version of playing hard to get. She wasn't very good at it.

"Atmospheric. And unseasonably warm. That's what gave me the idea." As he said this, a warm gust of wind picked up through the trees, making them whisper a welcome.

"What are you up to?" She giggled as he grabbed her round the waist and pulled her to him in a quick embrace. She knew exactly what he had in mind.

"How about a little wander in the woods?" He glanced behind them, she assumed to make sure no one was watching, then he took her hand. There was still enough light filtering through the treetops to be able to make out where they were putting their feet. The birch and the maple trees, still naked after the winter months, swayed in the soft breeze, the buds of their spring mantles trying to burst through. The rustling of the leaves masked the sound of their quickening breath as they half walked half ran through the forest. He was right. It did feel warmer than usual. She didn't need the jacket she was wearing. Their feet crunched down on the ground, a well-maintained snake of silvery gravel creating a narrow path through a world that had existed for a thousand years. Kali felt her heart starting to beat faster and her hand warm in his.

Noah had a more unorthodox view than Andy when it came to venues for making love. That was part of the excitement, part of what enthralled her with him. She ignored the voices at the back of her mind telling her that she was playing with fire. This was too much fun, and she didn't want it to stop.

"Here. This is the spot I was thinking of." After a few minutes, he pulled her to one side and off the gravel trail. Pulling back the bush, he

When the Universe Called

made space for her to slip through to an opening, out into a small clearing where the undergrowth was only ankle deep. A couple of old trees were lying horizontally across the forest floor, covered in downy moss, like ready-made seats. To one side stood a huge oak, the trunk so wide and gnarled it must have been centuries old. Its branches hung low as though each year of life weighed heavily. Noah led her over to the oak, then while still standing, started kissing her insistently, pushing her against its trunk. She felt the gnarled bark dig into her back but was too lost in his embrace to feel discomfort. First he removed her jacket. Then he reached his hands to her side and slowly unzipped her dress. As she felt it slip to the ground, she stepped automatically out of it. She shivered yet didn't actually feel cold. As his mouth made its way down her neck, she tugged at his shirt. He stopped and stared straight into her eyes. Their eyes remained locked as he took off his shirt, shoes, jeans … She giggled.

"You still have far too many clothes on, young lady." And she felt his hands gently move over her until all she was wearing was her sandals. She felt him move into her, and she braced her feet against the rocks wedged flush against the tree trunk. He started to moan as his hands moved slowly down her sides.

And that's when it happened. He touched her ticklish spot, on her left side just above her hipbone. She flinched and laughed at the same time, and her foot slipped on the moss on the rocks. She lurched, accidentally pushing him backward, but managed to pull herself upright.

"You know I'm ticklish there!" She knew she had been smiling when she opened her eyes because she felt the muscles in her face change instantly and tense into an expression that hurt as she looked around.

She'd heard a thud and a crack, and had expected to see Noah rolling around on the forest floor, laughing, or at least swearing at the prickles of brambles and branches sticking into him. She was aware of a weird sound and realized the yelping was coming from her.

"Noah?" she whispered, not quite sure why she felt the need to keep her voice down. He was sprawled on the ground on his back, not moving. The light had started to fade, but she could see from the position of his body that something wasn't quite right. Dark blood was pooling out from the

Maggie Denhearn

back of his head, and his eyes were wide open, staring. His expression was contorted, a mixture of pleasure and pain.

She whispered his name a few times. No response.

Tentatively, she bent down and put her hand on his shoulder and tried to shake him gently. He still didn't respond. Taking his wrist, she felt for his pulse. Perhaps it was just because she had started to shudder so violently and could hear her own heart pounding in her head that she couldn't find any sign of life. It was all so surreal. She tried to convince herself that if she stared at him hard enough, he would miraculously come alive again, grin at her, and start laughing.

The wind had picked up more, gliding over Kali and giving her goose bumps, reminding her that she was completely naked except for her favorite strappy blue sandals. She searched about on the ground in the half-light and managed to find her underwear and her dress. Hugging herself to try and stop herself from shaking, she looked around to see if anyone was watching. Apart from the creaking of the trees bending back and forth, it was eerily quiet.

Grabbing her jacket, she reached for her cell phone. One bar of signal was all she needed. She was starting to feel very cold. She shouldn't have worn those sandals. When she had been leaving the house, she'd almost put on her walking shoes, but hadn't wanted Andy to know where she was going. It was all her fault. A split second decision, that's all it had taken.

She looked over at Noah again, still hoping that he would move, that he was only unconscious. Her mind racing, her heart thumping wildly, the sound of her own breathing clashed with the howl of a sudden gust of wind. What should she do? Call the police? A feeling of panic rose within her at the thought of having to explain to some irritating young cop what they'd been up to. Nor could she just leave Noah there. Perhaps she should try and get his clothes back on him at least. That might wake him up. He couldn't be dead; she was overreacting.

She bent down and started picking up his things. She had to jump up to try and get his shirt, which somehow had got caught in the lower levels of the branches of the oak. She was lucky it didn't rip as she pulled it down. She felt like she was moving through molasses, doing things in slow motion as though she was acting out some bizarre scene of a play. She got his jeans

When the Universe Called

and started to try and put them back on him. He was heavy, very heavy, a dead weight, but somehow she found the strength to begin to move him.

He sighed. She screamed and jumped back, her hand instinctively covering her own mouth in an attempt to stifle any more noise she might make.

"Noah?" Everything sounded so loud, and she felt like the whole world could hear her. She realized the sound was probably air escaping from his lungs. That meant he had to be alive, right? Or perhaps he really was dead and that was his soul exiting his body. She'd heard that some people could actually see that happening. She had thought that sounded ridiculous until now.

She glanced upward. Nothing. This was way too macabre. She couldn't bring herself to continue trying to dress him. Picking up his wrist, she felt around again, then put her fingers to his neck, desperate to find a pulse, any faint sign of life. Nothing.

She needed help and quickly. She wondered whom she could call. Who would understand that she couldn't go to the police, even if this had just been some dreadful accident? Andy would kill her. She picked up her cell phone again and managed to find a spot back on the main trail where there was some reception.

"Maria, you have to come and you have to come now!"

Kali put her phone away and started to sob.

*   *   *   *

Luke hadn't particularly wanted to move to Eagle Cove, but over the years the place had grown on him. Situated on the east coast of Vancouver Island, Eagle Cove boasted an odd population of locals: retirees looking for an island paradise, and a thriving local artist community. Everyone was welcome. Other than the brief flurry of tourism in the summer and forestry, the local economy relied on people working on the mainland, coming back for a couple of weeks at a time, and spending their hard earned money.

Luke was one of the few who worked locally. He barely had a thirty-minute commute along the old highway that meandered along the coastline to get to the offices of the law firm where he'd been working now for more

23

Maggie Denhearn

years than he'd ever thought possible. There was something about Eagle Cove that stopped people from leaving.

Luke glanced around as he got out of his car. The dark blue car was nowhere to be seen. The tension in his body made him wince as he moved. His shoulders had been sore for weeks now, and he knew it wasn't just from spending time in front of the computer. The nebulous shadow of the Consortium was moving in on him. He hoped Brina would have some news—some good news. He looked at his watch: 8:00 p.m. Maria must have gone out about an hour ago. He was counting on her being gone a while, wherever it was she'd disappeared to, so he could get back home before she did. The dull, tympanic rhythm of his footsteps seemed loud and out of place as he walked the short stretch from the parking lot to the coffee shop. The mall was deserted. Everything was closed except the Kavama.

The Kavama Coffee Shop and Emporium was situated right at the end of the strip mall in Eagle Cove. The storefront was set back a couple of feet from the rest of the stores, and there was a gated courtyard to the right-hand side, accessible only from inside the Emporium. This lent it an air of being set apart from the rest of the mall, either as a late addition or because it was there before all the other stores. The storefront was a mixture of turquoise, emerald, and red. In good weather, a couple of small tiled tables with wicker chairs were set outside the front, and the side courtyard would be open, with soft couches and chairs under umbrellas to provide shade from the sun. Lush greenery seemed to grow out of everything, leaving just enough space for people to sit and relax. The Kavama wasn't the kind of coffee shop where you bought a drink to go.

Luke glanced around to see if anyone was watching him. No one. To the left of the Kavama was a little bakery and deli store and beyond that, a bank, a library, an art gallery that sold exclusively the artwork of local artists and artisans, and at the other end of the mall, the local grocery store. All the windows were dark.

Luke paused, his fingers lightly touching the smooth wooden door handle, cold to the touch. Anxiety like an unrelenting vine was snaking its way through his veins. Staring through the window of the coffee shop, he could see shelf upon shelf of jars containing every kind of tea or coffee imaginable along with various herbs, spices, and tinctures on the left-hand

When the Universe Called

wall. To the right, books, Buddha statues, packets of incense, stones and gems of various kinds, candles, and all the other paraphernalia one expects to see in a metaphysical store filled a huge oak cabinet that spanned from the floor to the beams above. From the ceiling, swaths of cloth in vibrant colors and textures hung down, making it seem as though it were covered in sumptuous pillows. There were no customers this evening. He looked behind one more time before opening the door.

The bell over the door tinkled as Luke walked in. He hadn't called ahead to see whether Brina's assistant Tullia was working this evening or whether Brina would be there. He saw the heavy purple velvet curtain behind the counter move; Brina appeared. She was a small woman, although her slender yet sturdy frame and upright demeanor made her seem taller. Her long gray hair was neatly brushed and pulled back gently into a soft ponytail that hung over her left shoulder. Her long, loose, graceful clothes were unusual for Vancouver Island. They spoke of a European refinement, a unique and innate poise. Even the cane she used to help her walk had elegance. It was made of arbutus, with rosewood inlay on the handle and tiny gems of moonstone and black onyx. She didn't seem to limp so much as float along, and her cane seemed more of a whimsical accessory. Today her face looked serious. There was something about Brina's expression that reminded him of another time. It was an odd look, one of shock but without the surprise.

"What's up? I've not seen that look on your face since the first time I ever met you." He felt his insides contract.

"You mean when you wandered in here late one Christmas Eve, looking for a last-minute gift for Maria? I hope you've got better at doing your Christmas shopping."

"Not really. What's going on?"

"When was that?" Brina had a faraway look in her eyes.

"A long time ago. I almost didn't come in."

"I bet you're wishing now you hadn't."

"Well, yes and no." Luke remembered the tinkle of the bell and the smell of warm cinnamon wafting past as he'd opened the door that very first time.

"The look on your face when you saw me!" Brina laughed gently.

"Well, the same with you. You looked like you'd seen a ghost."

"I had." They both stopped and stared at each other, hesitating.

25

Maggie Denhearn

"I guess you didn't come here to reminisce."

"No. And judging by the look on your face, Brina, I'm assuming you have news."

"I do." Her expression was grim. Luke waited for her to continue. Slowly she brought over a tray, poured green tea into two small cups, and handed him one. He sat down in his usual chair. It was significantly more threadbare than it had been the first time he slumped down in it fifteen years ago.

Brina breathed in deeply before speaking further. "The Consortium has moved things up. They're planning on moving Bill 267 through when they come back after the Easter recess. I was sure it wasn't going to be for another couple of months, but Mary called me this morning and said that somehow the Consortium has managed to arrange it for sooner. Most of the MPs will have been too distracted by the holidays to have read the bill properly before the first day back after the recess. They clearly haven't so far as it's made it through to the third reading and it passed the standing committee review. Mind you, all the committee members were Consortium members. No surprise there. They're rushing it through so no one will see exactly what they're up to."

"I still can't believe that no one will notice." Luke clenched and unclenched his fists underneath the table.

"Well, there's democracy in action for you. They've made the bill so long, attaching so many amendments, who's going to make it to page 120 and think to question a drug trial from FPH? They've been going for decades, and everyone trusts them. Frost Pharma Health is a household name."

Luke wanted to throw something, but there was nothing on hand that wouldn't break, so instead he sipped the tea. He was fairly sure Brina put something strange in it, but he preferred not to ask. He needed its calming effects. The time he and Brina spent biding their time while collecting information had somehow made working for the legal firm representing FPH and having to pretend that he wanted a relationship with his father bearable. That his dissimulation could eventually help bring down the company and along with it all the politicians, judges, business people, and police officials that had come together to form the Consortium was what kept him going. The thought that the Consortium, an organization comprised of Canadian high society's most powerful, were milking the governmental system yet again

When the Universe Called

and continuing to earn millions of dollars from the nefarious experiments of a corrupt pharmaceutical company filled him with an anger he had no idea what to do with. At this moment he felt powerless and like a failure.

"So what do we do? Can't we go to the press now? Surely they'd have something to say about an organization of corrupt rich people trying to influence government? Surely there would be an outcry about a bill that would essentially make it legal for the government to force DNA testing on people, even if it is aimed at convicted criminals? And then using that as an excuse to give them drugs that turn them into zombies. They're bent on drugging the general population into a state of docile compliance, that's for sure."

"You know was well as I do that we have to bide our time. The Consortium has members in all walks of life, including the media. We do need to stop the new legislation and keep Torporo from being legalized, but unless we protect ourselves at the same time, all our efforts to end the Consortium will have been a waste of time. It's not just about winning this particular battle; it's about winning the war. Don't forget: A lot of lives are on the line. Plus there are some people who believe the idea that DNA predetermines who we are. Remember that article by the professor in the States who claimed his research showed that some people have a gene that predetermines they'll be more disposed to criminal activity? A lot of people believe that. They'll think that drugging convicted criminals will stop them becoming recidivists, and that it's a good idea. People fall for the pharmaceutical company brainwashing tactics hook, line, and sinker. They don't see that it's a plot by Big Pharma and governments. They don't stop to think that this won't stop at convicted criminals. Soon the government will be finding any excuse to force the drug on all kinds of people to make them submissive."

"What about the side effects of Torporo? Surely people will at least worry about those?" Luke slammed his hand on the table in frustration, causing the teacups to quiver, the delicate pottery rocking side to side.

"Pharmaceutical companies feed and cultivate people's fears. Fear of crime outweighs fear of personal freedoms surreptitiously being eroded."

"But doesn't new research show that our genes or our DNA, or whatever, are more like a blueprint and that it's our thoughts and our environmental

Maggie Denhearn

influences that activate how they develop? That the whole genetic predisposition view isn't as definite as scientists have been thinking? That's what I've read, anyway, in some article about epigenetics. That explains how some people might get sick from something and others not, even though they have the same genes. That means that we *do* have some control and influence over our health and our lives."

"Precisely. And this is just what the drug companies don't want to hear. Imagine if people could take their health into their own hands and didn't need to rely on pharmaceuticals so much? These companies would lose billions. And so would all the rich people who currently have shares in them. Those companies want us to be scared, docile, to think we have no control over our lives. So do governments. If you claim someone is a criminal because of genetics, that means there's no responsibility of the individual, and it's an excuse for the government to drug people for the so-called common good. You know that."

"I know. I'd just rather not believe it. But I did manage to get hold of the results of the trials of the most recent iteration of Torporo."

Luke drew some papers out of the inside pocket of his jacket and unfolded them, reading out loud, "Of the fifteen individuals who survived, ten suffered severe panic attacks, suicidal ideation, and extreme anxiety. Depersonalization is a major side effect that has not yet been fully eliminated across the series of trials of the drug that have been conducted thus far."

"Remind me what depersonalization is again."

"It's a dreamlike state, feeling distanced from reality, wanting to distance oneself from others."

"How many were originally in this particular trial?"

Luke paused, trying to hide the fact that his voice was breaking up. "This time, twenty. There were twenty. Five died. They've been taking people from the homeless shelter again. And they've stepped up doing testing on specific groups. I've managed to find the paper trail that confirms that. They've been doing a pretty good job of hiding it."

Brina placed her hand on her heart, locking eyes with Luke.

"You mean?"

"Yep. People have been going missing from Indian reserves all over British Columbia for the last three years."

28

When the Universe Called

A look of horror flashed through her eyes. "Haven't the police noticed?"

"Most of the top officials belong to the Consortium, remember. They're turning a blind eye, saying they're runaways who have just left home. Police Commissioner Petturi is livid. He's trying to figure out a way around it, but too many of the top brass around him stand to gain if the legislation goes through and if FPH gets approval to sell Torporo. He knows he has to tread carefully or he'll be ousted from being police commissioner, and then he won't be any help to us at all."

"How good is this new evidence?"

"Emails, lab reports. FPH has been getting complacent in its practices, at least in front of me. I think my father finally trusts me. Plus they've had to pay off a few families, and that's where the legal department has become involved. Thankfully, that's not involved me. I'm not sure I could handle that."

"Okay, we have to stop this. It's time."

Luke sighed. "Fifteen years of hiding, of pretending everything's okay when it isn't. It's making me sick, the thought of what my father has been doing. You know that, right?"

"I know. And I admire the way you've managed so far to gain his confidence."

"He makes my skin crawl." Luke shuddered. He had a physical feeling of revulsion any time he thought of his father, one reason among many why he and Noah had decided to use their mother's name, Morgan, rather than their father's name, Frost. He wanted as little association with him as possible.

"I know. I hope you can stop doing this soon and go and give legal counsel to people who really need your help, like the homeless and the drug addicts Frost has been exploiting all these years."

"I'm not sure after this I'll want to continue being a lawyer." Luke felt so jaded, like he was wearing a heavy coat with stones in the pockets.

"So how do we stop the bill from going through? That essentially gives us until the twenty-eighth, a couple of weeks at the most. I don't see how we can do it. Seriously, can't we just go to the press?"

"Too many Consortium members. It's not safe. None of the regular organizations are safe. We need to find a more off-the-grid strategy."

Luke fell silent, avoiding Brina's gaze.

29

Maggie Denhearn

"There's something else going on, isn't there?" She put her hand on his knee. "Look at me, Luke. There *is* something else, but you're trying not to let me see that you're worried." Brina was peering at him over the top of her reading glasses in that way she had when she was trying to burrow into his thoughts. Luke paused and lifted his piercing blue eyes to meet her gaze, focusing his energy on not letting her into his head. He was much better these days at blocking her, at not letting her hear his thoughts. It had taken a lot of practice to know when and how to keep her out of his mind. She looked older this evening somehow. Her usual aura of vitality had faded, and she was starting to look thin.

"Noah's disappeared." Luke felt his voice tremble again.

Brina did not respond, but took a sip of tea and gazed out into the darkness. After a few moments she sighed wearily.

"I'm sorry to hear that. I guess it really is time then."

Friday evening, August 2, 1963

Anja closed the front door behind her and carefully turned the key to lock it, struggling to pull across the bolts at the top and bottom of the door. She had never used them before, and they were stiff from lack of use. She stood for a moment, leaning her back against the nicotine-stained door that she still hadn't got around to painting. The last occupant of her cramped bachelor apartment must have been a heavy smoker. Anja had never tried a cigarette, but right now she rather wished she could. The last light of the evening sun was finding its way through the blinds, shafts of light casting long shadows along the walls, which she had also been meaning to paint. That wouldn't happen now. Her room seemed cold, lifeless, and drab, despite the rays of the summer sun. There were no pictures on the dirty cream walls, and the dark brown sofa was threadbare and could easily have been mistaken for a dead animal lying against the wall. It was like she lived in sepia rather than in color. Her bed was unmade from this morning, and there were clothes strewn around the floor. She hadn't realized how untidy she was. Lately she had barely been home. There were grease stains on the only carpeted area, near the bed, darker brown shapes contrasting with

When the Universe Called

lighter brown, almost creating a pattern. The pale sun highlighted the dust bunnies on the linoleum and the dust building up layers on the bookshelf. This wasn't a home. At least it wouldn't be too hard to leave.

Breathing deeply, Anja kicked off her sandals and felt the cool of the floor beneath her feet as she padded to the fridge and took out a bottle of brandy. She liked it cold. Pouring a couple of fingers into a glass, she swilled it round, focusing on the brown liquid a moment before lifting it to her lips. She needed that feeling of headiness that came from the first sip, then a second. Feeling the warmth trickle down her throat and into her stomach, she closed her eyes and mentally replayed the events of that afternoon. It didn't seem to matter how many times she went over what she'd seen—at least ten times or more on her walk home. The results and the conclusion were the same. Putting the glass in the sink, she picked up her leather satchel that she'd dumped beside the door and pulled out the manila file. She knew she shouldn't be bringing this home with her. It was bad enough that she'd seen it. Frost would be livid if he knew that she'd taken it from the lab. But she needed to check the information one more time.

Anja threw the file onto the coffee table. The slap of the paper on wood made her start. She went to pour herself another drink. One brandy clearly wasn't going to be enough. The sofa creaked as she sat down, the way it always greeted her, but it made her flinch nonetheless. She couldn't shake the feeling of walking along a narrow pier and knowing that she could fall off or be pushed off any minute. Taking another gulp, she spread the contents of the file across the table.

There were lists of names, photos, dates, times, drug trials. The way the notes were put together made it seem like any of the hundreds of files they had on regular drug trials, unless you looked a little deeper. There were no consent forms. The people involved were all listed as "of no fixed abode," status "drug addict," "prostitute," or "Indian." There were various acronyms written against most of the names, and it took a while for Anja to figure out that they indicated what other non-pharmaceutical drugs the trial subjects were taking, the side effects of the particular version of the trial drug, and also the reason for death for those subjects who did not survive each trial. There had been three unofficial trials of FERISIT. According to the paperwork in the manila file, over twenty-five percent of the subjects of

Maggie Denhearn

the third trial had either died or suffered permanent serious brain and liver damage. None of this was documented in the final report.

Taking out another file from her bag, a blue one, she pulled the papers out of it and began lining them up next to the ones from the manila file. The paperwork in each matched, but with crucial differences. The names of the subjects were the same, but in the blue file, each suddenly had a regular address and occupation: housewife, plumber, office worker. Rather than records of whether they were using cocaine, heroin, or alcohol, instead subjects either had "N/A" checked against their name or a note that they were taking headache medication or something for blood pressure. None of the subjects, according to the blue file, experienced any major side effects, and none of them died. There was no evidence of the major psychoses, manic episodes, or suicides that were documented in the manila file. And according to the blue file, the subjects who had died according to the manila file were marked down as "moved out of province," where a current address was also noted. The blue file was the official one used to make the entries into the official company ledger, which was kept for audit purposes. The blue file she was familiar with. She knew there would be no record of the manila file. Officially, it would not exist.

Anja drained her glass of the remaining brandy and burst into tears.

CHAPTER 3

MONDAY MORNING, APRIL 14, 2014

John Frost stared down at his breakfast plate in disgust and pushed it away.
"Mary! Mary!" He hissed, banging his fist on the table. "Mary!"

Mary, who had been dutifully standing on guard by the breakfast buffet, waddled over to him. She was a short, rotund woman in her late sixties, with a dodgy hip and a permanently haunted look on her face. She had been working for Frost for over forty years. She was his maid, housekeeper, cook, and butler. She was used to his moods. When he was younger, he could issue a deep bellow if he was dissatisfied with something, but at eighty-four years of age and with a recent partial laryngectomy, the most he could manage was a hoarse, raspy whisper. The years of smoking Gauloises had finally caught up with him.

"Sir? Sorry, sir. What is it, sir?"

"I can't eat this. Take it away."

"So sorry, sir. What's wrong with it? Can I make it again for you?"

He waved his hand at her dismissively. "No, no, nothing's wrong with it. I've just no appetite this morning. Just pour me more coffee."

Mary shuffled back to the breakfast buffet for the coffee jug and brought it over to the table. She poured more into his cup, being careful not to let the slightest drop escape onto the bright, white tablecloth. He grunted his way of saying thank-you.

He glanced over at the clock on the mantelpiece. It was an Albany, manufactured around 1866, with mahogany casing, roman numerals, and

Maggie Denhearn

gold inlay hands that clicked gently as they marked the passing of each minute of every hour. It was a family heirloom and still kept perfect time. Alexis Bailey and Judge Rawley would be arriving in about ten minutes. He sipped his coffee, brooding. He wasn't sure why they were so keen to see him, but he suspected the reasons were not going to please him. Most of their communication was either by telephone or the occasional carefully crafted email. They met face-to-face only when there was a problem.

He heard the front doorbell and watched as Mary hobbled over to answer it. He preferred a limited staff these days, his distrust of almost everyone having turned into something of an obsession. Mary did most things for him around the house, and he had other staff to take care of the grounds, plus a driver and an on-call nurse.

He had spent all his life accumulating wealth, only to find that he now had no idea what he was going to do with everything when he died. He wasn't sure whether he still wanted to bequeath everything to his once-estranged sons. The ten years when they had not communicated had caused a rift between them that had not entirely healed after years of being reunited, and mistrust remained on both sides. Efforts at rebuilding a connection and time passing had not managed to completely chip away at the rock of resentment sitting between them. Perhaps all fathers and sons were like this. Perhaps theirs was a perfectly normal relationship. He was under no illusion that it would get any better than it was. There wasn't enough time left for that.

Their relationship now involved a level of bitter tolerance and sour disdain, yet it worked. Frost retained his power as the head of the family and the respect to which such a position entitled him. He toyed with the idea of bequeathing everything to charity, one last opportunity to get one over his sons, but he realized he wouldn't be around to enjoy the victory. Besides, he couldn't think of a charity he would like to leave anything to. Thus far his misanthropy was keeping him going, and he didn't believe he was going to die quite yet, so he had time yet to revise his will if he chose. For the time being, his sons would have to remain his official benefactors. In the first flush of their reunion after a decade of silence, he had called his lawyer and changed his will but had regretted this show of weakness ever since. He took another sip of coffee.

When the Universe Called

The sound of Mary shuffling back into the breakfast room with footsteps close behind her broke into his thoughts. The sun was shining through the bay window overlooking the lush green lawn, perfectly mown within an inch of its life. Rays of light danced across the tablecloth, refracting through the crystal lamp on the oak dresser.

"Judge Rawley." His voice was particularly scratchy this morning, and he noticed how Judge Rawley winced at the sound of him. He knew people found it painful to hear him speak.

"Frost." The judge nodded, curling his upper lip back and biting his lower lip. It was a nervous tick he displayed when he was agitated, which the judge clearly didn't realize he had, although it had earned him the ridiculous nickname Bugsy. Rumor had it that occasionally he would find a raw carrot on his desk at work. This behavior toward a superior court judge was somewhat disrespectful, but apparently he'd never yet managed to find the perpetrator, and Darcy, his trusted secretary, had been unable to identify the culprit. Frost smiled to himself. He'd rather be feared and make people feel uncomfortable than be an object of derision. The judge had a bulging gut, gray hair, and yellowy orange bumps on his hands, sure signs of elevated cholesterol. Frost wasn't the only one from whom age was stealing time.

Alexis Bailey, however, defied the stereotype of men aging better than women. At seventy-eight and much older than the judge, Bailey could pass for being in her early sixties, still glamorous and apparently without having resorted to plastic surgery. She would outlive them all, if for no other reason, just to spite them.

"So what is it you want? It must be important if you've come around here." Frost couldn't be bothered to hide his ill humor or the strain in his voice. Up to this point, Bailey had yet to speak, merely nodding in greeting. She glanced over at the judge, who was carefully studying his fingernails. Clearly he was too cowardly to speak up. She cleared her throat and stared squarely at Frost.

"We think we've found Anja."

Frost was holding his coffee cup up to his mouth just as she spoke. The cup seemed to hover in midair, then to take on a momentum of its own, falling onto the table, splattering coffee everywhere. Mary hurried over, picked up the cup and saucer, and pulled the coffee-stained part of the

Maggie Denhearn

tablecloth away from him, all the while apologizing. Frost froze. He felt the blood drain from his face and beads of sweat start to form on his forehead. The judge and Bailey didn't move. They were watching him, waiting no doubt to see any further reaction. Frost wanted to smash the contemptuous smile creeping up onto Bailey's face. These days she did little to hide the disdain she felt for the men around her. More than once Frost had fantasized in minute detail how he would wipe that sneer off her face for good.

"Mary, might you bring us all some fresh coffee? And some brandy for Mr. Frost."

Mary glanced over at Frost for his approval, then nodded at Bailey and shuffled as quickly as she was able out of the room. When she was gone, Bailey continued.

"We realize this must be somewhat of a shock to you. We had no idea that she was alive either until a short while ago."

"Shocked? *Shocked?*" Frost wanted to shout, but the most he could manage was a croaky whisper. Bailey's predilection for understatement was infuriating. *Shocked* didn't begin to cover it. "I shot her. She was dead. I saw her. I saw her go down." Breathy words erupted out of him, spewing out as though he were about to throw up.

"Apparently you didn't. Well, not dead, anyway."

"But ... but she ... I ..." The blood was returning to his cheeks and he started to splutter. His hands shook as he reached over to a glass and tried to take a sip of water.

"We're still trying to establish the facts. So far it appears that you had only injured her. Another police officer found her and helped her." Bailey's manner was cool, a glint of enjoyment evident in her eyes.

"But ... But how can that be?" Frost couldn't stop his hands from shaking, almost spilling water everywhere. Bailey put her hand on his in an apparent effort to calm him and to stop the water from pouring out of the glass. In spite of the loathing he felt for her, a feeling of sexual attraction seared through him, which he did his best to ignore. There was a time when they had been more than business associates. His body had a mind of its own more and more these days. He could see she was enjoying every moment of his discomfort.

When the Universe Called

"There's more." Bailey paused. Mary appeared and handed him a glass of brandy. He gulped it straight back, dropping the glass back down on the table. Mary recoiled, then reached out and took the empty glass.

"The coffee is just coming," she mumbled and shuffled out again. Frost stared at Bailey, his eyes rheumy.

"Spit it out, woman."

"We have reason to believe that Luke knows her, has known her for quite a while. She goes by the name of Brina these days. She runs some kind of coffee shop on Vancouver Island, in Eagle Cove. The Consortium is still investigating their potential connection. We've been watching him for a few months. It could just be a coincidence."

Frost slammed his fist down on the table, sending a teaspoon flying across the tablecloth. A coincidence was unlikely. He didn't believe in coincidences, not ones that great at any rate.

"Why didn't you tell me any of this before?"

"I … We didn't see the point in troubling you until we were closer to getting more information."

"I'm still the head of this consortium. Remember that. And I will remain so as long as I'm still breathing." Unfortunately, at that precise moment he started coughing, and was unable to catch his breath. Mary, approaching with a silver coffee pot, waddled over and poured him more water from the jug in front of him, holding the glass up to his mouth. Feeling as though that made him look childlike and weak, he batted her away and the glass fell to the floor. The carpet cushioned the thick cut crystal. It didn't break, just rolled underneath the table. Frost watched Mary bend down awkwardly to recover it. Then she backed away and began busying herself with pouring the three of them more coffee.

"You were too soft. You should have let us deal with her." Bailey uncrossed and then crossed her legs, letting one of her very high shoes dangle. "So we're dealing with her now."

Frost stared past Bailey and across at the rhododendron bushes by the window, not quite in bloom. They would soon come out in a burst of red, the exact color of the shoes Anja had been wearing the last time he had seen her, a constant reminder of the blood he had on his hands. Or at least had thought he had. He remembered that he had the gun in his hand and pointed it straight at her heart. His hands were shaking and he couldn't steady them. He didn't want to shoot her, yet he had no choice. She had betrayed him to the police. He closed his eyes and pulled the trigger. When he opened his eyes she lay crumpled on the ground like a rag doll, the sound of the shot echoing in the alley. She didn't move. She looked dead. He was sure she was dead. He heard voices and footsteps coming their way and fled the scene, not daring to look back. She was the one weakness he had ever shown in his life. And she was back from the dead.

The judge sighed but said nothing.

Frost tried to focus on the here and now, but his mind kept wandering back to that moment with the gun.

"We need to act. Promptly. There's no time to be wasted. We have our sources in the police still, and in the press, but clearly I would like to limit my involvement in that regard." Bailey curled her lips as she spoke, looking as though she had just eaten something distasteful.

Frost held up his hand. "No. Not yet. If she's not done anything, leave her for the time being. Just keep an eye on her and on Luke." The judge and Bailey exchanged looks. They must have thought he was blind. They were up to something and thought he was too senile to notice. He would bide his time. No one got the better of him.

"Then there's nothing more to discuss." Bailey got up and started to leave.

"Wait. What about the bill? Where are we on that?"

"You mean 267? The third reading is being brought forward. The twenty-eighth. Once the legislation is in place for the compulsory DNA testing of convicted felons, we'll be able to roll out mass production of Torporo. We're just waiting for it to get FDA approval." She glanced over at the judge.

"Our distinguished judges will see to that, won't they, Judge Rawley?"

Judge Rawley met her gaze, but still said nothing. Frost sneered. The judge was such a coward.

"Okay. Goodbye then." Frost stared again at the rhododendrons.

*   *   *   *

When the Universe Called

It was almost lunchtime by the time Bailey sat down at her desk and began scanning through her email, her fingers deftly tapping the keyboard as she scrolled through her messages. Although she had retired several years ago as police commissioner for British Columbia, the first woman ever to hold such a post, she continued in various advisory roles and had extensive speaking engagements. Today there were 103 emails in her inbox—not an unusual amount. Typically her secretary would go through them first and highlight the ones to which she should pay particular attention. That was for her regular email. She also had a private account, one few people knew about, not even her secretary. It was this account she next started to read through.

There was another message from Andy McDowell. She would read that later. The mayor seemed to have an overblown sense of his own importance that Bailey found rather tiresome.

She continued scrolling down until she reached a message from Heeley, the Consortium's go-to man for any less savory job it needed handling, but with which it could not be seen to be associated. She paused before opening it, reflecting on her meeting with Frost that morning. Frost had totally screwed up all those years ago and had been lucky to avoid both prosecution and scandal. Bailey didn't relish the idea of a repeat performance. The possibilities and implications reverberated around her mind like pinballs whizzing round a pinball machine. She opened Heeley's email, scanned a few lines, then picked up the phone.

"Heeley? It's me. I got your email."

"And?"

"It's time. Get Luke. The bill has to be pushed through on the twenty-eighth. We can't afford any glitches. And Heeley … dispose of Brina. I don't care what Frost says. She knows too much."

"Got it."

"And you're sure Luke hasn't figured out Charlotte is working with us?"

"I am. He hasn't a clue. We've got her under surveillance too, just in case she decides to change her mind about where her loyalties lie."

"Hmm. Good idea. And where are you on finding out if Petturi is involved with them?"

"Nowhere so far, but working on it."

39

Maggie Denhearn

"Keep at it. This whole thing reeks of his hand."

She ended the call and stared out of the window. From her office in the Harbor Centre, she could see the whole of the Vancouver skyline. It was one of her favorite views. She liked the idea of being able to look down on people, to be able to see the protective wall of mountains off in the distance, to feel as though she were above everyone else. The idea that Brina and Luke and whoever else thought they could somehow destroy the Consortium was laughable. It wasn't possible. Still, it was better to play it safe. There was too much at stake. Bill 267 needed to go through or billions of dollars would be lost, and there would be several angry members of the Consortium, powerful men, asking what on earth had gone wrong. And Bailey would take the fall. Seeing as Frost owned FPH, they could hardly go after him. And besides, he was clearly on his last legs, so what would be the point? No, as second in command of the Consortium, second only to Frost, who was weaker by the day, it was her reputation on the line and more. She knew what the Consortium did to people it no longer needed. Picking up the phone again, she hammered the numbers in irritation.

"Judge? It's me. We need to act. Frost is weak. It's time. Get everyone together and meet me at the club, let's say Wednesday evening at 8:00 p.m. That'll give people time to convene. We'll do the vote then." A bloodless coup. Well ... almost.

5:00 A.M. SATURDAY, AUGUST 3, 1963

Anja had been up all night, poring over the papers, desperate to find anything that would indicate that she was wrong. Nothing. After half a bottle of brandy and only a couple of slices of toast and butter to eat, her head was pounding, and the overwhelming urge to throw up wouldn't go away. She made herself some coffee and added three heaped teaspoons of sugar. Although she wasn't quite ready to face it, she knew exactly what she had to do.

She started to cry again. Was she crying for herself or for Frost? Both probably. She loved him. He'd said he would leave his wife, that he'd get a divorce. Anja had believed him. Perhaps he still would, but it didn't matter

40

When the Universe Called

anymore. She wasn't proud of herself for having an affair with a married man. It was something in the way he looked at her that she'd been unable to resist. For the first time since her mother died, when Anja was eighteen, she had felt safe. He took care of her, gave her the security she had been hankering after. Or so she had thought. Perhaps that was what she had actually fallen in love with: safety, security.

Reading the manila file had shattered all of that. There was nothing safe or secure about being with John Frost. If she had been in any doubt that he had known of the existence of these unofficial trials, the handwritten notes and annotated documents in his handwriting left no doubt at all. Gulping back the coffee, she pulled out some clean clothes from the wardrobe and got changed. If she didn't go to the police now, she might not have the courage later.

Anja looked up as the police officer handed her a handkerchief. She had tried to remain composed, but the moment she started to explain why she was at the police station, she broke down. She was surprised to see a woman. She was good-looking, even in a uniform obviously designed for a less feminine physique. Her dark brown hair was pulled back neatly into a ponytail. Everything about the way she wore her clothes was organized, considered. Her hazel eyes were intelligent but cold. Anja glanced down at the floor, focusing on the stains on the tiles.

"I'm sorry, I think I need to speak to a detective. It's kind of serious."

"I'm Officer Alexis Bailey."

Anja realized she must have shown her surprise as Officer Bailey continued, "There aren't many female police officers around, I know, but the Vancouver Police Department is somewhat more enlightened than other places. So tell me what's going on and we'll see if you need to talk with someone more senior. Has someone hurt you?"

"No, not me." Anja scanned the waiting room. She couldn't talk here. The policewoman was intuitive, noticed her desire to speak elsewhere.

"How about we find somewhere more private?" Anja nodded. Taking a deep breath, she followed Officer Bailey into a side room. The walls were so white the color hurt her eyes. There was a tiny window high up on one wall that allowed a trickle of daylight to seep into the starkness of the room. It smelt of ammonia and cigarettes. Officer Bailey pulled out a metal chair and

41

Maggie Denhearn

motioned for Anja to sit down, while she pulled out another and sat opposite her. On the bare, gray table between them, she put a notepad and pencil, and pushed a lukewarm glass of water in Anja's direction.

"Have a sip of water. That'll make you feel better. Take your time."

"I'm not sure where to start." Anja truly wasn't. Pulling her satchel onto her lap, she took out the two files, one blue, one manila.

"I discovered something where I work, at FPH—you know, Frost Pharma Health. I found this yesterday." She pushed the files toward Officer Bailey and watched as she opened the files and started to read.

Anja took a gulp of water. It tasted sour. She waited, watching Officer Bailey's face. Her expression betrayed nothing. It wasn't the reaction Anja had been expecting.

After about ten minutes, Officer Bailey finally spoke, her tone matter of fact.

"You'd better leave these with me."

"Do you understand what these mean? They're not reporting all the drug trials. They're experimenting on people!" Anja heard that her own voice sounded oddly hoarse.

"I understand the possible implications of the material you have brought in. I'll make sure this is dealt with appropriately."

"Okay, but I can't leave the files. I have to put them back at work. I shouldn't have taken them from the laboratory in the first place. If it's noticed they're missing, I'll be the first person who's suspected of taking them." She didn't feel safe; none of this was safe. She shouldn't have come here.

"I'm sorry, these are police evidence now." She paused, eyeing Anja in a way that made her feel like she was somehow the criminal. "Okay, I'll see what I can do about getting them copied. You'll still have to leave them with me, though. Let me take down some contact details."

"What's going to happen?"

"We'll deal with this. You've done the right thing by bringing this to our attention. You can leave it with us now."

"But what do I do?" A lurching feeling in Anja's stomach was making her feel dizzy.

When the Universe Called

"Go back to work and pretend you don't know anything. Don't worry. No one will know how this information was brought in."

Anja hesitated. She'd never been to the police before, but she'd imagined that she would have to speak to a detective or someone with more authority, not just a police officer. She tried to push the doubts to the back of her mind, to ignore the feeling in the pit of her stomach. She was overreacting. It was probably because she was upset and they'd sent the only woman around to deal with her. That was why she'd not seen a detective. That had to be it. Officer Bailey smiled coldly at her and said goodbye. As Anja was fastening her satchel and heading toward the door, she heard a male voice call out.

"Bailey, so what did that young woman want?"

"The usual. Said she was being abused by her boyfriend but then wouldn't press charges. Typical."

Anja froze. Not daring to turn around, she started fumbling with her satchel again as she walked, trying to make it look as though she wasn't paying attention to anything else. Walking out into the sunshine of a warm, bright Vancouver morning, she started to walk briskly, then run down the road.

CHAPTER 4

Around 7:30 p.m. Monday, April 14, 2014

Maria didn't miss a beat. Whatever Kali had got into had to be kept secret. As director of communications for the mayor, Maria couldn't let anything harm McDowell's reputation. She had worked hard to get to this position. She might be about to lose her marriage. She wasn't about to lose her job as well. If McDowell lost the election because of some scandal to do with his wife, Maria would be out on her ear. All those years of dealing with the mayor's boorish behavior and indiscretions, of making sure McDowell found her to be indispensable, first of all volunteering at his campaign office, then working her way up from admin assistant to doing something more interesting, had to count for something. Before coming to work for him, she'd been a journalist on one of the local newspapers, so she knew exactly how the media worked. One whiff of a story, no matter how tenuous, and the hounds would be unleashed.

Apart from anything else, she didn't want to move. She loved living in Eagle Cove: the quiet, the community, the escape from the rest of the world. Decent jobs were hard enough to find generally on the Island, even harder to come by in Eagle Cove.

As she drove to the trail where Kali had said to meet her, the world—her world—seemed very different. Over one cup of tea her life had changed, and judging by the hysteria in Kali's voice, hers didn't appear to be going too well either. Maria felt heavy. The blood flowing through her was getting thicker, moving more slowly. She wasn't prone to superstition, but she couldn't shake

44

When the Universe Called

the feeling that something bigger was afoot, with Maria and Kali as pawns in some big game. An image of herself dressed as a chess piece with a giant hand reaching down from a dark cloud and moving her across a chess board popped into her head.

There was a strange energy in the air. The fact that a bizarrely warm wind was blowing and that the storm had yet to break did not help her mood. She stopped herself. She was being melodramatic and it didn't suit her.

She pulled into the parking lot. Only one other car parked; it was Kali's. Maria started to walk along the trail. It was dusk. She'd never come here at this time of the day before. Sure, they would sometimes go out for early morning runs, starting out when it was barely light, but somehow day breaking was invigorating. Night falling was entirely different. The leaden sky cast long shadows through the trees, and what little light remained danced around in odd shapes as the leaves and branches swayed and swished in the wind, playing a lugubrious song.

Maria felt the hair on the back of her neck stand on end, and she shuddered. She wasn't sure which she was more afraid of: coming across someone other than Kali, unlikely as that seemed, or meeting the local wildlife. At least animals would keep silent, would not pass on anything they had seen.

Crunch, crunch, crunch. She heard the sound of her feet on the gravel. Every sound was amplified, echoing back to her and signaling to the world her arrival. The trees watched her march past, waving balefully in the breeze. Fortunately she knew the trails well enough that she had a good idea of the spot Kali had described, even in the half-light. As places go for a secret assignation, she could see why they had chosen that particular clearing. It was rather magical, otherworldly. Maria had the sense that if fairies or magical creatures existed, that's where they would hang out.

Turning a bend in the trail to where the bush was beaten back, she saw Kali sitting on a fallen tree, staring vacantly into space. She turned to look at Maria and jumped up, flinging her arms around her.

"I'm so glad you came!" Maria tried to step back and disentangle herself from Kali. She wasn't a fan of hugging, and this was no time for sentimentality.

Maggie Denhearn

"So what's all this about?" Maria didn't need Kali to answer. The second the words were out of her mouth, she saw Noah's body. She clasped her hands over her mouth.

"What the ... Kali, what's happened?" She bent down to feel his pulse, but from the dark stain, just visible in the dim light and which she assumed to be blood, she knew there was no life left. Only then did it register that he wasn't wearing any clothes.

"Kali ... were you ...?" Maria wasn't quite sure why she couldn't bring herself to ask out loud whether they'd been making love. Was it because Noah was Luke's twin brother? It was the most bizarre feeling, seeing a man identical to her husband, collapsed naked on the forest floor.

"You see why I couldn't say more over the phone."

Maria suddenly felt embarrassed seeing Noah naked, exposed. It seemed disrespectful. She tried to avert her eyes, but she couldn't help taking another look. She hadn't realized what great shape he was in. Evidently Noah was a man who took care of himself. She wished Luke would work out a bit more often. He seemed to be letting himself go. It did seem strange that someone as young as Charlotte would see anything in Luke.

So it seemed Noah and Luke were both having affairs. Maria had always found them very alike. But this? For a moment she wished it were Luke who was lying dead and cold.

She snapped back to where she was when Kali started to snivel. Noah was definitely dead, very dead indeed. This was not his best look: his jeans half on one leg, his body twisted in some painful-looking pose, and the blood. It looked like he was playing some kind of Halloween prank. None of this was real. Memories of family get-togethers started to prance through her mind, different images of Noah. She took a deep breath. She had to stay composed.

"Kali, you need to try and pull yourself together and tell me what happened."

"We ... Well, Noah texted me to ask if I ..."

"The brief version. How did Noah end up like this? Did you argue? Was he trying to hurt you?" Maria was already going through the various possible scenarios in her head.

"Of course not. He wouldn't have hurt me. How could you say that?"

46

When the Universe Called

"Kali ..."

"Okay, well I guess it's obvious seeing as he's naked, and so was I. Well, I got dressed. But, well, one minute we were ... it was all so amazing, and then I don't know what happened. My foot slipped or something, and he fell, and I guess he hit his head on a rock. Or on something hard, anyway, by the looks of things. It all happened so suddenly. He was dead, but I wasn't sure. I couldn't find a pulse, but ... and then the blood ..., and ... I didn't know what to do, so I called you." Her voice speeded up and became more high-pitched.

"Did you call the police?"

"No, not yet. Do I have to? Andy can't find out about this. He'll kill me." In the little remaining light Maria could see her trembling. She wasn't sure if it was from the shock of what had happened to Noah or the thought of what McDowell would do to her if he knew what she'd been up to.

"How long have you and Noah ... erm ... Have you been together long?"

"A few months."

Maria sensed that numb feeling creeping over her again. Noah had been carrying on behind everyone's backs too, and so had Kali. At least Noah wasn't married. But he knew Kali was. And Maria hadn't noticed anything was up with either of them. She felt sick.

"What *were* you thinking?" Maria's voice raised then lowered as she realized how the sound was echoing around the forest. Another ten or fifteen minutes and it would be pitch black. The discussions of the whys and wherefores would have to come later.

They couldn't leave him like this. Apart from this position not being the way he would want everyone to remember him, it seemed a little unfair that some poor, unsuspecting hiker or runner might come across him like that. At least she knew their running group the WOECs wouldn't be out in the morning, so there was less danger of one of them finding him. It needed to look like he'd had an accident. He had, she was sure. She couldn't imagine things had happened any other way than how Kali had described. They just needed to make sure that it didn't look suspicious, which was a bit tricky, given that he was naked.

"We've got to get his clothes back on."

"I've tried." Kali was trying not to cry again. Maria would have dearly liked to slap her for a variety of reasons, but didn't.

"Okay, you've got to pull yourself together. You can disintegrate later, not now. We've got work to do. Give me a hand. Where are his undershorts?"

"He wasn't wearing any."

"Okay, okay." Together they somehow managed to get his jeans back on. What should they do about his shirt? If he'd been wearing it when he died, it would surely have blood on the outside, not the inside. If they put it on him now, any blood on his body would get on the inside of his shirt. Better to leave it off. They left his shoes to one side and opted for leaving his shirt by the other side of him.

"Where are his socks?" They looked around. "Forget it, there's no time to look for them." Maria tried to touch as little as possible, directing Kali to move things, and putting on her running gloves that she remembered she'd left in her jacket pocket when they were putting the jeans back on his body. Kali's DNA was already all over him, and at least she had some explanation for it, if it came to that. They both hoped that it wouldn't.

The next issue was where to place him. Somehow, leaving him where he was didn't seem like a good idea, but moving the body didn't seem much of a plan either. The question was whether they should hide his body or not. If they left him where he was, it would look like the accident that it was. Yet he seemed so exposed.

"We could pull some branches over him. That wouldn't be so bad." Kali sniffed.

Maria rolled her eyes. "A corpse can hardly pull branches over itself! Do you want to be arrested for murder?"

"Good point."

"Look, the only option is to try and leave him back in the same position he fell in and to try and make the ground look as undisturbed as possible."

They had to move him this way and that to get his jeans back on. They rolled him onto his back again and placed his head so it was twisted at the peculiar angle Kali had first witnessed when she had opened her eyes, his head resting against a sharp and now bloodied rock. It was disconcerting to see his eyes open. Maria tried not to catch his eye.

"Won't the ravens get him, or the bears?" Kali wailed.

When the Universe Called

"Not a lot we can do about that, I'm afraid. Just don't think about it. His body will be discovered sooner rather than later. There are enough locals who come along here. We do."

There was a somber silence between them. The implications of what had happened were trickling down, one by one. Questions would be asked. Who knew what evidence they were leaving behind? Maria wasn't entirely sure they were doing the right thing, but it was all she could think of right at this moment. The thought of them being the topic of gossip of their local running group, of Luke's affair even, would surely be the least of their problems. What on earth was she going to say to Luke? How would she tell him? He'd be devastated. What would happen when Noah's body was found?

Maria looked at Kali, wondering where her mind was going. Her expression was like that of a stunned fawn who's just seen its mother hit by a truck.

"Don't go there, wherever it is you're going. It won't help, not right now. It was an accident; I believe you. It wasn't your fault. Let's go."

They tried to fiddle with the undergrowth to make it look less trampled down. They could hope for rain to cover some of their tracks. Although it hadn't rained for weeks, the storm had to break sooner or later. The air was thick. They had to trust that the forensic people were good at their job and could tell an accident from a murder. A poor guy was out on a walk and somehow slipped and banged his head—while removing his shirt and shoes? Rather a long shot, but truth was often stranger than fiction. In her head, Maria was already imagining the official press statement.

*   *   *   *

Maria felt like she was made of stone by the time she got home. She couldn't risk feeling anything, not about Noah, not about her flailing marriage. It was just after nine thirty, and Luke was in the living room. She didn't bother going in, even though not to do so was unusual and could potentially draw attention to her if he noticed. She couldn't face him so went and sat down in her home office. The list of reasons to avoid him had increased exponentially over the last couple of hours. Luke having an affair seemed petty in comparison to knowing his twin brother had just died,

49

Maggie Denhearn

but how could she tell him without him knowing she was complicit in hiding what had happened? And why exactly was she doing that? She wasn't sure how much was to help her friend, how much was to save McDowell's reputation and by implication her job, and how much of it was some kind of warped passive-aggressive retaliation against Luke for being an adulterer. Or was she just acting on autopilot, turning into a robot?

Luke came to the doorway of her study. He ran his finger slowly up and down the doorjamb, a gesture that would have appeared casual if it weren't for the forced way in which he was doing it. Now he was the one being unusually attentive, asking if she was okay. Odd, seeing as it was she who had gone out unexpectedly and not told him where she was going. He didn't even ask where she'd been, a sure sign he was feeling guilty about something. She mumbled something about having a headache and turned back to her computer. He wandered off into the kitchen and she heard him put the kettle on.

Maria stared at the computer screen in front of her, but nothing was registering. She was playing through her mind the events of the last few hours. How had she gone from making tea to discovering her husband was being unfaithful, then to helping Kali cover up the death of her brother-in-law, Noah? She couldn't say she was exactly shocked about finding out that Noah and Kali had been having an affair, but she was certainly surprised. Maria clearly wasn't as good a judge of character as she thought she was. She wondered what could have possessed Kali to get involved with him. Of all the people to cheat on and of all the men to choose to cheat with, she couldn't have made it any worse if she'd tried. Too young to know any better it would seem. Noah was a good few years older than her too. He should have known better.

As she shut down her laptop and flipped the lid down, she caught sight of her wedding photo. She worked in her home office nearly every day of the week, but it had been ages since she had noticed that photo. It wasn't one of the official ones. It was one Noah had taken when Maria and Luke weren't looking. They both looked so happy. Somewhere between work, work and the silence of a house large enough for a family that never came, they had drifted apart. It was like they were shouting across a huge lake at each other, neither able to hear the other. It wasn't that she disliked Luke. Far from it. In fact, finding out he was having an affair had jolted her into realizing that she still had far more feelings left for him than she realized.

When the Universe Called

The problem was that of late she just found him incredibly annoying and frustrating—and boring, so utterly boring. He didn't used to be so stifled, so stiff. Would things be different if they'd had children? Sometimes not getting something you wish for is the actual blessing. Children aren't exactly known for their ability to bring couples together. Now at least, she had only herself to think about. Yet the pain of not having a child was like a sore that wouldn't heal. In spite of herself, in spite of her husband, she loved him, or at least was still in love with who they used to be together. She couldn't get the thought of Luke and Charlotte being together out of her head, nor the image of Noah lying on the forest floor with a blood-splattered head. Even if she didn't confront Luke about Charlotte, she knew she should tell him about his brother. She couldn't find the words. Each time she tried to formulate the sentence in her head, the words evaporated and her mind went blank. This was what her father's Alzheimer's must be like, knowing what you want to say but the words slipping away from you, unable to gain any traction in your mind.

*   *   *   *

"You know, I have to go away for a couple of days on business." She heard Luke's voice seeping into her thoughts as she walked into their bedroom.

"What?"

He was suddenly behind her at the bedroom door, fingering the doorjamb again.

"I've got a last-minute business trip, so I have to go away for a couple of days."

She paused, trying to read his expression. He was playing it cool and giving nothing away. Here it was. While she'd gone out, he and Charlotte must have cooked up some plan or other to have some time away together. Or worse. She glanced over at their bed to see if it had been slept in or remade. The silky blue covers were smooth and neat. It didn't look like it been disturbed from the morning when she had made it. The top sheet was turned down exactly the way she liked.

"Ah. Where?"

"The mainland."

"That's a big place."

Maggie Denhearn

"Well, just outside of Vancouver. I thought I'd got out of going, but Paul is sick and I have to go in his place. I wanted to tell you earlier, but Charlotte was here, and then you went out."

"I didn't think lawyers had emergency business trips."

"It's hardly that. Just all the heavy guns getting together, and they need someone from the legal department to be there. Big account stuff, an excuse for everyone to stay at a swanky hotel and write it off to tax."

Maria scrutinized him. He seemed to be trying too much to sound offhand. His forehead was creased the way it did when he was thinking too hard.

"Well, have a good time."

"Sorry, darling."

"Why would you be sorry? I go away all the time. It'll do you good to get away for a bit." She caught herself and tried to sound casual. "Who else is going with you?"

"A few of us." Maria couldn't work out whether his vagueness was deliberate. She tried not to roll her eyes. It occurred to her that his going away might actually be good. It would give her and Kali a little more time to figure out what to do, would delay the inevitable terrible conversation just a little while longer. It was beginning to dawn on her that she would have to come up with something exceptionally creative to explain why she had helped Kali with Noah's body and not told him.

"Well, I hope it's not too boring and that you have a good time." She wandered off into the bathroom to wash her face. The cool water and the tangerine smell of the face soap were reassuring. She buried her face in her hands, the tips of her fingers touching the crown of her forehead and the edges of her cheekbones as though she were physically trying to keep her mask in place. One slip and the river of dark thoughts and emotions might all come pouring out of her.

He had broken his habit of having the radio on while they went through their usual nighttime routines. He was trying to be solicitous. Usually the buzz of the radio annoyed her, but this evening she almost asked him to switch it on. Engaging in this polite conversation was excruciating. Maria was usually calm, good in a crisis, could keep her head. This Maria with her mind a torrent of—of what exactly? This Maria she didn't recognize.

52

When the Universe Called

Finishing up in the bathroom, she was about to come back into the bedroom but stopped. She heard Luke on the phone. It was late, past 10:30 p.m. He wasn't crass enough to be talking to Charlotte. He sounded angry.

"No, I'm being serious, I've not heard from him all day. ... I know, but there's not a lot I can do about that. ... Okay, okay, I'll call him again. I've already left three messages. I'll leave him another one. ... No, no, I'm sure there's a perfectly reasonable explanation."

A few moments silence, then, "Where are you? Why aren't you returning my calls? You know who's been calling me, looking for you? Call me as soon as you get this message."

Maria remained standing in the bathroom doorway, rubbing her shoulders.

"Is everything okay?" She wandered back into the bedroom and watched him pacing up and down. He stopped when he saw her, like he'd been caught in the act of doing something he shouldn't.

"Erm yes, fine."

"You look agitated."

"It's nothing, forget it."

Maria stared at him. He turned away and carried on packing his things, then slowly turned back, his tone softer.

"Look, I'm stressed about something at work. That's all. I don't want to talk about it. Let's just go to bed." He sighed, a shock of hair falling over his forehead. She saw the man in her wedding photo, not the man she'd been married to all these years. She caught her breath.

Neither spoke as they finished their bedtime ablutions and switched off their respective bedside lamps. Maria lay on her back in the dark, occasionally looking sideways at the stony back of her husband. He may as well have placed a brick wall between them right down the middle of the bed. Something felt wrong, really wrong, but she couldn't put her finger on it. She knew why *she* felt like the world was crumbling around her, but he seemed unusually on edge too. There was something going on with Luke, and her intuition was telling her this wasn't just about Charlotte.

*　　*　　*　　*

Luke lay there thinking. He knew Maria was awake and staring at his back. He felt her eyes burning into his spine. He wasn't sure what part of his conversation Maria had overheard, or if she'd heard all of it, what she would then be thinking. She couldn't find out. Not now, not after all this time, and not like this. He'd managed to protect her all these years from his father, from the Consortium. He couldn't bear the thought of everything now falling apart. He'd hoped one day, once the Consortium had been brought down, he could explain everything to her.

Although he wasn't sure whether she loved him anymore, he still loved her. He'd just never been quite sure how to show how he felt in a way that she understood. They had always spoken different emotional languages. His involved ensuring there was a protective layer around himself and not getting too close. He had lost too much in his life early on. As far as he could tell, being close to people only ended in pain for everyone. Maria was wrapped up in her work and he in his. Somehow they had made it work. He had known what he was doing was risky and that one day everything might come tumbling down. He had this awful feeling that the time might be now.

If the Consortium were to find out that he and Noah and Brina were trying to stop them getting Bill 267 through, they would come after them. He had known he was being watched for a while, but there had been little he could do about it. And now Noah wasn't answering his phone, which wasn't normal and didn't make sense. He feared the worst. And yet he was the one who was being followed, not Noah, at least not that either of them had noticed. And Luke was getting calls from his father asking him where Noah was, summoning them both to the mainland. That seemed strange too. Why was he so keen to speak to them? Something was wrong, very wrong indeed.

SATURDAY EVENING, AUGUST 3, 1963

Anja hadn't known how to get out of going to the special dinner. She didn't want Frost to have even the slightest idea something was up, and she needed a couple more days to figure out how she was going to leave Vancouver. Her only remaining family consisted of distant cousins back in Ljubljana, far away in Yugoslavia. She remembered the sky the morning her

When the Universe Called

mother had dressed her in her best blue coat and they'd caught the train that took them away from there a couple of years after the end of the Second World War, never to return. It was a rage of color, a fanfare to bid them farewell. Her mother had told her they were going to start a better life. At eight years old, she had believed her.

Now she was alone. A few years after they had immigrated to Canada, her father had been murdered on his way home from work by an angry co-worker who had accused him of being a communist. Although she had only technically become an orphan at eighteen when her mother died, Anja felt she had lost both her parents the day her father had been taken from them. From the age of eleven she had learned how to be self-sufficient. Frost had offered her the dream of security.

Now that dream had been shattered into hundreds of tiny pieces, each one engraved with the name of someone who had been hurt or worse during one of Frost's illegal drug trials. Reading those files was enough for her to realize this was not a man you crossed—and not the man she had been in love with.

She looked across at him as he undid his tie and started taking off his shoes, slumping down onto the bed. They were in their usual hotel room, the dinner now over. She knew what came next. This was what she would usually long for all evening, to have him hold her in his arms, to feel his fingers lightly caress her skin. She lingered, trying to delay the inevitable and to stop herself shaking.

The phone rang. Perhaps it was his wife, and he would have to leave. How strange to be hoping for the very thing she used to dread and dreading the very thing she used to long for. Everything was upside down.

"Great news! Ha, I knew it!" He slammed down the phone in triumph and beamed.

"Knew what?"

"FERISIT, it's been approved. Well, it will be Monday. That was Senator Miller just confirming. Time to celebrate."

He lit a cigarette, and the unmistakable smell of Gauloises Bleues drifted over to Anja. He poured some champagne into two thin cut crystal glasses, and they drank deeply, him in toast, she to fortify herself. He drew her toward him and down onto the bed, pulling her mouth to his. He tasted sour.

55

Maggie Denhearn

Anja closed her eyes and shuddered as chills cut through her. Her body was screaming no; he didn't notice.

When it was over, Anja waited for the sound of him sleeping, then pulled on her cerise silk slip and walked across the darkened room to the window to look out at the city lights. She used to think of them as fairy lights, twinkling below, lighting up her fantasy world. In the cold, hard face of this breaking dawn, those same lights now laid bare the harsh world she had fallen into. She had been desperate to escape the poverty and privation of her childhood, to avoid the pain her mother had experienced. Anja had thought she could—*would*, do better. She had thought Frost a boring, older rich man looking for a young woman to brighten up his arm while his wife led her very separate life. She hadn't realized that he was merely looking for another toy to amuse him. It was the oldest of stories in the world, one that gets repeated generation after generation, century after century, and never seems to change. The actors in each drama are different, but the plot line remains the same. Anja had unintentionally become part of that chronicle, had become ensnared, a gangster's moll who would be thrown to the wolves if he ever found out she had betrayed him.

CHAPTER 5

Sunrise Tuesday, April 15, 2014

The tremor in her hands and arms from the force of the axe hitting Trevor's skull and slicing through bone and brain surged through her, and with it, a flood of relief. Up until this point, it had only been the stuff of dreams. Each time her husband's fist had connected with her cheek, her forehead, her stomach; each broken bone and line of stitches; each time she had dreamt of the moment she would finally find the courage to stand up to him. And yet, she had not actually planned to kill him that particular morning.

Last night he had come home drunk. Again. A few months ago she had tried counting how many times he returned home in an extreme state of inebriation, but she gave up after losing count. So many times he had fallen against the front door, waking her up as he thudded around, fumbling with his door key and staggering into the hallway. In days gone by she would have got up to see if he was alright, but since her trouble was invariably met either with abuse or amorous advances, neither of which were particularly attractive coming from a man who stank of stale beer and could hardly stand, she had taken to pretending to be asleep and to ignoring the flailing human being staggering around their cottage in the early hours of the morning.

Last night had been different. The universe works in mysterious ways, Iris thought, or perhaps mysterious only to her because she hadn't been paying sufficient attention. Brina kept telling her of the importance of staying conscious, of keeping her attention in the present moment. At this moment

Maggie Denhearn

in time, looking over at a now deceased Trevor and wondering quite how she had got to this place, she was starting to understand why.

Iris had woken up at the precise moment of a lunar eclipse. The moon was a coppery red, looming down from the sky—a blood moon. She was gazing sleepily out of the bedroom window at the heavens above, wondering if there was anything up there, when she heard Trevor come in. For some reason, she decided to go and see what he was doing. He'd already lurched into the house, knocking over anything in his way, including her favorite vase, which she had thought safe enough, as it was placed high up on the shelves in the kitchen. She wasn't sure how he had managed to knock it down, but there it was, in several pieces on the kitchen floor, waiting to cut her bare feet.

When she first came into the room, he didn't even acknowledge her. Iris sat for a while on the sofa, staring at him slumped in the armchair. She stared at the debris on the kitchen floor and the newspapers strewn around the living room. Both of them watched the night fade away to the breaking dawn. Memories of their wedding day sauntered in and out of her mind like ghosts looming, taunting her. The man she had married was not this worn-out intoxicated shell. The woman he had married was not the woman she saw in the mirror these days.

Then Trevor began to stir. She had been too caught up in her own thoughts to notice that he was already upon her. He was clenching her hair and was breathing foul, stinking breath into her face. She pulled on his hand to try and loosen his grip, but his grasp was strong, and he pulled her off the sofa and down on her knees. She screamed, kicked, and tried to use her hands to push him away. He placed his free hand around her neck and started to squeeze. She couldn't breathe. Her arms dropped. She crumpled and lay prone on the hardwood floor. Her instinct for survival kicked in, and she stopped struggling. His breathing was heavy, the smell of his sweat sour.

"Keep still, bitch." His voice was raspy, guttural. There was no presence in his eyes, only a drunken, vacant stare. She was on her back, and he was on top of her, legs splayed either side of her hips, pinning her down. She coughed violently and gasped for air as he let go of her throat and began fiddling with his fly, trying to undo the zipper on his pants. Glancing wildly around her, she caught sight of the axe by the fireplace. It was just within her grasp.

58

When the Universe Called

Trevor was too engrossed in his drunken fumbling to notice Iris reaching her arms behind her head. She managed to grab hold of the axe handle with both hands, and with a strength she did not know she possessed, she swung the axe over her head and down onto Trevor with incredible force. His hands dropped from his fly, and staring at her in surprise, he keeled over, banging the side of his head on the fireplace and crumpling in a heap, the axe jutting out of his forehead.

Iris lay panting on the floor for some minutes before she dared to move. She felt warm liquid splattered over her, and in the growing light she realized it was Trevor's blood.

It felt to Iris as though someone else had taken her place, someone drawn, shadowy, and angry. And yet, here she was. It was she who had wielded the axe. There was no one else here. Blood was everywhere. Human detritus and goodness knows what was all over the floor, all over her. *Be careful what you wish for; pay attention to your thoughts.* Brina's words echoed in the back of her mind. It was as though she had been standing outside of herself and watching someone else bringing down the fatal blow. How peculiar to be able to feel something as though someone else were doing it. Iris felt nausea suddenly rising from deep inside and ran to the bathroom, bringing up a lifetime of pain and sorrow.

As she sat on the bathroom floor, leaning against the bathtub, Iris felt tears sting her eyes, tears of both relief and apprehension. The image of her granddaughter's smile popped into her head, and she put her hands to her neck, feeling where Trevor's fingers had squeezed. What would she tell Charlotte? How could she explain this to such a dear young girl? Charlotte, who had only just come into her life, the granddaughter who had been given up for adoption without Iris's knowledge, had to be shielded from all of this. Charlotte had not met Trevor; Iris made sure he wasn't around the few times Charlotte had visited and made excuses for his absence. She had been unable to protect her own daughter, Ena; she would not let anything happen to Charlotte.

She wondered what she should do. The sensible course of action of course would be to call the police, but to do so would be to admit to the world that she was a victim. They would ask if she provoked him. They'd

59

ask why she hadn't just left him. They wouldn't understand that she hadn't known how, and she would be blamed.

Trevor had been one of those people who pushed and pushed again, then would stand back and laugh as you tried to maintain your sense of self. He thought it was a game. He liked to taunt, like a cat playing with a mouse, literally torturing it to death. That's what he had been doing with her all these years. She hadn't noticed at first; the assaults on her sense of self had been small, incremental. A comment about what she was wearing, stony silences when she said she had plans with her women friends. Eventually it had just been easier to wear what pleased him and not to go out too often.

Life was easier when he was in a good mood, when she was there when he got home, dinner waiting on the table, TV remote control close at hand. Gradually, over the years, the attacks had become more open, flagrant. If he didn't like what she had cooked for dinner, he would throw it across the room if she was lucky; at her, if she wasn't. She gently ran her right index finger across her clavicle, feeling a small bump; all that remained of the physical injury from Trevor pushing her down the stairs and breaking her collarbone. The emotional pain lived on.

Rinsing her face in cold water and carefully avoiding looking at her reflection in the bathroom mirror, Iris went back into the living room. Trevor was collapsed in a heap by the fireplace, the axe sticking out of him. Iris glanced at the clock on the wall. It was barely fifteen minutes since he'd drawn his last breath, but Iris felt like time was standing still. She went over to the fridge, took out the gin and tonic, and poured herself a large one. Taking one big gulp, then another, she surveyed the mess. She'd better start cleaning it all up. She emptied the cupboard of every cleaning product she had and started to read the label on each one, looking for which would be the most effective at getting rid of blood. She wondered whether it was true that blood could still be seen with some kind of special light, even if you'd scrubbed it off, or if that was just the stuff of TV dramas.

As she started to scrub, she was grateful they had hardwood floors rather than carpeting. She examined walls, baseboards, pictures, everything in the room for even the faintest speck of blood. She still hadn't touched Trevor's body. It remained there, a silent accusation. If she waited until rigor mortis set in, she presumed that no more blood would spill, but she wasn't sure. It

When the Universe Called

was not something she'd ever given any thought to until now. The downside would be that the body would be stiff and hard to move. She wasn't sure which would be better, but it didn't really matter.

The overwhelming relief she was feeling at that moment was more intoxicating than the early morning gin. A huge burden had been lifted from her. It was as though the weight of his spirit that had been crushing her for all those years had now risen and evaporated into the ether.

She stopped cleaning and took another large gulp of gin and tonic and raised her glass to the sun, now streaming through the window. "To freedom!" she whispered, then sank down onto the sofa, drifting into a dreamless slumber.

*   *   *   *

Iris felt like she had been asleep for hours, but as she got up stiffly from the sofa and glanced across at the clock, she saw it was 6:45 a.m. She'd been asleep for only five minutes, but it seemed as though she had traveled the universe in her sleep. Time was elastic. For a brief moment she forgot what had happened and wondered what time she would be starting work, then remembered that she didn't have to go in.

Then she saw Trevor's body and cleaning bottles and rags strewn around the floor. She wasn't dreaming or having hallucinations. She needed to get rid of the body. Various ideas ran through her mind. The best bet seemed to be dumping his body somewhere out in the bush, but she had no idea how she was going to manage that. She was a strong woman for her size. She had inherited her grandmother's Scottish sturdiness. But Trevor was not a small man. He wasn't that tall, but what he lacked in height, he made up for in girth. She also wasn't entirely sure how she was going to get him out of the house without anyone seeing. It might be early, but you never knew who might be watching. Most people were early risers around here.

She checked out of the side kitchen window that looked out on to the drive. Trevor's truck was backed into the driveway, close up to the backyard gate; that was a good start. If she could somehow get him out of the house via the back and into the truck, it was unlikely anyone would see.

Maggie Denhearn

She opened the patio doors to the deck and propped open the backyard gate. She made sure the truck was unlocked and opened the back passenger door. She'd have to put something on the seat to protect it. Garbage bags—lots of garbage bags.

As she went into the laundry room to get them, she saw Trevor's hockey bag on the floor by the dryer. She'd been meaning to move it for ages, but hadn't wanted to start an argument. He hadn't played hockey in a couple of years, and his stuff was all clean and put away. There was nothing like the dreadful smell of used hockey gear. Well, perhaps the smell of a dead body might be worse. She had an idea. Only the sticks were still in it. She pulled them out, flinging them to one side. Just how she was going to get him inside the hockey bag, she wasn't sure, but it would be worth a try.

She went over to his body and hesitated. She grimaced, gritted her teeth, grabbed the axe handle with both hands, and pulled. There was a sound like meat being sliced as the axe moved. She nearly fell back as she yanked it out. Carefully, she placed it on top of the rags she had got out to clean up. Next, she went to his side and bent over to pull his arm to move him away from the fireplace. His body was even heavier than she'd expected and also not as stiff as she'd thought it would be by now. He'd only been dead for half an hour or so, but she'd imagined rigor mortis would already be setting in; apparently not quite.

The strange sounds as she moved the dead body made her want to throw up again, but she didn't have time. She had withstood his brutality all these years. She wasn't about to let him get the better of her now.

There are things you never imagine you'll be doing when you grow up. Stuffing her husband's dead body into a hockey bag had certainly not been part of her girlhood dreams.

She put the hockey bag next to his body, pushed him on to it, and then began the process of stuffing body, limbs, and finally what was left of his head into the bag. More mess. She had at least thought to put on her marigold gloves and her cooking apron to minimize how much more blood she got on herself. She was already imagining the hot steaming bath she would relax in later, with candles—vanilla scented candles.

Trevor didn't quite fit into the bag enough to zip it all the way closed, but enough so that she could move him. She remembered they had a dolly

When the Universe Called

in the garage, and used that to get him out to the truck. Climbing into the truck from the other passenger side, she hauled the bag up onto the back seat.

She breathed in deeply. The first step was over. Iris felt empowered; she'd managed all on her own. Life was going to be different, very different. She hadn't quite figured out how she was going to get away with this, but there had to be a way. Within minutes she was driving down the street and out toward the trails.

Iris knew exactly where she was going to take him—the perfect spot. Luckily there were no cars parked when she got to the trail entrance. Hopefully there would be no early morning runners madly prancing around in Lycra. She knew at least that for her running group, the WOECs, it was a rest day. With some effort she got the bag out of the truck and onto the dolly again, and proceeded along the trail with her cargo. It was hard going. The dolly churned up the gravel on the trail, leaving a sharp groove in its wake. It was all she could do to keep the bag from toppling off the dolly. She should have used some kind of straps. She'd know better next time.

Next time? She wasn't planning on going on a violent killing spree, but anything had to be more interesting than continuing to work on the checkout at Fun Foods Supermarket. She couldn't go back there, not now, not after this.

After about ten minutes, her arms were sore and her back was burning. She would have to stop where she was. She had been hoping to take him deeper into the forest, but here would have to do. She was almost at the clearing with the old oak. She wondered whether she should leave Trevor in the bag or take him out. If she left him in the bag, it would most definitely look like he'd been murdered, but then an axe wound to the head was also probably a bit of a giveaway. Then she remembered she'd written his name and their address inside the bag. Although logically she knew the police would find out soon enough who he was, there was no point in making it any easier for them.

Trevor's final resting place: We come from the earth and go back to the earth. He now lay in a green tomb of branches and leaves that she had hurriedly tried to pull over him. She shivered and thought about saying some kind of prayer, but couldn't bring herself to do so. She didn't want to imagine there was a god for someone like Trevor. Besides, the morning was

Maggie Denhearn

marching on and people would soon be around. She half walked and half ran back to the truck, feeling the sudden need to speak to someone, to confess. Brina—she could tell Brina.

*   *   *   *

Maria reached a weary hand over to the nightstand to feel around for her phone and tapped it until the alarm stopped sounding. It said 6:30 a.m. Again. That time of day seemed to come around quickly these days. She had not slept well. Her mind had spent the night offering up a cinematic extravaganza that kept her adrenaline pumping all night long.

Dreams are sometimes strange. There are those where you can tell your mind is mentally filing experiences and feelings, and processing the day's events. And then there are the ones that make absolutely no sense and leave you wondering if your brain is about to implode. Maria wasn't quite sure which category her dream last night fell into. It wasn't hard to find an interpretation of the piano falling from the sky and landing on top of Luke in their back garden as he was mowing the lawn, creating a large crater. Even the bright orange gnomes, who then stepped out of the bushes and started singing Oompa-Loompa songs, like in the *Charlie and the Chocolate Factory* movie, could possibly be explained as a metaphor for the endless thoughts that were now marching incessantly through her brain.

What was less easy to figure out was the part of her dream when millions of ants had been crawling all over her. She could see herself thrashing around as she stood a few steps away from the chanting gnomes, trying to bat away millions of tiny ants that were crawling all over her bare arms and legs and getting tangled up in her hair.

When she woke up, she was flailing around. She looked across at Luke. He was snoring, still sleeping the sleep of the innocent. Except that he wasn't. She wondered what he was dreaming about. His sleeping expression gave nothing away. Not this time. She felt nauseated at the idea of him being with another woman. This was not how she had imagined her life panning out. She liked order, neatness. There was nothing neat and tidy about this.

Maria dragged herself out of bed and went downstairs. The sun was already up. She looked at herself in the hallway mirror as she went into the

When the Universe Called

kitchen. She bore a remarkable resemblance to a zombie at that time of the morning. She wasn't usually an early riser unless it was a running day, but after last night she was surprised she'd managed to get any sleep at all. On autopilot, she began making coffee. Caffeine was usually a good solution to any problem. She couldn't face food just yet.

Instinctively she looked out of the window to check out the backyard. No large crater, no sign of any gnomes, orange or otherwise. She couldn't feel any ants on her, although she did feel kind of itchy. She reached for some hand cream. Maybe last night hadn't happened. Maybe Noah wasn't dead. Maybe Luke wasn't having an affair. No, he was, she was sure of that. Although there were lots of maybes at the moment, in her mind, that was not one of them. She'd known her husband too long. He was a hopeless liar, or so she'd thought. She'd always been able to figure out what he had bought her for Christmas or a birthday present if she asked sufficient questions. She'd learnt not to. It avoided disappointment—some kinds of disappointment, anyway.

She waited while the coffee machine chugged away, feverishly brewing up the black liquid that would jump-start her body and jolt her awake. She squirted some of the cream into her hands and began to rub them gently together. There was something different that she couldn't place. Her wedding ring—it wasn't on her finger. Her hands started to tremble, and suddenly she felt light-headed. When had she last noticed it on her hand? She never took it off, not even at night.

"Crap!" She started at the sound of her own voice.

A plan. She should come up with a plan: immediate, short- and long-term. That was the best way of dealing with any situation. She grabbed a pen and paper to write a list. Not a good idea. Some things were better committed to memory. There could be no paper trail.

*   *   *   *

"Look, I swear to you, I've still not heard anything. ... Okay, okay, I know, I'm going round there now." Luke hung up and slammed his phone down on the table in the hallway. Maria, still in the kitchen, was sipping coffee and staring out of the window. When Luke came through, face dark, she forced a smile, deliberately not asking about his latest phone call.

65

Maggie Denhearn

"All set for your trip? Anything I can get you?"

"No, thanks, I've got to go."

"Want me to put some coffee in a thermos for you?"

"No. Wait ... Yes, thanks." His expression was meek, as he flicked a lock of hair out of his eyes. "I'll phone you when I get to the mainland."

She glanced up at him, searching his face to find any clue about what was going on in his mind. A deep, dull ache had settled into her heart since finding out about him and Charlotte, making her wish she could stay lying down to bear the weight more easily. It used to be that his arms around her could make anything feel better, but the thought now of him touching her made her cringe. She tried to sound casual as she handed him the thermos of coffee, keeping him at arm's length.

"So is anyone else going with you on this trip?" She was counting on him forgetting she'd asked him that last night. Either he'd forgotten she had, or he was playing along.

"A few from the office, no one interesting." Absentmindedly, he bent down to kiss her on the cheek and she had to stop from recoiling. He walked out the door without glancing back, leaving Maria nursing her cup of coffee.

*   *   *   *

Luke couldn't get out of the door quickly enough. Playing the part of a boring tax lawyer was starting to become too much. He thought he had mostly grown used to it, had integrated it into his persona, but there were more and more days recently when he desperately wanted to stop the pretense, to tell Maria everything. The cloak of dissimulation he wore daily had grown heavier of late, and he was tired, ready to put aside the mantle.

When he first met her, all he wanted to do was protect her. That meant keeping his father as far away from her as possible. So he had entered their marriage on a lie, telling her that both his parents were dead. An initial deceit, so innocent in the beginning and meant to be easier for everyone, soon became much more complicated than he'd ever intended or envisaged. When he had been estranged from his father, it had been fine. But once he met Brina and agreed to help her infiltrate the Consortium, that's when life became far more entangled than he had ever thought possible.

When the Universe Called

There is a critical point in time when you're at a crossroads. One direction leads to truth and all the messiness that comes along with that. The other leads to falsehood. One lie, then two, then three, and so on— lies heaped upon lies, or rather below, each one bolstering up the original fiction until the mountain of deception is so high it's impossible to climb down from. Luke had already reached most of the way up the mountain by the time he met Charlotte. Now he had no idea how to tell the truth or what the actual truth was.

Right now there was something going on with his brother, and he had to get to the bottom of it before he could even begin to think about what he was going to do about Maria. Noah never took more than a few hours to return Luke's messages, especially not when Luke had made it very clear that he needed to talk to him. As he pulled out of the driveway, he began to dial his brother's number on his hands free set.

"For goodness' sake, pick up the damn phone, will you? I need to speak to you. I'm coming round to yours now, so get rid of any woman you've had staying over. We need to talk—in private." Luke slammed his fist against the dashboard. Their father didn't like to be kept waiting, and if he was insisting that he see them, anyone with any sense would make sure he was available so as not to raise suspicion. He thought his brother had figured that out by now. John Frost was not someone you messed with.

Noah had been told all they knew about the Consortium and their father's criminal dealings before he'd agreed to help Luke and Brina. He knew the risks as well as Luke did, and that meant keeping up the appearances of a happy family for as long as it took them to get the evidence and support in high places that they needed to stop their father once and for all. Given that their father had become exceptionally good at hiding his involvement in anything illegal, particularly since the episode with Brina, this was proving much harder than they had imagined. For fifteen years they had been trying: Luke infiltrating his father's legal affairs, Noah researching individuals involved in the Consortium, Brina creating a web of trusted informants from among the faceless people who serve those powerful individuals. If the Consortium or their father found out now that they were secretly trying to sabotage them, they all knew their days would be numbered.

Maggie Denhearn

He would have to take the later ferry over to the mainland. He needed to swing by his brother's place first to see what he was up to. Luke was annoyed at how responsible he felt for him, even though they were both grown up and into middle age. Although he was born only five minutes sooner than his brother, he'd always had the feeling that he should be taking care of him; Luke had always been the older brother.

He pulled into his brother's driveway. Noah's car was there, so he must be home. That irritated Luke even more. If he was home, why wasn't he picking up his phone? Luke rang the doorbell. No answer. He rang again, then walked round to the window and, shading his eyes with his hand, peered through the glass. He couldn't see anyone, and the place looked as neat and tidy as always.

His brother was a bit of a neat freak. Although they were physically identical and hard for most people to tell apart, there were some things they didn't have in common. Luke liked things to be tidy, orderly, but not in this OCD way. With baby brother, everything had a precise place, right down to the last millimeter. No wonder he'd never got married. He would drive any woman nuts with his obsessive behavior about how the towels should be hung and which way round the toilet roll had to go on the holder. He somehow managed to keep his compulsion to himself when he visited him and Maria, but Luke could see when his brother was clenching his teeth, trying not to say anything when the table wasn't set with military precision. Sometimes Luke would deliberately make a mess just to watch Noah tense up and not say anything.

There was still no answer. He took a key out of his pocket and unlocked the door. The house was quiet and felt empty, like it had been empty a while. Luke walked into the kitchen. Everything was clean, nothing out of place. The living room was the same. He slowly walked up the stairs, listening for any sound to indicate someone was home. Perhaps he was in bed with his latest paramour and wasn't picking up his messages. It wouldn't be the first time he'd accidently walked in on him in flagrante. Haltingly, he opened the main bedroom door. The bed was made and everything was where it usually was. If he had been there last night, that would mean he had left early this morning. Or perhaps he hadn't come home last night. It was 8:30 a.m. He checked the closets. Clothes hung in an orderly row, according to color and

68

to season. His briefcase was neatly standing at attention by the door. He never went to work without that. He'd not gone away and he couldn't have gone to work if his briefcase was still there.

The knot in Luke's stomach turned one notch tighter. There was nothing he could do. He would just have to get the ferry as planned and wait for him to get in touch. Noah would have to eventually. He closed the front door behind him and noticed a car parked across the street, the dark blue car that had been following him constantly this last little while. Luke walked down the path, pretending not to notice, and got back in his car. This was not the time for confrontation.

9:30 P.M. MONDAY, AUGUST 5, 1963

Anja turned the key in the lock to her apartment door one last time and hurried down the stairs, outside into the warm August evening. One small, shabby red suitcase, that's all she brought with her. A few clothes, one book of family photos, and her satchel. Glancing around the street, she turned left and hurried in the direction of the bus station. She had the feeling she was being followed, but each time she looked around, no one was there. The same had happened yesterday. She was being paranoid. All she needed to do was to keep it together long enough to get the bus to the ferry terminal and then take the ferry out to Vancouver Island.

She had enough savings to last her two to three weeks, maybe a month if she was careful. Long enough to lay low for a while. Vancouver felt dangerous, alien. It was a beautiful evening, yet few people were milling around. Taking to the side streets, she looked back quickly every few minutes. She felt like she was being hunted. She had planned to leave early the next morning to catch the first bus out to the ferry. There were no buses or ferries at this time of the evening.

But she was afraid. For some reason, Officer Bailey was covering up what Anja had told her. Why would she lie to a co worker? Or was Bailey afraid some of her fellow officers were somehow involved with FHP? So many things didn't make sense. Anja had no idea who to trust. Her apartment was no longer safe. Nowhere was. At least if she spent the night at the bus station,

Maggie Denhearn

it was a public place. No one would dare hurt her in public. Passing down the back alley of the jazz club Scott's, she stopped to listen to the refrain of music lilting its way out onto the night air. It was her favorite song, "Someone to Watch over Me." Putting down her case, she stood listening. Then she turned around. Frost was standing a few feet away, pointing a gun directly at her.

CHAPTER 6

Around 8:30 a.m. Tuesday, April 15, 2014

"**B**loody hell! Ouch!" An explosion of expletives poured forth from Vanna as she felt her foot catch mid stride and planted face down in the dirt. "Ow!"

She lay there for a few seconds, stunned and winded, then pushed herself into a sitting position, wincing as she did so from the pressure on her wrists, which had broken her fall. Her hands were covered in dirt and slightly grazed, and her knees were dirty and bloodied. It was the rule of the running club she'd just joined that after April first everyone had to wear shorts, regardless of the weather. Right now she was beginning to regret that particular sartorial decision. Her right shoulder was now making its presence known with a shooting pain coursing through her right arm. When she'd reached out her hands to break her fall, her fingers had bent right back on a rock. She wiggled them around. They hurt, but not enough to be broken. She'd be fine.

She turned around to see where her dog, Morris, was. He hadn't even noticed that Vanna had fallen over and was still running ahead on the trail, nose to the ground, assiduously searching out smells. Vanna should have been paying more attention to where her feet were going. She was still finding it hard to remember that trail running involved picking your feet up much more than road running. She had been too enthralled in looking around as she jogged through the forest.

71

Maggie Denhearn

It was like stepping into another dimension. There was an other-worldliness about the trees on Vancouver Island that was hard to explain. She'd just passed through her favorite part of this trail, where a steep embankment just off the trail led down to a freshwater creek. Salal and fern graced hemlock, maple, and Douglas fir, the trees leaning sideways, intertwining here and there, as though bowing down in homage to some invisible spirit. There was a hush that made it seem as though you were in some ancient natural cathedral, protected, removed from the rest of the world.

Her fall had brought her abruptly back to earth in every sense of the word. Picking herself up, she began brushing the dirt off her hands and knees and pulling leaves out of her hair. She glanced around to see what she had stumbled over. There was a large tree root crossing the trail, defying the man-made gravel path. How could she have missed that? She'd have taken some ribbing from the WOECs if anyone had been around to witness that particular nosedive. The WOECs were a fun bunch to run with, and rather hard-core. Minor cuts and bruises were part of the deal. She could hear Maria's voice saying, "Suck it up, princess." She wasn't sure what the acronym WOEC stood for. Something of Eagle Cove, naturally, but the others would just grin and change the subject when she asked what the *W* and *O* stood for.

Vanna laughed to herself and started after Morris. It was never a good idea to let him too far out of sight. He'd stopped sniffing and was pulling on something determinedly. From a distance it looked like he was trying to drag a log, which was rather out of the league of a twelve-pound dog, but that didn't seem to be putting him off.

She stopped. It couldn't be, could it? It looked alarmingly like a boot. She couldn't be seeing straight. She didn't wear her glasses when she ran. She squinted at her running watch. Although it was already 8:30 a.m., she still didn't feel fully awake. She must be imagining things. She hadn't had her first cup of tea of the day.

She had reached the point on the trail where the bush on one side was beaten back, and behind, a breathtaking clearing was evident, sun now streaming through the treetops, pouring through like water through a sieve, casting streams of light and shadow.

When the Universe Called

"Holy mother of ..." Another stream of expletives poured forth. She was stuck in a swearing loop and didn't seem to be able to get out of it. There it was. A boot. It was definitely a boot, or a foot, to be more exact, as it was attached to a leg—a leg poking out of branches and leaves. She felt tingles go up her spine, and although she desperately wanted to move, she remained rooted to the spot. Tentatively, she pulled back some of the branches. She felt her stomach heave as she fell on her knees and threw up. The water she'd drunk before her run made a reappearance. Morris scampered over to her, waging his tail and barking furiously.

"Oh my God!" Scrambling up and backing away from the body, she half ran, half walked further along the trail, calling Morris to her. She felt like she'd suddenly stepped into one of the detective programs she loved to watch on television. Only this was not how she had imagined it. Vanna had seen quite a few dead bodies. Having worked in long-term health care, it was sort of an occupational hazard. This was not like that, nothing at all. She had never seen anything like this, not even in her nurse training. Vanna had sometimes joked with friends that she knew this would happen one day. Sooner or later she'd find some random dead body. Look at *CSI* or any of the crime dramas. It was always the runners or the dog walkers or workmen who found them. As a runner and a dog owner, the odds were stacked against her. But her prediction had been exactly that, a joke. She had never really thought it possible. She retched again then started coughing. Morris had lost interest in what Vanna was doing and had gone back to the foot and was playing tug of war.

"Away, Morris, away!" Bloody dog.

"Away!" Trying not to give in to growing panic, she went to grab Morris, but he did his usual little dance and darted away. She reached in her pocket and dug around for her baggie of dog treats.

"Morris, come!" She rattled the treat bag, hoping the sound of rustling plastic would tempt him. A vague hope flashed across her mind that perhaps the foot was attached to someone who was just sleeping or unconscious for some reason, but that hope was fleeting. Even with the quick look she'd taken it was very obvious there was no sign of life. The head was all but obliterated. No one could be alive with a head like that. She should call the police. She felt around in her other pocket to get out her cell phone. No signal. Typical.

Vanna gasped, jumping backward and nearly falling over again. There was a rustle from the undergrowth. It was probably a bird or some kind of animal, but what if? At that point she couldn't decide which would be worse; coming across a cougar or bear, or meeting the murderer. Murderer? Her mind was jumping ahead. Her imagination always did seem to leap around. More innocuous explanations could be possible; she hoped. Morris started to pull at the boot again.

"Away, Morris, away." She knew she sounded like a screaming banshee but she couldn't help it. "Come, Morris, come. Oh no!" Too late; Morris had already raised his leg and was scent marking the body. She felt herself getting tearful and knew Morris would never take any notice of her if she started to cry. She jiggled the treat bag, but he danced away and began chewing some grass. She held her phone in the air, trying desperately to get some reception, wincing as she'd forgotten she'd hurt her shoulder.

Maybe it wasn't a suspicious death. Maybe it was just a cougar or a bear that had … She didn't want to finish that line of thought. It wasn't fabulous. None of this was fabulous. It also didn't make sense. An animal would have made more of a mess. It also wouldn't have thought to cover the body with branches.

The stabbing pain in her stomach was turning into a sickly feeling, a fitting accompaniment to the taste of bile in her mouth. Morris seemed oblivious. This surely was a more positive sign. He'd bark if there were someone or something around. Usually, if they were out and he sensed something like a bear, his ears would be pricked and pushed back, and that white, fluffy tail of his would be tucked right down, his little bottom would sag, and he'd refuse to move. As it was, he was merrily sniffing away, fortunately at the moment, farther into the clearing.

He seemed to be distracted by something else. He was growling, focused intently on whatever it was that had now got his attention. Vanna jogged to catch him up, checking her phone every few strides to see if she had finally got some reception.

She screamed. It was another body—another soulless dead body. Naked torso, smart jeans, shoes, and shirt seemingly carefully placed by the body.

When the Universe Called

Had she stumbled on some kind of ritual killing? Morris was busy sniffing around the bloody head. Before she even realized what was happening, she was bent over, convulsed, vomiting, only narrowly missing her running shoes and Morris, who at that moment decided to finally come over to her. Her stomach lurched, and her eyes stung with salty tears as she tried to stifle a sob. She threw up again, her insides burning. Fear was starting to feel like a physical entity, taking over her body, clutching at her limbs.

"Morris, come, come on, Morris. Good boy, come here." She forced her legs to move and started to run awkwardly, like she was just learning how to move her legs for the very first time. This time she headed back down the path they had originally come along. It would be quicker to get back to the parking lot that way.

"Morris, come here!" Finally the little terrier seemed to get the message that perhaps he should take notice, and he began to follow her. After about twenty meters, she was able to tempt him with a treat and get him back on the leash. For some reason, at that moment she suddenly stopped to listen, but was able to hear only her own heart pounding and her heavy breathing. She looked down at her phone: one bar of a signal. She tried to call the emergency services. After about three attempts, one of which had failed because she'd dialed 999, forgetting she was no longer in England, she managed to get through. She'd never called them in Canada before and was bizarrely nervous, as though she was the one who'd done something wrong.

"What is the nature of the emergency?"

"Erm ..." Vanna was taken off guard. "I've found two dead bodies."

"What is your location?"

"The trail behind the community center."

"Where?"

"Oh, er ... Kwalicum Bay or Eagle Cove? I'm not sure. Somewhere in between." She felt embarrassed at getting so flustered and not being more certain where she was. She could hear her voice wobble as she tried to fight back the tears and panic.

"Sorry, I'm not sure. Can't you tell where I'm phoning from?"

"You must be calling from a pay-as-you-go cell phone, so no, unfortunately we can't. What's your number?"

75

Maggie Denhearn

Her mind was blank. She'd just switched to a Canadian SIM card and hadn't memorized her number yet. The only way she knew how to check would be to hang up.

"I don't know. I've just got this phone. Listen. I was running along and …" she heard her voice speeding up as she proceeded to try and explain what had happened.

"Try to stay calm. Let me transfer you. Are you able to stay with the bodies?" She hesitated. She really wanted to just run home and pretend none of this had happened.

"I guess I could stay a bit longer. How long do you think it'll be before someone comes?"

"I'll transfer you, ma'am, and someone will be able to help you. We'll be there as soon as we can." That wasn't a helpful answer. "As soon as we can" could mean right away or after we've finished our coffee and donuts.

"I have to get home."

"We really need you to stay where you are. What's your full name?"

The line went dead; she'd lost reception. She'd not realized that she'd been pacing up and down. Crap. She looked at her phone. There was barely anything left in the battery. It was probably better to wait until the police actually arrived than to call back.

Wandering back and forth between the two dead bodies, she kept looking at the time on her phone. Each minute that passed felt more like an hour. She'd always thought it odd how time could bend and twist. A minute could feel like an hour, a day could feel like a month or disappear before you'd even noticed.

Morris kept pulling on his leash, trying to get to some smell here, something icky to chew on there. Now that she'd stopped running, she was starting to feel chilled, and her body was aching, partly her body cooling down, mostly due to the fear and shock that had made itself at home inside of her. The day was warming up and she could see patches of intense blue as she looked up to the sky and beyond the treetops. The beauty of the forest juxtaposed against the violence that the bodies bore witness to felt surreal. The line between reality and her imagination was becoming blurred.

9:45 P.M. MONDAY, AUGUST 5, 1963

Anja lay with her eyes closed, holding her breath. She felt the cold of the pavement beneath her and something warm and damp on her hip. She didn't remember falling, just the sound of a gunshot reverberating through the air. Tentatively, she opened her eyes and lifted her head. In the moonlight she could see a dark patch growing on her white cotton dress. Her hand shook as she reached down to her hip and touched the blood seeping from an open wound, wondering why she couldn't feel anything at all. She tried to pull herself up onto one elbow to look around. Someone was bending down over her. It wasn't Frost.

She heard a voice tell her, "Lie still." Nausea flooded through her as she felt herself being dragged into the unconscious.

CHAPTER 7

Early Tuesday morning, April 15, 2014

Violent coughing and wheezing woke Frost up most mornings. This morning was no exception. His sleep had been more fitful than usual, and at around 3:00 a.m. he'd given up trying to stop his mind racing. At some point he must have drifted off again. He tried to pull himself up onto his pillows, but the effort made him start wheezing again. Right on cue, Mary simultaneously knocked on his bedroom door and entered. The knock was a relic of formality that no longer had any meaning. Physical infirmity had put an end to any privacy he once had.

Getting old was the hardest role he'd played in his life. This morning he felt particularly weary. He didn't want to believe that his son had betrayed him, but Bailey was no fool and would not make up such allegations. He had never thought that estrangement could curdle into such duplicity. He was too old to feel the kind of anger that used to fire him up, too old to feel the rancor that had fueled much of the building of his empire, Frost Pharma Health, and the Consortium. He'd almost had enough—almost. There was shame and dishonor in his son's actions that had to be addressed quickly. There was no time for sentimentality. While Mary was busy helping him sit up and propping him up on various pillows, he growled orders at her.

"And bring me some coffee!"

"Yes, sir. I'll bring that right away."

Frost watched Mary shuffle off and sighed. He knew he would have to give the command for Luke to be taken down. As this thought passed through his mind, he caught sight of the photo of his long-departed wife, Leonora, next to his bedside lamp. She was smiling broadly, her head thrown back. She'd had this way of laughing with her whole body that made her good humor contagious. He felt her reproach from beyond the grave. She would have forgiven her son anything. She would have forgiven Luke, but not Frost.

Reaching out, he grabbed the photo and flung it across the room. The glass shattered into tiny pieces. Mary burst back into the room, a look of alarm on her face. Muttering something under her breath, she disappeared into the hallway to find a dustpan and brush in one of the cleaning cupboards. These days it was easier for Frost to sleep on the ground floor rather than negotiate the stairs, so one of the drawing rooms had been converted into a bedroom. He'd had an elevator installed in the house at one point and for a while had continued to make full use of the house. Yet of late he felt the desire to be closer to the earth. He liked the view better from the ground floor. He could see the rhododendron bushes from the drawing room.

Like Hamlet, he imagined blood on his hands. He looked down. His knuckles were gnarled and boney, his nails long and uneven. They were the hands of an old man, and for a moment he thought they belonged to someone else.

He lay back and closed his eyes, feeling the cool softness of the down pillows. An overwhelming fatigue washed over him. He wished Bailey were wrong about Luke, but the evidence she presented to him when she called him late last night seemed undeniable. She also forwarded Heeley's email. Under other circumstances, Frost would have been furious to learn that Bailey had used Heeley without first getting permission from him. As much as he felt his vitality ebbing and his physical power diminishing, he clung to the reins of power of the Consortium. Over the years, corrupt politicians, public officials, police, and bankers had been carefully selected, groomed and brought together to fund, facilitate and promote the work of his pharmaceutical company. Without the work of the Consortium, FPH would not have received the level of financing that it had, nor indeed got away with much of its experimental work. They were on the brink of a major breakthrough with a new drug. To find out that Luke had been working both for and against the Consortium to undermine this work was devastating,

Maggie Denhearn

both professionally and personally. Frost brushed a tear from his eye and snarled.

*   *   *   *

Vanna shivered. It was eerily quiet in the forest. The early morning song of the birds had faded as though the whole forest had hushed and was waiting with her to see what would happen next. Mother Earth was waking up after the winter months, and the pungent odor of skunk cabbage drifted along the air. Bears eat skunk cabbage. Bears would be waking up too. She had been told that they leave you alone if you make a noise, at least the ones on the Island would. No longer able to stand either the silence or the thought of being breakfast to some wild animal, she started to sing. She considered starting to look around while she waited for the police, anything to give herself something to do and to keep Morris busy, but changed her mind. She might destroy the crime scene, and she'd be in trouble for that. Morris had already left behind a fair number of his own contributions to the evidence. Much as it didn't make much sense, she couldn't help worrying that the police might think she was somehow involved. She carried on singing, her voice wavering and echoing in the air. Morris looked up at her, tilting his head to one side, staring at her with a "what on earth is that?" expression in his eyes.

The chill and numb from the shock along with hunger pangs were taking over from the feeling of nausea as Vanna fought back tears.

It had been ten minutes since she'd called the police, and there was no sign that anyone was coming. She'd sung her song at least four times, and it was doing little to alleviate the rattled feeling in her stomach. Morris yawned and carried on his endless sniffing around. Random thoughts continued to pop up in her brain, like devilish imps, leading her in this direction and that, all the while holding up warning signs of trouble ahead. Brina had been teaching her the importance of conscious awareness, of the power of breath and meditation to help keep you in the present moment. No amount of concentration seemed to be able to stop her mind whirling and going in all the darkest directions.

When the Universe Called

This had been the longest ten minutes of Vanna's life. She was starting to think she was stuck in a time warp. One would hope that a woman alone in the forest with two dead bodies would be a priority. She couldn't imagine there was anything much more pressing going on in the neighborhood. It wasn't exactly the Bronx. Perhaps the police hadn't believed her, had thought hers was a prank call. Maybe she was actually imagining all of this. She'd read somewhere that there was no *one* reality, that what we experience is what we create in our own minds.

If that was the case, maybe this was just a figment of her imagination, and she would find out that it had all been a dream, just like Bobby or whoever it was in Dallas, who'd been in the shower and had thought he'd been abducted by aliens. She'd been very young when that had been on the television. She remembered sneaking into the living room and making like she wasn't there so she could watch it. She knew everyone at school would be talking about the show the next day, and had been determined not to miss out. It was hard enough for her to fit in at school as the only brown girl without also being the one who never knew what was going on in the soap operas.

Her mind drifted back to the bodies lying in the undergrowth. Plucking up courage, she shivered, took a deep breath, and headed back toward them. She forced herself to take a long look at the first body she had tripped over. She tried to take in all the details, feeling once again the queasiness rising within her. She couldn't fathom how a head could become that mangled. Although she tried to take a good look at the second body, after only a brief glimpse, she retched again, an involuntary reflex. It didn't make sense. The first body definitely had the air of some malintent, like the man had come to some untimely end, but the second, he was different.

Then it struck her. There was something familiar about him. As her mind slowly clicked into gear and realization came to fore, she screamed.

"Holy crap!" She realized she knew who he was. Life and soul departs from a body no longer breathing and faces change. She had seen that in her nursing work. Sometimes people could look completely different when they are no longer breathing, but in this case she was sure. The man with the naked torso, who looked almost surprised to be dead, was Luke, Maria's husband. This was definitely Luke. She thought of Maria and how she would feel. She didn't know Luke well, had only met him a couple of times. He

Maggie Denhearn

was not the most interesting person on the planet, but being boring wasn't a crime. Poor Maria would be devastated. Vanna was just beginning to get to know her. They ran together with the WOECs running club a few times a week, and she seemed to be happily married. Maria and Luke had been together a long time; that much she knew. And she also knew what it was like to lose a partner so abruptly.

Vanna was starting to feel light-headed. Her mouth was parched, and she desperately wanted to clean her teeth to get rid of the sour taste in her mouth. Edging away from the bodies and heading back along the gravel trail, she felt a deep guttural wail trying to push its way up and out of her. She was hungry and had started to tremble. Morris was looking bored and was biting at her ankles. She kept telling him to get off, but as usual he thought it was some kind of game.

She tried to breathe deeply to stop herself from hyperventilating. She heard Brina's voice in her head reminding her of the importance of mindful breathing. Vanna had left England barely six months ago to escape to Vancouver Island to heal her grief in the tranquility and beauty of the rain forest. Right now it was not the idyllic escape she had imagined. As she shivered and stared up at the century-old trees, her heart ached. One minute her husband Jai had been there, the next, gone. He had been talking to her on his cell phone and had stepped out into a busy street without looking.

She started to sob, but was brought abruptly back to the present by the sound of Morris whimpering. She looked down to see him shaking and jumping up, trying to get in her arms. She froze, listening intently, the hairs on the back of her neck standing on end, tingling. Her stomach lurched. There was a rustle coming from behind her. This was it. She couldn't run; her legs wouldn't move. She held her breath and slowly turned around.

"Maria?" Vanna put her hand on her heart and almost started to laugh. Morris ran up to Maria, wagging his tail and barking. Vanna tried to collect herself, wiping her eyes.

"Vanna! What are you doing here? I mean, running, I see that. It's just not one of our regular mornings. ..." Her voice hung in the air. Vanna flushed.

"I ... er ... I know. Morris needed a run." Instinctively, Vanna glanced back in the direction of the bodies. She was about to tell Maria not to

When the Universe Called

continue on the trail but stopped herself. A little voice inside Vanna told her that something in Maria's demeanor was suspicious.

"What's up? You look spooked." Maria's casual tone sounded forced.

"What? Really? No, no. Really? No. Just Morris being annoying. How come *you're* out?"

"Me? Oh, just fancied a walk. I didn't sleep well last night and thought some air might wake me up." Maria didn't look like she was just out for a walk. Most people don't wear pink sling-back sandals with an inch heel to go walking in the rain forest.

"In those?" Vanna pointed at her shoes.

"Oh, right. I just grabbed the pair nearest the door. I wasn't thinking."

"Is … er … everything okay?" Vanna studied her friend.

"Yes. Yes, why wouldn't it be?" Maria's response was too quick. She was frowning and biting her bottom lip, and playing with her ring finger. Her wedding ring was missing. Instinctively, Vanna took a step backward. It was too much of a coincidence that she should be out walking in ridiculous footwear near the exact spot where her husband lay dead and minus her wedding ring. What if Maria already knew Luke was dead—was involved in his murder?

"Morris, away! Away!" Morris liked shoes and had decided the pink straps of Maria's sandals were far too enticing not to start pulling on. Maria was now doing a little dance trying to shake him off her, but he was clinging on. Vanna pulled his leash and started to move away from Maria.

"Sorry, Maria. Morris you little … stop it!" Vanna could hear her voice was starting to squeak.

"Sorry, Maria. Morris is being a brat. I should get him home."

"Sure, no worries."

Vanna didn't look back as she pulled into a run, leaving Maria walking toward the dead bodies.

*　　*　　*　　*

Maria glanced back at Vanna as she jogged away, unable to shake the feeling that all her friends knew about Luke's infidelity. Then the penny dropped. Perhaps she had a bigger problem. If Vanna had gone off the trail

83

Maggie Denhearn

and headed into the clearing, Noah's body would have been only meters away from her and in full view. Surely if she'd seen him, she'd have said something, though.

No, this whole business with Luke was making her neurotic. It was a lucky escape, and she needed to get back to the body as soon as possible and find her wedding ring. It must have fallen off her finger when she'd taken off her running gloves. In her haste to get back to retrieve it before anyone found the body, she'd not considered she might run into someone. Hopefully her ring would be easy to spot. An itchy agitated feeling was growing inside her. It still didn't seem quite real that Noah could truly be dead, and she'd half convinced herself that when she got to the clearing, there would be no body.

She made her way along the trail to where the bush was pulled back and stopped. She saw a boot jutting out of the undergrowth. This didn't make sense. They'd deliberately not covered Noah in branches because it needed to look like the accident that it was. And Maria had never seen Noah wear boots like that. Yet here was a shabby black work boot attached to a leg and a body protruding out from under some branches. Either some branches had been cleared away, or the body had not been properly covered.

It was a dead body—but not Noah. The head was smashed in and covered with dried blood. She gasped and nearly stumbled as she instinctively backed away. Turning, she hurried further into the clearing to where she thought they'd left Noah, still hoping not to find him. But there he was. That was definitely Noah, although already looking less fresh than the night before. So who was this other body? Goose bumps started lining up along her spine, and her breath quickened.

She stopped, not willing to investigate further. What should she do? Nothing. She could do nothing. If she did something, anything, it would be harder to lie, to pretend she knew nothing about how Noah had come to be in the forest.

She headed to where he lay. Trying the best she could not to disturb the undergrowth any more than it already had been, she hunted around for her ring. At first she couldn't see anything. Then a ray of sunshine suddenly shot through the branches overhead and she saw something glint on the ground. There it was, next to Noah's glasses. Somehow they seemed such a personal object to leave behind, yet she couldn't bring herself to pick them up.

84

When the Universe Called

A wave of grief washed over her, and she caught her breath to try to stop herself from crying, but tears started to trickle down her cheeks in spite of herself. She reached over and picked up her ring, avoiding looking directly at Noah's body. As she did so, Maria stepped on something. She moved her foot and looked down. It was a packet of dog treats, the exact kind of bag Vanna brought along every time on their runs. They'd all had their stint of helping to catch Morris and entice him with the goodie-bag.

Vanna had seen the body. The *bodies*. She must have seen them. Maria started to feel dizzy, her hands trembling. She was hyperventilating. Did Vanna have anything to do with the other body? Surely she couldn't. But it wasn't like any of them knew much about her. She could be telling them anything about herself, and there was no one around to verify who she really was.

Maria felt unsteady. She tried to walk quickly, but kept tripping over tree roots and then sliding on the gravel. Her breathing felt labored, and she had this strange sensation of everything around her being distant. She finally got back to her car. Her hands still shaking, it took a few attempts to get her key to unlock the door and then into the ignition. She focused on breathing deeply for a few minutes, trying to shake the lightheadedness. Thoughts buzzed through her mind like insects trying to fly through cotton wool, each getting stuck, flailing and fighting.

Who was the other body? Had someone been watching them last night? Was Vanna responsible for murder? Maria suddenly felt exhausted and nearly had to pull over, afraid she would lose control of the car. She had to get ready for work. She couldn't call in sick. She never did that, so to do so would draw attention to her. She could go in late, though, give herself time to regain her composure. She had to act as though everything was completely normal. Normal? Maria couldn't remember what that felt like.

* 𝅃 ⺊ 𝅃

Vanna poured food into Morris's bowl to distract him from following her into the bathroom. She switched on the shower. The cold sweat made peeling off her sticky running clothes harder, and she banged her shoulder against the wall as she was yanking off her top.

85

Maggie Denhearn

She started to cry again. Stepping into the shower, she let the water pour over her as she tried to wash away the early morning's events. It would not end there. It would be only a matter of time before the police would be knocking at her door. Despite the fact she'd not actually done anything wrong, the feeling that life was about to take a desperately bad turn enveloped her like a gray, musty shroud. This had to be her karma keeping her company.

It was more than a little perturbing seeing Maria like that. What did she really know about Maria, or anyone else around here for that matter?

The water on her skin was warm and soothing, the smell of the shampoo comforting. Concentrating on bodily sensations was better than giving room in her mind to the unsettling thoughts swirling around in her head, each one competing fervently for her attention.

It was almost 10:00 a.m. by the time she stepped out of the shower and was drying off. She heard the customary scratching. Morris, as usual, was clawing against the bathroom door. He succeeded in opening it and skipped in, then started to lick off the moisturizer she had just applied to her legs. After a few licks and a couple more cursory ones to her wet feet, he lost interest and scurried off.

"Oh to be a dog." As she dried herself off, she realized there was no way of avoiding the conclusion that maybe, a strong maybe, her new friend might have killed her husband.

TUESDAY EVENING, AUGUST 6, 1963

Anja slowly opened her eyes and felt the pain that seemed to have seeped into every cell of her body. The room was dimly lit, and her first view was of a ceiling she didn't recognize. Turning her head slowly and wincing as she felt her neck stiff and sore, she tried to make sense of her surroundings. The room was sparse and decorated with nondescript colors designed neither to offend nor appeal. There was a tall oak dresser in the corner by the door, a small night lamp on the chair by the bed in which she was lying, and a threadbare brown woolen rug on the parquet floor. Her mind was processing

When the Universe Called

this information at a frustratingly slow speed. Where was she? What had happened?

After a few moments, she recalled the street, the pavement. Flinching, she raised herself up on a thin, damp pillow. There was a window high up on one wall, the half-light of dusk barely making its way through the dusty pane. If she could muster up the energy to get up and look out, she might be able to figure out where she was. As she attempted to pull herself up to a sitting position, she swore and slumped back. Pain like she had never experienced coursed through her hip.

Only then did she remember the shot. She breathed in sharply, clasping her hand to her side, not daring to touch her wound. Was Frost holding her captive? The room could easily be mistaken for a prison type accommodation. Her pulse quickened as an avalanche of scenes and emotions of the last few days cascaded over her. Shutting her eyes to try and block out what she was feeling only seemed to intensify the emotions, so she opened her eyes again just in time to see the door start to open. She froze.

Officer Petturi edged open the door to his spare room, carefully easing his head round the frame so he could peer into the room. The hinges creaked, reminding him that he'd been meaning to oil them. He squinted into the dim light, as he had been doing every couple of hours for nearly twenty-four hours. A sigh of relief washed over him as he saw that the young woman had finally regained consciousness. He'd had no idea what he would do if she didn't survive the gunshot wound. As a newlywed, he was still in that phase where he woke every morning thanking God for bringing his wife Grace to him, the absolute love of his life, and serendipitously a nurse. She had attended to the young woman's wound and had known not to ask any questions. Anja was slumped, half upright, her eyes filled with fear.

"It's okay. I'm not going to hurt you. You're safe here."

"Where am I?"

"My home. No one knows you're here. Well, except Grace, my wife."

"I don't understand."

Officer Petturi slowly entered the room but remained at a distance, sensing that any sudden movement on his part would startle her.

"You were shot."

"I remember—vaguely. Who are you?"

87

Maggie Denhearn

"I'm a police officer. Officer Petturi, Joe Petturi. I found you." He could see from her expression that she remained confused. "I found you in the street behind the jazz club. I know who shot you. I also know that if I tell anyone else in the police, he'll probably find you and come after you again."

"What?" Her voice was strained.

"You need to rest. We can talk about this later."

"No, no, I need to know what's going on." She tried to sit up but fell back on the pillow, pain etched across her forehead.

"Okay, but then you need to sleep again. I was one block over when I heard the shot and came running. I saw Frost running away and was about to chase him but then looked back, and you were slumped in the street. As I got closer, I recognized you. You came in on Saturday to the station. Bailey left the file that you brought in on her desk for a few moments, and I took a look when she went to the washroom. I knew she was lying when she said you were a domestic abuse case. I saw you stop suddenly when you were leaving the station. You heard her. I knew something wasn't right. I don't know what this is all about, but I'm fairly sure that if Bailey finds you, so will Frost. And another time he might be a better shot."

"But how do you know Frost?"

A feeling beyond anger and fury became lodged in Petturi, a tight, thick thread of emotion that was gradually weaving itself into the fabric of his inner life. He was learning to keep it in abeyance most of the time. But the mention of Frost was enough for the twine to start reaching out, twisting around his heart and lungs, constricting his breathing, the lack of oxygen making it hard for him to think.

"You need to rest. There's food and water on the chair. I'll bring you some tea." He paused, staring at this young, pale creature barely making an imprint on the bed.

"You're safe. I promise. I won't let him get you."

CHAPTER 8

EARLY TUESDAY MORNING, APRIL 15, 2014

Ever since she was a small child, Brina had liked to watch the morning sunrise. It was the best time of the day. It was a time of stillness and contemplation. Most people were still sound asleep, and she felt like she had the world to herself. One of her few good memories of the Second World War in Yugoslavia was of the dawns, which would offer a peace rarely felt at any other time.

This morning the world had woken up to a blaze of pinks, blues, and yellows, a multicolored backdrop to the tumult of activity of the ocean. Sea lions were bobbing around, barking noisily, and the gulls were on the hunt for breakfast. The impending storm of the evening before had drifted away without breaking. Although it would be summer soon, there was still a cool in the air, a remnant of the chill of winter, lingering like a soft veil, gently caressing the skin until it finally gave way to the warmth of a new spring day. Birdsong had broken the dawn, and the woodpecker behind her cabin was back. Brina was relieved that the signs of spring were on their way.

She was thinking about Luke's visit to the coffee shop last night. There was symmetry to his visit, a closing off to the circle. They were at a pivotal stage in their work together, and they needed to take immediate action. But how? She closed her eyes and started to meditate. She needed to quiet her mind, tune into her intuition. Only later in life had she truly come to trust her abilities, the fact that sometimes she "knew" things, had a sensitivity that other people did not. She was still honing her skills and had limitations

Maggie Denhearn

that were more than frustrating at times. She had spent the last twenty years practicing.

As a young child growing up in war-torn Europe, her special gifts had gone unnoticed by her parents. Her mother, Alenka, worked all hours, and her father had been called up in 1940, the year she was born. She didn't meet him until she was five years old. When they immigrated to Canada in 1947, after the war and escaping the surge of communism, she had thought they would be a family again. They were, briefly.

Even at eleven years old, the irony of her father fleeing the communists, only to be accused of being one, was not lost on her. Brina had known it was going to happen, that her father was going to die that day, but hadn't known how to tell him in a way he would believe, or how to stop it happening. That morning, when he had left for work, she asked him to stay home, begged him, told him she feared something bad was going to happen to him. He laughed and promised her he would be safe and would always keep her safe.

Brina lost both her parents that day. With her father gone, her mother had been forced to work days, evenings, and weekends, and Brina had been left to her own devices. With no other family close by and no siblings, she got used to spending much of her time alone. Brina knew that her mother wasn't absent just because of work. She was avoiding her daughter. There was a look of both anger and sorrow in her eyes. She had heard her beg her father Josef not to leave that day. Brina wasn't sure whether her mother was angry with her for not preventing her father's death or feared her because she had known something was going to happen to him. From that moment Brina began to actively ignore the messages she would intuit, to hide from who she was.

The years of practicing denial had convinced her on that fatal evening with Frost that she had an overactive imagination, that he wouldn't dare to hurt her. All roads had been leading here. If her father hadn't been murdered, if she had learned to listen to her intuition, she never would have got involved with Frost. And she wouldn't have spent the rest of her life trying to bring down the Consortium.

A mulberry-colored patchwork knitted blanket keeping her warm, Brina sat on her deck, enjoying the salty fragrance of the ocean gently embracing her senses. She poured herself another cup of coffee and stared out into the water, her eyes dancing across the line of the horizon.

When the Universe Called

She knew Luke would not hear from Noah, that something had happened to him. She just couldn't figure out what. There had been no point in telling that to Luke last night without more evidence. Her intuitive abilities fluctuated and were highly dependent on how close she was to someone. Those whom she counted among her friends she could read more than she would ever dare tell them. Luke, Noah, Maria, Vanna, Iris, Kali: they were like an open book unless she got too emotionally involved or they really did not want to be read. It was something she had realized over the years and which still caused her much frustration.

It was hard not letting emotion get in the way of being fully conscious, and she hadn't figured out a way of getting past someone who was blocking her. Both Luke and Noah had become quite proficient at not letting her into their thoughts. Although she didn't know Noah as well as she knew his brother, she felt a bond with both of them. She knew what it was like to grow up with distant or lost parents. She didn't want to believe anything bad had happened to Noah. But something must have because she couldn't even feel his presence anymore, which usually meant only one thing.

But if he was dead, why was she sensing that whatever had happened, it somehow involved Kali? She knew Kali was having an affair with him, had known for a while, but Kali didn't have it in her to take a life. For now the images and feelings that were fading in and out of her mind didn't make sense. There was little she could do, only to wait and see.

Brina had a phone call to make. She was supposed to call Darcy only in emergencies. As Judge Rawley's secretary for the last fifteen years, Darcy had been an invaluable asset in keeping them informed of the dealings of the Consortium. It was important that her involvement with Brina, Luke, and Noah be kept at a minimum. A tall, dark woman in her early forties, her manner was quiet and unremarkable. She had the ability to slip in and out of rooms without people noticing. Her very ordinariness was the perfect cover. Darcy understood the art of dissimulation. Brina had learned that worrying about things was fruitless, yet the urgency of the situation was clear. Her hip ached. It ached only when there was negative energy around. Darcy was supposed to have called either Luke or Noah by yesterday evening at the latest to let them know how close FPH was to finally getting FDA approval for Torporo. Brina needed to know. If it was a still a while away, there was a

91

Maggie Denhearn

vague hope that Bill 267 would be stalled, that the Consortium would wait until the drug was actually ready for market.

She was about to pick up her phone when a flash of light caught the corner of her eye and a loud crack sounded in the distance. She glanced up and caught a streak of lightning barely visible in the bright morning sky, followed by another boom of thunder.

At first Brina thought it was the morning mist clearing as she glanced over the treetops, but then she noticed that it was becoming denser rather than evaporating. Smoke—thick, dark, gray smoke was snaking up above the roof of her cabin and curling its way high into the air, stretching itself out and trying to reach the mountains looming in the distance. As she contemplated the scene unfolding before her, she felt her skin begin to tingle, and the energy in her root chakra start to vibrate. This was not a campfire or someone in a backyard burning garden debris. This was a forest fire. The scent of destruction was in the air. She shivered. It had been an unusually dry winter. There had been no rain for weeks, and there was no rain coming down now. A dry thunderstorm? Here? The forest would be like tinder. It wouldn't take long for fire to take hold.

Her cell phone rang. She couldn't tell who it was from the number flashing up and so didn't answer it. It continued to ring, the sound shrill and piercing, splitting the uneasy quietness, beating in time to the billowing smoke that was spewing more and more urgently into the air. As if Brina and the rest of the world had become alerted to cries of the trees at the same time, the sound of sirens screaming came within earshot, becoming louder and louder. A rescue helicopter flew overhead, the blades cutting through the air. Her phone continued to ring, insistent, demanding that she pay attention. The tingles on her skin were now spreading up her spine to the back of her neck. Her whole body was alert, waiting to decide on fight or flight. She picked up her phone and pressed the answer button.

"Brina?"

"Yes." Silence on the other end. "Is that you, Vanna? Are you okay, dear?"

"Not really." Her voice was choked with tears that she was trying to fight back, although not succeeding very well.

"Start from the beginning."

When the Universe Called

"I'm not sure where to start, but I think I'm in trouble even though I've not done anything wrong. I don't know what to do."

"Breathe, dear, breathe. ... That's it. ... Breathe in for one, two, three, four. Hold. ... Now breathe out, one, two, three, four." Brina talked her through a few rounds, until the tear-filled hiccupy breathing had stopped. "I'm at home. Come round."

"I can't, not yet."

"Well, tell me what's wrong then."

"I can't, not over the phone."

"What's going on?"

"I'll tell you later. I'll come round as soon as I can." Vanna hung up, leaving Brina staring at her phone. She'd known Vanna only a few months, and she'd never heard her sound so distressed. Closing her eyes, she breathed in and tried to calm her mind. All she could see behind her closed eyes was Noah, surrounded by darkness. And Iris?

Brina opened her eyes and stared at the smoke, thick dark palls billowing up into the air. The sea lions were gone. The gulls had disappeared. Deserted ocean, deserted forest. Her phone rang again. She was about to pick it straight up, assuming it was Vanna calling back, but she noticed that this time a name flashed up. It was Kali. She changed her mind. Right now her head was too crowded. If she was to be of any help to Kali or Vanna, she needed space to think; and to tune into their energy without the cloud of emotion. She wasn't comfortable with the Noah–Kali connection in her head and didn't want to speak with her just yet, not until she'd figured things out. Eventually the ringing stopped.

A few moments later, the phone rang again. It had become a live creature, vying for her attention. This time it was Maria. Again, she let it ring out. Her world was being turned upside down and shaken. And not just hers. It didn't take much to figure out that they must all be calling about the same thing. It couldn't be a coincidence; there had to be a connection. The universe has laws; like attracts like; whatever you place your thoughts on grows. For every thought there's a manifestation. Whether we intend it or not, everything we think and do affects the universal energy in ways often far beyond most people's comprehension. Of this she was sure. The question now was, what was going on this morning that had the forest burning and

93

Maggie Denhearn

her phone constantly in motion? When in doubt, take time to sit quietly and think.

The air was acrid, bitter from the increasing amount of smoke in the air. The sirens had stopped.

*　　*　　*　　*

Vanna turned her cell phone to silent mode. She hunted through her wardrobe, wondering what to wear. Despite the chilled morning, it was going to be another warm day, unusual for the time of year. Since it hadn't rained in ages, it seemed unlikely it would today. She breathed in deeply, remembering to focus on expanding her diaphragm. In, out, in, out. Calm energy—she needed calm energy. Brina had been teaching her meditation, but she was still struggling with the whole calming her mind thing. No amount of meditation could get the image of the dead bodies out of her head, nor of the feeling of nausea.

Vanna was just negotiating closing her front door without letting Morris out when she heard someone coming up the steps to her deck and turned around.

"We have to talk." It was Maria.

"Oh, Maria. We have to talk now?" Vanna's mouth went dry, and she felt herself go cold. She thought her new friends on the Island were good people. Now she wasn't so sure. She daren't make eye contact with Maria, so busied herself with putting her bag in the car.

"Yes, *now.*"

"I'm sorry, I'm on my way out and I'm in kind of a hurry." Vanna felt Maria scrutinizing her. She started to say something, but Vanna interrupted her.

"I've really got to go, Maria. Sorry, I'll call you later." Vanna got in her car, avoiding her gaze. She drove off, glancing at Maria in her rearview mirror as she stood watching her turn round the corner.

*　　*　　*　　*

Maria stared as Vanna drove off. She got in her car and decided to follow her. It felt like today wasn't going to get any better than yesterday. Even if she assumed for a moment that Vanna had nothing to do with the other dead

When the Universe Called

body, and on reflection it did seem rather bizarre that Vanna could possibly have anything to do with it, Maria still wondered whether she could be trusted with the knowledge of what Maria and Kali had done. Yet, she'd have to risk telling her. Otherwise it was distinctly likely she would go to the police. If she was innocent, why would she not? That could even be where she was heading now. Vanna must have seen something. She had definitely been there. The last twenty-four hours had crushed Maria's sense of being good at reading people, and although she was used to taking gambles, she didn't like the odds on this one. Like it or not, they had to get hold of Vanna. Maria pulled out her phone and dialed Kali's number, putting it on speakerphone so she could drive hands free.

"Kali, we have a problem."

"What on earth else?" Kali's voice was creaky and hoarse.

"You sound awful."

"It's not been a great night. I can't get Noah's last expression out of my head. And I've been dreaming all night of what it would be like going to court, everyone standing there, looking at me, with the judge passing sentence."

"Don't go there. Try to stay present. You know what Brina says, and she's right. What you're imaging doesn't exist yet. Besides, we have a more immediate problem." Maria heard Kali sigh on the other end of the line. There was never going to be a good moment to tell her this, so she may as well get it over with.

"Vanna was in the forest this morning. She must have seen something."

"What were you doing going back there?" Kali's voice became more high-pitched.

"I had to go back and retrieve my wedding ring. I realized it must have fallen off last night when we were ... Anyway, I only noticed this morning. So I went back, and there was a bag of dog treats on the ground near to ... you know ... just like the ones she has for Morris. You know, those disgusting ones she's always carrying around. But when I bumped into her she didn't say anything at all about having seen ... erm ..." Her voice trailed off. She was afraid to mention Noah's name over the phone. There was silence for a moment on the other end of the line.

"Kali, did you hear me?"

Maggie Denhearn

"Surely she'd have said something if she had seen something. Maybe she didn't. And anyway, Vanna knows about me and … him. So if she did see something, she'd come and talk to me, right?"

"What? How does she know? How come *she* knows and you didn't tell me?"

"I … I'm sorry. I couldn't tell you. You're his sister-in-law. It was up to him to say something, and he was adamant about keeping us quiet. I had to tell someone, I was fit to burst."

Maria's head spun and she almost felt again like she would have to pull over. Nothing in her life was as it seemed—nothing. And she had been too stupid to notice.

"Well has she? Have you actually heard from Vanna this morning?"

"No. And look, don't be angry. I thought it would just make things complicated for you with Luke if you knew." Maria reddened at her mention of Luke's name. Now was not the time to ask if Kali knew anything about *his* affair.

"Well. We have to do something about Vanna."

"Like what? Maybe she's about to call me. It's still early. We should give her more time."

"Time to go to the police?

"Well, someone's going to find … him." Kali started to snivel.

"Kali, look, I know. I know this is hard, but you've got to keep it together. You've dragged me into this now. We're both complicit. I'm not sure what that means, but I'm guessing it's not good. But it's done, so we have to deal with it."

"Don't go to the police. Please don't go to the police. Andy will kill me!"

"I won't. Look, I was at Vanna's place just now, and I'm following her in the car. She refused to speak to me and looked decidedly shifty. She just drove off. Don't you find it odd that she hasn't called you yet? Wouldn't you be the first person she'd call, apart from maybe the police?"

"Well, maybe she didn't see anything. And are you sure she'd call the police?"

"She's English. And besides, I told you, there were Morris's dog treats on the ground. She saw, I'm sure of it." Maria paused. There was no way of avoiding telling Kali, even though she was sure she would not react well.

96

When the Universe Called

"Maria, what aren't you saying?"

Maria paused, then cleared her throat. "This morning when I went there … there was another dead body near … you know … I'm positive Vanna has seen everything. She was acting very oddly this morning. … It's just possible that she had something to do with that other body."

"What? You can't be serious! Vanna?" Maria moved her phone away from her ear as Kali began shrieking. She waited a few seconds then tried to interrupt her.

"Calm down, Kali, calm down! Enough. We need to talk to her, find out what she knows. Find out if she's gone to the police, or whatever else is going on."

"Maybe it's too late. Maybe she's already called them. Or maybe she's a killer. Oh no, this is awful, just too awful!" Kali wailed.

"Seriously, Kali, I can't think with you screaming and wailing. Get off the phone, slap some cold water on your face, and call Vanna. Pretend we haven't had this conversation and that you're calling to chat. Ask her round; find an excuse to get her to your place. Anything. I'm going to keep following her to see what she's up to." Maria hung up before Kali had time to reply.

Even by Maria's standards of having worked in PR for so long, events were getting out of hand. She'd handled her fair share of scandal for McDowell but nothing quite approximating this. This situation was getting messier by the hour.

Trying to follow Vanna at a distance wasn't easy. She'd never tailed anyone before. There was a garbage truck between them, and she hoped it wouldn't pull off, leaving her exposed to view. She needed to see where she was heading. At the same time, she was leaving Vanna a message.

"Listen, it's me. We need to talk. Don't do anything, just call me, okay?"

As she clicked off her phone, she caught sight of Vanna's car taking a left turn as the garbage truck continued on. Vanna was pulling into the parking lot of the strip mall in Eagle Cove. Maria slowed down as much as she could, turning and pulling up outside of the bank, watching as Vanna headed into the Kavama. Maria switched off her engine and settled down to wait.

Maggie Denhearn

WEDNESDAY MORNING, AUGUST 7, 1963

Frost summoned his secretary, Gina, into his office. She scurried in, notebook and pencil in hand, a wisp of hair escaping from a tightly wound knot of limp, copper hair. Hovering in front of his desk, she waited for him to speak. He watched her, wondering if he needed to be suspicious of her too. The all-too-apparent fear seeping out of her thin frame made it clear that it was highly unlikely that she had anything to do with Anja's betrayal. He sighed.

"I need you to send out a company memo expressing our condolences for the tragic and untimely death of our young intern Anja Oblak." Gina shuddered and fell back, catching herself with her hand on the door handle, the little color she had evaporating from her face. He coughed, trying to clear his throat of any trace of emotion, studiously ignoring her reaction.

"Traffic accident it seems. Very sad. Off you go." He began shuffling papers. Glancing up briefly, he saw her still in the doorway, staring at him vacantly.

"Gina. Go."

"Oh, er, yes sir." Her voice was tearful. Damn woman.

He was about to pick up the phone when footsteps and voices caught his attention. Glaring back in the direction of where Gina had been standing moments ago, he saw a uniform, a police uniform.

"Officer Bailey. Come in, come in." He got up and moved round to the front of his desk, gesturing for her to take a seat.

"Hold my calls and don't disturb me!" he yelled and shut the office door.

"I was about to call you."

"I thought it better we speak in person."

He liked her self-assurance and the fact that she was extremely attractive despite the uniform. The masculine cut could not hide the contours of a fabulous figure.

"So. I trust you have managed to ... deal with the matter."

"We have. It would appear that after the ... er ... accident, a new officer found her and took her immediately to the emergency room, but she was dead on arrival." The color drained from Frost's face. This could not be good, having others involved.

When the Universe Called

"Don't worry, sir. I was able to have a fruitful conversation with the other officer. He understands his position most clearly."

"Good. And ... er ... Anja?"

"Dealt with. As she has no family, the provincial authorities will deal with her burial. The death registry will state accidental death."

"And the other officer ... What's his name?"

"Petturi, Joe Petturi."

"And Petturi is cooperative? You're sure of that?"

"Very, once I clarified his situation. He's sorted out everything with the body. If he should change his mind at any point, he would face criminal charges, as he is now complicit. I doubt he will, though. He clearly values his future in the force."

Frost relaxed his shoulders and unclenched his jaw. "Thank you, Bailey. Your loyalty will not go unrewarded."

"Thank you, sir." She got up to leave. He appreciated the fact that she knew her place. He turned and stared at the bright blue morning sky, saying nothing further as he heard Bailey leave, closing the door softly behind her. It was over. Damage contained. He had been careless; he would not be so again.

CHAPTER 9

TUESDAY MORNING, APRIL 15, 2014

Luke arrived at the Nanaimo ferry terminal just in time. He parked his car in the lot and ran into the terminal building. He was the last foot passenger onto the ferry. He sent Charlotte a text to let her know to meet him over on the mainland in just over an hour and a half. The ferry was packed; it felt to Luke as though it was close to carrying its 1500 passengers capacity. Daily commuters with their laptops and phones beginning their workday, tourists milling around above and below deck, throngs of strangers abruptly thrown into close proximity for the hundred minutes it took to cross the thirty nautical miles of ocean between Vancouver Island and mainland Canada. The sun was shining brightly, and the water was flat and blue. The dull throb of the engines provided a constant background hum. The ferry had barely left the harbor, and children were already ensconced in the children's play areas and the video zones, while parents were forming long lines in the cafeteria.

As was his usual routine, Luke joined the line in the smaller café to buy a coffee and the morning paper. He needed caffeine to stop the skittish feeling he had inside. He'd left the thermos Maria had given him in the car. His cell phone vibrated. Glancing at it, he saw that the number was withheld. He was about to answer it and thought better of it. If it was urgent, whoever it was would leave a message. He let it go to voice mail. A moment later a text transcription of the voice message popped up. He was used to these texts sounding somewhat bizarre but the message didn't

100

make any sense at all. Luke quickly clicked on messages and listened. The message was half cut off:

"And then we'll get your brother's wife. And if we do, she will die if you don't tell us where he is." That was it.

Luke felt a cramp in his chest. The voice sounded unnervingly familiar. He wracked his brains as he tried to remember who it was. The message didn't make sense. His brother didn't have a wife. Noah didn't even have a regular girlfriend. He tried his brother's number again; still no answer. He had no idea what he was supposed to do. Even if he did know where Noah was, how was he supposed to respond if there were no instructions as to how and whom to contact?

"What can I get you?"

"Pardon? Oh, er, coffee please, cream and sugar," he hadn't realized it was now his turn in the line. He heard the groans of the person behind him. He turned around. He wasn't in the mood to take any crap from anyone.

"Is there a problem?" He turned to look behind him, not bothering to try and hide his hostility.

"Just give your order, buddy. Some of us want to get served too, ya know." Luke was about to tell this individual exactly what he could do, but he caught himself. He smiled sweetly and turned back to the server.

"And a bagel with cream cheese, please. Oh, and I'll pay for this paper too." The man behind him groaned again. This time Luke ignored him. He wasn't worth it, and he couldn't afford to draw attention to himself. He took his coffee and bagel and managed to find an empty table in a corner, away from the windows. It was a stunning day, and most people were either out on deck or sitting as close as they could to the windows to soak up the vista. Hiding in a corner suited Luke much better. He stared at the front page of the newspaper but wasn't reading the headline. All he could think about was his brother.

"Crap!" The couple a few seats away glanced quickly across at him, and he pretended to be engrossed in his newspaper. He hadn't realized he'd suddenly spoken out loud.

The voice that had left the message—he knew who it was. It had to be Heeley. He'd only ever spoken to him once, but he had a voice that was hard to forget. It had a raspy edge reminiscent of dry sandpaper rubbing across

Maggie Denhearn

concrete. Luke felt himself physically cringe. He knew only too well that the Consortium used Heeley whenever they wanted something illegal to be done and didn't want to be directly involved. In the last ten years working as a tax lawyer for FPH, pretending to rebuild his relationship with his father, all so that he, Brina, and Noah, could find out as much as possible about the dealings of FPH and its connections with the Consortium, he'd been privy to enough to know exactly how Heeley's services were used. He had no idea what the Consortium knew, but they evidently knew or at least suspected something and were clearly after Noah. And if they were after him, that could only mean he was alive.

Luke breathed out slowly. He tossed aside his bagel, his appetite gone. The danger was still there, and his brother remained missing. How had Heeley got Luke's number? He had two phones. The only people to whom he'd given the number to this one were his brother, Brina, and Darcy. Not even Maria knew it. To admit to it would mean peeling away layer upon layer of untruths that he had been telling her ever since they'd met, all in order to keep her safe. But Charlotte. He remembered now; he had given her the number too.

There was only one person who could possibly have betrayed him. His brain buzzed like one of those plasma balls. He sipped his coffee. Everything was undoing before his eyes. He picked up his phone and dialed. He heard the phone pick up at the other end.

"It's me. What's going on?" Luke's voice was icy.

*   *   *   *

The skin on Kali's hands was red and raw. She had been rubbing them together nervously and couldn't stop as she paced back and forth in her kitchen. Thank goodness Andy had left early in the morning. She'd heard him pottering around and had been waiting desperately for him to go so she could get up without having to face him.

She hadn't slept. The shock of what had happened with Noah cast a dark shadow that she was unable to escape. She had this feeling she was walking on quicksand and that any minute now she would be sucked under. Her chest felt constricted, and she had to continually focus to be able to get any air. The image of his dead body wouldn't leave her mind. Neither would the fear and guilt.

Had she somehow managed to create this situation with her thoughts? What if what Brina said about energy and thoughts and manifestation were true? She hadn't wanted Noah to die, but what if somehow she had accidentally caused this to happen? The idea was too horrible to conceive.

She was thankful that today was one of her work at home days, so she could hide at home while the nightmare played out in her head. The academic semester had just finished. Last Friday had been the last day of classes. Maybe she should go for a run to take her mind off things, though not in the forest. She doubted she would ever be able to look at the trails again in the same way.

Kali remembered the first time Vanna had come out with the WOECs. She'd just moved to the Island and had found out about their running group from Brina when she'd dropped by the Kavama, which was the first place most people went to when they either visited or moved to Eagle Cove. Kali and Vanna had instantly become friends. Only now did she consider the fact that she still didn't know Vanna that well. And who knew if what she said about herself was true? No, she refused to believe that Vanna had been dishonest with her. There was no way she could be mixed up with the other dead body. She just didn't seem the type to be hiding anything. Maybe she should call her to try and explain, like Maria had told her to. Surely she would believe Kali when she told her about what had really happened to Noah. Her hands shaking, she grabbed at her phone.

"Vanna, you'd got to call me. Call me. Please. As soon as you get this, call. Bye."

What if that message was used in evidence against her? She hadn't actually said anything incriminating, but the anxiety in her voice was clear. This was all getting to be too much to think about. Maria had to sort this out. She just had to. That's what she did; that was her job. Maria would make it all go away.

Kali looked at her running shoes and thought better of it. Coffee and cookies and closed curtains seemed a much better idea. She needed sanctuary. She slumped down on the sofa and switched on the television. Time to watch something inane. The music for *Murder She Wrote* came blaring out. Cursing Andy, she hit the mute button.

Maggie Denhearn

"Thanks, universe!" She switched channels. Hopefully, watching the home design channel would remind her of nothing except badly chosen wallpaper.

*   *   *   *

Vanna sat in the Kavama, nursing a cup of chai. She'd felt too unsettled to stay at home, but then hadn't known where to go. She needed time to process all the strange thoughts going round her head before going to see Brina. She didn't feel up to seeing her quite yet and wasn't sure why she'd called her when she had. If Brina was at home, that meant Tullia would be working at the coffee shop. Brina had a way of knowing what Vanna was thinking, and she couldn't face her reading what was going on in her head at this particular moment. She needed to get more of a grip on herself.

Tullia was busy humming and making sandwiches. The old guys who always came in were huddled in the corner as usual, making one coffee each last for hours. The normality of the scene was reassuring.

Vanna looked at her phone. There were several messages, mostly from Maria, and one from Kali. She wasn't sure if she wanted to hear what Maria had to say. She didn't want her worst fears confirmed. She liked Maria. She'd seemed nice, normal—until now. Maria was a frequent customer at the café as she organized the running club from here. She was a friend of Brina. No one had told Vanna yet what WOECs stood for. Clearly it was an in-joke, and as a newcomer it seemed she was yet to be privy to that. But what else weren't they telling her?

And if Brina and Maria were friends, did that mean she couldn't trust Brina either? Vanna didn't know quite what to make of this strange older woman. Brina's intonation could sometimes make a question sound more like a command. With most people you could catch a glimpse of who they were if you looked hard enough into their eyes, but with Brina's there was something odd, and you couldn't do that. Even so, she had an aura about her that Vanna found reassuring and on the Island, she was the only person she could think of to turn to. She had the wisdom of the crones that was so much overlooked these days, although not within Vanna's family. Her grandmothers and great-grandmother held sway over the family in a way

When the Universe Called

that she realized was unusual. A pang of homesickness passed through her like a ghost. She shivered. Looking again at her phone, she picked it up and dialed Kali's number.

"Hi Kali, what's up?" Vanna heard Kali swear and some scrambling around.

"Vanna? Sorry, the phone nearly fell in my coffee."

"Yeah, hi. You left me a message. I've not had time to listen to it. How's things?"

"Thank goodness you called! Listen, you need to come round. I can't talk to you on the phone."

"What's happened? You sound upset."

"Vanna, please, just come round."

Vanna hesitated. She wasn't sure she was up to putting on a party face and pretending everything was fine. No matter what she thought Maria might have done, it didn't seem right talking to Kali about it before she'd found out what was actually going on. On the other hand, it didn't feel right leaving her friend in the lurch either.

"Pleeeaase!" Kali sounded tearful.

"Okay. I'll come right over." At least whatever was going on with Kali would take her mind off things. Kali could be such a drama queen sometimes.

*   *   *   *

"Don't lie to me," snarled Luke. "Heeley is sniffing around. He's one of your hounds. You must know something about that. If you have a problem, why not come out and say so? Is that why you want Noah and me to come to the mainland so urgently all of a sudden?"

Frost curled his lip in disdain. He didn't care for Luke much. Of his two sons, he found Noah the least annoying. Luke reminded him too much of his late wife. She used to equally frustrate him. Excessive displays of emotion of any kind made him feel uncomfortable. In a woman, such lapses in behavior were tolerable, perhaps occasionally endearing. In a man he found them repugnant. But, up to now, he had to admit that Luke had been good at what he did. He had got FHP out of countless legal wrangles and continued to ensure that they got away with somewhat gray financial dealings. Frost had

Maggie Denhearn

opted to tolerate him. Now, however, it seemed he might no longer be the asset he once was—worse even, a traitor.

"Good morning to you too, Luke. I don't know what you're talking about. And is it wrong that I should want to see my sons?"

Frost genuinely didn't know what the deal with Heeley was, although he could guess. He had a shrewd idea Bailey was up to far more than she had let on. They would be having words later. As for summoning his boys over, he wanted to talk to them before she did.

"If you've done nothing wrong, why would we be sending Heeley after you?" He decided on a double bluff to see what Luke might let slip.

"What's that supposed to mean?" Frost sensed his son's confusion at the other end of the line.

"Guilty conscience?"

Luke snorted. "*Whatever*, Father."

"Luke, my dear boy, I truly don't know what you're talking about. Perhaps another skeleton is coming back to haunt you? We're not the only ones to whom Heeley offers his services."

He heard Luke hesitate. Frost tried to sound casual.

"Look, I'm sure it's nothing. If it was Heeley calling you, he's not doing so on my account. I'll look into it. In the meantime, don't worry about it."

Technically, he wasn't lying. He would investigate, but with a rather different agenda. Bailey was keeping something from him, and he wanted to know what. He didn't trust her; he didn't trust anyone. Wheezing, he decided to plant one more seed of doubt.

"Perhaps you might want to rethink how much you trust Charlotte."

"What?"

"I'll be in touch." Frost hung up and started coughing. Mary scurried into the room, glass of water in hand. He grabbed the water from her and waved at her to get out of the room. He needed time to think. Her continual hovering could be disconcerting.

*   *   *   *

Luke banged his fist on the table, sending his coffee cup clattering to the ground. Other passengers turned round and stared in his direction.

106

When the Universe Called

Leaning down and picking up the smashed pottery, he tried to regain his composure. He stared out of the ferry window, watching the mainland rise up into view, avoiding the looks of those around him. His father's comment about Charlotte felt like a hand grenade exploding in his stomach. Surely Charlotte would never betray him? They were getting on fine. Too late; the shards of doubt were now firmly embedded. How else could Heeley have got his phone number? He'd have to tread carefully when she picked him from the ferry. They'd agreed that it made sense to go in one car to the hotel, and since she had decided to go over to Vancouver on the late ferry last night, she offered to come and get him from the ferry terminal once he arrived on the mainland. He'd have to pretend everything was normal until he could figure out what to do.

He got up and went out onto the deck. It was cool, and there was a crisp breeze as the vessel chugged along. He breathed in deeply. The salty air was invigorating. His stomach continued to churn. Focusing on one of the mountain peaks in the distance, he inhaled slowly, held his breath, then gently exhaled. He continued doing this as the ferry came into dock. Positive. He had to remain positive.

"Like attracts like," he whispered to himself. Given what was happening right now, he clearly needed to be paying more attention to his thoughts than he had been doing. A garbled announcement over the ferry's loudspeaker and people suddenly milling around indicated that they were nearing shore. Luke lined up with the other foot passengers, considering his options. It would appear that he couldn't even trust his own daughter.

As he came out of the ferry terminal at Horseshoe Bay and walked out into the sunshine, he saw Charlotte over in the parking lot. She was staring right at him. He waved hello and started toward her. Then he stopped. Something in her manner wasn't right. She was rigid, unmoving. Even at a distance he could see that her mouth was set, like she was holding back from saying something. As he got closer, he saw a man sitting in the back seat of her car, his arm leaning out of the window, something in his hand poking Charlotte in her side. A gun—it had to be a gun.

Confusion and adrenaline made him drop his bag. Trembling, he bent down to pick it up. Slapping his forehead theatrically, he tried to make it look like he'd forgotten something, and pretended to head back in the direction

Maggie Denhearn

he'd come. He hoped the gunman was after him, in which case he'd see
Luke going in the opposite direction and come after him, leaving Charlotte
to escape. Glancing back, Luke just made out that the man had got out of
the car and pushed Charlotte to one side. Good. If he could lead the man
back onto the boat, Charlotte would have time to get away. He ran back up
the gangplank, pushing past people, glancing back quickly every now and
then to make sure the man was following him. Yes, it was definitely one of
Heeley's men, and he was catching up: dark, tall, thin, cheap suit, tacky
sunglasses—hard to miss.

"Sir, you can't go back on."

"I left my cell phone."

"Okay, but make it quick."

"Sir, sir!"

Heeley's man ran straight, pushed the ferryman out of the way, and
barged his way through the crowd. Various people were cursing him. The
ferry was the usual warren of different levels and staircases, with doors
leading in all directions. Luke bounded up two flights of stairs, ducked in
behind one of the doors, and then looped round and ran back down the
stairs on the other side. If he was quick, he could be back off the boat before
Heeley's man realized he'd been given the slip. Running back down the
stairs, he realized he'd gone too far. As he came rushing out of the door at
the bottom, he ran into the side of a car. He'd come down as far as the lowest
deck, and the final cars were being driven off the ferry. The startled driver
behind the steering wheel slammed on his brakes.

"What the ...?" As the driver wound down his window, Luke jumped
in the back seat of the car.

"I'm so sorry! I was asleep and I thought I was going to miss getting off.
Would you mind just giving me a ride off?" Luke smiled sweetly, as his heart
pounded in his ears. Too stunned to respond, the driver merely nodded and
carried on driving. As they came out into the sunshine, Luke scanned the
parking lot. Charlotte was still waiting there by her car, craning her head,
it would seem, looking for him.

"Thank you!" Luke jumped out of the car and ran over to Charlotte. By
the time he got to her, she had jumped into the driver's seat and started the
engine. He was just able to slip in beside her as Heeley's man came running

When the Universe Called

toward them, his face dark with fury. There were too many people around for him to pull his gun. Even Heeley's men weren't so stupid as to draw that kind of attention. Charlotte's car screeched out of the parking lot and into the line of traffic. Hardly a speedy getaway, but with so many people and cars around, Heeley's man stared at them helplessly as they pulled out of sight, his cell phone already to his ear. They wouldn't have much time. Luke tried to get his breath back.

"Are you okay?"

"Shouldn't I be asking you that question? Charlotte, what's going on? Why didn't you get away when you had the chance? You shouldn't have waited."

"What, and leave you to that thug?"

"I could handle him." Luke loosened his tie.

"Well, I didn't know that." Charlotte glanced across at him. She seemed genuinely concerned.

"Nice to know you have faith in me. Who was he? Are you okay? He didn't touch you did he?" The doubts he'd just formed about her were now drowned in an overwhelming paternal instinct to protect his daughter.

"What? Eew, no! I got out of the car while I was waiting for you, and he just came from behind and grabbed me. I wasn't going to argue, seeing as he stuck a gun in my side. I've no idea who he was, but he definitely seems to know you. What are you mixed up in?"

"Nothing. Nothing." Luke briefly took his seat belt off and struggled out of his jacket. He was perspiring and needed something to drink.

"Got any water?"

"On the back seat. I'm impressed you managed to hold on to your bag."

"Me too. I think I've wrenched my shoulder, though." Luke started to massage his left shoulder and concentrated on his breathing again. If Charlotte had given his number to Heeley, then why would his man need to hold her at gunpoint? That didn't make sense. He watched her drive. She kept glancing in the rearview mirror.

"Is anyone following us?"

"Not that I can tell."

Luke glanced back and then wished he hadn't. His neck was seizing up and starting to feel sore.

109

Maggie Denhearn

"So you're sure you didn't know this guy?"

"Of course not. Why would I?" She paused. "What, do you think I had something to do with this?"

"What? No, no, it's just that ..." Luke let his voice trail off. "Forget it. I'm just, it's not every day someone chases me with a gun, alright?"

"Me neither!"

"Sorry. Are you okay?"

"Yes. Stop asking me."

They drove in silence, winding their way through the thick morning traffic. They were crawling along at a frustratingly leisurely pace. Luke continued looking out of the window, glad Charlotte had to concentrate on driving. It was peculiar, feeling fatherly toward a grown woman as though she were still your little girl, yet having no memories of her as anything other than a strong, independent adult. He knew he had no right.

The randomness of the universe had got them working together, her as a junior paralegal on his team. Unwittingly, he had recruited his own daughter to work with him—indirectly. Someone else had done the interviews, but he had reviewed her resume. He'd had no idea who she was. He had known he had a child somewhere, but had long ago opted to believe it was an old story, a myth lost in another time. The moment she had walked into the meeting room on her first day of work, he had realized she was Ena's child; and his. Over the last six months, he'd got to know and like her, had begun to muse ever so slightly on what he had missed out on. It wasn't that he would change the outcome of the situation, but if he had a chance to do it all over again, he liked to think he would handle it somewhat differently.

She was like him in so many ways and like her mother in so many others. He hadn't seen her mother Ena for twenty-three years. That was just before Charlotte was born and years before he'd married. He'd never seen the point of telling Maria about that particular episode of this life. What was the point of telling anyone about previous love affairs? And he didn't think Ena was his biggest fan. He believed keeping his distance had been better for all of them. Now he had a chance with Charlotte. This time he wanted and needed to protect her.

But what if she had betrayed him in some way? There it was, that doubt, planted by his father. He regretted ever telling Frost about Charlotte—a

110

When the Universe Called

momentary slip that had cost him. All his father had done so far was to use her existence and the fact that no one else knew of their true relationship in a power play against his son.

They were nearing Vancouver's city center.

"We can't go to the hotel conference center. That'll be the first place they'll go. I don't imagine they're going to give up looking for me that easily."

"True, but they would assume we wouldn't go there precisely because it's too obvious, so going there might actually be the safest option. Everyone else from the company will be there. At least if we stay in the group, they can't get us. Anyway, why don't you call the police?"

Luke hesitated and opted to sidestep the question in the hope that she wouldn't pursue it. "What would I say to the police? I can't prove anyone was after me. They wouldn't believe me. The police can't do anything."

"Okay, how about we at least go to the hotel initially? That'll buy us some time to think of what to do. Surely if we stay in public, we'll be safe?"

"We?"

"I'm assuming that whoever it was is going to be mad at me now too for not letting his man get you. I don't feel safe anymore." Her voice trembled.

"I know, but they're … Whoever it is, isn't after you. It'll be dangerous if you stay with me until I know exactly what's going on. I'm sure it's some big misunderstanding. Some of our clients are powerful people, as you well know, and can be rather paranoid sometimes." He'd never told her about the Consortium and he wasn't about to right now. Even if it turned out that she had given his number to Heeley, he had to believe there was an innocent explanation.

"Sounds like gangsters to me. Just tell someone when we get to the hotel. All the company bigwigs will be there, and you are the son of the owner of FPH, after all. Surely they can do something. And I still think we should call the police." Luke tried to ignore the tears in her eyes.

*   *   *   *

They sat in silence for a few moments as Charlotte continued to negotiate the busy city traffic. She was enjoying playing the ingénue. Luke was falling for it hook, line, and sinker. Charlotte deliberately glanced briefly across at

Maggie Denhearn

him, using the girlish sad look that had always worked on Carl, her adopted father. She was a virtuoso and she knew it. Luke seemed to find it hard to meet her gaze when she looked at him like that. Charlotte saw she was wearing him down.

"We don't have much time, and the hotel is only another fifteen-minute drive away, even going this slowly. We need to try and get at least some things figured out before we get there. I've got my passport and some cash."

"You've been watching too many movies. How did you get time to get that with a gun pointed at you?"

"I always carry my passport and extra cash with me. Don't you?" She carried on chatting as though this were the most normal conversation in the world.

"Okay."

Good, her plan was working. For a while Charlotte thought he might have found her out, but it would seem not. She knew she was running out of time and that before long he would begin to suspect her. She had to act fast.

"Where's Maria, by the way?" Distraction seemed a good plan.

"At home. She doesn't usually come with me on business trips."

"I swear she thinks we're having an affair."

"What?" Luke snorted, then burst out laughing. "That again? Don't be stupid, of course she doesn't! How on earth could she think that? You're young enough to be ..." He trailed off, his cheeks flushing crimson.

"To be your daughter? How true and how true! I'm not wrong, though. Didn't you see the looks she was giving us yesterday?"

"She was just in a funny mood. She's often like that. You read too much into things."

"Whatever. It's not important. I guess you'll tell her eventually." Or never. She wasn't so sure, and Luke didn't respond.

"Poor Maria. I would have thought she would have cottoned on by now. I thought she was smarter than that." Glancing sideways, she caught Luke arching his eyebrows, but he didn't rise to the bait.

"What can I say? I'm a good liar," he said simply.

"Clearly." An awkward silence fell between them. The traffic continued to crawl along. Charlotte wished they were already at the hotel. In a single moment something had shifted. She was starting to feel acutely

112

uncomfortable. If she carried out her plan, this was likely the last day she would ever see her father.

FULL MOON—TUESDAY, SEPTEMBER 3, 1963

Anja watched the mainland melt away on the horizon amidst the glow of an orange sunset. The pulsing of the ferry engines steadily edged the boat further out into the expanse of the ocean. It was a clear evening, the sky a limpid blue. The last rays of gentle sunshine were hanging on as the soft blanket of night was starting to unfold, the moon still only a faint silver slither in the pale sky. Time to look forward.

Holding on to the rail, she moved to the other side of the deck, tentatively, her hip still sore, her legs not quite steady. Vancouver Island was not yet in sight. Closing her eyes, she focused on the caress of the breeze on her cheeks, signaling a new freedom. She had spent nearly a month in the Peturris' sparse, colorless spare room. The color had been switched back on. She hadn't realized how much she'd missed it. Although she had not quite recovered, they, she and Petturi, had both agreed that it was time for her to disappear. Since she had been officially pronounced dead and actually buried, neither of them could afford her to be discovered. Petturi had used the unidentified body of young woman who had died in the hospital where his wife worked, as part of the ruse to convince the world that Anja Oblak was now deceased.

So far the plan seemed to have worked. Anja felt it an odd sensation—so near to death, yet not quite dead, not yet. A chance to start again. What would she do differently? Many things. She wished she could bottle how she felt right now, keep it as a reminder for when the nightmare of the last month had faded. Once the novelty of starting afresh wore off, she didn't trust herself to be able to resist any flashes of hope of returning to her former life that might spark.

Opening her mouth, she breathed in the briny ocean air. Her family had managed to create a new life by coming to Canada. She could reinvent herself again. She would need a new name. She would have to give that some consideration. It was four, perhaps five years since she had returned to the cabin on Vancouver Island where she had spent the last years of her

Maggie Denhearn

childhood. As she had never told anyone about it since she'd left, it seemed safe enough to return there. She could smell the wood and see the view from the deck in her mind. As she disappeared that night and slipped into the shadows, she awoke to a new understanding of who she was.

CHAPTER 10

Around lunchtime Tuesday, April 15, 2014

Charlotte pulled up in front of the hotel. She had been praying that they would get a parking spot and wouldn't have to park miles away from the entrance, leaving them vulnerable. Somehow she managed to find a place right in front of the main lobby. A concierge was ready to greet them.

"You go and check in, and I'll be right there. I'll meet you at the front desk."

"Okay." She watched as Luke walked quickly up the steps and into the hotel, scanning the people around; he looked conspicuously on edge. Everyone seemed engrossed in their own business. She pretended she was searching through her bag on the back seat, slipping her phone from her pocket, and starting to dial.

"So far so good?"

"Yes." Charlotte whispered, even though Luke was too far away to hear her.

"Okay. We'll be with you soon. Follow the plan and sit tight." Charlotte ended the call and stuck her phone back into her jacket. Luke hadn't looked back once to see what she was doing. He trusted her. This was good, very good. Not long to go now.

It had been a long road, trying to find her father, although it hadn't been that hard to track him down—too easy, in fact. It's incredible what information people are prepared to give a complete stranger. Charlotte had

Maggie Denhearn

hesitated at first to call him. She was too scared to pick up the phone. What do you say after so much time has elapsed? It was hard to quantify the sense of disconnection she felt. She'd decided to write him a letter. It would give them both the time to come to terms with the idea of meeting.

His response had been guarded. He didn't think he was her father, and even if he was, he couldn't do anything to help her. He had nothing to offer. She knew he was referring to money. That was not what she was looking for. She wanted answers, and she was prepared to be persistent.

Now here they were. Charlotte couldn't remember the exact moment when she had decided to get revenge. It was as though her anger had been metastasizing like a tumor without her noticing, taking her over from within, a rage so strangely volatile and real she knew she needed to do something with it or it would devour her. Once she had decided to consciously give her fury space, it started to consume her every waking moment. She had chosen the same profession, law, long before she knew that her father was a lawyer. A few months after she tracked him down, she found FPH. She began envisioning what it would be like working there, thinking about it all the time. It became an obsession.

It hadn't taken long for an opportunity at his firm to come up. It was meant to be. She used her adopted name on her resume, knowing he wouldn't recognize it. There were advantages sometimes to having two identities. When she contacted him again and he finally agreed to meet, she passed it off as bizarre coincidence that she happened to have started working at the same law firm where he worked. He seemed to believe her, or chose to. He apologized for not reacting more positively to her letter months before. Incrementally they became more intertwined in each other's lives. No one at work knew of their connection except Luke's father. It worked.

She wanted to hurt him, though, to make him feel pain, to make him pay. She wanted him to know hurt, anger, and isolation and was prepared to bide her time to ensure that happened. Initially she'd had no idea exactly how she was going to enact her revenge on him, but she had faith that if she waited long enough and focused, her time would come, and she would know what to do.

When the Universe Called

And it did. It landed in her lap, just like that. Alexis Bailey. She was on to Luke. She knew he was defrauding FPH in some way. Charlotte didn't hesitate. It was the ready-made opportunity she had been praying for.

* * * *

As Vanna pulled into Kali's driveway, Maria pulled up and parked right behind her, blocking Vanna's way. Her heart sank. If she wanted to leave, she wouldn't be able to. This seemed too much of a coincidence, and she had the distinct feeling she was being set up.

Did this mean Kali was up to something with Maria? Perhaps there was more to this running club than everyone had let on. Perhaps that was why they were so secretive regarding the meaning of WOECs. Maybe she had secretly joined a cult without realizing. The Island seemed to attract alternative types. She stared at Maria but couldn't bring herself to engage in the usual pleasantries.

"Maria."

"Vanna." The tension between them was palpable.

"Shall we?" Maria had taken charge and with arm outstretched, ensuring there was only one direction Vanna could walk, was ushering her up the path through the front door. Kali must have been looking out of the window because she was on the doorstep before they had even both got out of their cars. Silently she motioned for them to follow her into the kitchen. Coffee and cake were laid out on the table, adorned with a freshly laundered embroidered tablecloth and Kali's grandmother's coffee service. Vanna knew Kali got that out only when she was trying to impress.

"Would someone mind telling me what this is all about, please?" Vanna tried not to sound as worried as she felt. She had thought they were her friends, but now she had no idea who they were. She felt vulnerable and confused.

"It's not what you think," Maria started.

"How do you know? What do I think?"

"Well, I think you found a dead body in the forest and you think that I might have had something to do with it."

"Well, didn't you?"

Maggie Denhearn

"In a manner of speaking."

Vanna felt her eyebrows shoot up to the top of her head, and she felt light-headed. She so didn't want it to be true that her friend was a murderer.

"Hang on. It's not in the way you're clearly imagining. Besides, I could be equally suspicious of you. There was another body which I—we—had absolutely nothing to do with."

"What? So you think I did? I was just out for a run! Next thing I know, I'm tripping over dead bodies all over the place." Vanna glared at Maria. She knew what she had seen. If Maria was going to try some kind of psycho trick on her to convince her she'd imagined everything, she could forget it. Vanna was not that susceptible.

She was about to say something else but stopped herself. Perhaps she was in danger. That hadn't occurred to her until now. She shivered, feeling cold sweat beading on her forehead and her hands getting clammy.

"Okay, I'm going to explain my—*our* end of things, and let's see where we are after that. Kali, as you know, has been having an"—Maria paused— "has been having a 'friendly' shall we say 'relationship' with Noah." Maria was good with euphemisms and had a remarkable way of italicizing the spoken word.

Vanna's mouth gaped as Maria proceeded to give the edited highlights of Kali's intimate exploits that had led to the untimely and unfortunate demise of Noah. And of how, since Noah had genuinely cracked his head against a rock, they hoped that the matter would be smoothed over and that Kali and Andy could be kept out of the whole lamentable affair.

"Kali? You did what? Is that why you called me just now? Why didn't you call me before?" She looked back to Maria, totally bewildered by what she had heard, trying to dry her sweaty hands on the tablecloth without the others noticing. "I don't understand why were you in the forest this morning though."

"I helped Kali dress Noah, but my wedding ring slipped off in the process. I didn't notice I'd lost it until this morning."

"But I still don't get it. I'm sure I saw Luke. I know I did. I know I've not met him very often, but it was definitely Luke. I didn't recognize the other guy. His head was too bashed in to see."

When the Universe Called

"Noah just banged his head. He wasn't all bashed up. This doesn't make sense. Who is this other guy anyway? Surely not Luke ..." Kali wasn't doing a very good job of fighting back tears and grabbed a tissue to blow her nose. Mascara-stained spidery black tears were running down her cheeks, but she was too distraught to wipe them away.

"Kali—breathe, then drink some coffee." Maria pushed Kali's mug closer to her. "Maybe you should put some brandy in that." Kali took a sip, hugging the mug with her fingers that hadn't stopped shaking since Vanna and Maria walked through the door.

"I saw Luke this morning, so the other body can't have been him. At least I don't think so. ... He did leave rather early, though." Maria paled. A strained silence fell between them.

They were missing something, something important. Maria suddenly started laughing, like she was deranged.

"I don't see what's funny." Vanna was losing patience and made a move to leave. Maria was sounding unhinged and Vanna was feeling distinctly threatened.

"Vanna, wait! Sit down, please." The weight of Maria's hand on her arm made Vanna pause, then slump back down in her seat.

"Listen, I don't know why I didn't think of it! Okay, so you, me, we both saw the body with the bashed-in head. I don't know how that got there and if I'm to believe you ... and I do," she added hastily, "then someone else has been up to something. But the other body is definitely Noah, not Luke. Noah is—*was* my brother-in-law and Luke's identical twin brother. Didn't you know Luke was a twin? That has to be it."

Vanna stared at her, astonished. "No! You've never mentioned that. And I've never met Noah ... so ..." She looked across at Kali, who nodded meekly in confirmation. She didn't seem to think this as amusing as Maria appeared to.

"So no wonder you thought it was Luke! I should have thought of that before." Maria laughed again.

"Oh my goodness. I *so* thought it was Luke. And then I saw you, and didn't know how to tell you, but then you ..." Vanna trailed off, various pieces of the puzzle falling into place, one by one. "Hang on, though. How did you know I'd seen the bodies?"

119

Maggie Denhearn

"There was a bag of dog treats by Noah. They looked like Morris'. And then you wouldn't look me in the eye when we bumped into each other, and it dawned on me afterward that you must have seen something. I couldn't figure out why you wouldn't warn me about dead bodies in the forest unless you thought I'd had something to do with them." For a few moments no one said anything, each of them assiduously avoiding the gaze of the others.

Maria finally broke the silence. "Thanks for the vote of confidence, by the way. Nice to know you trust me."

"Sorry." Vanna felt herself blush, wringing her hands. "It's just, well, it's not often one finds dead bodies. Never, in fact. And I don't know anyone very well here, and ..." She squirmed in her seat.

"There's still that other dead body, though." Kali got up to get a bottle of brandy from one of the cupboards and was pouring a slug into her coffee, holding up the bottle as a silent offer to the others. Both shook their heads.

"I know."

"Hmm."

"No idea who he is," said Maria.

"No idea either," said Vanna. "I'm sorry about Noah." She didn't know who to feel worse for. Kali stared down into her mug as though she was trying to do some kind of tealeaf reading with coffee grinds. Maria nodded, tears welling up in her eyes.

"I have no idea how to tell Luke. I don't want to believe it. I keep thinking none of this is real. I mean, you know how Brina is always telling us that we create our own reality? Maybe if I could just think different thoughts, all of this would go away." Vanna reached out to touch Maria's hand, but she pulled it away.

"I'm sorry, I'm okay. I just need ... I need to not think about how I feel. If you're nice to me, I'll crumble, and that won't do any of us any good." Avoiding eye contact with Vanna, Maria poured herself some more coffee.

The three of them sat there for a few minutes. Maria was the first to speak, her voice peculiarly wobbly.

"We need a plan. If the police come and ask us questions, we need to get our stories straight."

"Police?" Kali turned white.

"It's a suspicious death."

When the Universe Called

"I know, but I was kind of hoping ..."

"I know ... that your relationship wouldn't come out. You might be okay. I'm a relative, though, so they're bound to ask me something." Vanna felt a lurch in the pit of her stomach.

"I er ... well ... I er ... I called the police from the trail."

"What?"

"Well, wouldn't you? What else would you do?"

"Yeah, okay. So what did they say?"

"That someone would come. But I got cut off and they didn't, at least not by the time I left."

"Did they get your name and number?"

"No, at least I don't think so." Vanna was surprised and not a little alarmed that her memory of events was starting to blur already. Surely she should be able to remember? Was she in shock? Her body did feel very strange, almost like it didn't belong to her anymore.

Maria sighed. "For once in my life I have no idea what do to, I really don't. Lying to the police is never a good plan. I've been in PR for a long time, and I realize some people think it's a shady business, but I've never had to cover up any dead bodies. We'll have to think of something, though. And in the meantime, pray for some kind of divine intervention."

"I've been doing that all night!" Kali sniffed. "Cake anyone? I made it especially." She cut three slices and handed each of them a piece. Vanna picked at her slice with her fingers, breaking off small pieces at a time. She let the sweetness dissolve on her tongue.

"I think we should talk to Brina. She'll know what to do."

*   *   *   *

"Do you really hate me that much?" Luke was like a caged creature, gesticulating and pacing back and forth in the hotel room.

"I don't hate you." Charlotte had thought she did, but realized now this was not hate. It wasn't even dislike.

"You must if you're turning me over to Heeley's men!"

"You betrayed me. Now it's my turn." This sounded more petulant than she felt. Luke looked blank, not understanding what she was talking about.

121

Maggie Denhearn

Then his expression changed as the realization of what she meant seeped through.

"Not just me, my mother. You deserted us." Charlotte looked away. She'd thought this moment would feel different. She'd thought that when she finally revealed how she had tricked him, she would feel happy, relieved, overjoyed even, anything but how she was actually feeling right now. The hurt was still there. She'd thought that would disintegrate, crumble the moment she got her revenge. It remained, like a sharp stone digging into her ribs. This didn't make sense. It wasn't supposed to be like this.

"Don't you know they'll kill me?"

Luke looked at her pleadingly. She didn't know what to say.

"Is that what you want? Is that what you really want? And you say you don't hate me."

Charlotte stared past him to the window and out at the fluffy white clouds scudding across an opalescent sky.

"Charlotte, look at me. Look at me! So I did a dumb-ass thing when I was your age. Your age! And maybe I wasn't Mister Sensitive when you first found me. I'm sorry. Is that what you want to hear? I'm sorry! I'm sorry!"

"Easy to say that, now your life is at stake."

"You're behaving like a whiny child."

"Patronizing me, good call."

"Charlotte. Seriously, this is my life on the line. I am sorry, *truly*. I didn't know what to say when you wrote to me out of the blue. And I thought after the last few months we'd got past that. I didn't think I needed to say anything. I thought I'd made up for things. You know I'm sorry. If you were that angry with me, why didn't you say something before now?"

"I thought you wouldn't have listened. Or cared."

"You didn't give me a chance."

Charlotte thought for a moment. She wasn't convinced that she believed him, but at the same time, she suddenly had this awful feeling she'd been playing with fire and that now he wasn't the only one who was going to get burnt.

"Tell me what to do then. I don't know how to get out of this."

"Well, start by telling me how you got into this in the first place. How on earth do you know someone like Heeley?"

When the Universe Called

"I don't, exactly. It was a woman called Bailey who approached me out of nowhere."

"Oh my God, Alexis Bailey? Have you any idea how dangerous that woman is?"

"No, but …" Charlotte bit her lip to hold back the tears that were forming in her throat. She was confused. She'd thought Luke was the bad guy, but now she had this lurching sensation in her stomach that was making her wonder whether she had completely misunderstood the situation. "Don't shout at me. That doesn't help."

"What? Sorry, look, I really don't think you understand what you've got mixed up in. Tell me what you agreed to. How come she knows I'm your father?" He sat down opposite her, his left leg twitching as though it had a life of its own.

"I can't remember. I think Grandfather told her about me. She said all I had to do was do as she said, and she'd give me five thousand dollars a month for life."

"For money? Really, this is all over money? You told me you got a large inheritance when your adopted parents died in an accident. Was that a lie?"

"No. It's just … I wanted revenge. The money was a bonus, and it didn't seem like such a big deal. She was only asking me to keep an eye on you and to tell her where you went." She flinched as Luke glared at her. Was he going to hit her?

"I can't believe you were that naïve. Did you honestly think, at that price, that would be all she would want?"

Charlotte felt herself redden. Yes, she had been that callow. She'd thought Bailey was just out to blackmail him, to make his life difficult, not to kill him.

"What about the guy at the ferry terminal? Was he really threatening you, or was that all an act?"

"You were right about him being one of Heeley's men, working for Bailey. He was supposed to catch you though. And if he didn't, the back up plan was for me to bring you here. He knew that you wouldn't question coming with me." She watched her father, waiting for him to explode. His leg had stopped twitching and he was staring over her head at some invisible

123

Maggie Denhearn

spot on the wall. His silence was more frightening. His breathing was heavy, like it was a huge effort to get oxygen.

"Okay, so at least I know what I'm up against." He got up and moved over to the window and pulled the netting back a fraction, she assumed, to see if anyone was outside looking up at their room.

"Have you told them we're here?"

"Yes." A whisper was all she could manage. He paused, then came back and faced her.

"It's up to you." He went into the bathroom and shut the door.

*   *   *   *

Luke slumped down on the bathroom floor and leaned against the door, trying to focus on his breathing, anything to stop his mind going off in several alarming directions. He'd thought they were getting to know each other, but evidently he had no idea who Charlotte was at all. He wasn't proud of some of the things he had done in his life, but now, with the work he was doing with Brina, fighting the Consortium, working within FPH to finally expose his father and everyone involved, surely that had to count in his favor.

There were much bigger issues at stake, far greater than he or Charlotte and their small lives. Since Charlotte had come into his life, he'd been trying in his own way to make it up to her. He'd never told her that it was he who had spent the last few months helping her career. Sure, she had the ability, but having the right connections helped. He'd never told her. He'd wanted her to feel good about herself, to feel like she was succeeding on her own merit. He was proud of her, had started to grow very fond of her. Never had he imagined that she could be capable of such deceit.

His stomach was hurting. He got up, filled a glass with water, and gulped it down. Splashing his face with cold water, he dried himself off and walked out of the bathroom. Charlotte was sitting on the bed, exactly has she had been moments ago, staring off into space.

"There's still time to stop this if you want."

"How?" She looked up at him, and for a moment he imagined her as a small child. In spite of himself, the instinct to protect washed over him again.

"I'm not sure. But we can go ahead and try to figure a way out of this."

When the Universe Called

"You're lying. I can't believe you'd want to help me after what I've done."

"You're my daughter. I don't want to die, and I don't want you to, either. If you stick around, Bailey will eventually send Heeley after you too. She won't want to leave a trail. You can't escape her on your own. She has the power of the Consortium behind her."

"The Consortium?"

"I'll explain later. Just take it from me, she's powerful and knows lots of people in high places. If you go ahead and do what she wants now, you'll still never be off the hook. There'll always be something else she wants you to do until you're no longer of any use to her, and then Heeley will do her dirty work for her."

"You mean ..."

"Yes. You're not indispensible."

"Crap. Why did I ever get mixed up in all of this?" Her face was drained of color, and she looked like she might keel over.

"Look, we need to get out of here fast. We need to get to somewhere safe and then contact Brina."

"Brina? You mean that weird woman who owns the Kavama? What can she do?"

"If you stop this and come with me, I'll explain everything. There's a lot you don't know." Luke saw that Charlotte was thinking, considering her options.

"We're family. You might not like me, but I'm your father."

"You honestly would help me, after what I've done?"

"Yes, yes! Look, there's no time for this. You have to decide." Luke was trying not to squirm visibly as he kept looking at his watch, seeing the seconds of his life slipping quickly away. "Time's up. If you don't want to come, fine. But let me go. Pretend I escaped."

"They won't buy that."

"They will. You're a kid. Sorry, but you are. They'll be angry, but if you play along, you might just pull it off. For now at least."

"You don't know that."

"No, I don't. It's a risk. But you made a deal with the Devil, so what did you expect?"

125

Maggie Denhearn

Vancouver Island, Fall, 1997

Gathering a few essentials in her tattered scarlet cloth travel bag, Brina set off north along the Vancouver Island Highway, following the twists and turns of the road as it snaked along the coast up to Campbell River, following the line of the ocean. The water was a dull gray, reflecting the November sky. The mainland was securely concealed behind a curtain of mist. When she took the road west to Gold River, lakes and mountains entered the stage, stately players in the vast theatre of the landscape. She was heading to a small village called Tahsis.

Although it was now forty years since her mother had passed, she had woken that morning to a feeling of overwhelming grief that she had never gotten to know either of her parents very well. Her chest felt crushed by a lead weight. Her usual remedy for emotional turmoil was to go on a road trip for as long as it took for her equilibrium to return. She wasn't sure why she chose Tahsis. It was fall and not exactly tourist season. For some reason she had felt compelled to do so. Lately she'd been intuiting more and more, and the messages, or whatever one would call them, were becoming more and more insistent. The feeling that she had to come to Tahsis had been too compelling to resist.

Situated in a fjord in the Nootka Sound, Tahsis was one of the most remote and breathtaking places on the Island she had yet to experience. Nestled between snow-capped mountains and a never-ending ocean, everything human or manmade seemed Lilliputian by comparison. Parking up to go into the one open store to buy a map, she stopped to contemplate the vast panorama.

"Anja?"

Brina froze, her heart starting to race. She turned slowly. A withered elderly man was staring at her. His clothes were tattered and dated. He looked like he'd stepped out of a movie set from the 1930s.

"Anja, it is you, isn't it? Joseph and Alenka's little girl? Not quite so little any more, but still beautiful."

"Jakob? You're my father's friend Jakob, right?" Her muscles relaxed and her heart rate started to slow down again.

"That's me. You remember after all these years."

When the Universe Called

"I nearly didn't recognize you." She hesitated, unsure, then added, "I'm called Brina now, not Anja. Call me Brina."

He eyed her and didn't ask the obvious question. His expression revealed that he knew not to.

"Well, my dear … Brina. I would recognize you anywhere. You've not changed since you were a child. Won't you come round for tea?" He smiled with his eyes, filling Brina with both joy and sadness. The last time they met was at her father's funeral. Jakob had taken her hand, as he was doing now, squeezing it gently. She fought back the tears as memories started to flood before her, marching past like soldiers of the past, parading fragments of her former life before her.

"I'd like that."

*   *   *   *

For three days she stayed with him. Jakob lived alone in a two-room log cabin. A tall yet frail man with shocks of white hair springing up all over his head that gave him the air of a mad professor, he had an unquenchable thirst for storytelling, the years unable to diminish either his memory or his acuity. He took her back in time, regaling her with story after story. He brought her parents back to her and answered all of her unspoken questions.

On the morning of the third day, Brina shivered as she got up to make coffee for them both. It had been a beautiful few days. She shivered again as she waited for the kettle to boil. The embers of the fire were all but dead, and there was a chill in the air unusual even for this draughty cabin. Pulling her long woolen cardigan tightly around her, she padded around the kitchen, finding clean mugs from the cupboard and getting milk out of the fridge. From the corner of her eye she noticed Jakob, slumped in his armchair by the cold fireplace. He must have fallen asleep before making it to the pullout bed he usually slept on by the hearth.

"Jakob?" He didn't move. Moving slowly toward him, she realized he was no longer there. His wizened body was cold to the touch, his soul having departed as the full moon rose in the early morning sky. As she gently kissed his forehead, the lead weight that had been clutching her heart since the morning she left Eagle Cove fell away.

127

Maggie Denhearn

Driving back toward home, Brina reflected on the days now behind her. It was time. She could no longer keep pretending that she didn't have particular abilities. It wasn't just that she was becoming more and more able to tune in to what some people were going to say or do before even they themselves knew, a gift from her childhood that over the years after Frost she had decided to try and recultivate.

There was more. It was as though her thoughts were developing some kind of creative power, as though by thinking something she could make it happen. If she happened to wish for a parking space, she always found one, no matter how busy it was. She never lost anything anymore. If she wished she could find it, she did. Since initially it only seemed to involve the insignificant, she had not wanted to believe it. But meeting Jakob so randomly and after over forty years left her with little doubt. He had given her the knowledge of her family that she had been seeking, just when she had desired it most. What if she was to try to create with her thoughts using *conscious* intention? Up to now, she had not consciously been trying to make anything in particular happen, and yet what she wished for was increasingly coming true. Was it possible that she could make things happen on purpose, or was she just travelling as an accidental tourist along the universal highway? She needed to know.

As she pulled up to her cabin and felt the joy of being home, she made a decision. She would try a series of experiments to see if she could make her thoughts become reality.

CHAPTER 11

Tuesday afternoon, April 15, 2014

Frost eyed Bailey as she slid the brown manila envelope across the tablecloth to just within his reach, her bright red fingernails looking like blood stains moving across the white linen. He looked at her, hesitating to take it. Two visits to his home within a couple of days. This did not auger well.

"It's all in there: names, dates, documentary evidence, even some photos, just in case you didn't believe me when we spoke last night, or Heeley's email. There's no doubt."

Frost continued to stare at her, wondering how much pleasure she was taking in this. He wanted to wipe that disdainful smile off her face. No doubt she would not be alone in finding gratification in this whole affair. The sharks were circling, waiting to devour him. He had known for a while that he was under siege, but had avoided thinking about it. He didn't need to open the envelope to know what it contained: his downfall, Luke's demise.

Frost had always believed there was a way out of every situation, no matter how dire. Most of his life he had been able to buy his way out of any predicament, without having to devote too much brainpower to figuring out a more cunning approach. No amount of careful investment was going to get him out of this one. Yet he wasn't sure he had either the energy or the will for the strategizing it would take to avoid what appeared to be the inevitable. Much as he would never admit it to anyone, he was tired, very tired indeed.

*   *   *   *

Maggie Denhearn

Bailey edged the envelope closer to him, urging him quietly to pick it up. She had been collecting evidence for a while now, and their conversation the night before had opened her eyes to the fact that Frost was never going to cede power willingly. The Consortium needed new leadership, to cut away the rot of the Frost family. Luke and Noah may have taken their mother's family name, Morgan, but they were Frosts by blood, and that sanguine connection was about to be the downfall of the entire Consortium if someone—if *she*—didn't act fast. Out of feigned respect, she pretended she was asking for his permission.

"I realize this is hard, Frost, but everything will go much more smoothly if you are in agreement that I can bring Luke in." She had already given the go-ahead to Heeley to bring in both of the sons now. Whether Frost approved or not was a moot point. She was just keeping up the pretense that he was still in charge. If the meeting at the club tomorrow night went exactly as she planned and the core group of the Consortium Committee agreed to back her, Frost's days as head of the Consortium would be numbered. He would have no choice but to step down.

She stared at him, listening to his wheezing. His mind seemed elsewhere. She could wait. Finally he nodded his head, not uttering a word. A nod of the head or the bullet of a gun; did he know that in that moment he had just signed the death warrant for both his sons and that he may as well be the one pulling the trigger? She wasn't sure and didn't care. He looked old and wizened. He shivered, pulling the blanket on his knees toward himself, then spat viciously on the floor.

Bailey cringed but neither responded nor made any attempt to move. She didn't mind admitting that part of her was very much enjoying this. She used to find Frost's arrogance erotic. Now it was just odious. There was no hint of imperiousness in this moment, though. Was that the smell of resignation or fear? It was hard to tell. It was over for him; surely he knew that. She was already imagining the governance meeting. Frost would be out of the picture by the end of the month. She ran the tip of her tongue over the back of her teeth. This is what power tastes like.

*   *   *   *

When the Universe Called

Brina closed her eyes and tried to start meditating, but thoughts kept flooding her mind. She was finding it hard to focus. The Consortium was days away from pushing Bill 267 through parliament, and right now it didn't look like there was anything she, Luke, or anyone could do to stop it.

The fact that she still hadn't heard from Darcy was worrying. Although she had planned to call her instead, she changed her mind. She didn't want to put Darcy in unnecessary danger. It was unlikely that Judge Rawley would have discovered his secretary's deception after all this time, but they couldn't afford to be complacent. Darcy had been feeding Luke and Brina information about the machinations of the Consortium for years, and they had all been extremely meticulous in how they communicated. So what else could account for her silence?

A soft breeze brushed her cheek, and she opened her eyes and stared at the view around her. The last traces of smoke from the forest fire clung to the air, filling her with apprehension. Brina loved her home and she loved the Island. She was grateful for each new day and knew she had been lucky to make it this far. Whatever happened next was going to happen, but she wouldn't go down without a fight.

Closing her eyes again, she began her daily routine of calling on the universe. Shifting her body weight into a comfortable position, she allowed the soft, silky cushions of the swing chair to hold her as she relaxed each muscle of her body in turn, feet planted firmly on the deck. She focused on her breath, counting in and out to slowly bring her heart rate down. After a few minutes, she managed to silence the chatter in her mind, to close her senses to the world around her, and to center herself. Then she pictured in her mind what she desired: the Consortium dispersed; all involved held accountable for their illegal activities; Frost on trial; FPH shut down; Bill 267 stopped. Holding her hand on her heart, she sent love and peace to all the victims of the drug trials, and of the dangerous pharmaceuticals that had been allowed to go to market.

"So shall it be done, and harm no one." Opening her eyes, taking one more deep breath in and out, she got up and went inside. She'd barely eaten all day and felt dizzy; her spirit weighed down by what she feared was yet to come.

*   *   *   *

Maggie Denhearn

Luke switched off the radio and paced back and forth in the hotel room. He was glad Charlotte was not with him at this precise moment. According to a CBC radio report, he'd been found dead. That was a strange thought, a very strange thought indeed. He wondered what his obituary would read. There were still so many things he wanted to achieve in life.

Then it dawned on him: If it was thought it was his body and he was still alive, it had to be Noah's that had been found. Heeley must have got to him. Luke collapsed down into an armchair, grief punching him squarely in the stomach. Lurching forward, he just had time to grab the garbage can nearby and to vomit into it. He retched again, then slumped back in the chair and started to cry. His baby brother, his poor baby brother. Noah could annoy the heck out of him sometimes, but wasn't that how it was supposed to be between brothers?

It all began to make sense now why he'd not heard from him. He'd never just disappear. He let the tears roll down his cheeks, watching moments shared with his brother, his closed eyes acting as a movie screen for the memory projector whirring desperately in his head. If he didn't store up the memories now, they would slip away like those of his mother, leaving only outlines and shadows.

He opened his eyes abruptly, startled. He wasn't sure if he'd been sitting there for minutes or hours. He looked at his watch but it had stopped. It was easier to wind up if he took it off. As he undid the gold buckle, he flinched, sucking in his breath, feeling another body blow of grief. The room around him was moving, swaying, his whole world in motion. The engraving on the back read *Noah Morgan*.

"Stop, stop!" Startled at the sound of a voice, it took a few seconds for him to realize that he was the one who had cried out. His mind flipped back to the moment before he heard the radio announcement, and he stood up precariously. He had to hold it together. If nothing else, if all else failed, he had to avenge his brother.

He wondered how the police could make such a mistake. Then it dawned on him. If he had Noah's watch, Noah must have been wearing Luke's when they found the body. They must have got their watches mixed up when they were getting changed last week after they'd been playing tennis. The watches were identical, except for the engravings on the back. Their

When the Universe Called

maternal grandmother had given them each an Omega gold dress wristwatch for their twenty-first birthday, watches she had bought in 1969, the year of their birth, ready for when they came of age. And the fire. The radio announcement had mentioned something about a forest fire. Was a watch all that remained of his brother? A spike of nausea shot through him but he held his breath and managed to stop himself from throwing up again.

Why Noah? From his conversation with Charlotte, it seemed Bailey had definitely been trying to get him, not Noah. So if it was on the news he was dead ... But the phone calls the last few days had been from Heeley looking for Noah. Something didn't stack up. Come to think of it, they'd just said they were after "his brother" and had mentioned "his wife," which he'd thought was odd at the time. Had they gotten them mixed up? It wouldn't be the first time someone had. They had always been extremely alike, down to identical mannerisms and the same laugh. Even their father would get them confused sometimes. Their mother had been the only one who could always tell them apart.

Luke had a growing pain in his head like someone had hit him over the head with a sharp rock. He winced and reached out for his bag. He usually carried some aspirin with him somewhere. He often got headaches, but not usually this painful. An intense throbbing like a drumbeat was now pounding away behind his forehead. He couldn't think. He rummaged around in his bag and eventually found the aspirin. Gulping a couple down dry, he went into the bathroom to get some water and to splash cold water on his face again. Looking in the mirror, he saw a man with a five o'clock shadow and bloodshot eyes, his hair, usually combed neatly, completely disheveled. He needed a haircut. The harsh bathroom light made his graying temples more noticeable. Lately he had been debating whether to dye his hair. The idea seemed so superfluous now, so stupidly frivolous.

Focus, he needed to focus. That's what Brina was always saying to him. "Where your attention goes, the energy flows." He had to stay focused on the fight against the Consortium. For the moment, he would have to put his grief on hold. Splashing more water on his face, he tried to fix his mind on what he needed to be doing right now.

It had been a long day, a very long day. He had no idea of what the implications could be of the radio announcement that he was dead or what

133

Charlotte would decide to do. She'd gone out, leaving him barricaded in the hotel room. She'd said she needed some air and went out, he didn't know where. Her expression as she left was as blank as an empty page.

He didn't know why he was waiting for her to make her mind up. He had to escape immediately. He grabbed his bag and checked that he had his phone. There were several messages and missed calls from Maria. He'd not dared pick up or answer it since the ferry. He had no clue what he was going to tell her. Better to wait until he had an idea of how everything was going to play out. As long as she had no idea what was going on, the greater the chance she would stay safe.

He pulled back the net curtains at the window and looked down into the parking lot. As far as he could tell, no one suspicious was hanging around. Heeley's men were fairly easy to spot. He'd always wondered about that. It was like Heeley didn't care, and thought he himself had the ultimate power. It was odd that the Consortium didn't rein him in more; one day he would attract far too much attention, and his connections to them would become public knowledge. The Consortium was getting complacent.

* * * *

Charlotte sat in the lobby, sipping a latte, staring into space. She was at an impasse and had no idea what to do. Be careful what you wish for, isn't that what they say? Handing over Luke had seemed like the only way she could finally free herself of the anger, the pain, that had taken root inside her like some kind of pestilent weed that was gradually choking her heart. She'd invested so much energy into avenging her mother and herself. She never stopped to consider whether revenge would really be the antidote.

She traced the lines of embossing on the paper napkin in front of her, her finger moving slowly over each bump, one by one, each bump a memory. Playing on the swings in the park, the butterflies in her stomach as she went higher and higher, afraid she would lose control and fly over the top, hoping she would lose control and fly over the top. She was out of her depth, and there was no one there to help her, guide her.

This decision was hers and hers alone. If she didn't hand Luke over, Heeley would come looking for her and would still want Luke. It would

When the Universe Called

never end. At least she could save herself if she gave him up. She took a last sip of her latte and picked up her phone.

"It's me."

*   *   *   *

Luke slipped quietly out of the hotel room and tiptoed along the corridor. The room was on the sixth floor, so it wouldn't be too far to walk down the stairs. That seemed like a better option than coming face-to-face with someone he didn't want to in the elevator. As far as he could remember, the elevator doors opened directly into the middle of the ground floor foyer. If he took the stairs, maybe there was a way he could slip out of the back, perhaps via the kitchen or laundry room. But then what? Luke had no idea.

Charlotte had been driving, so no doubt she still had the car keys. He didn't feel like going back and checking the room for them, just in case she came back. Self-preservation. Part of him wanted to give her the benefit of the doubt; part of him couldn't. The latter part was winning the day.

He could order a taxi to come to the back entrance. That was a good idea. Typical—there was no cell phone reception in the stairwell. He'd have to risk getting outside and ordering a cab from there. Everyone from the company would have arrived for the meeting by now. They were supposed to convene for a business dinner that evening, with the main events starting in the morning. He was supposed to be arriving early that day to have some preliminary meetings with one of the main honchos. People would be wondering where he was.

No they wouldn't. They would have heard the news on the radio by now; they'd think he was dead. In which case, it would cause quite the confusion if they saw him. This was getting far too complicated.

"Luke?" He turned around. It was Stephanie Manning, head of accounting, from the head office Of all the people he had to bump into, it had to be her. He stopped but said nothing, trying to pretend he didn't recognize her.

"I'm sorry, I mistook you for someone else. You look so like him. But then you can't be. He's dead." The woman burst into tears. "I'm so sorry," she said, as she pulled out a tissue from her purse and started to wipe her eyes, "it's just such a shock. And to hear it over the radio!" She continued sobbing. Luke stared, not knowing quite what to do or say. The thought of trying to comfort someone who'd heard he'd died was rather surreal. All his life he'd never quite been able to remember whether or not people knew he was a twin. It didn't seem relevant to either him or Noah, but it had got them into some interesting situations.

"I'm sorry you're upset." He turned and continued down the stairs. "I'm sorry," he said, again over his shoulder. Hopefully she would think she was imagining things and not mention to anyone else that she thought she'd seen him. She'd sound crazy if she did. "Wait!" she called after him. He didn't turn around.

*　　*　　*　　*

Luke started to dial Maria's number then hung up before it started to ring the other end. He was being selfish, wanting to talk to her. What exactly would he say? Both he and Brina had decided it was safer for her not to know anything about their work. The Consortium was dangerous enough without giving them reason for Maria to be a target. He had to stay strong, to keep protecting her. This had been Luke's risk to take, not hers. She was bound to find out soon, though, but now was not the time to be worrying about that.

Standing under cover of the doorway of the kitchen at the back entrance of the hotel, pretending to staff he was sneaking a cigarette away from his girlfriend, who'd thought he'd given up (which he actually had), he'd been wracking his brains over what to do next. Right at this moment, he wished a car would magically arrive and whisk him away. He wanted to head straight to the airport and get on a plane to anywhere far away, but he couldn't. Brina needed him. They were so close to bringing down the Consortium. He was sure Brina would come up with an idea how they could stall the bill from going through in a couple of weeks. He couldn't run away. Noah deserved justice; they all did. Hopefully, Darcy would have some news for them soon. He got out his phone again and started to text Brina.

"Consortium after me. Will call when safe. News from Darcy?"

He couldn't bring himself to mention Noah. To do so would be to make his death real, concrete, irreversible. Perhaps she already knew, in

When the Universe Called

that strange way of hers, or from the radio. Hitting the send button, the swooshing sound of the message winging its way through the air sounded like leaves rustling.

He stared across at the trees near the dumpsters, beauty and ugliness hand in hand. Luke expected to see branches swaying in the wind. They were still, yet bursting, desperate to come to life again, the faintest green buds just barely visible. He wished he hadn't given up smoking. Nothing else could calm his nerves in quite the same way, except Brina's tea.

A black sedan with tinted windows rolled slowly round the corner. Luke watched as it pulled up in front of him. This was it. He should run. He couldn't. He was rooted to the spot. He had no idea that your legs could literally seize up if you were afraid. The door swung open, a signal for him to get in. Luke faltered, his legs numb. Consciously focusing on moving his feet, he folded himself into the vehicle. There didn't seem any point in running, and he couldn't have anyway. Maybe he didn't want to. He didn't fancy a chase through the hotel and some kind of showdown. He might still have a chance if he could talk his way out of things. He could offer Heeley a deal. That was it. He needed to come up with something juicy enough for Heeley to bite. People always had a price.

"You!" Luke was incredulous.

"Who did you think it would be?" Charlotte glanced back at him as he closed the car door and she put the car into drive.

"Well, clearly not you. Is this how you're selling me down the river then?"

"No. Change of plan. I just heard the news on the radio playing in the lobby. I called Heeley. He thinks you're dead too."

Luke exhaled slowly, not sure quite what to say.

"Really? But what about his man who saw me get off the ferry?"

"It seems there was a bit of a mix-up. The hit was on you. Bailey wanted to bring you in. Heeley was calling you, thinking you were Noah. Apparently one of Heeley's men isn't the brightest light bulb and got your contact details mixed up. Anyway, I said that you'd set me up and that it was Noah on the ferry pretending to be you and that I let him go because he wasn't you. Heeley bought it, although he's pissed because apparently now Bailey wants him to get both of you. So now he has to tell her that Noah got away. It'll buy you some time at least."

"But ... okay, well." His thoughts trailed off in the direction of his brother. There was silence between them for a few moments. Charlotte seemed content to focus on driving.

"So how did you get the black sedan?"

"I 'borrowed' it, if you see what I mean. The hotel is full of people who'd recognize you and who'd start asking questions, awkward ones. You need to get out of here. And you'll need a makeover."

Charlotte laughed, but the reflection of her expression in the rear view mirror showed her face etched with concern. Luke noticed, but the observation flew straight out of his mind as another thought popped up, ideas tunneling like gophers in his brain with a randomness he was finding hard to control.

"Aren't these cars supposed to come with a chauffeur?"

"And risk involving anyone else in all of this? Do I look that stupid?" No, she didn't.

"I er, I'm sorry about your brother."

Luke bit his lower lip to stop it quivering, unable to respond. He had no idea and didn't particularly want to think about that right now. Nor did he want to break down in front of his daughter.

There was still something that didn't make sense, and it was disturbing that he couldn't figure out what it was. He leaned back as she turned the car around and drove them out of the hotel complex. There was champagne in the bucket in front of him, already open. He didn't suppose it had been put there intentionally for him, but he took a glass and poured some anyway. The dryness of the liquid hit the back of his mouth, and he sank back in his seat, focusing on the tingling feeling sliding through his body. He could hear Brina's voice in his head reminding him to concentrate on his breathing. He had this habit of holding his breath when he was nervous or anxious, each inhalation getting more and more shallow without him noticing.

He stared out of the window as they slowly beetled their way through busy city traffic. The noise of engines, sirens, and people shouting made him feel like he was in a cage, hemmed in. He already missed the quiet of the Island. Vancouver was always crowded, throngs of people pouring along the city streets like a human tidal wave. He was glad that he could see out of the tinted windows and that no one could see in.

He pondered the question hanging between them. If he'd not been suddenly presumed dead, would she have ratted him out? He didn't know, and she wasn't saying anything. A song came on the radio that reminded him of the day they'd first met: "The Meeting." It hadn't exactly turned out the way it did in the song; theirs was clearly a relationship in negotiation.

Vancouver Island, May, 1998

It was a bright, clear morning, the kind that chills and energizes. The sky was already a deep azure, even though it was barely 8:00 a.m. The gray wisps of clouds of the day before had scuttled off to dim some other horizon. Brina sat on her deck, eyes closed as she inhaled the fragrant air, lost in meditation. For weeks now she had been getting up half an hour earlier every morning to meditate and to practice *manifestation*. So far she had succeeded in conjuring up small things, like finding the exact book she wanted at the library or getting more customers for her coffee shop. She'd stopped phoning friends and manifested talking to them instead. Invariably now, the person she wished to speak to would call her shortly after or send her an email.

Lately she had been focusing her attention on something grander. The Kavama was doing fine, better than she'd dared hope, but she could do with a cash injection to redo the décor and update most of the kitchen equipment. She had no idea where she would get that kind of capital, other than going to a bank. Brina decided to try manifestation. First of all she wrote a list of the things she needed and how she would redecorate the coffee shop if she could. Closing her eyes each morning, she would imagine the vibrant colors, the comfy sofas, and all the new herbs she would source. A feeling of excitement and passion filled her as she envisioned how she could transform the place, how she could help people who wanted an alternative to the Western approach to medicine. Although Brina had qualified at university as a pharmacologist, she was afraid to go to a hospital when she still had problems with her hip months after being shot because it would be clear to anyone what kind of injury she had. She found an Ayurveda practitioner on

Maggie Denhearn

the Island who helped her. Inspired, Brina turned to alternative medicine, and after years of study, now practiced Ayurvedic medicine.

Brina focused on her dream of a renovated coffee shop and an expanded Ayurvedic practice. It was just a question of time. Opening her eyes, she took in one more deep breath and was about to go inside to get more coffee when she decided to walk to the end of her drive to check her post. She didn't usually at this time of day, but she hadn't checked her mail for a few days now, and her hip was stiff and she needed to stretch out.

Reaching inside the mailbox, she felt a bunch of letters. Flicking through them in the sunlight, one in particular caught her eye. The envelope was large and cream colored, with a return address she didn't recognize. Tearing it open, she pulled out a sheet of paper that was thick and felt expensive to the touch. With a gold embossed letterhead, Mr. Damon Foley, Attorney at Law, Gold River, was writing to inform her that Mr. Jakob Grohar's estate had finally been settled. With no living relatives, he had named Brina as his sole beneficiary. Jakob had left the entirety of his fortune to her; and it was substantial. Brina stared at the letter with a sense of both excitement and fear. Her hands shook as she stuffed the letter back into the envelope and walked back up the path.

Brina couldn't focus on breakfast or anything much for the rest of the day. All she could think about was the letter. Was it coincidence, or had she actually managed to *manifest* this? She wanted to believe it was her doing, but she didn't quite dare.

When she arrived home that evening from the coffee shop, just rounding the corner about twenty meters from her driveway, her truck ground to a resounding halt. She tried the ignition several times, but there was no sign of life. She sighed and walked the final stretch home. Luckily, hers was the only dwelling along the street, so she could wait until morning to get someone to tow her truck, which was unceremoniously stuck in the middle of the dirt road. Iris had to maneuver around it when she came over for a visit about an hour later.

"So what's the deal with your truck?" Iris pulled a blanket over her knees as she reached for her glass. They were sitting on the deck, sipping red wine and watching the sunset. Brina liked Iris. They had known each other maybe ten years, and she was probably Brina's closest friend, if she had such a thing.

When the Universe Called

There was an inner unspoken sadness to her that she could somehow relate to. Both of them assiduously avoided speaking too much about their own lives, although Iris divulged somewhat more of hers than did Brina. Brina had consciously perfected the art of seeming to answer questions but in a way that deflected the attention back to the person asking. It was safer that way.

"Well, I knew it was only a matter of time before it was going to die. I was just hoping it would be later rather than sooner."

"What are you going to do?"

Brina paused, examining Iris closely. "Iris, have you ever had the experience where what you've been thinking about comes true?"

Iris looked puzzled. "Well, sometimes when I've been thinking about someone they call. Everyone has that, though, right? Why?"

"Well, here's the thing. For the last little while, things I think about have been coming true."

"Really? Like what?"

"Oh you know, wanting to hear from someone and they call. Needing something in particular at the store and suddenly it's in front of me. But bigger things too."

"For example?"

Brina had told no one about Jakob. To do so would mean she would have to explain aspects of her history she had never revealed to anyone, not even Iris.

"Just stuff. So here's the thing. I've been trying these experiments, to see if I can create something just by thinking about it."

Iris's eyes widened.

"I know it sounds peculiar, but ... I've been hoping I could renovate the Kavama, but that would take quite a lot of money."

"And now you have to fix your truck too."

The moment was gone. She had been about to confide in Iris about the letter she had received that morning, but it sounded so ridiculous to say out loud that she had conjured it up. She should wait for more evidence.

"I know, I know. But, well, I can either focus on what's wrong with the situation, or can decide to trust that everything will work out. Miracles happen every day. Something will come up." Brina avoided looking at Iris.

Maggie Denhearn

She couldn't admit that something already had. She would have to find another way of explaining how she could afford to get her truck fixed.

"I could do with a miracle to get rid of Trevor. Want to focus on that too?" Iris's laugh was bitter. Brina knew she wasn't joking. She touched her friend's hand, but said nothing.

"Sorry." Iris gulped more wine. "Okay, well, let me know how your little experiment goes."

Brina could hear the skepticism in Iris's voice. She didn't expect her to understand. She wasn't entirely sure she did herself. She obviously wasn't completely convinced, or she wouldn't be looking for more evidence.

She'd started reading about the *Law of Attraction* a few months ago. The idea that you can create your experiences by what you think about took some getting one's head around, even if her experiences were already showing her that it was true. The streaks of crimson and gold in the sky made her existence seem so insignificant in comparison to the power that could create such a vision, what she was reading about the universe had to be true. She couldn't find any other explanation. In comparison her life, her worries, seemed like tiny particles of dust floating in the atmosphere.

CHAPTER 12

Tuesday evening, April 15, 2014

It was nearly dusk by the time Vanna finally appeared on Brina's doorstep.
"My dear, you look awful! You're so pale."

"Thank you" she said ruefully. "At least you're honest. I know it takes some doing for me to look this pasty."

"Sit down. Let me get you something to drink."

"A cup of tea would be nice, thank you."

"I'll put the kettle on. Come inside and tell me all about it."

Inside, the cabin was dark and cool. The sweet notes of incense burning away seemed an odd contrast to the smell of the ocean and the acridity of smoke lingering in the air. Music was gently playing in the background. Vanna recognized the sound of the sitar. Her heart suddenly ached with an intense longing. It reminded her of her childhood and sitting on her grandmother's lap, listening to the music of her parents and grandparents. For her it conjured up a vision of India as a mystical land that seemed unreal, far removed from her life and what she knew in England. She'd felt safe sitting with her grandmother, at least with her paternal one. She wanted to feel that security now rather than what she actually felt—like she was walking on a fault line, waiting for the earth to crack beneath her. Brina motioned for her to sit down on the sofa, which was lost under a pile of cushions and fabric. Better to be swallowed up by color rather than darkness.

"Kettle's on."

143

Vanna wasn't sure quite where to start. She'd never had to casually introduce into a conversation that she'd found one dead body, let alone two, and was now worried about what she was mixed up in. Despite some relief at discussing events with Kali and Maria, her anxiety had returned.

"It all happened this morning when I went out for a run with Morris." She proceeded to explain to Brina what she'd found on the trail, her conversation with the police (what she could remember of it), and how she'd bumped into Maria and then ended up round at Kali's.

"Ah." Brina pondered, her face grave.

"Ah? What do you mean ah? Am I in trouble?"

"Hmm."

"You're not inspiring me with confidence."

"Well ... that does explain the phone calls."

"What phone calls?"

"The ones right after yours—from Kali and Maria. You all called me this morning." She paused. "I did try and call the others back this afternoon, but as I couldn't get hold of them I presume that they were with you. How do you like your tea?"

"Strong, milk, and a little honey if you have it."

Brina busied herself making the tea. Vanna sat in silence. Brina seemed the sort of person who would have the ingenuity for any kind of crisis. She had an air of calmness about her, a presence that was reassuring, almost hypnotic. At the same time, there was something unnerving about her. She had a look that could pass straight through you, past any facade, to see whomever might be hiding underneath. Vanna wondered how old she was. She could be anything from sixty-five to ninety-five. She was hard to place in every respect.

"There, drink that. I've put extra honey in it. You look like you could do with the sweetness."

"What am I going to do?" Vanna tried not to weep, but didn't quite succeed. Brina looked at her sharply, then her eyes softened.

"You didn't do anything wrong. No harm will come to you."

Vanna wasn't so sure. She stared into her mug of tea, sipping the hot, sweet liquid and cupping her hands around the solid brown pottery. A flood of self-consciousness washed over her, and she started to fidget. There were

When the Universe Called

times when it seemed as though Brina could read your thoughts, knew what you were thinking about. She sincerely hoped this wasn't one of them. Her bright green eyes could hypnotize you, hold you under a spell so you couldn't look away, then would draw you in, like a lake pulling you away from the safety of the water's edge. Before you knew it, you were lost in her gaze, and it was as though she was taking your thoughts directly out of your mind. Brina was humming, a habit she had that Vanna found peculiarly disconcerting yet comforting.

"So," said Brina. Vanna felt Brina's eyes bore into her. She felt the heat rise in her cheeks, her emotions raw.

Vanna paused; "I know I should probably go to the police, but I don't want to get my friends into trouble." Brina did not respond.

"Is this ... is this some kind of bad karma coming back to bite me?"

"Do you think that you deserve bad karma?"

Vanna looked down at the floor—anywhere but at Brina directly. Vanna *did* think she deserved it. Somewhere along the way she had lost her moral compass. Now she was trying to get it back, and it was hard to make sense of the last few years of her life. It was as though she'd stopped paying attention for a while, hadn't noticed what was happening. When she finally woke up to what was going on, she didn't recognize her life or who she had become. She thought that coming somewhere new where no one knew her, some quiet place, would mean she could escape everything and start again.

"You feel guilty, and you think you deserve this even though you've not killed anyone."

Vanna started to sob, a sound coming from deep within her that she didn't recognize as herself, like someone else was crying inside her. "I guess so. I know that doesn't make sense and I'm overreacting. But I can't shake this feeling that somehow I brought this on myself."

"We're all here to learn different karmic lessons."

"Do you mean this *is* karma, that I did something crappy and now it's coming back to haunt me?"

"Not exactly. We all have karmic lessons. That's not the same as punishment, which is what I think you're saying. Life is a process of learning, and everything that happens to us is part of that learning process."

Maggie Denhearn

"I'm struggling to understand what the lesson could be from stumbling across dead people."

"It doesn't necessarily mean you did something wrong. It might mean your lesson is to show courage or loyalty to your friends. It'll become clear soon enough. It could also mean that you need to be more conscious of where your attention is going. Remember what I've said about how we can create with our thoughts."

"I know, you tell me that often. Clearly I'm not doing a good job, or this morning wouldn't have happened. I thought I was trying to focus on positive things."

"Remember the *Law of Attraction*. Where our attention goes, the energy flows. If we focus on good things, more good will come. If we focus on the bad, we'll get more of that."

"I know, you keep telling us." Vanna couldn't hide her resentment. "So you're saying that I attracted all of this, that it's my fault? Why on earth would I want to attract *this*?" She bridled, feeling blamed, shamed for something she had no control over.

"That's not exactly what I mean, and I'm not blaming you. The *Law of Attraction* is the idea that we get what we think about. If you've been focusing on all the drama in your life and wishing you didn't have so much, guess what you'll get more of? Exactly what you've been thinking about, even if it's experiences you don't want. And the universe will find its own way of bringing that to you."

Vanna inhaled deeply, trying to quell the anger she was feeling. "So you mean that by focusing on, for example, 'I don't want more drama,' then I actually attract *more* rather than less, even though I thought I was being positive for *not* wanting drama?"

"Yes. Inadvertently, yes. It doesn't mean you asked for it, just that if you're not paying attention, you might get things you don't want rather than what you do."

"But that doesn't make sense. Surely I wouldn't get more drama if I've been focusing on *not* wanting it."

"The universe only knows what you're focusing on, not whether you want it or not. It works in positives. Think of the number of times you can't find your car keys. If you keep saying to yourself 'I can't find my keys,' chances are you won't. Or at least it'll take you much longer to figure out where you last put them."

Vanna thought for a moment. "That does seem to be true; about keys, anyway."

"Many times we focus on what we don't want, on what we fear. The energy still flows in that direction, and then we end up getting just what we didn't want."

"So if I was afraid something bad might happen when I was alone in the forest and was hoping it wouldn't, by focusing on what I don't want, I end up getting just that?"

"Exactly."

"But how do you get around that?"

"By focusing your thoughts using positive terms. Instead of thinking 'I hope nothing horrible happens,' think 'I am safe and supported'."

"It still feels like you're saying I brought this on myself because of the way I was thinking."

"We're culturally conditioned to think in certain ways, and most of our thoughts are unconscious unless we pay attention and practice being more mindful. Also, many of us absorb so many negative messages growing up that it takes conscious effort to reprogram how we think. That's all I'm saying. Reprogram the way you think, and your life will open up in much more positive ways."

Vanna considered what Brina was suggesting. "But how do you explain the fact that lots of people really do want to win the lottery, but don't?"

"*The Law of Allowing.*"

"Allowing ..." Vanna repeated, trying to make a mental note.

"Lots of people wish for things every day of their lives, but don't really believe they deserve them. The universe hears the negative subconscious thoughts as well as the positive, and if the negative ones are stronger, guess which ones will be heard?"

"The negative?"

"Exactly. Plus, chances are, most people aren't specific enough. They think they want money, but what they really want is the freedom that money can buy or the financial security. If they focused on, say, having the freedom to quit their dull job and become a full-time artist, they'd have more chance

Maggie Denhearn

of attracting the circumstances into their lives that would make that possible, which are infinite and not just dependent on a lottery win. The universe is far more creative than we can possibly imagine."

"So I need to practice thinking positively?"

"More than that. Think of the life you'd like to create and how it would feel, and focus on that, the *feeling*. In the meantime, I'm not sure you'll have too much to worry about. Did you notice the fire trucks today? Did you hear the local news at all?"

"No, I've not had time. What trucks? And what's that got to do with anything?"

"There was a forest fire this morning."

Vanna stopped, trying to figure out the connection. She felt her expression change from dejection to utter amazement. "You mean ...? I thought I could smell smoke as I came in but I presumed you'd been burning something in the garden. Are you sure the forest fire was in the same place as the bodies? This is all just too bizarre ... and rather too convenient."

Her brow furrowed. She felt like she was trying to compute a difficult equation.

"Okay, let me get this straight in my head. You're now suggesting that there's been a forest fire which has potentially destroyed any evidence of all this?"

She shuddered even though she wasn't cold. She felt like something or someone had walked straight through her. Brina continued to eye her while stirring a pot on the stove—slowly, thoughtfully. A few moments passed silently before Brina spoke again. Vanna sipped her tea, trying to process the conversation.

"Where does the fire come into what you're saying about the *Law of Attraction*?"

"Were you hoping for some kind of miraculous way of escaping all of this, focusing lots of energy on wishing for a way out? Were Kali and Maria?"

"Of course."

"There you go."

"But what about all the people who think 'Forest fires are terrible; I hope we don't have one'?"

148

When the Universe Called

"Exactly what I was just saying. In focusing on not wanting fire, they're thinking about fire. So fire is what they get. Anyway, I doubt a forest fire would have been on too many people's minds this morning at this point in the season. But you, Kali, and Maria, have been highly focused on a way to get yourselves out of this situation."

"True, but I don't see how between only the three of us we could have managed that alone."

Abruptly, Brina stopped stirring the large pot, the sweet fragrance of orange and cinnamon still wafting up from the steaming liquid. Something in her expression told Vanna she was about to tell her something she might not like.

"What aren't you telling me?"

"Nothing, dear." She stared out of the window, seemingly distracted by the tenebrous sky. The sun had long since set, and the stars were sparkling like tiny jewels. The moon was bright.

"What? You're scaring me." Clutching her mug like a life preserver, Vanna started to well up again.

"It's fine. Don't worry, I just need to go somewhere."

"Sorry, I didn't know you were going out." Vanna got up to leave too, her legs feeling decidedly unsteady.

"Neither did I until now. It's alright, you don't need to leave."

Vanna stared at the peculiar old lady. Words kept forming in her mind and then evaporating before they became sound.

"Be a dear and continue stirring, will you? The mead needs a little longer. Keep it simmering for about another ten minutes, then switch off the stove. It'll be fine for when I get back." With that she donned her cyan velvet cloak, leaving Vanna stirring the pot and wondering what exactly had just happened.

*   *   ⋏   ⋏

Charlotte pulled the sedan into a long tree-lined driveway. The crunch of the gravel under the tires caused Luke to squint out of the window. He didn't recognize where they were, and the dim twilight left little visible.

"Where are we?"

Maggie Denhearn

"It's where I grew up."

It was beginning to dawn on Luke how little he actually knew of his daughter's life, how little interest he'd shown.

"Come in." They both got out of the car, but Luke remained hovering on the threshold. He followed her into the house. It was the typical kind of home one might expect of two working professionals with only one child: bigger than your average family home, with more expensive furnishings and ornaments. Various expensive pieces of artwork hung on the walls, and the sofa in the living room was white. It felt more like a set from some design magazine than a home.

"Is this how it was when you grew up?"

"Yes. I've not changed anything. I barely stay here anymore. I just haven't wanted to sell it either; not yet."

"It's ... er ..."

"Not very homey? No, it's not. I was always getting into trouble for spilling things on the beige carpet. I could never have a pet either. Too many hairs."

Feelings of discomfort were burrowing into Luke's stomach. He changed the subject.

"How about we eat something? Got any food in? I'm starving."

"There's always stuff in the freezer. I'll go take a look. I could probably whip us up some pasta and prawns if that works."

"Sounds good to me. Mind if I go and take a look around?"

"Be my guest."

*   *   *   *

Charlotte took out her phone. Making sure Luke had made his way upstairs and wasn't within earshot, she started dialing. "We're here and he's bought my story. I know you know exactly where we are. Can't we just get this over with?" Her voice was tense, nervous.

"All in good time. Just make the pasta. It sounds delicious." Charlotte tried to muffle a gasp. They must have the house bugged. They weren't kidding when they said there was no way out. She really did have no choice.

150

When the Universe Called

She went into the kitchen and looked at the various bottles of wine in the wine rack. There were some vintage pieces that had been her parents', ready to drink for the perfect occasion, worth hundreds of dollars apiece. The right time for them had never come.

She picked up a bottle of 1986 Chateau Mouton Rothschild. She figured this one had to be worth at least a thousand dollars. Charlotte wasn't a wine expert, but when she'd recently had the house valued for insurance purposes, along with the contents, she'd been shocked at how much expensive wine her parents had bought. She carefully opened the bottle and poured the thick red liquid into a cut crystal glass. She knew she was probably committing some kind of sacrilege by not decanting it first or letting it breathe, but there was no time for that. She needed a drink. She took a large sip and closed her eyes. It tasted warm and velvety. Taking another large gulp, she began rummaging in the freezer to see what there was. She knocked back the rest of the glass and poured another, letting the warmth and headiness of the alcohol numb her senses.

Vancouver City Centre homeless shelter, Wednesday night, May 19, 1999

Brina sat by the bedside, holding the young woman's hand. The woman's breathing was shallow, labored. Brina felt the hand in hers: bony, clammy, callused. It felt like the hand of an old woman, yet the woman was no more than twenty-five or twenty-six. Brown, scraggly hair lay like a spider's web across a thin pillow. With black ovals under her closed eyes, her face was sallow and sunken, the skin jaundiced. She lay on a dismal threadbare mattress, covered in a thin gray blanket. A shaft of moonlight was trying to battle its way in through the small window at the top of the wall, casting an eerie shadow across the otherwise unlit room. The walls were bare, the only furniture the bed and the sharp wooden chair bedside it, on which Brina was perched.

Outside, the noises of the city continued, oblivious to the last struggles of the soul finally freeing itself of this particular earthly incarnation. Brina listened as the woman's breathing lessened and the crackle of the death rattle began. She held her hand until she was sure there was no life left, then said

151

Maggie Denhearn

a silent prayer and laid the hand on the woman's chest. Leaving the room, she went out into the cool air of the evening. There was a bench across the road where she sat down and cried silently. How many more times would she have to witness this?

A figure came out of the shadows and sat beside her.

"You were of great comfort."

Brina looked up at Darcy, as she sat down on the bench beside her.

"We have to do something, Darcy. Frost is killing people—actually killing people with these drug trials."

"I know."

"Your boss is protecting him."

"I know. That's why I'm helping you."

There was silence between the women for a moment, both lost in their own contemplation.

"Who was the young woman?"

"A drug addict. She'd been one for years, poor woman. She has a child somewhere, gave her up for adoption a few years ago, and that just seemed to send her further into addiction. It's what Frost plays on." Darcy spat, then lit herself a cigarette. "Want one?"

"No, thank you."

"I know, not a good habit. But I can't seem to kick it. Too much horror in this life. I need something to block it out."

"You're doing all you can. If you weren't helping them escape the labs and at least rest here for a while, there'd be nowhere for these poor souls to go. What was her name?"

"Ena. She was called Ena."

Brina felt her stomach tighten. It was an unusual name. What were the chances?

"Was she originally from the Island?"

"Yes. How did you know?"

"Did you know her mother's name?"

"She didn't talk much about her parents. I only remember her mother's name so clearly because of my grandmother. She had the same name. And it seemed so odd that there was something too about Ena that reminded me of her. Her mother was called Iris."

152

CHAPTER 13

TUESDAY EVENING, APRIL 15, 2014

Iris stared at herself in the mirror. She couldn't remember the last time she'd actually really seen herself. Every day she would do her hair and apply her makeup, what little she wore, but it was as though she could do it blindfolded. She rinsed her face in cool water and stared at the lines and contours on her forehead and around her eyes. Her skin was starting to look like a relief map, a saggy one. All the amazing skin cream in the world can't stop the sands of time. She wondered why everyone, including herself, was so obsessed with trying to stop or slow down the inevitable. What would life be like if she just accepted that she was getting older? She didn't recognize the woman staring back at her. She wasn't Iris. In her mind she was still seventeen years old, still waiting for life to start, still hopeful that one day …

She could no longer finish that thought; she'd forgotten. At one point, there had been something that came after "one day." Gradually that had turned into "when Trevor is gone …" And now he was. It didn't feel real.

She had come back from the forest and cleaned up again, and then cleaned one more time, just to be sure. Then she cleaned the whole house, top to bottom. Eight hours later the house gleamed, now more sanitary than an operating room.

Her back ached, and the skin on her hands smarted. She was tired in that way that oddly precludes sleep so decided to run a bath. As the hot water swooshed into the tub, steam rising and bubbles growing, she continued to stare at herself in the mirror. She watched her face gradually disappear as

Maggie Denhearn

the mirror fogged up with the steam. She was being erased. At that point in time, she wished she could be. Would it be possible to start again, truly wipe the slate clean and start afresh?

She wanted to speak to Brina, to confess, to confide, to be consoled. Her soul hurt. At first she thought that it was because she had taken the life of another human being, but if she was honest with herself, that wasn't it. Right now she didn't feel guilty. Try as she might, she couldn't feel bad about what she'd done to Trevor; not because she thought it had been the right thing to do, but because she knew it had been the only thing she could have done to save herself. If she hadn't brought the axe down at the precise moment that she did, she would have evaporated right there and then.

This would be hard to explain and to justify to anyone else. Why hadn't she left him? Why hadn't she filed for a divorce? Why hadn't she gone to the police? She could hear all the questions she would be asked. They all made sense, were perfectly reasonable questions unless you were living in her skin, unless you had spent the last forty-three years in her life.

Small hurts, minor abuses, build up and snowball, becoming compounded one on top of the other. They get bigger and bigger, yet you don't notice. You can't or you won't get through the day if you take the time to see what is happening. And although you may not notice, your body does. Your mind rationalizes what you endure to keep going, to keep getting up in the morning and going to work, to keep the kids in school and food on the table. It's called getting by. Since there are good days—or passable days at least—you fool yourself that things aren't so bad and that it'll get better. You even think *I'm imagining it. It's not that bad.* Your mind plays tricks, and all the while your tolerance level for unkindness and anger builds until the protective shield you've built to keep yourself safe becomes the weight that slowly starts to crush you.

Iris had felt this weight bearing down on her ever more so the last few months. She felt like she was in a movie scene that went on for days, weeks. She was playing a part, acting, with no idea of her next line or what the ending would be.

She switched off the tap and tested the water. Perfect. Lighting some candles, she took off her bathrobe and climbed slowly into the hot water. The tension in her body began to dissolve as she eased herself in and lay there,

When the Universe Called

listening to the bubbles crackle. She closed her eyes and tried to pretend this was just a normal evening after a day at work at Fun Foods Supermarket. She was Iris, checkout woman. She was reliable, dependable, and predictable. She was Iris.

"I am Iris. I am Iris." She said her name out loud. If she heard her name, then she existed. She was real, not the ghost of the woman she had become.

*   *   *   *

Luke kicked back on the sofa. He'd said he was afraid that he might spill red wine over it, expensive red wine at that, but Charlotte just laughed and said it didn't matter.

"I've always hated this sofa. It's not even particularly comfortable. My parents rarely sat on it because they were hardly ever home." Charlotte stared off into the distance, her face morose.

"Lovely dinner. I didn't realize you could cook like that."

"I enjoy it. It's a kind of therapy. It relaxes me."

"I guess we may as well rest here for the night and decide where best to head in the morning."

"That sounds like a plan."

"In the meantime, you can give me that makeover you were talking about. I definitely need a shave, that's for sure. Any good at cutting hair?"

"I'll give it a go. And I've got some hair dye around somewhere, I'm sure. I did a lot of experimenting when I was a teenager."

"Just with your hair or other things?"

Luke suddenly wished he hadn't asked that. He didn't want to know what a teenage daughter did. He was very well aware of what he'd got up to at that age.

Charlotte didn't respond. He couldn't place what it was, but in this moment she seemed different. Maybe it was just being in the family home. It was bound to feel a little uncomfortable, even if her parents weren't around anymore. He felt awkward. He poured himself more wine, hoping the haze descending on him would obliterate thoughts of his brother. There was no time for him to allow himself to be swallowed up by the pain that had taken root in his chest.

155

Maggie Denhearn

Charlotte got up.

"I'll go and check in the bathroom to see what I can find."

"You okay?"

"Fine, just tired." She blushed and glanced away, as she headed upstairs. Maybe she was embarrassed by his grief.

*　*　*　*

Iris shivered; she had fallen asleep. Something woke her, and she wasn't sure whether it was the chill of the tepid water or something else. She hurriedly got out of the bath, grabbed a towel, and quickly dried herself off. She grabbed her robe and put her ear next to the bathroom door. Out of habit she had closed it and locked it, even though no one else was home or would be coming home.

There it was. It sounded like someone or something was downstairs. She felt her stomach lurch and the chill of fear. For one brief moment she thought Trevor was back, that putting the axe in his head had been just a beautiful nightmare after all. The events of the day had made her jumpy, and she was being irrational. In all the time she had lived in this area, nothing untoward had ever happened. The most excitement seemed to be when the deer ate the plants or there was the occasional bear sighting in the park close by. Nothing had ever happened—until now.

Iris unlocked the door and called out, "Who's there? I'm just in the bathroom. I'll be right down."

She figured that at worst, it was probably kids trying to steal something. Calling out would warn them off, and they'd disappear. She crept down the stairs, first cautiously peering around the door of both the bedrooms, just to be sure there was no one in them. Approaching the bottom, she heard a chair scrape across the kitchen floor and screamed. Not sure what to do, she grabbed a wooden statue that was on the table in the hallway, as she saw a shadow cross the doorway to the kitchen.

"Sorry, Iris, did I startle you?"

"Brina!"

"Yes, dear. Who did you think it was?" Brina stared at the statue in Iris's hand, then at Iris's startled expression. "Did I frighten you? You seem jumpy."

When the Universe Called

"Brina, oh my goodness, it's just you."

"I hope you don't mind my letting myself in. I knocked and there was no answer, but the light was on, and I assumed you were home."

"How long have you been here?"

"Only a few minutes."

Iris tried to compose herself. She felt disoriented from just waking up. She had a sense that she'd been dreaming about something when she was in the bath, but she wasn't sure what. Something was different, and she couldn't place what it was.

"Is everything alright, dear?" Brina's intonation gave away that she knew it wasn't. "You look like you've seen a ghost."

"No, no, everything's fine. Well, it isn't, but anyway." Iris felt the color of a spoken untruth flushing her cheeks.

"I got your message and came straight over. Something's happened." Iris looked at her friend, trying to read her face. She wasn't asking a question.

"In a manner of speaking." Iris was still confused. For the life of her, she couldn't remember calling Brina. It had crossed her mind to do so, but then she hadn't. She'd decided that until she had an idea of how she was going to explain what had happened, it would be better not to say anything to her. She was sure she'd not called. How could she have forgotten that?

"I'd forgotten. I was in the bath and fell asleep." Brina was looking at her steadily. Iris glanced away, unable to hold her gaze.

"I'll make you some tea. Herbal? What would you like?"

"Chamomile I think." Out of the corner of her eye she saw that Brina was continuing to eye her quizzically. There was silence as Brina busied herself with putting the kettle on and finding mugs and tea bags. Iris was glad to be waited on. Any movement suddenly seemed like too much of an effort.

"Have you eaten? Can I make you a snack?"

When Brina said this, it occurred to Iris that she had no idea of the time. She tried to look casual as she turned around to look at the kitchen clock. It was 9:00 p.m. Late. Had she asked Brina to come round at this time, or had she just come after Iris had allegedly telephoned her? She felt off kilter. The whistle of the kettle provided some distraction and briefly filled the space between them.

Finally Iris spoke. "What's going on with you these days?"

157

Maggie Denhearn

"I'm fine. But you don't need me here to make small talk with you, do you?" Brina had a way of cutting straight to the point that wasn't exactly impolite, yet had a directness that often knocked people off balance.

"I guess not." Should Iris admit that she couldn't remember calling her?

"Brina, look. You know, I've had a really stressful day, and the truth is, well … I don't remember calling you." Brina looked at Iris, but didn't respond.

"It's lovely to see you, though," she continued, desperate to fill the silence.

"I know you didn't call."

"What?"

"I said I got your message. I didn't say you called."

"Sorry, I'm not following."

"No, dear, apparently not. Why don't you tell me what's going on?"

Iris looked at Brina, really looked this time, and realized she already knew everything. There was nothing left to tell.

"You already know, don't you." It wasn't a question.

Brina hesitated, then said, "Yes, I do. Do you want to tell me about it?"

"How? How did you know?"

"You know me. There are some things I can't help knowing, no matter how much I'd prefer not to."

Iris caught her breath. Brina had her peculiarities, and there were times when she seemed to be able to read her thoughts. But this—this was something else altogether. This was beyond the bizarre experiments Brina had been doing, which Iris had found hard to believe. There was no point in any dissimulation.

"I didn't mean to. Well, I know I can't say it was an accident. I can't exactly say 'the axe slipped and fell out of my hand.' I just don't know what came over me. I just couldn't take it any more … couldn't take *him* anymore."

Iris slumped down in her chair and started to weep. "What am I going to do?" Brina got up and hugged Iris until her chest finally stopped heaving and she was able to breathe more easily.

"Drink your tea. It'll steady your nerves."

Tea, the panacea of all ills.

"I'm not sure a cup of tea is going to fix things. I could do with a brandy."

158

When the Universe Called

"Chamomile tea and brandy. Why not?" Brina got up and went into the living room to the small dark wood cabinet. Iris didn't bother asking her how she knew that particular cupboard was where she kept her brandy.

"One slug or two?"

"Two." She didn't miss the irony. All the times that Trevor had come home drunk, all the damage done in their lives by the abuse of alcohol, now she was finding comfort in the sweet, thick liquid and the sting of inebriation she felt from just a couple of sips. She could gladly have drunk herself into oblivion.

"Not too much, dear, you still need a clear head." Brina put the top back on the bottle and put it back in the cabinet.

"Tell me exactly what happened."

Iris didn't know where to start because she wasn't entirely sure where it had all begun, although in truth, she knew the seeds were planted years ago. Last night was no different from hundreds of others. She had come to despise Trevor long ago. Maybe it was that he had broken her favorite vase, but since he had broken her nose and three of her ribs, along with her wrist and their wedding photo, the vase was really nothing more than a casual addition to an already-long list. Something had changed, though, and she was desperately trying to identify what that was. Maybe it was this acute sense that she was disappearing.

She searched for the words. "I'm not sure what, how, or exactly when, but I saw Trevor lounging drunk in his chair. I saw the mess he'd left everywhere. I looked at the beautiful sunrise and I just couldn't pretend anymore that everything was okay. I couldn't pretend I wasn't angry. And I needed to feel like I exist. And when then he …" Brina said nothing, just held her gaze, a gentle hand resting on her arm. Iris tried to look away, but somehow couldn't. Facing Brina was like facing herself, and it was excruciating.

"Brina, I have to ask. Did I … I mean, you're always telling me about the *Law of Attraction*, that we attract all our experiences into our lives. Is this my fault? Am I to blame for everything Trevor did?" Iris felt her face crumpling.

"No one is ever to blame for someone being violent toward them. Sometimes when someone is so caught up in negative energy, it's too hard to focus on the positive, so more bad things happen. That's the *Law of Attraction*.

Maggie Denhearn

Where your attention goes, energy flows. Talking about blame isn't useful because it implies responsibility." Iris listened quietly.

"You're not responsible for Trevor's actions. If you had a mindset where you believed you deserved to be abused, you'd get more of the same. That doesn't mean you deserve it or are to blame. It means you're deserving of compassion and kindness so that one day you can change your thoughts enough to be able to attract more positive experiences."

"But I *am* responsible for what I did to him."

Iris saw Brina hesitate. "Yes. Yes you are," she said simply, squeezing her hand.

* * * *

Maria leaned into the wall of the shower stall and closed her eyes, letting the thick drops of hot water wash over her like heavy rain beating down. Peace. It had been a long twenty-four hours. She tried to find solace in the belief that things couldn't get any worse.

The doorbell rang. It was an odd time of the evening for someone to be calling round. Probably Vanna or Kali. She'd been looking forward to relaxing with a glass of wine after a long, soothing shower. Her car was in the driveway, and the lights were on in the house. No chance of pretending she wasn't home.

The doorbell rang again, this time for longer. Cursing, she wrapped herself in a towel.

"I was in the sho ... shower." It wasn't Vanna. It wasn't Kali. It was the police.

"Ms. Cartright?"

"Yes?" Maria pulled the towel closer around her, goose bumps spreading all over her.

"Ms. Cartright, Ms. Maria Cartright?" Maria nodded.

"Can we come in?"

"What's this about?" They must have discovered Noah. Party face. She had told lies often enough, in public; she could do it now.

"Ms. Cartright I'm afraid we have some bad news. Can we come in? Are you alone?"

160

When the Universe Called

She led them into the living room. "Mind if I put some clothes on? I'm feeling slightly underdressed." Somehow she didn't feel like she could keep up the pretense if she wasn't dressed. She ran upstairs and grabbed a sweatshirt and sweat pants.

When she returned, one of them asked, "Is there someone else here?"

"No. What is it? You're freaking me out."

"Please sit down, Ms. Cartright. Have you heard the radio at all today?"

"What? No, why?" She saw the detectives exchange looks.

"When did you last see your husband?"

"This morning, early. Why?"

"We're so sorry to have to tell you that we have reason to believe that the body of your husband Luke has been found in the forest." Maria looked at them.

"What? And what's that got to do with the radio?"

"A body has been found in the forest near the community center and it's believed to be that of your husband. Unfortunately, a reporter decided to publish the story before we were able to get hold of you."

"But it can't be Luke. He's in Vancouver on a business trip. He was on the ferry this morning."

"Did you speak to him after he left?"

"No. But ..." Maria felt her heart sink and her stomach tighten. Even though it was entirely possible the police were getting Noah and Luke confused, it was more than unusual that Luke hadn't called her to say he'd arrived safely. He always called when he went away. She had been so preoccupied that she'd not even thought about it. An unsettling nagging feeling started to form at the back of her mind.

"I don't understand."

"Is there someone we can call to come and be with you?" What if something really had happened to Luke? She didn't know what to feel. The woman detective looked at her pityingly. Maria wondered how many times the detective had broken bad news to someone. Old enough for that to be many times over by the look of her creased face. Her male colleague looked equally beleaguered.

"I ... er ... I don't know what to say. I don't know what to do." She got up and began pacing back and forth, rubbing her hands together. She felt

161

Maggie Denhearn

peculiarly light-headed. This was not what she had expected. The other body. Doubt. She had thought she would be trying to act the performance of her life, pretending she knew nothing of Noah's demise. Not this. Anything but this.

"Ms. Cartright?"

"What?"

"Are you sure we can't call someone for you?"

"Yes. No. Yes. Would you mind leaving?" They got up.

"We'll be in touch. The thing is, though ..." The female detective hesitated. "There was a forest fire. The body is badly burnt. We still need someone to try and identify him, just to be sure. You'll need to prepare yourself."

"Fire? So you're not sure it's Luke? Why would you say it is when you're not sure it's my husband? Surely it could be anyone, then. And how come this reporter got hold of the story? Aren't you supposed to stop those vermin?" Indignation had ignited within her. The detective put her hand on Maria's shoulder but she brushed it off.

"We're sorry. The reporter is being dealt with. The body was wearing a watch. An engraving on it was still partially visible, and it had Luke Morgan engraved on it." The detective paused. "If you have it, it would also be useful to have the name of your husband's dentist."

Maria fell back into the armchair, holding her stomach to stop her gagging. She didn't respond. His dentist? Her mind was blank. She'd had her fill of dead bodies. She refused to believe this one was Luke. The detectives let themselves out. She felt lost, like her limbs were missing. Catching sight of her cell phone on the coffee table, she picked it up.

"Luke, it's Maria. Call me. It's urgent." He didn't pick up. Hands shaking, she reached for the wine bottle, poured herself a glass, and barely managed not to spill half of it all over the table. She took a large gulp and closed her eyes, falling back into the warm embrace of the sofa.

The doorbell rang again. She hoped it wasn't the police coming back. Maria needed more time to collect her thoughts. The doorbell rang again. Somehow she managed to get up and go to answer it.

"Brina? What are you doing here?"

"Well, you called, didn't you?"

When the Universe Called

"Yes, but I wasn't expecting you *now*."

"I thought you might need me. Am I wrong?"

Maria was starting to feel dizzy and shivery with shock. "No, no. Come in."

*   *   *   *

Charlotte came back downstairs carrying a basket of various packets of hair dye.

"Which color do you feel like trying?"

"None of them look particularly great."

"Take a look while I go get a towel and find some plastic gloves. I'm sure there must be some somewhere. Mother was meticulous about not getting her nail polish chipped."

Luke started to examine the different packets: natural blond, beige blond, ash blond, using "color technology." Who knew dying your hair could be this complicated? He'd assumed you just dabbed on some bleach and then washed it off. Charlotte had put her cell phone down on the table, and he couldn't resist taking a look.

"So did you decide which ...?" Luke saw Charlotte blanch at the sight of her phone in his hand. He felt his face flush and his lips quiver. It was taking all his energy not to grab hold of her and start shaking her.

"You have some explaining to do, young lady!" He expected a litany of excuses, tears even, but instead she began rolling her eyes and pointing to her ears, then frantically gesturing around the room, to the light fittings, the home phone, mouthing something.

"What are you ...?"

"I know, I know, the colors are all rather dated." She was grimacing at him and gesticulating wildly. She mouthed something to him again.

"What on earth?"

"I know; can you believe I used to use this stuff?" Her eyes were pleading. The penny dropped. The house was bugged. She carried on desperately.

"I used to look ridiculous. I tried pink at one point too but my parents went ballistic. Luckily it was just a phase."

163

Maggie Denhearn

Luke pulled a face, which he hoped was communicating, "Will you get on with telling me what on earth is going on?"

"That's exactly what I was thinking." He attempted to play along, trying not to give into the concoction of anxiety and fury rising inside of him like some bizarre chemistry experiment.

"Let's try the downstairs washroom. Come here and I'll wash your hair for you. It needs to be damp before you can use the dye." She grabbed his hand, and Luke followed her into the bathroom, where she switched on the taps at full blast, whispering, "I had no choice! I'm sorry. I thought we were in the clear when Heeley called off his men, but then I got a call from Bailey. She said they'd kill both of us if I didn't hand you over. She's been after both of you—you and Noah, that is—all along. Her people are everywhere, watching us. They've even bugged the house. What was I supposed to do?"

"Tell me for a start!" Luke hissed.

"But I couldn't. I didn't get a chance. They were the ones who sent the sedan. I thought it could be bugged. I never thought the house would be, but they heard me say I was going to cook pasta. Anyway, more to the point, what the hell are you doing mixed up with gangsters?"

"I'm not, not how you're thinking. But there's no time to explain right now. You're going to have to trust that I'm one of the good guys. And I guess I'm going to have to take a leap of faith that you don't really want me dead either."

Charlotte reddened and looked away. She was trying not to cry. He tried to soften his voice. Much as it could cost him his life, he couldn't bring himself to believe she wasn't telling the truth.

"Is there a back way out of here? We'll have to get out on foot. It's too risky to take the car. Let's carry on talking as though you're dying my hair. That'll buy us some time. When did they say they were coming?"

"They didn't. I've no idea how much time we have. They could be here any minute."

Luke gritted his teeth. This was it. He knew this day would come, but he'd rather hoped he would have been better prepared than this. No time to get their things. He had his passport and his wallet in his jacket pocket. Back in the living room, he showed his passport to Charlotte to silently ask if she had hers. She did, in her purse.

When the Universe Called

"Let's put some music on. May as well get into the spirit of my teenage years again. I can't believe some of the dross I used to listen to." Charlotte's attempts at joviality were forced and high-pitched as she quickly flicked through some CDs and put on The Black Eyed Peas.

"This was good though. I used to listen to this a lot and dance around the living room when my parents weren't home. More wine?"

"Please."

"I'll open another bottle." They made the appropriate noises, then quickly snuck out of the back door and into the darkness.

EAGLE COVE, FRIDAY, MAY 21, 1999

Iris sat on the floor in the kitchen, legs pulled up to her chest, hugging herself and rocking back and forth. She had to keep moving, afraid that if she stopped, she would disintegrate into a thousand pieces. It felt safer on the ground. The cold of the hardwood floor just about registered in her body, reminding her she was still alive.

At this moment she wished she weren't. She thought that she had endured the worst pain imaginable when her daughter left home. Guilt is an odd emotion. For Iris it would take on different shapes and weights, depending on the day. Some days it would be a dull ache in her stomach and others it would be a lead weight in her heart that made her breathing feel labored and shallow. Whatever shape or form, she carried it with her, always, an Ena-shaped hole that the presence of her daughter used to fill. Ena had left the moment she turned eighteen and not returned for nearly five years. No phone calls, no letters.

Even then she came back for only a few days, a shadow slipping in and out. Luckily Trevor had not been home when she had turned up out of the blue. Iris had run Ena a bath and bathed her grown-up daughter as though she were a little girl again, combing her long, thin hair and singing softly to her. Iris had ignored the marks all over Ena's arms, making them look like a pincushion—the bruises and the cuts, the track marks between her toes, the scar on her abdomen. Iris chose not to see any of this. Ena would never explain why she had not come to Iris for help when she got pregnant. A few

Maggie Denhearn

days later, just as abruptly as she had reappeared, her daughter walked out of the front door. She never returned.

Iris had thought she was still alive—could not imagine it any other way. Unwittingly, she had chosen her husband over her daughter. She thought she'd been protecting her.

The thought that Iris had a granddaughter somewhere on the mainland filled her with both hope and sorrow—mostly sorrow. It was unlikely she would ever get to know her. But the thought that part of her daughter lived on in some way was of some meager comfort.

The police officer had been as comforting as she could be, made Iris a cup of very sweet tea, and sat with her, holding her hand as she explained that her daughter would not be coming back. The feel of another human being's touch had been too painful, like someone sticking pins in her flesh. She didn't deserve such kindness. How could she go on breathing when her daughter was no longer walking the earth?

Iris wasn't sure how long she remained huddled on the kitchen floor. At some point it had grown dark outside. She remembered that. She heard someone knock softly at the door. She was unable to stand up. The door creaked open and Brina walked in. Unable to kneel, Brina reached down a hand and coaxed Iris up to sit on one of the kitchen chairs. Iris remembered staring into Brina's eyes and seeing such sadness reflected back. Yet she couldn't tell if it was her own or her friend's.

"My daughter ..." Iris heard herself speak.

"I know."

"I have a granddaughter somewhere." She looked around the room as though the child might appear out of one of the corners or cupboards.

"I'll help you find her, I promise. I promise."

CHAPTER 14

WEDNESDAY MORNING, APRIL 16, 2014

Frost switched off the radio and lay back against the pillows. The tiredness he felt was overwhelming, yet it had nothing to do with needing to sleep. He was tired of life, tired of breathing. There is no good way to hear about one's son's death, but from a radio broadcast is less than ideal. So Bailey had gone ahead and dealt with the "situation" without consulting him. He realized a long time ago that she was ruthless, but even he was shocked to discover quite how merciless. He wasn't sure how he felt. He'd imagined feeling some sense of righteous vindication, bringing Luke in, letting him know that his father always had the upper hand. He'd thought he would have one last chance to have a conversation. Bailey had denied him that—had denied him everything.

A surge of rage coursed through him, sending him into a paroxysm of coughing and wheezing. Lashing out to try and catch hold of the emergency cord next to his bedstead, he barely managed to find the strength to pull on it. Then he lay back, staring at the ceiling. Would death take him now? The swirls of the plaster on the ceiling started to dance around, taking on a life of their own, as he slipped under a dark cloud of delirium.

*   *   *   *

Vanna hadn't slept. She'd tried, but every time she closed her eyes, all she could see were the two dead bodies. Morris seemed equally restless and kept alternating between wanting to sleep on top of the bedcovers right on

Maggie Denhearn

top of her feet and then wanting to come under the duvet and lick her face to get her attention if she didn't lift the duvet quickly enough for him to let him get back under. She couldn't be bothered to fight him, so went to put the kettle on. It was already 6:00 a.m., so she may as well get up.

Everything seemed quiet, but a different, eerie kind of quiet. It was always peaceful in the dark. That was one of the reasons she liked where she lived so much: no noise, no light at night except what the moon and stars could offer. Occasionally Morris would hear something and would start barking, which would freak her out, as she could never hear what it was. Thinking that the sound of the radio might lighten her mood, she turned it on in time to hear the local news.

> Fire officials are still trying to establish the cause of a local forest fire that swept through the trails near Nile creek yesterday morning. Fortunately, some local residents who were out fixing the trails alerted the authorities in time for the fire to be contained within a quarter mile radius, with the forest sustaining only minimal damage. It is reported that two bodies have been found.

Vanna jumped up and switched off the radio. Hearing the rest of that report was not going to make her feel any better, even if what Brina said was true about it destroying evidence. The kettle came to a boil, and she made a cup of tea. Mug in hand, she went back to bed and curled up next to Morris. His gentle breathing was reassuring. She stroked his furry stomach, and he rolled over sleepily on to his back, a signal he wanted her to continue petting him. Maybe Brina was right. She should just focus on positive thoughts and it would all be okay. And in the meantime, going to work early to distract herself couldn't hurt either. She threw some clothes on and called to Morris that they were going out.

*   *   *   *

Vanna continued shouting down the beach as Morris danced his little jig and looked like he was having the time of his life, completely ignoring

When the Universe Called

her calls for him to come to her. She was really not in the mood for his usual antics. Eventually she managed to catch up with him and, only by snarling, got him to stop long enough so she could put him back on the leash.

He smelt less than fragrant. The white fur on his back was now completely brown with runny, oozing bear scat. She dragged him back to the holiday cottage she was supposed to be cleaning and dumped him straight in the shower. He struggled briefly then cowered under the water that was having little effect at washing away the brown gunk. She hunted in the kitchen, and the only thing she could find to wash him in was dishwashing liquid. She gave a good squirt on his back and began lathering him vigorously. It took a few minutes, but gradually the deep brown water pouring off him became clearer. By the time she'd finished washing him, much of the bear scat had transferred to her, and she was drenched. The showerhead was strategically placed so that the water shot straight out of the shower cubicle door and, since the door was open, all over her and the floor. She rubbed Morris dry and took off her top and pants, shoving them in the washing machine, hoping she could get them washed and dried while she cleaned. She left Morris in the bathroom to dry off so he wouldn't prance around the house and leave the malodorous whiff of wet dog.

At least cleaning distracted her from everything else that was happening in her life. She carried on making the beds and sorting out the linens. She was just walking past the hall window when she caught a glimpse of someone coming down the driveway. Not wanting to be seen naked, she ducked down before she could see who it was.

*   *   *   *

It had been a cold and damp night. The thin veil of early morning dew glistened in the light of dawn and made everything twinkle. The coolness of the air was sharp. Charlotte couldn't stop shivering. She wasn't entirely sure how much of it was because she could no longer feel her extremities and how much was due to out-and-out fear — a dread filled mixture of both, most likely.

Luke had done his best to keep her spirits up, which, all things considered, was very good of him. They'd finally had the chance to have a

Maggie Denhearn

long conversation about "things." What else were they going to do, huddled in some outbuilding they'd managed to find in the complete darkness? Luckily, Charlotte had spent a lot of her childhood roaming the area and knew it like the proverbial back of her hand. Even in the dark she had managed to navigate them to what she was fairly certain was the deserted barn up by the lake. She'd spent many an afternoon there as a child, either with friends or alone—mostly alone. She had no idea who it belonged to.

As far as they could tell, no one had followed them. The Consortium, Heeley, and whomever Bailey had sent after them must know they were missing by now. Charlotte had put the CD on repeat, but the fact they were no longer talking was probably more than a bit of a giveaway that they'd left in a hurry. They should have pretended they were going to bed, but they'd been so keen to get away, it didn't occur to them until later. They didn't have much of a head start; that was for sure.

Quite what they were going to do to get out of all this, neither of them had figured out. They'd come up with various scenarios, but so far each one seemed to have a fatal flaw that most certainly would lead them back to being caught. The best option (*best* being a relative term) seemed to be to return to Vancouver Island. Maybe the perfect thing to do would be to do exactly what would be so obvious and therefore ruled out.

*   *   *   *

Kali lay in bed, staring at the wall. She'd been staring at the same wall for hours, yet if she'd been asked to describe the color and the pictures that were hanging on it, she wouldn't have known. Her mind was racing with thoughts she couldn't control, each one almost tripping over the last in its haste to get into her head and torment her. They were like wasps on crack, buzzing around in her brain.

Sunlight was beginning to seep in through the blinds, signaling the dawn of another new day. Life would march forward regardless of whether she remained hiding under the duvet.

She couldn't go to the university like this. She was a mess. Luckily, she knew her voice sounded awful from all the crying she had been doing, so calling in sick wouldn't be hard. She wouldn't have to fake sounding

When the Universe Called

dreadful. It was a strange combination of being upset about Noah and self-interested fear of what was going to happen to her. If all this got out, Andy would totally freak out. He wasn't a violent man, at least not that she'd ever witnessed. But she knew some of the things he had been prepared to do to get where he was politically, and had a feeling that she didn't know the whole picture.

She needed Maria to call. She looked across at the clock: 7:00 a.m., a little early. She would steel herself to wait a little longer. She stuck her head under a pillow and started to sob again.

Her phone rang. It was Maria.

"Are you okay?"

"Not really," Kali sniffed.

"Is Andy still away?"

"Yes, for another two days, I think. Why?"

"That gives us time. What time do you have to be at work? Can I come over quickly? The police came round last night."

"Oh crap! Really? What did they say? Maybe I should just come clean and see what happens."

"Hang on, hang on. They've found a body, but they think that it's Luke's."

"Well, we know it's Noah. I'm going to call in sick. Come round."

"I'll be getting a call any minute to go and identify the body. I'm just worried that, well, what if it *is* Luke? There was that other body, remember."

"It's hardly likely."

"True, true. I'm being ridiculous. Okay, I'll be right over. If the police can't find me, they'll just wait, I guess. Do you know where Vanna is?"

"It's her cottage cleaning day."

"Is she still doing that? I thought her BC nursing license was all arranged."

"Not yet. She's still waiting for immigration to do something or other."

"Okay, I'll call her later. See you in a bit."

Kali hung up and dragged herself out of bed. She wanted to look vaguely respectable when Maria turned up. She switched on the shower and let it run for a bit until it was warm enough, then stepped in. She tilted her head back and soaked her hair. This was normal. She was taking a shower. Normal people take showers in the morning. One foot in front of the other, everything will be okay. She closed her eyes, enjoying the sensation of the

Maggie Denhearn

water running down her back. She began to feel better, as the smell of vanilla-honey soap revived her senses.

Kali must have been in the shower longer than she'd realized as her doorbell was already ringing. Maria. Kali switched off the water and quickly toweled herself dry, grabbing her bathrobe. The doorbell rang again.

"Hold on, Maria, I'm coming!" she yelled down the stairs. Kali stepped back as she opened her front door. It wasn't Maria.

Two men in dark suits and sunglasses stood on Kali's doorstep, two very large men. They couldn't have looked more conspicuous if they'd tried. No one wore suits in this neighborhood. If they were trying to blend in, they clearly hadn't been paying much attention to local sartorial norms.

"Where is he?"

"Excuse me?" One of the men pushed her out of the way and started scanning round the hallway. Kali tried to maintain her composure but it didn't take much to work out that these were definitely hired thugs who were unlikely to stand on politeness.

"You *heard*. Where is he?" Thug number one bent down and stared menacingly at her, his finger jabbing at her chest. "Don't waste my time."

Recoiling, she found herself pressed against the wall. "Andy's away … He's away on business. Honest. He won't be back for two or three days." In her head she was already calculating how much time Andy would need to get further away.

"Don't lie to us."

"What? I don't understand. I'm not lying."

"We've been watching you."

Kali gasped. Did that mean they'd seen her in the forest with Noah?

"I don't know what you mean." If she stalled for time, maybe Maria would turn up. Maybe that would scare them off. Surely they wouldn't do anything to her here, not in Eagle Cove, not with witnesses?

Thug number two pushed past her and started wandering around the house, first downstairs and then heading upstairs. Kali tried to sound indignant rather than scared witless.

"What are you talking about? Who are you looking for? You must've got the wrong house. Would you kindly leave or I'll call the police!"

"Don't be stupid. Just tell us where he is."

When the Universe Called

"Andy's away on business. I don't know where, really I don't."

"Cut the crap. Just tell us where he is and we'll leave you alone. We want him, not you."

Kali started to cry. "I don't know, I don't know. I've not seen him since yesterday."

Thug number one stared at her and she tried to hold his gaze.

"I hope he's worth it. You're coming with us."

"What? No I'm not! I've no intention of ..." He grabbed her arm and bent it behind her back. "Ow, you're hurting me!"

"We'll do more than that if you don't cooperate. Put some clothes on." He shoved her sideways and she banged her shoulder against a bookshelf.

Realizing she'd better do as she was told, Kali went upstairs to get dressed, closely followed by thug number two. Maria had to be here soon. She'd see something was up and call the police. Crap. They didn't need the police involved. For a moment she weighed up both options in her head, wondering which would be worse: the police or going with these thugs. Thug number two was glaring at her.

"Do you mind? I'd like a bit of privacy to get dressed."

"Seen it all before, darlin'," he snickered but turned away long enough for her to grab her phone off the dresser and stuff it in her jeans pocket. Cringing at the sight of him leering, she dressed as slowly as she could, desperately stalling for time.

"Come on." Thug number two pushed her roughly downstairs, almost causing her to fall. She barely had enough time to put on her shoes when they were hauling her out of the door and pushing her into the back of a dark blue van. Surely some neighbor would notice her being abducted? It just couldn't happen that she was being taken away against her will in broad daylight, and no one was doing anything about it. They hadn't tied her hands or gagged her. Perhaps they were amateurs. From the back of the van, she could hear the faint conversation of the thugs in the front. That meant that they would be able to hear her if she called anyone. She'd have to text. Switching her phone to silent mode, she texted Maria. A few minutes later a text came back.

"What? Where r u. Am @ your house."

"Been abducted!"

"Where r u?"

Maggie Denhearn

"In blue van."

"What?"

"?? Don't know!"

"Who?"

"Nasty thugs want Andy. Help!"

"License?"

"849 V??"

"Where r u going?"

"Huh?"

"Switch on GPS."

Of course! She'd been too panicked to think about that. She didn't usually have it switched on.

She had one bar of signal. No wonder her phone seemed to be taking an age to think about it. Her battery was also getting low. She'd better switch it off until they got to wherever they were taking her and try again then.

Kali stuck her phone into her bra, glad she'd chosen to wear a large old sweater that was bulky enough to cover any odd looking bumps. Her head pounding, she tried to listen to the conversation at the front, but the thugs had gone quiet. She could hear the radio, CBC local news. It must be 8:30 a.m.

> Fire officials are still trying to establish the cause of a local forest fire that swept through the trails near Nile creek yesterday morning ...

A fire in the forest? She heard the channel being switched, and then very loud rock music blasted out. Kali slumped back in the van. Just when she thought things could not get any more bizarre.

Kali tried to think about what people did in *CSI* or other crime dramas when they were kidnapped. Mostly turned up dead. She wasn't a fan of that scenario. She tried to pay attention to which way the van was turning and when it stopped. As far as she could tell, they'd turned right, which meant they were heading in the direction of Friendship Bay. It didn't feel like they were going particularly fast.

When the Universe Called

She wondered what they were thinking of doing with her. If they had been after Andy and not her, then abducting her probably hadn't been planned.

They'd been driving for about twenty minutes, just going straight. The van suddenly slowed down, pulled to the right, then left, and came to a halt. Kali considered kicking and screaming when it came to them getting her out of the van in the hope that someone might hear her, but they had probably come somewhere far enough away from other people that it would be pointless and only antagonize the situation. She waited. Nothing, not even voices. Then she heard them.

"What are we going to do now?"

"Dunno. Let Heeley figure it out."

"He's not gonna be pleased."

"What else could we do? She'd have warned him if we'd let her go. At least if we've got her, that'll show him that Heeley means business."

"I don't like not sticking to the plan."

"Shit happens. Get over it." Silence.

"Better get her out then and into the shed. She'll be fine there for a while."

Kali remained seated. When they opened the van doors, she pretended to be inspecting her nails, as though she'd not been trying to listen to their conversation. As casually as she could muster and trying to hide the shake in her voice, she looked at thug number one.

"So, what are you going to do with me?"

"That'll be for Heeley to decide."

"Who's Heeley?"

Snide laughter. "Do we look stupid enough to tell you that?" She said nothing.

"As long as you do as you're told, you won't get hurt." One thug in front and one behind, she was marched past a dilapidated, low-slung house set to one side near a wooded area at what appeared to be the end of a crescent. The shed was at the back of the property. She tried to gather as much information as she could by looking out of the corner of her eye without making it too obvious she was trying to figure out where she was.

175

Maggie Denhearn

"In there." Thug number two pushed her inside the wooden outbuilding that was listing precariously to one side. The wood was rotting. She heard the door being locked behind her and their footsteps trailing away.

It took a few moments for her eyes to adjust to the dim light. A faint stream of sunlight was sliding through a small grubby window, spotlighting trails of dust in the air. She coughed. It smelt musty and damp. There were garden tools, a couple of propane tanks, and a rickety old lawn chair. She pulled out the chair and sat down. Time to think.

She inspected all the tools to see if there was anything that looked remotely like she could use it to break the lock on the door. Probably, but if she did that immediately, they would just come after her. It would be better to lay low for a while and wait until she heard them going out—assuming they did, of course, and assuming they both went together. She'd take her chances, though. In the meantime, she slumped down into the lawn chair and switched her phone back on. She started to text Maria.

"Trying GPS now. Think 20 mins from Eagle Cove, Frdship Bay drctn, off old hwy. In shed back of old run-down house." Given how many old houses there were, that possibly wasn't very helpful.

"K. Hear anything?" Kali listened. Birds. There were birds everywhere. Not helpful. Ocean. She could definitely hear the ocean.

"Ocean, ravens, eagles." Not exactly narrowing things down a heck of a lot, but it was a start. At least it was clear which of the only two Island highways she was close to. There were times when being somewhere so unpopulated was a definite advantage.

"Can u talk?"

A map sprang up on her screen, then blackness. Punching a few keys didn't help. The battery was dead. Throwing her phone on the floor in frustration, Kali slumped back in the chair and closed her eyes. If she ever got out of this alive, she would make sure her phone was *always* fully charged. Now what should she do?

She looked around quickly for a mirror, then closed her eyes again. Unexpected abduction had left no time to do her hair and make-up. To cap it all, she needed to pee and had not had breakfast, so she felt unbelievably hungry—in need of a cup of coffee and something to eat. Adrenaline pumped through her veins with nowhere to go. Her heart hadn't stopped pounding

When the Universe Called

since she'd opened her front door. Fight or flight? She couldn't fight and she couldn't flee.

With her phone dead, Kali had no idea how long she'd been in the shed. What felt like an hour might only be five or ten minutes. She felt both wired and exhausted, as though she'd run miles yet could keep on going. And she still needed to pee. Would the thugs remember at some point to let her use the washroom and possibly bring her something to eat and drink? She wondered whether to call out to them. Would they care? Maybe this was how she'd die: starving and with an exploded bladder ... and her hair a mess.

Perhaps she was in shock. She wasn't sure, but she wasn't ready to face the graveness of the situation she was in. It was easier to focus on the stupid little things that don't matter at all. Whatever Andy was mixed up in, this clearly wasn't any old business deal. A small ember of anger started to burn inside her.

Footsteps then voices grew louder outside. Kali quickly picked up her phone and shoved it in her bra. A woman opened the shed door.

"Hi."

Kali remained silent and just stared at her. The woman was in her mid-sixties, pleasantly plump, with short, cropped gray hair. Wearing an old T-shirt and dirty denim shorts that were far too tight for her, she looked like she'd been stuffed into her clothing. She had the air of a prison guard. Although she didn't smile, Kali could just make out a few black teeth at the front of her mouth. She shuddered, trying to hide her disgust.

"I've brought you something to eat and drink."

"Thank you. Erm, I also need the washroom."

"Use the bucket." Kali looked around, at first not seeing anything until her eyes stumbled upon a rusty metal bucket in the corner, covered in cobwebs. She grimaced.

"Can't I come out and use the bathroom in the house? I promise I won't run."

"Suck it up princess. The bucket is fine."

The woman closed the door and her footsteps faded. She left a tray on the floor with a bottle of water, a cup of coffee, and a couple of slices of buttered toast. Reminding herself that only a few years ago she had been an avid camper, Kali pulled out the bucket, brushed away the cobwebs, and

177

Maggie Denhearn

relieved herself. She found a small piece of tarp and covered it up, pushing it as far away from her as possible.

She took a slug of water and then started to eat the toast. After a couple of sips of the coffee, she started to feel so sleepy she couldn't keep her eyes open, so she lay back in the chair and closed her eyes, her head spinning. She did not feel well.

* * * *

Typical. No one ever came round to the cottage when Vanna was cleaning, and the one day she's stark naked, someone decides to knock on the door. Peering round to see who it was without being seen, she realized that it was Maria. She was beginning to feel stalked by her. There didn't seem to be anything more to say, especially now because of the fire. Vanna considered not answering, but then it dawned on her that her car was in the driveway, so she could hardly pretend she wasn't around.

"Just a second!" she called out. She didn't fancy chatting with her without a stitch on.

"Vanna, hurry up, it's urgent."

"Hang on, I just need to …" She ran to the laundry cupboard and got out a bath towel and wrapped it around her as she rushed back to the door.

"I've been trying to call you bu … why are you wearing a towel?" Maria looked around as she came through the door. "Are you with someone?"

"What? No. Why?"

"Well, it's not usual for people to clean house wearing a towel."

Vanna decided to ignore her comment. It was easier than explaining what had happened. "What's up?"

"I've been calling."

"Really? I didn't hear my phone."

"Luke's missing and Kali's been abducted." Her voice raised a pitch. Vanna had never heard anything remotely like panic in Maria's voice until now.

"What?"

"Luke is missing and Kali's been abducted."

"Kali's been …?"

"Kidnapped, taken, grabbed, snatched …!"

When the Universe Called

"Okay, okay, I get it. How do you know?"

"She texted me."

"She's been kidnapped and she managed to text you?"

"They put her in the back of some van. I was going round to her place and I must have just missed her."

"Who's *they?*"

"No idea. Didn't seem like she knew either." She paused. "They're looking for Andy."

"Why would anyone be looking for Andy? What's he got to do with anything?"

"Not sure."

Vanna stood for a moment, her mind blank. "I have no idea what to say right now. Is she okay?"

"How would I know? I'm not exactly used to friends getting kidnapped. This is the Island, not the Bronx."

"We should call the police."

"What's with you and the police? They're the last people we can call. How would we explain what's going on? This is all getting too weird."

"I know. What *should* we do then? And what did you say about Luke?"

"He's missing too. I've called and called. I just don't know what to do. The police came to see me, and they think he's one of the bodies in the forest. Logically I know it can't be him, but then there's that other body we found. What if it *is* him?"

Vanna couldn't think of anything remotely useful to say. Then: "Brina!" They both said her name at the same time.

"I saw her last night. She knows, you know."

Maria nodded conspiratorially. "I know. She came round to my place too. What did she say to you?"

"Not a lot."

"Me neither. I'll try her now." Maria pulled her phone out of her pocket, her hands shaking as she started to dial. "Maybe she'll know what to do about Kali or will get one of her visions. From what Kali wrote, she's still somewhere close. She was trying to use her GPS, but her phone died. At least I hope that's all it was. Something just doesn't feel right though. And

Maggie Denhearn

the police found Luke's watch on one of the bodies. I just don't know what to think now."

"Oh Maria!" Vanna reached out to put a comforting hand on Maria's arm, but she pulled away.

"Come on, Brina, answer, answer!" Maria stopped, holding on to the doorjamb, her face turning pale as she switched off her phone.

"The second body. It must be Luke's." Vanna grabbed Maria just in time as her knees started to buckle, guiding her to sit down on the stoop.

"When I went back for my ring, the other body was so mangled I didn't take a close look. What if it *is* Luke's?"

"When did you last see him?"

"At breakfast. Early in the morning, just before I saw you."

"That means he would have been taken and then left in the forest pretty much immediately after you saw him." Vanna carefully avoided using the word *murdered*. "Is that possible?"

"Anything's possible right now. I just don't know anymore. I can't think straight. And it's all my fault." Maria was shaking, her face ashen and her lips quivering.

"How can it be your fault?" Vanna was finding Maria increasingly hard to follow.

"It must be my fault. Remember what Brina says about us creating with our thoughts?"

"Yes, but what's that got to do with Luke possibly being ..." Vanna didn't want to finish that sentence.

"I was wishing him pain, harm."

"What? Whatever for?"

"You mean you don't know?"

"Maria you've lost me."

"He's having an affair with a young girl at his office."

"What?" Vanna wished she could stop saying *what*. "I mean that's absurd. He loves you."

"I don't know anything anymore, I ..." Completely drained of any color, Maria looked like she was about to pass out any second. Vanna pressed Brina's number on her own phone, and waited, reminding Maria all the

180

When the Universe Called

while to breathe deeply and to put her head between her knees. The last thing they needed was for Maria to faint.

"Brina's not answering. We'll have to go over to her place. I've got no clean clothes. They're still in the dryer."

Maria didn't respond.

"We have to go, Maria. The thing with Luke, I'm sure he'll turn up, and then you two can talk. I'm sure you've just got the wrong end of the stick." Vanna wasn't prone to giving false reassurance, but it was the only thing she could think of to say to get Maria moving again. She sensed the gears slowly moving in Maria's brain as she lifted her head and slowly stood up.

"Okay, I'm okay." Maria's breathing was labored, like she had to concentrate to get her lungs to work. "We'll stop by your place first so you can get some clothes."

"Oops, I forgot Morris is still in the bathroom. Hang on." Vanna ran to get him, grabbed her bag, and locked up the cottage. Getting in their cars, they drove separately to Vanna's cabin. Maria convinced Vanna—against Vanna's better judgment—that she was fit enough to drive.

Twenty minutes later they were at Brina's door. Smoke was coming out of the chimney, they could hear music faintly playing, and the door was ajar.

Vanna called out, "Brina, are you there?" No answer.

Maria tried: "Brina?"

"Maybe she's in the backyard," said Vanna. "Let's go round."

"I'm here." A disembodied voice called out to them. They looked around the yard, but couldn't see her.

Vanna peered through the back door. Still no one. "Brina?"

"Up here." Vanna and Maria looked up. Brina was sitting on her roof, staring down at them.

"What on …? What are you doing up there?" Vanna put her hand up to shade her eyes, blinking away the sunshine. Brina looked precariously balanced.

"Can you come down? We need your help. Kali's been kidnapped."

"I know."

"What do you mean, you know? Why didn't you call us then?" Maria's voice was shrill. Why are you just sitting up there on the roof?"

181

Maggie Denhearn

Vanna winced at Maria's tone. Brina didn't seem the sort of person who would take kindly to being spoken to that way. She slowly began climbing down the trellis from the roof, seemingly ignoring Maria's jibes. Vanna wondered how Brina was able to get on and off the roof with her dodgy hip, but she seemed to manage. Brina eyed her sternly, then her look lightened.

"I'm fine, honestly. I'm very careful."

"Sorry, I didn't mean to ..." Vanna stopped. It was more than disconcerting when Brina knew what she was thinking.

"Come in. I'll make some coffee." She turned to face Maria. "I needed to be able to see clearly. If we're going to get Kali back, I need to be able to see what we're up against. I can think better up there."

Vanna watched as Maria blushed, then followed Brina inside the cabin, while Vanna stood in the garden, staring at the sky.

Eagle Cove, Christmas Eve, 1999

It was late. Brina had meant to shut the coffee shop over an hour ago, but got sidetracked with puttering around. She wouldn't be opening for a few days, and she wanted to come back to reopen with everything in order.

The bell tinkled, signaling that someone had come through the door. Curious, she stepped out from behind the aubergine curtain. In the low lighting, the young man's similarity to Frost didn't strike her immediately, but as he walked up to the counter and she turned squarely to face him, she stopped, catching her breath. It was as though she had stepped back thirty-six years in time and Frost was standing in front of her. Shivers ran up her spine, and she had to steady herself on the counter, trying to maintain her composure. The scene of her last meeting with Frost flashed through her mind, leaving her giddy and slightly nauseated. This couldn't be happening.

The last few months, memories of him had started haunting her. She would wake from dreams certain he was standing over her bed, watching her. She would feel a cold breeze wash over her as she was sitting quietly in her living room, unable to shake the feeling that he had somehow just walked through her. The more she tried not to think about him, the more she was unable to focus on anything else. She tried to gather her thoughts into a

When the Universe Called

coherent sentence, but her throat was dry and she couldn't make a sound. The man was staring at her, a look of stupefaction on his face.

"You!" He spat the word out like a bullet. Instinctively, Brina's hand went to her hip, touching the scar that bore witness to Frost's attempt to kill her. She looked down; no red sparkling shoes. She paused, then looked up into what felt like Frost's eyes.

"You must be Frost's son." It was like witnessing someone rising from the dead.

"It's you!" His voice was hoarse, his face contorted as though he had eaten something bitter.

"You look like him. You could *be* him." Her voice was a whisper.

"I don't believe it!" He slumped down into a chair by the counter, jarring the table and nearly knocking over the vase of dried flowers that decorated it.

"I'll make us some tea." It was the only thing she could think of doing.

Brina tried to steady the shake in her voice and feign a calm she was far from feeling. Busying herself with boiling water and getting together a tray, she now and then cast a sideways glance at the man. He was tall, dark-haired, with striking blue eyes and strong features. He had a presence that would certainly command people's attention if he chose to exert his energy—just like Frost.

Tray in one hand, cane in the other, she came over to the table, slowly lowering herself into the chair beside his, minimizing the motion lest the slightest reverberation would cause him to explode.

"I'm right, aren't I? You're John Frost's son."

"Yes." The word was uttered through gritted teeth.

"You look just like him. I'm not sure how you know who I am, though."

Brina poured two cups of green tea, steam rising up between her and the man sitting opposite her. Glaring at her, he glanced at the tea but didn't pick up the cup.

"I suppose we could just sit here and stare at each other. Or you could tell me your name."

His fingers fondled the cup in the manner of someone admiring a butterfly they were about to crush.

"Luke, Luke Morgan."

183

Maggie Denhearn

Seemingly sensing her confusion, he continued, "I'm John Frost's son, but I use my mother's family name because my father and I are estranged."

"I'm sorry to hear that."

"Don't be."

"You clearly know who I am."

"You're the woman in the photo in my father's wallet, the one he seemed to value above my mother."

Brina hesitated. This didn't make sense.

"I don't follow."

"Really? You mean you had nothing to do with my mother's death, either?" Luke glared at her and Brina felt herself bridle, bracing herself to be attacked. She shouldn't be sitting down with him; it wasn't safe.

"I honestly don't know what you're talking about. When I last saw your father, your mother was very much alive and you weren't even born." She saw a look of disorientation cross his face, like he'd taken a wrong turn.

"But ... I ..."

"Please, drink some tea." He took a gulp. It was a special blend she used for calming nervousness.

"How about I tell you how I know your father? I think there might be some crossed wires here."

He nodded, suddenly mute, sipping from his cup.

"I was twenty-three. I'd just finished a pharmacology degree and got a position as an intern at your father's company. We had a brief affair. I'm not proud of that. I knew he was married. It didn't last long, I swear. Your mother was very much alive and well when it ended. You weren't born."

"When did it end?"

"August 1963."

Luke looked confused.

"I swear, I had nothing to do with your mother's death. I've had no contact with Frost since that summer. I've no idea about his life after that, or your mother's."

Luke took another gulp of the tea and poured himself more. Brina could see the muscles in his face visibly relax.

"And I don't understand why your father would be carrying a photo of me."

184

When the Universe Called

"He kept it in his wallet. I found it one time, and he went ballistic when he knew I'd seen it. He was more upset that I'd seen your picture than that I'd been going through his wallet."

"I don't know what to tell you." She didn't. She felt lightheaded and bewildered. "We parted on, let's just say, less than good terms."

"Well, clearly not that bad if he kept your photo." Luke's tone was derisory.

Brina hesitated. Would the truth help? "He shot me."

"What?"

"He shot me. That's why I walk with a cane. He shot me in the hip. He thinks I'm dead."

"But ... what?"

"I'm sorry, but I don't think I am who you have imagined me to be."

Brina wondered how long she should let the silence between them continue. She had gone from being shocked then afraid to now feeling acutely sorry for Luke. Being Frost's son could not be easy.

After a few minutes Luke spoke. "The photo, the one of you that he kept, was an old color Polaroid. It had ragged edges and white creases along the bottom. It was faded, but you could still see you smiling. You have the same ponytail, falling off your left shoulder. Your hair is a different color, so I didn't recognize you immediately, but something about your smile seemed familiar as I walked in. At first I couldn't place you. Then I saw the diamond shape birthmark on the back of your hand. ... He never kept a picture of my mother ..." He trailed off, staring down at his hands.

Brina wasn't sure how to respond. She'd thought she'd meant nothing to Frost. "I don't understand."

Luke looked up, staring at her intently. "Why would he shoot you if he loved you enough to keep your photo?"

"I don't know; I honestly don't know."

As he drank more, she sensed that the tranquilizing effect of the herbs she'd put in the tea was beginning to take hold.

"You don't seem shocked that he shot me, though. Don't you believe me?"

"I'm not sure. I'm not surprised that he might shoot someone. I know enough about him to know he's not a good man."

"You have your father's eyes."

Maggie Denhearn

"I hope that's all!" The timbre of his voice echoed both bitterness and grief.

"If it helps, there is more soul in yours."

As Luke's expression softened, she felt a visceral pain within. There were fleeting occasions when she had seen that look on Frost's face, when they had been alone and he had let his guard down. She had kept her feelings about Frost carefully locked in a box in her heart. Very occasionally she would take out the box, dust it off, and open it. She needed to feel the old pain from time to time to remind herself how she had got to where she was now—and why. It had been a while since she had laid those feelings out before her, like dried-up petals on white sand. Now here was Frost's son, and the box had flown open, scattering her emotions in all directions. She couldn't afford to crumble.

"Tell me about your mother."

An injured expression flashed across his face.

"She drowned; or so my father claims."

"You don't believe him."

"We were on the boat. I heard them arguing and went up on deck to see what was going on. I saw her fall into the water."

"How old were you?"

"Eight."

"That must have been awful." She reached out to take his hand, but he pulled it away. Seemingly embarrassed, he picked up his cup of tea.

"I'm sorry. I just … If it was an accident, why did you think I was responsible? I wasn't even there."

"I don't know, I just … after … I should have done something, called out, jumped in after her. … She fell over the rails. … He didn't do anything. He just watched. … I can't remember now if she fell or if he pushed her. … Then I found your photo a few months later. I don't know. I guess I somehow started to have a different memory, to dream that you were there on the deck too when she fell."

"I'm sorry about your mother. I really wasn't there, though. I promise."

He had tears in his eyes. Brina gazed at the young boy in the man's eyes, and felt the twinge of loss that rose like an invisible mist between them. She

When the Universe Called

wanted to reach out to him, but he was closing in on himself, collapsing inward.

"I see that now," he whispered. They remained staring at each other, both living their own versions of a story still unfolding, now metamorphosing into a completely different narrative.

"I just don't understand why he would shoot you," Luke said quietly.

"Because I wanted to end our affair."

"That can't be the real reason. It's not enough. I need you to tell me the truth." He stared at her, catching her with his gaze in a way that left her unable to look away.

"He's still your father." She blushed and picked up her cup.

"Was. We've not had contact for over ten years."

There was silence between them for a few moments. The music that had been playing in the background had stopped, and the inky blackness outside seemed to be deepening, wrapping around the coffee shop like it was about to swallow them up. "Why are you so sure he thinks you're dead?"

For nearly forty years she had remained silent. No one in Eagle Cove knew her story. The voice inside her chided her, cajoled her to break her silence. It was time.

"He thought he'd shot and killed me, that I was dead. There was a fake funeral for me. I changed my name."

"How did you manage that?"

"Someone found me right after I was shot. He got me away and protected me."

Brina regarded this stranger as she told him the secret she had never told anyone in her entire life. In doing so, she was risking her life, perhaps even signing her own death warrant, yet she couldn't help herself. He had already discovered her anyway. His walking through the coffee shop door had changed her life, regardless of what she did or didn't say.

"I still don't get it, though. Why would he shoot you for just wanting to end a love affair?"

Brina thought for a moment, eyeing him steadily.

"Because of what I'd found out about his work." She stared at him, looking for the slightest hint that Luke already knew. "Because I found out that FPH was illegally testing its drugs on vulnerable people, some of whom

Maggie Denhearn

died. The man who helped me, his sister, died in one of FPH's drug trials."
The expression on Luke's face told her all she needed to know.

"That can't be true! Surely you're wrong!"

"I wish I were. I went to the police and someone there betrayed me and told Frost, then covered the whole thing up."

"But haven't you tried to do something, anything, to stop him?"

"He's a powerful man with many influential friends. He's formed the Consortium."

"The what?"

"The Consortium. It's a group of rich and prominent individuals. They all get a cut of whatever FPH is selling, so long as they turn a blind eye to what the company does to bring its drugs to market. Pharmaceuticals are big business. I've been following Frost all my life, waiting for an opportunity to stop him." Brina checked herself, pouring them both more tea. She'd said enough. Luke remained quiet, his expression dark. They sat in silence for almost ten minutes, the ticking of the clock on the wall whirring like Brina's thoughts.

"He has to be stopped. People are dying. There's a homeless shelter in Vancouver where some of his victims end up. I'll take you there; show you. It's true ... I just don't know how to stop it."

Carefully, Luke put his cup back on the table, his hand shaking. Staring directly at her, he said, "I'll help you. I'll help you bring down this Consortium. And my father."

CHAPTER 15

WEDNESDAY MORNING, APRIL 16, 2014

"Sort it, Heeley, or I'll sort you!" Bailey slammed the phone down. "Of all the incompetent, stupid, idiotic …" She stopped mid rant as the phone rang again.

"What? … Oh, sorry, my apologies, I was expecting a call from someone else." Her violent tone turned to obsequious apology. "Of course, of course. I'll check into that for you, Minister. My apologies again … Yes, yes, by the end of the day."

She put the receiver down and let her head fall into her hands. Breathing in deeply, she sighed, then leaned back in her chair, her eyes still closed. She needed to stay calm. Everything would work out eventually; these were just minor bumps in the road. As soon as she was head of the Consortium, Heeley would no longer be in their employ. He had clearly outlived his usefulness. As head, she would not allow the eminent people of the Consortium to have their work jeopardized by such an imbecile.

How on earth had Heeley's men managed to get the two brothers mixed up? And if that wasn't bad enough, to kill one of them rather than bringing him in, and to let the other one escape? Then for Heeley to have the gall to lie to her on the phone and say he wasn't involved. Did he really think her that naïve? As for the forest fire, that was so obviously arson. She wasn't fooled.

Bailey was no longer sure which twin was which and who exactly was still breathing, although it didn't really matter. The one remaining brother needed to be brought in alive so they could find out just how deeply their

Maggie Denhearn

organization had been penetrated and who else was involved. Then they would dispose of him. Bailey was quite prepared to resort to unorthodox methods if that's what it took to get the information they needed. Not that she would engage in such behavior herself. She had people who would do that for her, and they did not include Heeley.

Thus far she had managed to use their contacts within the police to mitigate the damage, but this was hardly the time for the Consortium to get any unwanted publicity. There was always some unruly journalist who couldn't be bought off, wanting to gain fame and glory as a whistleblower. Two more weeks and Bill 267 would be law, and then nothing could stop them. Until then, they needed to tread particularly carefully. It was somewhat disconcerting that the minister had called her. Surely he should have called Frost? He was still head of FPH, after all. If anyone could get information regarding the latest developments with Torporo, it would be him. Opening her eyes, she reached across and started dialing.

"Rawley, It's me. Have you heard from Frost? ... No, I don't want to call him. ... Because, well, I just thought I'd see if you had. ... No, everything is fine; don't worry. I'll be in touch."

Judge Rawley was as useless as ever. She should have just called Darcy. His secretary was much more use than he ever was. Tapping a pencil on the desk, she tried to think. She really didn't want to speak to Frost, not after what had just happened with Luke. Even she had been somewhat discombobulated by hearing the news on the radio. She picked up the phone again.

"Darcy, my dear, I wonder if you could be so kind as to do me a favor? It's rather early in the morning to be disturbing Mr. Frost, particularly after such devastating news about his son. ... So you heard the news too. ... Yes, I know. Anyway, I need to know what the latest is regarding Torporo. The minister needs the information before Friday. Would you be a dear and see what you can find out? ... Thank you, much appreciated."

Bailey leaned back in her expensive leather chair and stared out of her office window at the early morning sky. If the security of the Consortium was truly under threat, she had no doubt that Brina was somehow involved. Forget what Frost had said. It was time to deal with her, and permanently this time.

*   *   *   *

When the Universe Called

"Well, that explains the other body, then!" Maria felt a wave of relief wash over her as Brina filled them in on what had happened with Iris. She almost wanted to laugh at the irony of it all, but caught herself in time. Relief turned quickly to sadness for her friend. How desperate Iris must have been. Maria had no idea that Iris's home life was that bad. Iris never talked much about Trevor when they were running together; Maria realized that it had never occurred to her to ask either. How odd that she could know so much about her friends and yet, apparently, so little. It did explain all those times that Iris didn't come running for a few weeks at a time. Trying to hide the cuts and bruises? Why hadn't Iris told them?

Vanna looked dismayed, but said nothing.

"Iris needs our support now more than ever." Brina was silent for a few moments before continuing. "And there's still Kali to find. Maria, has she texted back yet?"

Maria got out her phone and checked. Nothing. She sent Kali another text in the vague hope that her phone was working again. This was the third text she'd not responded to.

"Well?" Brina's eyes betrayed her worry.

"She's not answering."

Brina nodded, thoughtfully.

"Should we try and drive around to see if we can find her? We need to be doing something. We could ..." Maria looked at Vanna, who had started moving around as though she had something itchy on her back, then back to Brina to see what she thought.

Brina pondered this for a moment. "It's better than just sitting here. Action is important. Okay, let's go. Let's pick up Iris on the way. And let's go in my truck." Within twenty minutes they were outside Iris's house. As they pulled up, she was waiting on the stoop.

Iris got in the back seat of Brina's truck, next to Vanna. Maria turned to the back to greet her.

"Hi. You okay? I mean, not okay, I mean ..." Maria started to stutter and felt herself redden. In all her years of working in PR she had never felt quite so tongue-tied.

"So you've heard."

191

Maggie Denhearn

"I had to tell them," said Brina. "No one will say anything." Maria and Vanna both nodded. Vanna seemed to be carefully avoiding Iris's gaze, looking like a deer caught in the headlights. What must she think of the people on the Island?

"I'm not proud of what I did." Iris looked defeated. No one spoke. Maria was still in shock. And saying "he deserved it" didn't seem quite appropriate somehow, even though Maria thought that he did.

"I got your text," said Iris to Brina, like she was trying to push back the silence. "Not sure what I can do to help, but I'll come along."

"We think Kali's somewhere in Friendship Bay, or at least in that area." Maria offered. "That's what it sounds like from what she said when we last heard from her. We need to look out for a blue van, license plate 849 V or something along those lines."

"What can we do if we do find her?" Vanna sounded somewhat dispirited.

"Kali didn't mention anything about them having guns, and there's only two of them and four of us."

"Two that we know of. It's unlikely they're working alone. I'm really not convinced this is a good idea."

"Well, what else do you suggest? We can't just leave her. And no, Vanna, we're not calling the police."

"Okay, okay. I just think we need to be strategic about this. If we find the van and the house, we probably shouldn't just waltz in there. We should reconnoiter the place first and then come up with a plan that's not going to land all of us in trouble."

"Okay, so let's …"

Brina's mind wandered as she drove and the others talked strategy. Images flooded her mind, and she was trying to make sense of them. She could see Kali, but the image was too dark to give any distinguishing details. It was extremely frustrating that she was unable to tune in to see more. It didn't bode well. Kali was either unconsciously creating a block so Brina couldn't see, or she was unconscious—or worse.

"We need to focus hard on finding Kali."

"We are, Brina, that's what why we're driving around here, isn't it?"

When the Universe Called

Brina could hear the irritation in Maria's voice, but she didn't rise to it. They had talked last night. She knew Maria was still angry with her, believing that she knew more than she was telling her. All she had been able to do was to reassure her that Luke was not having an affair. It was up to Luke to explain what was actually going on. Brina couldn't interfere with that.

"I know," said Brina, "but I mean really focus: your mind, your energy. Imagine finding Kali and how you will feel when you do."

"Okaaay"

"I know you think what I'm saying doesn't make any sense, Maria, but humor me. It can't hurt, can it? And if I'm right, it could very possibly help."

"Well, this is Friendship Bay, and you say we're looking for a road on the right?" said Iris quietly. "Let's try the one coming up."

Brina flicked the indicator and they pulled onto a side road. She drove slowly so the others could scan either side of the lane, looking for a blue van in a driveway or a house that matched the brief description Kali had given. No luck.

They turned round and got back onto the main highway. Pulling into the next right turn, they went through the same routine. When they were almost to the other side of Friendship Bay, they found another road on the right. They were nearly at the end of it and starting to lose hope when there it was up ahead: a dark blue van, with the license plate 849 V2X, parked in a driveway on the left. They pulled up on the opposite side of the lane, fifty meters back from the low-slung, dilapidated house in front of which the van was parked. Brina killed the engine and closed her eyes. She felt the others looking at each other, wondering quite what to do, as they waited for her.

Vanna broke the silence; "I don't think it's a good idea for us to go charging into the house. We don't know how many people are in there or whether they're armed. We should sit tight and wait. With any luck, they might leave. Then we can go and get Kali. If they start to take her with them, we'll see and be able to follow them."

"Couldn't one of us go to the house and pretend we're selling something, just to check things out?" suggested Maria.

"Like what? What would anyone sell door-to-door around here?"

"We could pretend we're Jehovah's Witnesses," said Iris.

Maggie Denhearn

"Actually, that's not such a bad idea. It's an entirely plausible reason for knocking at the door," mused Maria.

"My grandmother converted to being a Jehovah's Witness when she was seventy-five," explained Iris. "I do remember some of the things she told me about what she believed, although I doubt they'll be asking us to come in if we've got the right house, and they've got Kali stashed somewhere. And if it's the wrong house, well, we'll figure something out."

"So which of us should go?" The tone of Vanna's voice clearly indicated that she was hoping she wouldn't be asked to go.

"Okay, let's try it. I think Iris and I should go," Brina said, finally opening her eyes. "Maria, you turn the truck around so we can make a quick getaway if we need to. Vanna, you stay with Maria." Vanna looked relieved. Brina climbed out of the truck with Iris and they slowly made their way to the house.

They were nearly at the front door.

"Which of us should speak first?" Iris looked to Brina for guidance.

"You, Iris. You can do this." Brina winked at her.

They knocked at the door. There was no answer and no sign of life. The blinds were firmly drawn at all of the front windows, like tightly-shut eyes, and not a sound emanated from the house. They knocked again, the sound hollow, echoing, as though the whole building was empty.

Brina leaned heavily on her cane. She felt stiff today, more than usual. The climb onto her roof was getting harder these days and leaving her more exhausted, but it wasn't just that. Her body was speaking to her more of late, and she didn't like the messages she was getting. She watched a cabbage butterfly skip around the wild flowers that were growing over the pathway leading up to where they were. It was early in the season for butterflies. It was a sign: transformation; metamorphosis; evolution. She felt the tension in her hip suddenly ease. This was a good sign; a very good sign. They were about to get a big stroke of luck.

"Let's try one more time." They knocked again. They were just turning around to leave when they heard the clatter of someone grabbing keys from a table and unlocking the door. A tall, lanky man wearing a shiny suit and a hideous tie greeted them disdainfully. Iris froze, unable to speak.

"Yes? What do you want?" He sounded irritated.

When the Universe Called

Iris took a deep breath. "How are you today?"

"What do you want?"

"We're in your neighborhood sharing some good news from the Bible. May I ask: Who do you believe Jesus was?"

They could hear a woman's voice from inside the house calling, "Who's at the door?" The young man turned around and yelled, "No one," then turned back to Brina and Iris.

"Get lost!" He slammed the door shut.

At least he tried. Brina stuck her cane out. Iris gasped. The young man turned an odd shade of puce and seemed about to hurl angry abuse but stopped. Brina scrutinized him, and that seemed to render him speechless.

"Young man. I'm feeling a little faint. May I prevail upon you to bring me a chair and a glass of water? I'm sure you don't mind helping a frail old lady." She knew she didn't look like she was remotely about to keel over or the least bit frail, but he obeyed her speechlessly. Brina had one foot over the threshold and was leaning on her cane, so he just pushed the door as far closed as he could.

"What are you doing?" whispered Iris anxiously. "Are you trying to get us locked up too?"

"It'll be fine." She winked at Iris again, eminently pleased with herself. A few moments elapsed, then the young man returned with a glass of water and a dining room chair, which he placed right next to the door, as close to the outside as he could manage without forcibly pushing Brina back over the stoop. It could not have been more obvious that he had no desire to let them inside. Brina estimated that he was in his late teens, early twenties, still exhibiting the teenage awkwardness and last throes of acne as his body tried to push him valiantly toward manhood.

"Thank you; you're a dear." Brina slumped theatrically onto the chair and gave a big sigh.

Turning to Iris, she said, "So sorry, Matilda, I'm just having one of my funny turns. You know how I get sometimes. I'm sure I'll be right as rain in a few moments, thanks to this kind young man." Brina flashed Iris a look as she could see she was trying to stop herself from shaking nervously.

Fortunately, the man seemed too caught up in his own discomfort to notice. He was shifting from one foot to the other, carefully studying the

195

Maggie Denhearn

hall carpet, a hideous seventies creation, dirty and threadbare, with a large, ugly, green and purple pattern that looked more like someone had vomited on it than actually designed it. He was obviously unsure how to get them to leave. It was also rather obvious that if he was a hit man or some hired thug, it was a new appointment and he wasn't very good at it.

"Can I get you anything … Miranda?" Iris started to play along.

"Thank you dear, I'll be fine in a little while. Although …" Brina glanced up slyly. "My dear … what did you say your name was?"

"I didn't …" he said, coughing. "Peter."

"Peter. That's a nice name. Did you know that means rock or stone?"

"No, I didn't." Peter continued to shift from one foot to the other like he had an itch he couldn't scratch, still staring at the dirt holding the threads of the carpet together. He was clearly hoping the carpet would swallow him up.

"So, Peter, do you go to church?"

"Erm …"

"That's okay dear, I know many of your generation think it's not relevant to you. But … how you live your life, the thoughts you think, they're important."

Peter glanced up long enough for Brina to see him roll his eyes, then he looked down again, as though if he caught her eye, he would turn to stone. Good, he was worried.

"So you see, Peter, it's something for you to consider …" Silence.

"And it's also important to remember that everything we do has an effect. You've heard of cause and effect, I presume?" Brina wasn't sure that she was particularly convincing as a Jehovah's Witness, but it was obvious Peter was none the wiser.

"Cause and effect—for every action there's a reaction. So you see, when you took Kali, there was bound to be a reaction."

Finally that got Peter's attention. He reddened, unable to hide his dismay. Brina met his gaze directly and smiled confidently. Iris gulped loudly.

"So you're … not … I thought you were Jehovah's Witnesses."

"No, we're not. We just want Kali. And if you'd kindly hand her over, we can all get on with our day. I believe she's in the shed at the end of the garden. I'm sure you've taken good care of her, but it's time for us to take her home."

When the Universe Called

Peter paused. He seemed to be weighing his options, although with a look of uncertainty that implied he probably didn't have many.

"I don't know what you're talking about. I think you need to go." Peter tried to slip back into thug mode, but Brina stared straight at him, holding his gaze and rooting him to the spot.

"Yes, you do. And we could argue about this all day, but I'm sure you have better things to be doing. I know we do. And by the way, Andy's on a trip somewhere or other. You'll have to wait until he gets back, although no doubt he's already heard about all of this and is long gone by now."

"We're not after anyone," he started to blurt out, then stopped himself. "What do you know?" He was angry now.

"Nothing, except that you've taken it into your head to abduct Kali."

"I, we haven't … Okay, say that's true, and I'm not saying it is. What's to stop us taking you two as well?" Brina tried not to smile at his attempts to sound menacing. There was no point in being unduly antagonistic, and it was evident that Peter was somewhat of a novice kidnapper. She was actually starting to feel a little sorry for him.

"What would you do with two old dears like us? You wouldn't gain anything, and if more people go missing, the more you will raise suspicion."

"Why didn't you go to the police if you're so sure we have … this Kali?"

"No one likes to involve the police. It just gets too complicated. You seem very reasonable, Peter. I'm sure we can work this out."

"Hang on." He went into the back room.

"What on earth are you doing?" hissed Iris. "Are you trying to get us killed?"

"It's fine. No one's going to get killed."

"You don't know that."

"No, I don't. But I'm fairly sure."

"Fairly sure? *Fairly sure?*"

Brina put her hand on Iris's arm.

"My dear, trust me. It'll be fine. Just breathe."

They waited. They could hear muffled voices in the back room. Then Peter reappeared. Brina didn't like the expression on his face. He looked far too smug.

Maggie Denhearn

*   *   *   *

"They've been gone an awfully long time." Vanna turned to Maria.

"Ten minutes."

"It feels longer."

Maria continued to stare out of the windshield. "We'll give them another five minutes."

"And then what?"

"I'll think of something!"

Vanna hoped she would, as she had no idea what they should do if Iris and Brina didn't come back. It felt like people were disappearing left, right, and center. The local population decimated in the space of a few days. She didn't know how Maria could be so calm about things.

"Aren't you worried?"

"What?" Maria looked across at her.

"Aren't you worried?"

"Of course. But forgive me for not leaping up and down or tearing my hair out." Vanna sighed, trying to ignore her own ever-increasing angst. She watched the minutes roll over on her phone.

"It's been five minutes now."

"I know." Maria exhaled loudly. "I guess we'll have to go over there too. Do you have any hair spray or anything like that?"

"Do I look like I use hair spray?" Vanna rummaged around in her bag. "Sorry. No, hang on. I do have some aromatherapy calming spritzer though. And let me see, I have this dog spray which is supposed to make dogs less itchy and get rid of fleas. It's a bit rancid smelling."

"That'll do. Hope your aim's good. Bring both. I've got some hair spray. Aim at the eyes and spray hard."

"They're pump sprays."

"They would be. Okay, well just get them pumping before you spray then. Unless you've got anything else we can use as a weapon."

"Not really. Hang on. What about that thing you use to change tires? Reckon Brina has one of those?"

When the Universe Called

"The tire iron? Good idea." They got out of the truck, and Maria opened the back passenger door, feeling underneath the seat. She pulled out the tire iron. Vanna looked at her dubiously.

"Would you actually use that?" Vanna suddenly wished she'd not made that suggestion.

"Well, as a last resort. We have to get the thugs before they get us. Aim for the eyes with the sprays. And when they're reeling, sharp knee to the groin. The tire iron can be backup if the sprays don't work. How good are you at tying knots?"

"Rubbish."

"Give me your scarf. Your job, keep kicking while they're down, and I'll try to make sure they're tied up long enough to something so we can get the others out of there." Vanna couldn't help thinking that Maria sounded like she'd done this before.

"Have you … how do you know this stuff?"

"Self-defense class at university. Didn't you ever do one?" Vanna hadn't and was beginning to wish she had.

They strode toward the house, and as they got closer, Vanna saw Brina sitting on a chair inside the doorway and Iris standing outside, looking around awkwardly. Iris spotted them coming. She shrugged her shoulders at them, palms up, trying to indicate that she had no idea what was going on. A man appeared in the hallway, a young, greasy-looking man. He looked across and saw Vanna and Maria. He was about to shout when Brina raised her cane and smacked him over the head with the handle. He hit the floor, no time to utter a sound.

Brina got up and signaled to Maria and Vanna to go around to the side of the house. Brina and Iris went inside as Vanna and Maria started running. There was the sound of yelling and some shuffling, then another thud. By the time Vanna was around the back of the house, Iris was rushing out of the back door. There it was: a shed at the bottom of the garden. Vanna tried the door. It was bolted from the outside, but the padlock hadn't been closed. Vanna pulled back the locks and opened the door. She gasped. Kali was lying motionless in a chair, with her face drained of all color. She looked dead.

"Kali, Kali!" Maria rushed in and started shaking Kali, but she didn't respond. "Kali!"

199

Maggie Denhearn

For a moment Vanna couldn't move, then she grabbed Kali's wrist, feeling around the veins, desperate for any sign of life. There it was—feeble, but there—a slow, gentle thump.

"She's alive, but barely. We need to get her out of here."

"Okay, you get her under one shoulder and I'll take the other. Iris, you get Brina back to the truck. Quickly," ordered Maria.

Just as they made it to the truck, Vanna turned back to see Peter propping himself up in the doorway, looking dazed and rubbing his head. They piled quickly into the truck, which lurched forward when Brina slammed her foot down hard on the accelerator.

"We'd better all go back to my place," said Brina calmly. "It's harder to find. I doubt we have much time before they come looking again." No one said anything. Kali lay across Maria and Vanna in the back, a dead weight, still unconscious. Whether they had tried to kill her or had just drugged her, either way, as far as Vanna could tell, she didn't look good. Her breathing was shallow, barely audible.

"She's not doing well." Vanna ran her fingers through Kali's hair. It was odd that she looked so peaceful. She would have expected her to look different somehow. She was trying to remain positive, but right now it was a struggle.

*   *   *   *

"Lay her down on the sofa and prop her head up on one of those cushions." Brina directed Maria and Vanna as together they carried Kali into Brina's cabin. Kali still hadn't regained consciousness. Whatever they had given her, it had truly knocked her out. Vanna was sure now that if they had been trying to kill her, she probably would already have been dead.

"I'll brew up some herbal tea. I think I know what'll help her." Brina flicked through one of her many old and moth-eaten books that remained strewn around her kitchen table, and started to mix together various herbs and tinctures. She lit the stove to boil some water and began slowly adding different strange-looking ingredients. The liquid began to give off a pungent vapor as it started to simmer gently, turning into a rich, purple viscous liquid. Vanna wasn't convinced that anything that color could help.

When the Universe Called

"How's she going to drink it if she's still unconscious?" Maria eyed the concoction with skepticism. "I'll put some coffee on for the rest of us."

"She'll come around eventually, but she'll be woozy. This'll help when she does." Brina took out a cold compress, soaked it in camphor, and placed it gently on Kali's forehead. They waited. Talking about the weather and making coffee and something to eat was a distraction from the larger issues they were all avoiding.

"I'm not sorry he's dead … Trevor, I mean. I can't be." Vanna stared wide-eyed at Iris. She couldn't help thinking that some elephants are best left sitting quietly in the corner of a room so everyone can dutifully ignore their presence. The others gazed at Iris, apparently also not knowing quite how to respond. "I just wish it hadn't been like that. I wanted him out of my life, that's all I wanted. I kept praying he'd be gone. And now look where it's got me."

"We need to leave," said Brina abruptly, already putting a few things into various baskets.

"What? Why?" Vanna stared at Brina. Her behavior was so brusque sometimes, disconcerting.

"They'll find this place soon enough, whoever 'they' are. We'll go to my cabin in the mountains."

"You have a cabin in the mountains?" Maria's voice sounded oddly high-pitched. "In all the time we've known each other, not once have you ever mentioned that you have another place!"

"I know. I needed it to be a secret. I knew one day I might need it. I'll keep an eye on Kali. You all go and get a few things that you need. Bring any food you have. And yes, Vanna, bring Morris. But be quick. Not more than a couple of hours. If for any reason I'm not here when you get back, call my cell. I'll give you directions how to get there. And stick together."

Eagle Cove, full moon—Saturday, September 17, 2005

Luke wandered into the Kavama and slumped down into his usual chair. He wasn't quite sure why he always sat in exactly the same place, but somehow he gravitated to its worn velour and odd contours. And it always

Maggie Denhearn

seemed to be empty whenever he entered the coffee shop. He didn't need to say what he wanted to drink. Brina saw him enter and immediately started preparing her proprietary green tea blend, which he found so soothing. Given the usual seriousness of their conversations, he invariably needed something to make him feel better.

"So?"

"Don't you ever get tired, Brina? Tired of hiding, of fighting?"

"There are moments for sure, but I don't let myself dwell on them. There's too much at stake. Why do you ask?"

"I don't know. I'm just tired. I hate lying to Maria ... and right now I don't feel like we're getting anywhere."

"You know you're only trying to protect her. The less she knows, the less anything can be used against her."

"I know."

"But there's something else, isn't there?" Brina paused, closed her eyes, then opened them abruptly. "Oh my god. FPH is starting the trial of a new drug!"

Luke gaped at her. "How on earth did you know that? I've only just found out. That's what I was coming to tell you!"

Luke had never seen Brina blush before. "What?"

"Please don't freak out or get angry."

"You're worrying me now. What is it?"

Brina hesitated, "I read your mind."

"Huh?"

"I can't always do it, only if I'm close to someone and they're open to me."

It was Luke's turn to blush.

"How long have you been reading my mind?!"

"Not long, I don't think. It's not intentional. If your guard is down and you're feeling strong emotions, it's like you're speaking out loud."

"That's really kind of creepy."

"Look, that's not the point right now. Tell me about this new drug."

Luke was about to express further indignation about the invasion of his mind and thought better of it. Apparently she already knew what he was thinking.

When the Universe Called

"It's called Torporo. According to Darcy, FPH is just starting preclinical testing."

"What's it for?"

"Allegedly anxiety and depression. But here's the thing. A version of Torporo has already been tested unofficially in the UK under a different drug name. I can't remember offhand what it used to be called. Originally it *was* created as an anti-depressant, but one of the side effects of the original formula was found to be extreme depersonalization."

"What's depersonalization?"

"It's when people feel disconnected from their body or physical reality. They feel detached from their thoughts and feelings, almost like having an out of body experience. It can lead to depression, anxiety, or self-harm—all the things the drug is supposed to be treating. That's not to mention the physical symptoms."

"So why would they bother continuing with it?"

"Well, here's the thing. Somehow the government got wind of this. Because of the side effect of depersonalization, they authorized an unofficial trial by the drug company on minor convicted criminals. In doing the follow-up study of the lifestyles of these criminals as part of a broader study on recidivism, they found out that those who were given the drug didn't engage in their communities. Part of identifying quantitative data to show levels of engagement was measuring participation in voting in local and national elections. Those who were given the drug didn't vote, even those who had done so previously and consistently, whereas minor criminals who were given supports that didn't involve medication were more likely to take an active part in their community, and did engage in civic actions like voting."

Luke could see Brina wasn't quite following.

"Bear with me. The British government then authorized another study, again secretly, of course, where they gave this drug—Torporo, as it later became known, to people with *any* history of antisocial behavior, people who hadn't been convicted of anything criminal, but who might have got an ASBO—an antisocial behavior order for civil offenses. While the drug did reduce reoffending, it again brought down the number of people voting."

"Really? How did they get away with this? And how come you know?"

"Government backing from both major political parties, backhanders to the pharmaceutical company, the drug reps, and the GPs, the doctors. ASBOs were introduced in 1998, but some people didn't think this was far-reaching enough. The findings of these unofficial studies played right into their hands. Enter a pharmaceutical company, the one which had been doing the unofficial testing all along, suddenly offering a wonder drug to reduce crime. And all with government backing. Guess who?"

Brina shook her head. "No idea. Go on."

"A subsidiary of FPH known as DUCO Health. And get this. As far as I can tell, officially the rest of the Consortium doesn't know about it: DUCO Health *or* Torporo. Nothing shows up in any documentation. Bailey doesn't even know about it."

"How's that even possible?"

"Frost somehow managed to hide everything from anyone else at FPH. I'm still trying to figure out how. Anyway, the British government, whichever party was in power, didn't matter as politicians on both sides had seen the potential benefits and invested in DUCO Health. Once the government saw the effects of the drug and how they could use it to their advantage to reduce the number of people they didn't want voting, they went ahead with manufacturing Torporo. DUCO Health was a great option as a Canadian company because there were all kinds of things they could then cover up. Any future backlash and they could blame a foreign company."

"So how on earth did you find out about all of this?"

"My father asked me personally to handle the legal aspect of transferring the rights to Torporo, and all the intellectual property associated with it, from DUCO Health to FPH. I was asking him various questions, and he was even more cagey than usual. So I told him I'd just ask Bailey. He got weird, and I realized he was hiding something from her, which seemed very strange. In the end, he had to tell me what I needed to know because, if I'd asked Bailey, that would have raised suspicion, and this was something he didn't want even her to know about."

Luke continued. "Then I did a bit more digging. If you look at the statistics for voter turnout in the seventies, under Mrs. Thatcher, you can see the decline. That's when the government was initially secretly testing this drug. They've been tweaking and testing the drug for decades, ever since

When the Universe Called

they found a direct correlation between lower voting and taking the drug. There was a minimal upturn in voting around the end of the eighties, and that's when they changed the formula slightly.

"They've now managed to make it even more potent. In 2001, only 58 percent of the entire British population turned out to vote compared with 84 percent in 1950. That's because they widened who was being given the drug. Anyone deemed to have any kind of mental disorder that the pharmaceutical companies could suggest it would allegedly help, anyone they could bribe or coerce doctors to give it to. And guess who was left going to the polls? Those most likely to vote conservative. The rates of voting are on their way back up again now, but only slightly. That's because DUCO Health keeps adjusting the formula. They keep trying different ingredients because of other side effects that they can't get rid of.

"With each new iteration, there have been problems with side effects, such as heart attack, suicidal ideation, and liver failure. The drug company pulls it before there is conclusive evidence that only Torporo could be the cause rather than anything else. They've been deliberately targeting vulnerable populations who are less likely to be able to stand up for themselves. And since the drug company runs its own investigations, there's a lot they can cover up."

"But why would the UK government try and drug its own people?"

"Power. Then money. As I said, many government ministers from both main parties have financial interests in DUCO Health. And both parties have also figured out that the fewer people who vote, the more likely whoever is in power will stay that way. They're willing to take the risk even if it could benefit the other party because of how much they stand to win."

"But that means they must be drugging millions of people," said Brina. "I don't understand how the government could manage that. That's a huge conspiracy. How on earth would they be able to keep that a secret?"

"MI5. MI5 can keep anything secret. And the country has a national health service, the NHS. If a drug is approved, no one questions it. The doctors just give it out. Up until now, there's been no central computer system for holding everyone's medical records. If a doctor has a few patients who die while taking Torporo, there are usually other contraindications that

205

Maggie Denhearn

could equally have been the cause. The drug company meanwhile has been keeping a check. Hence the various versions of the drug."

"So why would Frost be pulling Torporo out of DUCO Health and into FPH? Has the UK government banned Torporo?"

"Not exactly, as far as I can tell. In trying to handle the legal sale of Torporo to FPH, I discovered a guy who I went to university with, and who has been a lawyer in the UK the last ten years. He's helping bring a class action suit against DUCO Health by a group of doctors who have realized the dangers of the drug and how the company has been covering them up. He told me that the drug company is pretending to 'give up' on Torporo by selling the rights to it to FPH. But he knows Frost owns both companies. My father is just bringing it all back to Canada because of this class action suit. Only thing is, the main guy who started the class action died in a skiing accident a month ago, and my friend has been missing two weeks now. I can't get hold of him—no one can."

"So let me get this straight. FPH has actually been behind Torporo for years and is going to take over trialing it here in Canada. Meanwhile, MI5 is involved?"

"Yes."

"And are you thinking that FPH will try to get the Canadian government involved too?"

"Yes! What better way of keeping power than to stop people voting? And to convince law abiding citizens that their safety depends on drugging anyone considered vaguely antisocial?"

"But surely they'd have to drug more than the criminals or the antisocial?"

"Exactly. They managed it in the UK. So where does it stop? They'll find a way, I'm sure of it. Think about it. Think of the compulsory sterilizations in the US. Canada too. Eugenics. If that was possible and they got away with it, why not this?"

CHAPTER 16

WEDNESDAY EVENING, APRIL 16, 2014

K ali opened her eyes. Her head felt like it was going to explode, and her
mouth had the taste and texture of the bottom of a birdcage. She felt
dreadful. This had to be the mother of all hangovers. She had no idea where
she was or what had happened. Her mind tried to figure out what day it
was, but was too crowded with a thick soupy fog to be able to think clearly.
Thoughts popped in and out of her brain like slow-moving pinballs moving
through sludge. Staring at the ceiling, it slowly dawned on her that it wasn't
one she recognized. Wooden beams, dusty and covered in cobwebs, stared
back at her. She tried to move her neck and winced. She must have been
sleeping awkwardly. As she tried to sit up she became aware that she wasn't
alone. Brina was sitting on a chair nearby, staring intently at her.

"Don't move. You'll be fine. You'll just feel a little woozy for a while."

"Woozy? Like crap you mean." Kali's throat felt raspy, like sandpaper.
Brina put a glass of cool water to Kali's lips and she tried to drink. She barely
had the energy to raise her hand to steady the glass.

"You're safe, in case you're wondering."

"Safe?"

"You don't remember?"

Kali tried again to think. No, she had absolutely no idea what was going
on. She vaguely remembered being in the shower, then a song playing on
the radio. Nothing else.

"No … I'm guessing it involved too much wine, though."

Maggie Denhearn

"Not exactly. Don't worry. We'll talk about it later. Just rest." Kali lay back and closed her eyes. Her head was throbbing. She really needed to stop drinking.

*   *   *   *

Brina went out on to the deck. A fresh, cool breeze was blowing in from the west. It was a clear bright evening, and the sun was just about setting over the ocean. High up as they were, the mountains continued to rise behind the cabin that was nestled in the crook of some rocks. The smoke rising up from the chimney dissipated by the time it reached the treetops. It would be impossible for anyone to know they were here unless they knew exactly where to look. This was Brina's secret place. It wasn't far from Eagle Cove, but the route was sufficiently convoluted and involved enough dirt tracks that no one would have thought of coming here. It was an old loggers' cabin, long forgotten.

Brina and Luke had spent the last fifteen years trying to find ways to bring down the Consortium. She wasn't foolish enough to think that she was somehow immune from their machinations. She'd known that one day she would need a place to hide. She'd been wracking her brains where the best place might be. Then one night she had a vivid dream of traveling along twisting and turning roads through the woods. She wrote the dream down when she woke up. It was more out of fun that she decided to follow the directions of her imagination. They brought her to this place: a two-story, four-room cabin. It was peculiarly large, given where it was hidden, probably built in the nineteenth century—she wasn't sure. It took her years to renovate it, doing what she could on her own. Luke and Noah helped with what she couldn't manage alone. Other than her, they were the only ones who had come here until now. Vanna, Iris, and Maria were sitting on the sofa outside on the deck, nursing mugs of mead and quietly talking.

"She's come round," said Brina.

"Thank goodness!" Vanna looked like she might cry with relief.

"She'll be okay. She'll just need time to rest." Brina sat down next to them, staring off into the distance.

*   *   *   *

Maria was glad to be finally sitting down. Somehow or other, they'd all managed to get away from Eagle Cove before the police or anyone else caught up with them. They'd even managed to swing by Kali's place and put a few things in a bag for her too. Maria wasn't sure whether she'd done the right thing. Perhaps she should have stayed behind to do the identification for the police, go through the motions. Brina had convinced her that it could be dangerous. She couldn't quite see how, but she had been so convincing that she'd gone along with it. It was strange that Brina should be so insistent sometimes. She glanced over at Iris, who was staring into space. At least she wasn't her. Brina seemed engrossed in watching the moonrise in the dusky sky.

"What'll we do now?" Vanna asked. Maria couldn't think about that now, and no one else answered either. Maria still hadn't heard from Luke. The cell reception where they were was intermittent at best, but she had left her phone in the one reliable spot, just in case he should decide to call or to text her a message. He might not be dead in the forest, but something was very clearly up, and Brina would not tell her anything more. She wasn't totally convinced that Brina was right about Luke, yet she was right about most things, and Maria didn't think she was lying. There was definitely something going on between Luke and Charlotte, she was convinced, but if they weren't lovers, then what?

*　*　*　*

Brina busied herself making dinner while the others got themselves settled. Although she didn't do it often, she liked cooking for other people. The kitchen was small, almost an add-on to the open plan living room that looked out onto a deck running the length of the front of the cabin. She had mastered the quirks of cooking with an Arger oven. There was a small fridge, but a larger chest freezer outside the back in a lean-to shed. She had brought more than enough food supplies for a couple of weeks, although she always made sure there was food in the stores, wood enough for the fire, and propane for the generator to last a couple of months. There was a three month supply of water. She'd been careful all these years.

Night had fallen, and the cabin was enveloped in a heavy robe of darkness. Thick clouds now hid the stars and moon, and there was no light pollution

Maggie Denhearn

this high up, nothing to break the deep blackness that you could almost touch. Although Kali still looked extremely pale, Brina managed to get her to swallow a few mouthfuls of the purple viscous tincture that she had carefully prepared, and it seemed to be doing the trick. She was convinced Kali had been drugged with Rohypnol, probably laced with some alcohol. That would have made it easier for them to take her someplace else, if that's what they'd been intending. At the very least, if they had dumped her somewhere, she would have had no recollection of anything that had happened so would be unlikely to be able to identify them. She certainly remained hazy about events since waking up.

"All I remember is this guy who had a disgusting shiny tie." Kali frowned.

"That would be Peter," laughed Iris.

"Ladies! Shouldn't we be talking about something more important," snapped Maria, "like what we're going to do to get out of this mess?"

Brina carried on stirring a big pot on the stovetop. "Maria, I could do with a hand over here. Could you cut up some bread?"

Maria rolled her eyes and went over to the kitchen table where there was a large farmhouse loaf. "I was thinking of something *more* than making dinner."

"I know. But you can't think if you're not fed properly. So what's bothering you most? Not hearing from Luke, me not telling you what you want to hear, or worrying about your cat?"

Maria stared at her, mouth open, "I really wish you wouldn't do that. It's disconcerting having someone read one's thoughts. Not to mention intrusive."

"You didn't answer my question."

"Lady Black will be fine; cats are resourceful. I can't exactly bring her along with Morris the menace around."

"He's all Vanna has."

"I know," Maria groaned. "But sometimes ..." Brina looked fixedly at her.

"Okay, okay. I'm worried because I've not heard from Luke. And there's definitely something up between him and Charlotte, so if it's not an affair, what is it?"

When the Universe Called

Brina paused, closing her eyes and breathing in the fragrance of spices wafting up from the pot. She couldn't see Luke in her mind's eye. She knew he was alive, and not just because of the text message he had sent her. But he was blocking her out from something.

"He's okay. He'll call soon."

"How do you know? Oh wait, of course, you know everything," said Maria irritably.

"Not everything. In trying to hide who you are, Maria, you lay your emotions bare for me to see. I wouldn't be able to read your thoughts if you weren't letting me."

"So it's my fault?"

Brina breathed in deeply then exhaled. Maria could be exasperating. Vanna and Iris had sidled over to the kitchen area, looking discernibly uncomfortable.

"Could you both set the table? The food is ready." Brina pointed them in the direction of the cutlery drawer.

Maria started to hack at the bread while Iris and Vanna busied themselves with plates and cutlery. Brina felt their discomfort through the silence. As they sat down to eat, she eyed them all with that look of hers that she knew could cut through. It wasn't meant to be an unkind look, but it did tend to halt the conversation; that was her intention.

"Remember, where your attention goes, the energy flows." Maria, Iris, Kali, and Vanna all stared at Brina, not knowing quite what to say. The gentle clatter of spoons against crockery stopped.

She continued. "You get what you're thinking about, whatever it is, good or bad, whether you want it or not."

"Well, that's the end of the small talk portion of the evening, I guess," Maria responded.

"You don't agree?" Brina stared at Maria pointedly.

"No, no, you've shown me how that works. I'm just not sure why you're talking about that right now; there wasn't much of a lead-in to this particular topic of conversation." The others shifted awkwardly.

"We need to talk about this because there is a lot of negative thinking going on right now and that's not going to help the situation."

Maggie Denhearn

"I think I've a right to feel a bit negative at the moment, given everything I've been through." Kali's voice was feeble and weepy.

"Okay—first Maria. I can see why you think this is coming out of the blue, but unless we look at where our energy is going, anything we do from this point on has much less chance of working out if we're not careful about how we think and the energy we project. Kali, I'm not saying you're at fault for what's happened. I *am* suggesting that you think about what you've been focusing on recently. Do you remember what we talked about, how we can create our experiences with our thoughts?"

"I don't remember thinking about being kidnapped."

"It's not necessarily a straight correlation. Everything is made up of energy. The universe will find its own way to give you what you're focusing on."

Brina eyed the confused expressions of the women around her.

"Remember when we talked about the *Law of Attraction*? This is what I mean. It's not just some random theory. You need to be consciously applying the principles to your life, otherwise seemingly random things will happen that you don't necessarily want, the last few days being a good case in point."

"That's not helpful." Maria's tone was caustic. "Let's just say that between us, we have in some way contributed to what has just happened. It's not like we can just think 'Oh, I'd like everything to be okay' and that it all magically will be, anymore than you can think 'Oh, I might get hit by a car' and that will automatically happen."

"I know. But focusing on all the negatives right now won't help either. You know the work I've been doing."

"You mean your 'experiments?'" asked Iris.

"Yes, Iris, my experiments. I'm not sure how much you all believe me, though."

"Well it *is* a bit hard to accept," quipped Maria.

"I realize, Maria, that it's tough for you to consider reality in a different way. All I can promise you is that I've done several thought experiments with good results. That's what I've been encouraging you all to do too. I knew one day I'd need your help." She looked around the group of women. Between them they spanned three generations and four decades.

212

When the Universe Called

Vanna looked puzzled. "What could we possibly help with?"

"We'll get to that. But right now I really need you to think about what we've been talking about these last few months, and I need you to believe what I'm saying because it really matters now. I was hoping we'd have more time to work on this, but time is running out."

"What do you mean, 'time is running out?'" Kali dropped her fork in alarm, the clatter against her plate making everyone start.

Brina paused, sidestepping the question. "Kali, you were having an affair because you were bored in your marriage and wanted some excitement. Maria, you were feeling like you and Luke have drifted apart and have been secretly hoping something—anything—would happen to break the monotony. Iris, you were sick of your job and desperate to have Trevor out of your life. Vanna, well, you've not been thinking very positively for a long time now. Now you have what you were manifesting; whether you intentionally manifested or not. And it's brought you—us—together; don't you see? In the last few days, all of you have got what you wanted, what you were focusing on, although unfortunately not in the way you were probably hoping for."

They all stared at Brina in stunned silence, clearly shocked that she knew so much about what they had been thinking. Brina went on.

"All these months I've been trying to teach you all to *manifest*, to harness your powers, your ability to create with your thoughts. And it's working, you're doing it. Look at the forest fire. What are the odds that there would be a forest fire in the exact location you left Noah and Trevor, at that exact time, when it's not even forest fire season? Which of you was hoping for a miraculous solution so you wouldn't get caught?"

They looked at her, dumbfounded.

"All of you, right?"

"Chance?" suggested Maria.

"Do you really believe that, Maria, that the fire happened purely by chance?" Maria cast her eyes down, not responding.

"Let's try this. You've been bored lately with Luke and looking for reasons that your marriage isn't working."

"But, how did you know that?"

213

Maggie Denhearn

"Apart from the odd comments you make, I know. I can read your energy. And look what's happened? You suddenly think Luke is having an affair."

"Well … He's definitely up to something, that's for sure. You clearly know!" Maria stood up, pushing her chair back so hard that it fell over. Kali jumped nervously.

"Sorry!" She picked up the chair and went to get more wine.

"No, Maria, I don't know everything. You know I don't. I can't usually read people I don't know, and I can't read people when they actively block me. And no, I can't conjure up everything I want in an instant, but I'm getting there. And my point is: so are you. And right now I need you to be able to channel that energy into helping me. You have the ability; recent events show that. The forest fire shows that. It's now a question of channeling it more consciously."

"But …" Iris hesitated. "What about the fact I've done such a bad thing? Putting an axe in someone's head isn't exactly a positive thing to do. Aren't I in line for lots of negative energy now? Won't the universe now punish me for it?"

"The universe doesn't punish. That's a human interpretation. The universe works on energy."

"I don't understand."

Brina paused, choosing her words carefully.

"Trevor abused you. He certainly did a lot to attract a negative response from the universe. He had his own karma to face. Granted, you had a choice in how you responded, but your fear of how you would manage living alone made leaving him seem to be a worse option than staying. You were afraid. Just because we have choices doesn't mean they're easy or attractive options. Some people think that having a choice means that if someone stays in a difficult situation, they deserve the bad things they get. This type of thinking is just victim blaming and disregards the fact that some decisions are hard. And when we act out of fear rather than love, we can't always make the best decisions. There will be consequences to Trevor's death, cause and effect. What those are remains to be seen. If you continue to focus on the negative, you'll attract more negative energy."

"So what is it you want our help with?" Iris said simply.

214

When the Universe Called

"I need your full attention. I can't think clearly when there's clutter. Let's tidy up first, and then I'll tell you." Brina got up and started clearing dishes.

* * * *

Vanna's head hurt. The anxious feeling in the pit of her stomach that had faded slightly on arriving in the mountains started to return. She sucked her breath in, trying to block the pain, looking at Morris curled up, napping on her lap. The only thing he had to worry about was—well—nothing, actually.

"Morris, let's go out," Vanna whispered. Sleepily, he opened one eye then closed it again. As she put his leash on, he growled halfheartedly, and wearily got down from her lap, starting to stretch one leg at a time, like a ballerina carefully extending each leg in turn. He would not be hurried.

They went outside into the darkness. It seemed eerily quiet. She wasn't quite sure how this quiet was different from the quiet around her little house, but somehow it felt peculiar. She breathed in deeply the fresh night air. The sky had cleared somewhat, and a few stars were now visible, little dots of hope in the sky.

Morris snorted as he sniffed the grass, trying to catch some creature. Suddenly he stopped, his tail down, ears pinned back, uttering a low, fearful snarl. Vanna squinted but couldn't see anything. He must have heard a bear or a cougar. They should go in. Gladly he scampered after her, and she closed the cabin door tightly behind them. She turned the lock just to be sure. Logically, it couldn't have been a person. They were in the middle of nowhere, and no one knew they were there. Still, she had an uneasy feeling. The living room was silent except for the sound of the faint crackle of the fire in the wood burning stove. Kali was dozing again on the sofa. Maria and Iris were sitting at the table in silence, lost in their own worlds. Brina came and sat down with them. Iris leaned over and gently shook Kali, and she opened her eyes wearily. Vanna pulled up a kitchen chair.

"What's going on, Brina?" Maria, ever direct, crossed her arms and scowled at her.

215

Maggie Denhearn

GOLD RIVER, MONDAY, MARCH 15, 2010

Dr. Gagnon looked at the lab report and sighed, pulling off his glasses and rubbing his eyes, a habit of his whenever he was nervous. The exhaustion he felt had permeated into each of his cells and taken firm hold. He couldn't remember the last time he'd slept through the night, undisturbed by the worries that now haunted him each time he closed his eyes. He tried to read the report in front of him, but the lines were blurry, so he put his glasses back on. No matter how many times he read this, nothing would alter the results. More deaths. When he first become involved with the drug trials at FPH six years ago, he firmly believed that in research the end justifies the means. There is always a bigger picture to bear in mind.

That was until they started testing Torporo. Never in his entire career, now spanning decades, had he seen such a fatality rate, nor such a commitment by a company to plow on regardless of the cost to human life. He tried to convince himself that the lives of a few drug addicts and prostitutes were expendable if that meant saving millions of others from debilitating illness, but such a view was becoming harder to justify. He had taken an oath to do no harm.

He closed the folder and walked along the corridor to the boardroom. Frost and Bailey had been waiting for him for a quarter of an hour. It was never a good idea to keep these two waiting.

"Finally!" With one word Frost was able to cut the air in two. Gagnon tried not to flinch.

"I have the report, and it's not good."

"How so?" Frost peered at him. Gagnon glanced across at Bailey, who seemed to be taking some pleasure in his discomfort, judging by her mocking smile. Sitting next to Frost, she was caressing a cup of coffee like a cat toying with a mouse. He half expected the cup to break in two.

"More deaths. Three out of the fifteen of the current cohort ... I er ... with all due respect, erm ..."

"Spit it out, man!"

"Sir, it is my professional opinion that the trial of Torporo must be stopped. All the evidence and research thus far indicate that it's highly

When the Universe Called

unlikely that we're ever going to find a way of producing a version of the drug that's safe."

Frost paused, tapping his pen on the table, eyeing Gagnon coldly. "Out of the question. The financial investment has been too great. We're in no hurry are we? And there are plenty more subjects. It's not like we're going to run out of drug addicts now, is it? We're doing society a public service by getting rid of them, don't you think?"

Gagnon wasn't sure whether Frost was asking a question or being rhetorical, so he remained silent, opting to explore the pattern on the floor.

"Keep at it. ... And Gagnon ..."

"Yes?"

"You know I value you and your work."

"Thank you, sir."

"I would hate for anything to spoil such an impressive career."

"No, sir."

"And how are your lovely wife and daughter? Well I hope?"

"Thank you, yes." Gagnon swallowed, trying not to retch.

"You're very fortunate. Your predecessor was devastated when his family was killed in that dreadful car accident, and so soon after he'd decided he was going to quit working here. What an unfortunate coincidence, to lose everything overnight."

Gagnon pulled off his glasses and started rubbing his eyes again. His head was pounding, and he could hear the blood rushing in his ears.

"You're tired, Gagnon, I see that. I'm sure you'll feel more refreshed when we see you tomorrow."

Gagnon hurried out of the boardroom and into the men's washroom.

CHAPTER 17

Wednesday evening, April 16, 2014

Brina was trying to clear her mind. She didn't underestimate the enormity of what she was about to ask of the women around her. She wished they had more time, but they didn't. Unease hung in the air like a damp veil, touching them imperceptibly. Maria, Iris, and Vanna were sitting around the kitchen table. Still feeling unsteady, Kali lay prone on the sofa, facing the others. The fire stove crackled, and the dim lamps cast long shadows across the room. The fragrances of ginger and cumin from dinner were no match for the odor of mustiness that clung to the wooden beams and dusty rugs.

"Are we all ready?" Brina eyed each one of them individually.

They each nodded to her in turn.

"I'm in trouble. *We're* in trouble." Brina saw that Maria was about to speak and held up her hand.

"Maria, if you wouldn't mind, please let me explain first." Brina continued. "I asked the universe for help, and now we're all together, so I guess the universe called you." Greeted with blank faces, she went on. "I realize that you all find this hard to believe, but it's not an accident that we've all ended up here together. You see ..."

The sound of a phone ringing loudly startled all of them.

"What on earth ...?" Kali paled.

"Oh ... it's my phone." Maria jumped up. "I'm sorry, I really have to get this. I don't recognize the number and it could be Luke." She grabbed her phone from the windowsill and slipped out into the night.

218

When the Universe Called

*   *   *   *

Bailey hovered in the shadows by the door, watching the members of the Consortium's executive committee file into the boardroom at the Borealia Club on Hastings Street, downtown Vancouver, the city's most prestigious business club. Money was not sufficient to be a member. No one was permitted to join who did not have the requisite social standing. Being a member of the Borealia Club in recent years had become synonymous with being a member of the Consortium. Out of those prominent individuals who belonged, only twenty sat on the executive committee. This evening, only twelve members were in attendance, but it was sufficient for any motion put forward to be carried, should at least eleven of them agree.

The eighteenth-century chandelier hanging from the wood-paneled ceiling lit up the portraits of distinguished figures of Canadian history— all white, all male. Bailey mused that everything in the room seemed an anachronism, rather like Frost himself. Expensive wines and brandies were being poured by the wait staff as everyone took their seats around the conference table, which legend had it had been the site of negotiations between the British and the French at one time. Bailey coughed, bringing silence to the room and sending the wait staff scurrying out.

"You all know why we are gathered here this evening, and I thank you for taking the time to come ... as well as for your discretion." She stared at the nine men and two women, each looking at her expectantly.

"Since this is an extraordinary meeting, I'll keep it brief. Mr. Frost, owner and executive director of the foremost pharmaceutical company in the country, founded the Consortium fifty years ago with the intent of ensuring that everyone would benefit from the health innovations of FPH. We thank him for his endeavors. As the world moves forward, so must we. I believe it is time for us to lift the burden from our esteemed colleague, most particularly in his time of mourning. To save him further grief, I propose that as his second in command, the executive committee vote that John Frost be relieved of his position as head of the Consortium, and that I should be appointed his successor, effective immediately."

Bailey paused for effect, scrutinizing the expressions before her. "Will anyone second this motion?" She turned to look in Judge Rawley's direction.

219

Maggie Denhearn

His eyes cast down, he looked up at her as she paused. His hesitation was fleeting, but she caught it. She narrowed her eyes.

"I ... I second the motion." The judge's voice was quiet, lacking both weight and conviction. Bailey continued unabashed.

"It's time to cast your ballots. Please mark your vote on the paper before you and pass the papers to Judge Rawley." The sound of rustling papers and shuffling chairs echoed around the centuries-old ceiling. Once Judge Rawley had all the papers, he started to count.

*   *   *   *

"Maria, it's McDowell."

"Oh, hi!" Maria didn't know what to say. Shivering in the darkness, she sat down on the rocker on the deck, pulling a damp woolen blanket around her. The sounds of the night that she usually found comforting in their familiarity were not so, here in the mountains, and she felt tingles running down her back. Why would McDowell be calling her?

"I've been trying Kali all afternoon, but she's not answering. Is everything okay? Do you know where she is?"

"I er, no ... No, but I'm sure she's okay." Maria's intuition was telling her to keep Kali away from him. He didn't push her.

'Okay, well it's you I actually need to speak to. I er ... I er, I heard about Luke." Maria froze. The radio report the detectives had mentioned. Should she admit it wasn't true or play along? She opted for silence.

McDowell cleared his throat. "Well, erm, I'm sorry and all that. But this is a bit tricky. You know, and don't take this the wrong way, and I'm sure you're not involved with it all, but with the campaign and everything I just think that ..."

"What are you talking about? Involved in what?"

"Defrauding the Consortium. Like Luke. You know."

"No, I don't know." Maria felt like she had swallowed glass and was spitting out shards. "Enlighten me."

"Look, this is politics. Reputation is everything. I can't be seen to have any connection, however tenuous, with someone who might have got on the wrong side of the Consortium."

When the Universe Called

"The who?" As she listened to McDowell explain, Maria felt like his voice was getting further and further away, as though she were getting smaller and smaller, disappearing into nothing. He was still speaking when she hung up the phone and came back into the cabin. She'd been gone only a few minutes, yet it had seemed significantly longer. Maria felt the tension as she walked back in.

"So?" Iris looked across at Maria nervously. The haunted expression Iris had been wearing all day was still firmly etched across her face.

"Who was it?"

Maria looked across at Kali.

"It was McDowell, Andy."

"What?" Kali tried not to squeal. She'd forgotten all about him. "How come he was calling you and not me?"

"Well, he said he left you several messages but that you weren't answering your phone. I thought it was better if I told him I didn't know where you were. You're not in a fit state to talk to him. Anyway, he was calling about Luke."

"How did he know?"

"From the radio announcement, I guess. I didn't ask. That's not what he was bothered about."

"Oh Maria ..." Maria studied her fingernails; she didn't want to see the pity in Kali's eyes.

"It's okay. I know it's not his body that was found. It's just that I've not heard from him either for a while, and I don't know ..." Her voice trailed off. She slumped down into a chair and tried not dissolve into tears. She wasn't prone to crying, yet that's exactly what she wanted to do right now. "McDowell was more bothered about the negative publicity all this might cause for his campaign." She sighed.

"I wish something magical would happen and make this whole mess go away. I wish I could wake up and everything would be fine ... though I'm not sure what that would look like anymore." Kali's voice petered out. Brina nodded to Maria, indicating that she should carry on.

"There's something else, isn't there." Brina wasn't asking a question. There was no point in lying to her. Maria tried to hide the quiver in her voice. She had inherited her English mother's belief in the importance of

Maggie Denhearn

maintaining a suitably stiff upper lip and in not showing too much emotion in public. Right now she was struggling.

Maria continued. "Apparently our wonderful Mayor Andy McDowell has contacts in various interesting places with some rather unsavory characters. No wonder those thugs were after him … Sorry Kali." Kali just waved her hand feebly for Maria to carry on. "Anyway, there's a rumor going around that Luke was involved in some shady business deals that may have contributed to his murder." She paused, her voice lingering on that last word, which stuck in her mouth. "It would appear that my husband might not be the man I thought he was. Oh, Lord. I'm talking as if he's really dead. McDowell said something about him defrauding some group called the Con … something or other."

Brina must have read Maria's mind. She handed her a glass of brandy. Maria's hand shook as she took it.

"Appearances can be deceptive, my dear." Maria stared at her. The penny dropped. This is what Brina knew about Luke and wasn't telling her. She felt queasiness in her stomach.

"Well, I guess I have no concrete proof. And I have no idea about anything else he's seemingly been up to … really no idea." She looked at Brina expectantly, waiting for her to say what she knew. She held on to her glass to stop her hands from twisting. They seemed to have taken on a life of their own. Brina remained thoughtful.

"I don't know what to believe. He's certainly been behaving strangely recently. What do you think? How could I not know, though? How could he be completely another person?"

"It's amazing what we don't see," Brina finally responded. "And we see only what we can conceive of. But you're going only on what McDowell has said plus a feeling you've had with no evidence. Why would you choose to believe him over Luke?"

"You're always telling us to trust our intuition."

"Intuition isn't the same as taking what you see at face value. McDowell said more, didn't he?" So Brina *was* reading her mind.

"He said that the Con … Consortium—that's it—that they are a bunch of rich people who are very bad news if you piss them off, which Luke has done. Or so McDowell claims." Shock was starting to turn to anger. How

When the Universe Called

could Luke put their whole lives in jeopardy without a second thought for her?

"Have any of you heard of the Consortium?" Maria turned to the others. Kali, Iris, and Vanna all shook their heads, their demeanor showing they had no idea.

Brina paused, staring down at her empty teacup. "I have. It's because of them that I need your help."

"What?" Maria nearly dropped her glass. "What ...? But McDowell said they get away with all kinds of things. How would you know people like *that?*"

Maria didn't wait for Brina to reply. "Allegedly Luke was doing legal work for them and started stealing from them. What has he done? Oh my God, what has he done?" She looked at her phone, now on the table in front of her, her finger hovering over the call button. Her hands were shaking too much to be able to dial. "Say something Brina. You need to say something!"

"McDowell's right about the Consortium. They have power and reach across Canada. The group was founded decades ago by a man called John Frost."

Iris interrupted. "I've heard of him. Doesn't he run Frost Pharma Health? We sell a lot of their products at Fun Foods."

"He owns it, Iris. He built it up from nothing. And he's created a group that supports the company so that he can get around the law and cut corners to get his products to market, using whatever unscrupulous methods he sees fit. It takes on average twelve years for a new drug to be released to the public. FPH averages eight to ten. That says a lot."

"But how can he get away with that?"

"Anyone who belongs to the Consortium gets a cut of company profits. The company makes hundreds of millions. Politicians, doctors, they get paid off."

"Why do I get the feeling there's something else?" Maria had drunk two more glasses of brandy, and the room was beginning to spin. She sensed there was worse to come. "How come you know all this?"

"Years ago, I worked as an intern at FHP. I found out they were doing illegal drug testing on people."

"So how come you didn't do anything about it?"

Maggie Denhearn

"Iris, get Maria some water will you?" Iris followed Brina's command. Maria reluctantly accepted the glass of water and took a gulp.

"I've been trying, believe me, but it's not as simple as that. There are so many powerful people involved, and these are dangerous individuals."

"Brina, you need to tell us what you're mixed up in."

"I'm trying to, Vanna, I'm trying. I've been collecting evidence for years. One of the main people in the Consortium, a woman called Bailey, has found out what I've been doing. She's coming after me, I know it. And ..."

Maria felt like everything was happening in slow motion. She knew Brina was talking to her, but it felt like she was addressing someone else, and very, very slowly, like someone had hit a button to make time start crawling.

"I'm sorry, Maria. Luke was just trying to protect you. He's been helping me. Noah too. The Consortium has found out. He's not stealing money from them. He's trying to expose them. He's hiding out somewhere. I know he's still alive, I can sense that, but he's not letting me read him, so I don't know much else."

"I don't ... I don't ..." Maria felt her head shaking, bobbing up and down like one of those bobblehead dogs in the window of a children's toy store.

"John Frost is Luke's father. When Luke found out what his father was doing, he wanted to help me stop him."

Maria wasn't sure whether everyone had stopped talking or if the ringing in her ears was just drowning all other sound out. She was swimming in a wave of nausea. A white veil rose up in front of her eyes and everything went silent. Even the ringing stopped.

* * * *

Catch her!" Brina knew she wouldn't be quick enough, but Vanna was. She managed to grab Maria just as she toppled off her chair and before she hit the hardwood floor. Iris hurried to fetch her more water.

"Iris, in my bag in my room, in the red cloth bag, fetch me the little bottle marked smelling salts. That's it, Vanna, lay her on the floor with her feet up on the chair. That's it. Here, here's a cushion for her head."

"What happened?"

When the Universe Called

"She's fainted, that's all. She'll be fine. … Thank you." Brina took the small brown bottle that Iris handed to her and undid the lid, then leaned down and waved it under Maria's nose. Nothing happened for a few seconds. Then Maria moved her head slightly away from the bottle and started groaning.

"Keep her there, Vanna, make sure she doesn't move." Brina sat back down, keeping an eye on Maria.

"I'm not sure which I'm more shocked about: that Maria didn't know Luke's father owns FPH. None of us did, for that matter. Or that FPH has been illegally testing on people. Surely that can't be right." Iris was shaking her head in disbelief.

"I wish it weren't, but it is. And now the Consortium wants to take it one step further by getting Bill 267 passed, which would essentially make it legal to drug convicted criminals and do all kinds of DNA testing. There's no knowing where this could stop."

"I've never heard of Bill 267." Iris looked at Brina blankly.

"You wouldn't have. These people have their tentacles cast wide. The news and radio don't dare give it coverage either, or have been bribed not to do so. FPH and the Consortium aren't interested in cutting the crime rate. They just want to sell as many of their drugs as possible. What better way than to find some legal justification for drugging more and more people? Where does it end? Anyway, they've found out that we've been trying to stop them. They're after us, and they'll kill us if they get the chance."

"Surely not! Oh Brina, are you sure you're not overreacting?"

Brina stared at Iris. "The company has killed hundreds of people over the years through their drug trials. And …" Brina hesitated, then said quietly, "Frost shot me and tried to kill me before, years ago."

As the others gawped at Brina, Maria started to groan again and opened her eyes. "What happened?" Her voice was feeble.

"You fainted, my dear." Brina spoke gently. "Lie there for a few minutes."

"Ladies, I know this is a lot to take in. And I know you have more questions. Right now there's no time to discuss that. The bill is due to go through in two weeks, and we have to stop it, or at least delay it before Frost or Bailey find me or Luke."

225

Maggie Denhearn

"But if the Consortium is that dangerous, won't that mean they'll come after us too if they find out we're helping you?" Vanna's voice was almost a whisper.

"Yes," replied Brina simply, "so if anyone doesn't want to, I'll understand. Truly."

"What did you have in mind?" Brina glanced at Kali. It was the first she had spoken for a while.

"Well, I've been thinking about that. We need hard evidence that the drug they want to get approval for is dangerous, and video footage of the labs where testing is going on. If possible, we need to get testimony from people who have been part of the drug trials, though my guess is most would be too scared to speak up. Up to now we've been able to get only bits and pieces that wouldn't add up to enough—emails and such.

"Frost's lawyers would tear us to shreds in court, if it ever got that far. It's hard to prove who wrote an email, and since we stole the information, we're on tenuous legal ground. Plus they'd destroy any evidence we've found before anyone started investigating. And many of the court judges are part of the Consortium.

"So this is what I've been thinking. There's a lab up north, on the Island, in Gold River. If we can break in there and hack into the FPH computers, we might be able to get all the information on Torporo. If it's published straight onto the Internet, hopefully enough people will see it that the information will go viral before the Consortium finds us. No media or police. We can't trust either. And if we do it well enough, there's no need for anyone to know any of you were involved. The Consortium already wants my head, there's no changing that."

No one spoke.

"What bill?" slurred Maria, breaking the silence.

"I'll explain again later my dear. You've had a big shock." Brina ministered to Maria, putting a cold compress on her head, then with Vanna's help, got her up and sitting in an armchair by the fire. Brina felt the negative energy rising in the cabin. The look of horror on her friends' faces spoke more than any words they could utter.

* * * *

When the Universe Called

Bailey walked around Frost's office at the Consortium headquarters. Her long, silver fingernails played along the leather of the high-backed chair he used to sit in before infirmity forced him to remain in a wheelchair that could accommodate an oxygen tank for whenever he had difficulty breathing, which had been more and more the case of late. The office was spacious, with floor to ceiling windows along two sides, overlooking the ocean and a mountain view. The decoration was somewhat minimalist for Bailey's taste, but she would soon fix that. And then there was the on-suite bathroom with a large bathtub and state-of-the-art shower cubicle. Before his declining health, Frost had regularly stayed over in his office. The elegant couch was more than wide and long enough to provide a decent night's sleep. Bailey had always wondered why he preferred that rather than the comfort of staying at the Borealia Club.

He could be a peculiar man. No matter. His days were drawing to a close; her time had finally come. She had won the vote. This was her office now. She would wait a couple of weeks until after the bill went through before taking ownership.

Bailey had yet to have a conversation with Frost. It wasn't that she was afraid of doing so, rather that it would be awkward and he would be full of bluster. She would have to watch him struggle for breath and go that puce color that highlighted how thin and papery his skin had become. It was a scene she preferred to delay for the time being.

Picking up the phone on the desk, she pressed a button, then another, then sat on the side of the desk. Frost hated it when people did that. She smirked at her own childish enjoyment of such a trivial act of defiance.

"Yes, it's Bailey. Put me through to Dr. Gagnon ... Dr. Gagnon. How are you this evening?"

"Well, Ms. Bailey, thank you. I assume you're calling about Torporo."

"Indeed. I just need to know that everything will be in order in the next few days." She heard Dr. Gagnon cough. "Is there something I should know?" Like a switch being flipped, she changed her tone. It was important he take her seriously.

"Not at all, not at all. I'll have the required paperwork emailed to you by next Tuesday at the latest. I'm sorry it's not sooner, but with the Easter weekend and all that ..." He sounded cowed.

227

Maggie Denhearn

"See that you do, and that the documents are sent using the appropriate level of security. We don't want any errors, do we?" Dr. Gagnon coughed again. "And by the sounds of that cough, it seems you could do with some time to relax after working so hard. Please take a week off."

"It's kind of you, I'm sure, but ..."

"It's not an offer or a request."

She put the phone down before he could offer any further protests. She had never been entirely sure how much she trusted Dr. Gagnon. There was something in his manner this evening that seemed a little off. Even if she were being somewhat paranoid, this was not the time to take chances. Now that she was in charge, security would be tighter. And if there were any dissenters in the ranks, well, she would ensure they were dealt with accordingly.

The sound of her cell phone interrupted her thoughts. It was McDowell. She'd been avoiding him. She sighed and touched the accept call button.

"Yes?"

"I spoke to Maria."

"And?"

"She seems to be under the impression Luke is dead. And she clearly knew nothing about the Consortium, so you're in the clear. She now thinks her husband is a fraudster. No trace of Kali or Noah, though."

"Keep looking. ... Oh, and McDowell ... thank you. Your work will be rewarded."

She ended the call before he had chance to reply. She had no intention of doing anything for that village idiot, but she may as well make use of him for now. Her hand hovered over the desk phone receiver again. She picked it up and dialed another number. No one was answering.

"Heeley. Call me when you get this message. I need to know you've taken care of the matter with Anja. ... I mean Brina. And Noah."

*   *   *   *

"Brina, we need to talk about this," said Vanna, putting some more wood in the stove and fetching Maria some ginger tea. Right now she felt like she was the only one left other than Brina who could think straight. Iris seemed

When the Universe Called

subdued, and Kali had remained in a daze since she gained consciousness. Maria had barely uttered a word since coming around from fainting, a fact that worried Vanna the most. She was used to Maria being strong, in charge. She had never seen her like this. None of this boded well for whatever plan Brina might have in mind. Vanna failed to see how a handful of women like them could be any match at all for an organization like the Consortium.

"I know, Vanna, it seems impossible, but it's not." Brina laid a hand on hers.

"I er ..." Vanna wanted to tell Brina how creepy it was that she could sense what people were thinking but thought better of it. She obviously knew. Instead, she asked, "You mentioned this lab. What did you have in mind?"

"FPH has a laboratory up near Gold River. Friday is a national holiday, Good Friday. Everyone except security will be off work. All we need to do is break in to get the information we need about Torporo from the main computers. If we publish everything on the Internet and send it to websites that are overseas as well as in Canada, it'll be harder for anyone in the Consortium to stop it. It'll be international news."

"Assuming that's even possible for us to do, why would this be such a big story?" Vanna wasn't convinced.

"Because there's evidence we can use to show that something similar has been going on in England, evidence British security services won't be able to cover up any more."

Vanna put her hand firmly to her stomach, trying to crush the uncomfortable sensations that were simmering inside her.

"That's why you need me." Vanna turned and stared at Kali. Her voice was still shaky.

"I get it ... I can do it. There's not a computer system invented that I can't hack. I can do it; and I will do it. I'll be fine by tomorrow, I'm sure." Kali yawned, closed her eyes, and leaned back. Her expression indicated she felt anything but well.

Vanna paused. She could see how Kali would be useful, but she wasn't sure where she came into the equation.

Maggie Denhearn

"Vanna, I know this must seem all rather bizarre. But it's not. I've been manifesting for years getting the help that I need to thwart the Consortium. You're it. The universe has sent you all to me."

"I'm not clear where *I* fit in."

"You studied pharmacology, right?"

"Yes. Well, I studied pharmacology first, then changed to nursing."

"I studied that too, but I'm years out of date. When we find out the exact chemical breakdown of Torporo, you'll be able to tell us what that means, what FPH is hiding."

"I might. I'm not sure. The Canadian names are often different from the British ones. I'll do my best, though."

"What about me?" Iris looked older this evening, tired. Vanna couldn't imagine Iris killing anyone. The idea was too strange to fathom.

"We need a good driver who knows the Island. No one knows the roads better than you."

"I hadn't really thought of that. I suppose I do." A faint smile crossed her face.

"And me? Do I fit into whatever it is that's going on? Or am I just here because of Luke?" Everyone turned to face Maria.

Vanna looked between Maria and Brina. There was an extra layer of tension between them. Not surprising. It seemed rather incredible that Brina had managed to keep so much secret from Maria all these years. If she'd been Maria, she'd have felt furious, betrayed.

"We need someone who can handle the media, knows what works, what would make a story go viral. We need someone in PR."

Glaring at Brina, Maria did not reply.

Vanna got up and took Maria's empty cup, heading toward the kitchen. "I think it's time we all hit the hay, don't you? We've got a lot to sort out tomorrow." In her family, Vanna was the peacemaker. They were all tired, overwrought, and emotional. No good could come of talking about this anymore this evening.

* * * *

When the Universe Called

Maria and Iris headed up to bed in one of the upstairs rooms, just big enough for a double bed, a small wardrobe, and a dresser. The ceiling was barely high enough for someone to stand up. Iris was short enough not to bump her head, but Maria had to stoop a little. Every now and then as she was getting ready for bed, she would bang her head.

Maria still felt nauseated. She missed the comfort and orderliness of her own home—and decently high ceilings. This cabin was quaint to be sure: rustic, the usual euphemisms for an old, drafty log cabin in the woods, home to spiders and cobwebs. The sticky cobweb that she had meticulously removed from the bedroom window when she'd first arrived was back.

Iris was already lying on her side of the bed, waiting for Maria to settle, staring at the ceiling, lost in her own thoughts. Maria wondered if she was thinking of Trevor. She was thinking of Luke. The realization of the danger he could be facing was beginning to seep in, anxiety spreading within her like one of those spider webs. It was unlikely she would get much sleep. She could hear Kali already dozing on the sofa below. Vanna and Brina were moving around in the kitchen, making those bedtime noises so familiar yet so out of place given their circumstances.

It's a curious fact of life that no matter whatever major event is going on, the small aspects of life continue. Maria heard the kettle boil, then the sound of hot water being poured into a cup, bare feet padding around on the cold hardwood floor, a creaking bedspring. She wanted to find reassurance in the mundane, but couldn't.

Vancouver, Friday, August 8, 2013

Her whole life, Charlotte had felt as though the rest of the world was going on inside some kind of giant bubble from which she was excluded. When she saw her friends and how they resembled their parents, grandparents, and siblings, she felt lost. She looked like no one at all—a blank page.

Charlotte had read and reread Luke's reply to her letter, her hands shaking. His words burned. It was clear he was referring to money. That's not why she'd got touch with him.

Maggie Denhearn

He had suggested they meet in the foyer of the Fairmont Pacific Rim Hotel in downtown Vancouver, a public place. No doubt he feared she'd make a scene if they met in private.

Charlotte spent a half an hour in the washrooms of the Pacific Rim, doing her hair, her make-up, adjusting her clothes, anything she could think of to avoid the inevitable walk back out into the foyer. It was as though nothing fit her body and her body didn't fit her skin. A hot ball of anxiety vibrated within her. It shouldn't matter to her what he thought of her; but somehow it did.

She walked out into the bright lights of the lobby, squinting, and sat down in one of the large plump chairs. Pretending to read her book, she tentatively cast glances out of the corner of her eye: business people drinking wine and making deals, well-dressed couples draped over fine furniture, staff in uniforms designed to make them both stand out and blend in to take away their identity.

And then she saw him coming toward her. She had seen pictures of Luke at work in newsletters and other communications. She'd looked him up on Google to find out every last detail she could. Tall, slim, with salt and pepper hair, well-dressed, a typical businessman in a suit, he was one among thousands in the city. He had an aquiline nose, pale complexion, and extraordinarily blue eyes.

As he came toward her, he tilted his head to one side. He'd seen her. The world around her had stopped, and only the two of them were moving.

"Charlotte?"

"Yes."

"Luke." Stretching out his arm in greeting, she shook his hand. It was clammy. He sat down guardedly, staring at her, fiddling uncomfortably with his jacket pocket.

"You look just like my mother when she was your age." His voice was soft, sad. "Shall we get a drink?" He made a minute gesture and a waiter was by their table, ready to take their order. She was glad when he asked for a whiskey. She ordered a gin and tonic. They chatted about the weather, banalities, skirting around the real topic of conversation. They ordered food, but she couldn't eat. The questions she wanted to ask hung in the air between them like unexploded bombs, waiting to be detonated.

When the Universe Called

"So … what happened between you and my mother?" He squirmed noticeably. It seemed incongruous: this professionally dressed, middle-aged man, fidgeting in his seat like he was a small boy caught stealing candy. It felt like hours rather than minutes before he finally spoke. He looked straight at her.

"It was a long time ago, and I'm not sure I can explain it, at least not in the way you want me to. Life gets complicated sometimes."

"I'm well aware of that." She was as annoyed as she sounded.

He coughed and looked away.

"Look, it wasn't my finest hour, I know that now. We were young. I felt caught. I had plans, and having a child didn't fit into them. I'm sorry if that sounds harsh."

"Well at least it's honest." She bit her lip then took a large gulp of gin and tonic, trying to stop herself from tearing up.

Luke stared across at the young woman before him, hardly able to believe that she was his daughter. Logically he knew she was, there was no doubt. Her resemblance to his mother was both uncanny and eerie. There was something in her eyes, the slope of her nose, the cut of her cheekbones, and the way she held her cup and moved her feet nervously. It was peculiar to him what tiny details he remembered about his mother when he could no longer recall larger, more significant points in their brief relationship.

He had lied to Charlotte. He had to. How could he tell her that her mother was actually a drug addict, lost, on a mission to self-destruct? He had fallen in love with Ena in spite of himself and knew from the outset that she was troubled. For a while she managed to stay clean, then her behavior became erratic again and he realized she was back using.

One morning he decided he couldn't face another day with someone so bent on destroying herself, so he left without a word. He hadn't known Ena was pregnant. Not until years later did he find out through a mutual friend that there had been a baby. But if he *had* known she was about to have his child, would it have made a difference?

CHAPTER 18

THURSDAY MORNING, APRIL 17, 2014

Mary listened to the beep of the heart monitor and gazed at all the tubes and lines going into Frost. The paramedics had managed to stabilize him, and since he had access to enough medical equipment at home, they had agreed to let him stay where he was. For the last twenty-four hours he had remained unconscious, and there was no sign that would change any time soon. A round-the-clock nursing service had been lined up to watch him, but the current nurse had popped outside for a cigarette. The oxygen mask on his face seemed to engulf almost his whole head.

Mary hadn't noticed until now how withered he had become. She fingered the wires, caressed the tubes. It would be so easy to loosen just one, to pull it out as though he had moved in his sleep and it had become dislodged. No one would know. He had been unwell for some time. No one would question it. Her forefinger and thumb on the main line, she started to squeeze. The machine next to the bed started to make a hiccupping sound. She stopped and let go of the tube. Despite everything, she couldn't do it.

Dabbing his forehead with a cool cloth, she said a silent prayer and left the room. She took her cell phone out of her apron pocket, started to dial a number, hesitated, then pressed the call button. Putting the phone to her ear, she listened and braced herself to break the news.

*   *   *   *

When the Universe Called

It was barely morning; the sun strained to make an appearance in the hazy gray sky. The rain was hanging in the air, a cool mist in suspended animation, for the time being unable to fall. Vanna opened the door and went out onto the deck. Listening to the sounds of the early morning, she began a few stretches. A few moments later, Kali and Maria came out to join her.

"Are you sure you two should be running?" asked Vanna. Maria and Kali both still looked alarmingly pasty.

"I'm okay," mumbled Kali.

"I need to move. I have to get out of that cabin or I'll go crazy." Maria's tone was quiet but resolute.

"If you're certain. We'd better not be long though. I'm assuming we don't have much time."

Vanna wasn't sure that going for a run was a smart idea, but the energy in the cabin had been so tense when she got up, half an hour probably wasn't going to make a big difference in the grand scheme of things. Besides, Morris needed his morning exercise.

"Let's just keep it simple: out and back. I've got my Garmin." Vanna set her running watch to zero and they set off at an easy pace. The chilled air woke up their lungs, and within minutes they were running at a steady clip, Maria in the lead and Vanna bringing up the rear.

Vanna found it particularly challenging to orient herself on the trails. Each tree was so different yet looked exactly the same when she was trying to find her way around. The kaleidoscope of shades of green, hues of brown, and earthy aromas mesmerized each of her senses whenever she ran. After a couple of kilometers, they stopped in a clearing. Tiny buds were forming on trees, and here and there, white trillium flowers were popping up. Morris wiggled off, nose to the ground and sniffing loudly, then pranced back and started begging for treats. Everything seemed as though this were a regular morning's run.

"It's beautiful here," sighed Kali. "I don't want to have to leave."

"It's not safe. If the Consortium is as dangerous as Brina is making out and if they think Brina has told us anything, they'll be after us too. And it won't be long before they figure out where we're all hiding."

"Maria, are you, er, I mean ..." Vanna looked down at the ground, wishing she'd not started that sentence. While they were running, she and

235

Maggie Denhearn

Kali had filled her in on the details Maria had missed when she passed out. Vanna couldn't imagine what was going through her mind right now.

"I don't know. All I do know is that we have to help Brina. This is bigger than all of us. I'll worry about Luke and myself, and everything else afterward."

They fell into a silent run as they headed back to the cabin.

Vanna stared down at the mud on her trail shoes as though it were of great interest. A light breeze whistled through the leaves, and the birds were in full chorus with their morning song. The itchy, agitated feeling Vanna had gone to bed with was not subsiding, despite the expended energy.

They ran back the way they'd come. Everything looked different in reverse. Every now and then there would be rustling in the bushes, and Morris would growl and scurry off determinedly, returning a few minutes later with only a stick to show for his endeavors. By the time they got back to the cabin, smoke was once again billowing out of the chimney, and they could hear the clatter of plates coming from inside. Brina and Iris were busy preparing breakfast: toast, eggs, coffee, and tea for Vanna. Kali and Vanna sat down at the kitchen table while Maria wandered off to get a shower.

* * * *

"Want something?" Vanna pushed a plate of boiled eggs in Maria's direction.

"Just coffee, black." That was about as much as Maria could stomach right now. She sat down at the table, rubbing her wet hair with a towel.

"You'll waste away," said Brina.

"Hardly." Maria knew it was a control thing, but it helped her manage. If she controlled what went into her body, she was in control of the rest of her life. At the moment, everything was unraveling before her eyes. She knew she should eat, but the thought of anything other than coffee entering her body made her want to throw up. The latest revelations kept playing around in her head on an endless loop. And still no word from Luke. On the one hand, she wanted to confront him. On the other, she wanted to get as far away from whomever he was as she could.

236

When the Universe Called

Brina leaned over and switched on the radio. "We'd better see if there's a news update." Maria glanced at the clock on the wall. It was 7:30 a.m.

> And in local news, one of the dead bodies found in the forest on Tuesday morning between Kwalicum Bay and Eagle Cove has been identified as Luke Morgan. The identity of the other remains unknown. Police have not yet confirmed the exact cause of death but state that they believe the deaths to be connected. A freak bolt of dry lightning is now believed to be the cause of the forest fire that destroyed much of the area where the bodies were discovered. A campfire ban is being enforced, the earliest in the season for a decade. Police are appealing to anyone who was in that part of the forest yesterday morning to come forward with any information they might have.

Brina switched off the radio and turned to the women around her.

"See, I told you. That fire was no coincidence. Dry lightning at this time of year? Do you know how unusual that is? That's the power you have."

Maria shivered. The idea that they could have the power to cause something like that with their thoughts was still hard for her to comprehend. Iris dropped her mug.

"Crap!" She grabbed a tea towel, trying to wipe away the splatters of coffee on her pants.

Vanna picked up pieces of broken pottery and started mopping up the spilled coffee. Maria watched as the pool of liquid tried to outrun the paper towel Vanna was using to try and clean it up with. Morris started growling at the woodpile, then began barking furiously.

"Vanna, will you control that damn dog of yours!" Maria got up and poured herself more coffee and handed another mug to Iris. She was feeling jittery enough without Morris chiming in.

"Morris! Morris! Come here, come here!" Vanna tried to catch him, but he scampered into the back bedroom.

"I know," said Maria finally. "I've been thinking. It seems to me that like it or not, we're all on the run. Sooner or later the Consortium will figure

Maggie Denhearn

out we're all involved with Brina. We can't go up to the lab at Gold River until after it closes for the Easter weekend, so we have some time to kill. We could go and get more provisions and some things from home. We'll need to be careful, of course, but it would also give us a chance to find out more of what's going on. I know, Brina, that you'd said I shouldn't go back, but aren't I a potential suspect if my husband is dead?"

"Hang on," said Vanna, "on the radio it didn't' mention anything about the deaths being considered as suspicious. They usually do, don't they, if that's what they believe? Though I guess they could think it's a bit odd that you don't want to make certain they've got the identification right."

"Possibly. And they're bound to find out eventually that one of the deaths wasn't an accident." Maria glanced across at Iris, who was staring down into her fresh cup of coffee. She said nothing.

"What do you think, Brina?"

Brina met Maria's gaze thoughtfully. "I think you're right. Even if you don't go to the police, and I don't advise that you do, you and the others need to ensure that it doesn't look like you've just randomly disappeared. Otherwise, that'll draw unnecessary attention to you. Be careful not to bring back so much that it would look like you've run away, if anyone searches your house. There are members of the Consortium in the police too, and people know we are friends. If they think you've vanished, they'll know you're with me, or might suspect it at any rate. The longer the Consortium thinks it's just me they need to come after, the safer for the rest of you. There's only one person I know we can trust, and that's Police Commissioner Petturi. He's saved my life in the past."

"When? When Frost shot you?" Maria was realizing that getting to know Brina was like slowly peeling an onion. There was always another layer under the one you'd just removed.

"Yes. He was the first to find me, thankfully, after Frost had fled. He managed to spirit me away and he's been helping me ever since."

"But how do you know he's not been bribed or changed sides?"

"Because his sister died in one of Frost's drug trials. He's desperate to get Frost, but legally and for good."

"Lord! Okay, okay." Maria was pacing back and forth across the kitchen, focusing her attention on the floor, on how the hardwood felt against her

When the Universe Called

bare feet. She needed to feel grounded. Somehow it helped her think. She glanced across at Iris, who looked desperately maudlin and as though she wasn't hearing any of the conversation. "But Iris, do you really think *she* should go back? Brina?" Brina was now busy pouring various herbs and liquids into a pot. "What are you doing?"

"Making soup. I'm listening. Doing this helps me clear my mind. Iris, my dear, trust me on this one. You need to go back."

Iris nodded blankly.

"I feel like I'm in one of those crime films," said Vanna gloomily. "It's not quite so much fun being in one as watching it, I have to say. Give me a few minutes to get out of these running things and I'll be ready for whatever we decide to do."

Vanna disappeared into the back bedroom. Maria stared at Brina, chopping and dicing vegetables. It appeared she was getting messages again.

Brina smiled. "Kali? What are you going to do?"

"I don't want to go back. I can't face it. And I don't want to randomly bump into Andy. Besides, I called in sick at work the other day, so no one will think anything of it if I'm not around. I'll text Andy in a while and make up some excuse or other for being away. Maria, can I write you a list and you get stuff for me from my house?" Maria nodded.

Maria wasn't quite sure what she was feeling. She had done a lot of thinking in the night and not much sleeping. She could do with going back to her house, as she needed to get more clothes if they were going to be away for a while, and she'd forgotten her favorite lipstick. She felt naked without it. She'd need to figure out what she was going to do about the cat. Morris would clearly not approve if she brought Lady Black back with her, and she doubted Lady Black would be too impressed either. Vanna came back into the living room.

"That was quick."

"Shortest shower ever."

Maria looked at Iris. "So?"

"I'm coming. If Brina thinks I should go, I will because I trust her."

*　　*　　*　　*

Maggie Denhearn

Maria drove slowly up to her house. As far as she could tell, no one was around. The dark car was gone. Somehow it not being there seemed eerier than seeing it. She wasn't quite sure why she decided to slip in the back door rather than the front. She was supposed to be letting people see she was around, that everything was normal.

The house felt strangely empty. Normally when she went away, upon coming back, it felt like her home would welcome her with a loving embrace. This time she felt nothing. The life had gone out of the bricks and mortar that used to be her safe haven. The house was just a shell. She always thought it sad when she saw empty houses or buildings. Even if a place had been unoccupied for just a while, you could still tell. It would always look somehow forlorn, forgotten. It seemed like a house has a soul that departs with its occupants when they leave.

That was it; the soul had left their home. It was clear to her now that Luke knew he might be leaving for a long while when he left the other day. She hadn't seen it then, being too caught up in her own thoughts. She tried to remember the expression on his face, but she couldn't. Would she have looked harder had she known that might be the last time she would see him?

Everything she thought her life had been built on seemed to be a mirage, fading on the horizon: her husband, her job, herself. The mirage was evaporating, and with it everything she thought she knew, yet to be replaced by anything else.

It was too early for a drink, and there was a lot she had to do. First, find her lipstick. There was something about the crimson color and the way the smooth cream of it felt on her lips that felt oddly reassuring. With one application it created her party face, the one she presented to the world: strong, capable, cool. She had become so adept that she could apply it perfectly without using a mirror. She didn't usually bother with eye makeup, apart from mascara, and only occasionally applied powder. But lipstick—she definitely felt vulnerable without it. She could handle anything with that mask on. If people looked at her lips, they would focus on what she was saying and wouldn't notice that what she actually meant was hiding in her eyes.

Grabbing a few more clothes and shoes, she stuffed everything into a large duffle bag. Ordinarily she was meticulous about the way she packed.

When the Universe Called

Each item had to be carefully placed. There was no time. She already had her passport and a photo of her parents and her grandmother. She picked up a necklace Luke had bought her as a first anniversary gift—diamonds.

She went into her office. She couldn't place what it was, but something was telling her to go and have a look around, that she'd forgotten something. She rummaged through the papers stacked neatly on her desk. Nothing. She'd already taken her laptop with her and her iPad. The strange niggle telling her to keep looking wouldn't go away, even though she didn't know what she was looking for.

Delving into the drawers of the large dresser underneath the window, scanning the bookshelves, it hit her—literally. A large tome fell down from the top shelf, except it wasn't a book. It was one of those boxes disguised as a book. She didn't recognize it. It didn't look like anything she would buy. It was locked. She took it into the kitchen and, finding a screwdriver, managed to pry it open. There were some papers and a memory stick. She was sure this is what she had been hoping to find. Brina's startling news of the evening before had prompted her unconscious into wanting to find something that would give her some clue as to who Luke really was. She flicked through the papers. There was a sealed envelope, addressed to her in Luke's handwriting.

Nausea washed over her again. Clearly he had intended her to find this. A sudden noise in the kitchen made her jump. She stuffed everything back into the box and nervously headed to where the noise was coming from. When she saw Lady Black coming in through the cat flap, she let go of her breath. It was time to go, though. She would have to open the envelope later.

She was just in time. As she pulled out of her street onto the main highway, she saw a police cruiser turning onto her road. It was unlikely they were heading anywhere other than her house. She dialed Vanna's number.

"Are you ready?"

"Nearly. Are you okay, Maria? You sound odd."

"I'm fine. I'm on my way. Be ready in five."

* * * *

Iris stood for a few moments on the threshold, not quite daring to open the door. She hadn't realized how hard it would be to come back home. The

Maggie Denhearn

tingles on the back of her neck were growing, and her breath quickened. Was this how it felt for others who return to the scene of a crime? She glanced around the street. No one. Maria had dropped her off ten minutes earlier, and she still hadn't managed to get as far as going inside. Finally Iris slowly opened the door and stood for a few moments in the hallway. A faint aroma of bleach mixed with coffee wafted around the hallway in the breeze from an open window. She stopped. As far as she could remember, she hadn't left any windows open. She could faintly hear the radio on in the kitchen. She certainly hadn't left the radio on or the coffee maker. Was it the police? It would seem odd if they were making coffee and listening to the radio. Trevor was dead, so ... Iris quickly ran through in her mind all the possibilities of who it could be.

"Hi, Granny."

Iris jumped back a step and covered her mouth to stop herself from screaming.

"What are you doing here? How did you get in?" She'd totally forgotten about Charlotte.

"Sorry, I didn't think you'd mind. You left the back door unlocked."

"Did I? Oh. No, I don't, I don't mind, of course I don't. Sorry, I'm just surprised. How lovely to see you!" Iris eyed her granddaughter, who looked remarkably disheveled. It took some doing to look that bad. "Charlotte, are you okay love? You look, erm ..." Iris stopped herself, trying not to say anything tactless.

"I'm in a bit of trouble, Grannie. I need some help. And so does a friend."

"What is it?" Iris slumped down in one of the kitchen chairs, her initial gut-wrenching fear of finding the police or gangsters in her kitchen returning to exhausted anxiety.

"Well, I've kind of messed up." Her granddaughter sounded sheepish.

"Could you pour me some coffee, dear? Then tell me all about it."

As Charlotte briefly gave what was obviously the abridged version of the last couple of days, Iris tried to stay focused on what her granddaughter was telling her. It was apparent there was a lot she either wasn't telling her or was "adapting" to suit her grandmother's ears, and for that Iris felt oddly grateful.

Life was speeding up again, and right this minute it was going far too quickly. She couldn't keep up. All she could gather was that Charlotte and a

When the Universe Called

friend were trying to avoid someone they'd got on the wrong side of, for a reason she didn't disclose, and Iris felt disinclined at this point to ask. That would open a can of worms Iris wasn't at this particular moment capable of coping with.

Seeing her granddaughter, Charlie … Charlotte, evoked both pleasure and pain. It warmed her to see Ena reflected in Charlotte's eyes, and it broke her heart each time she was reminded that her own daughter was never coming back. She did not miss the irony of the years she had begged and pleaded with a God she didn't even believe in to bring her daughter back to her, to raise her from the dead. When Brina had started teaching her about manifestation, she had suggested Iris try it to bring her lost granddaughter to her. She had nothing to lose by trying. Only in this moment did it register that perhaps Charlotte turning up in her life wasn't the wonderful coincidence she had thought it to be.

It had been nearly ten years since Ena had died and less than three months since Charlotte had knocked at Iris's door. Iris had not told Charlotte exactly how her mother had died, only that she'd been ill for some time. She had managed to skirt around the exact details, and so far Charlotte had not asked anything further. It seemed she was not yet ready to hear. Ena had never said who Charlotte's father was. And Iris had not asked Charlotte if she knew. Iris didn't want to know. Nor did she want to know whether, in finding her grandmother, Charlotte had also sought out her father. If there was no face to imagine at which to vent her rage, she could keep it neatly locked inside, keep her fury safe from doing harm.

"Grannie?"

"I'm listening, dear. So if your car broke down in the middle of nowhere and you had to leave it, how did you get from the barn to the ferry and then to here?"

"Promise you won't freak out?"

"I don't have the energy."

"Well, we had to walk for ages. It took us most of yesterday to get to where we found a car that we could easily sort of 'borrow' without anyone noticing, and then drive to the ferry terminal. We slept in the car overnight and came over on the ferry first thing this morning."

Maggie Denhearn

Iris pondered this. Such behavior seemed somewhat extreme just for having upset someone. There were gaping omissions in her granddaughter's account.

"But we'll give the car back, I promise. We had no choice, honest."

"Well, stuff happens. Where's this friend of yours?"

"Well, that's the other thing. He's ... well ... he's a work colleague ... well, one of my bosses ... and erm ..."

"What?"

"Promise you won't lose it?"

"Of course I won't. Why would I do that? Why do you keep asking if I can control myself?"

"Well, I'm not sure you're going to be too thrilled to see him, that's all."

"Charlotte you're being silly. Why would I not like one of your friends?"

"Well, that's just it. He's more than a friend. ... He's also my erm, my biological father."

Iris glared at Charlotte, carefully putting down her coffee cup, trying to keep her hands steady. There had been times when, against every fiber in her body, Iris couldn't help but imagine having a conversation with this faceless, nameless man, the one who she believed had let her daughter down so terribly, who had left her to her own despair. Now she was afraid. Her anger had been let loose, and she wasn't convinced she could keep it in check ever again.

"I don't want to meet him." She got up and walked across the kitchen to pour another cup of coffee, tensing every muscle in her body as she tried to maintain her composure. More stimulation probably wasn't the best idea, but she needed to be doing something with her hands. At least if she threw hot coffee over him, that couldn't do too much harm.

"Look, I know this is awkward, I get it. I thought you might react like this."

"No Charlotte, you don't! And I'm sorry, but I don't want to meet him."

"Okay, whatever, but we're all here now, and he's upstairs. I'm sorry, I didn't know what else to do but to come here, and I couldn't leave him behind." Right on cue, Iris heard heavy footsteps coming down the stairs.

"Hello Iris." A man's voice came drifting in from the hallway, a voice Iris recognized.

244

When the Universe Called

"Luke?"

"I don't understand. Charlie, I thought you said it was your ..." Iris wondered if a light really did go on over your head when you had that sudden flash of clarity. It wasn't like you were ever in front of a mirror at the time to be able to check.

"You mean ...?"

Luke felt distinctly uncomfortable. He didn't dare sit down so remained hovering in the entrance to the kitchen. He had met Iris only a few times and had no idea until Charlotte brought him here this morning that there was any connection between his daughter and one of Maria's friends. Charlotte had never mentioned her grandmother once to him. He glanced over at his daughter, who seemed to be doing a fine job of avoiding eye contact with him. Iris was looking disturbingly flushed. Turning her back on Luke, she switched on the cold tap at the sink and began splashing water on her face. Slowly, she turned back around. Luke continued standing in the doorway, waiting, not sure what to do. Charlotte was still sitting at the kitchen table, now looking back and forth between him and her grandmother, suddenly looking very childlike.

"So do you know each other then? Have you met before?" Charlotte sounded dazed.

Iris stood still a moment, then through gritted teeth said, "You can explain, Luke. And then start talking to me."

Luke coughed, vaguely hoping that if he did so hard enough, a gaping hole would open in the ground and swallow him up.

"Iris and I have met, briefly, a few times. She and Maria belong to the same running group."

"So she knows that you're my father?" Charlotte turned to Iris, looking for an answer. Iris remained mute, stony faced.

"Not exactly. I didn't know that Iris is your mother's mother ... I mean your grandmother. Ena and I met in Vancouver. We never came over to the Island together, so I never met her parents, and she didn't talk about them." He shot a glance at Iris. "Sorry, I er, I honestly had no idea."

"Wow! No wonder Grannie looks like she wants to kill you."

Maggie Denhearn

"Apparently there's a lineup for that." Luke felt decidedly abashed. He studied his fingernails, doing everything he could to avoid looking at Iris. This could not be happening to him, not right now. And what was Maria going to say? Brina's words ebbed and flowed in his mind. He needed to stay focused on what was important at the moment. And at this precise moment, that was making sure all of them got clear of the Consortium.

"What do you want?" Iris expressed the question to Luke, her voice quivering.

"We need to hide here for a bit."

"I'm not sure that's going to work."

"Grannie, please. I wouldn't ask if I—we—weren't desperate. There are things I've not quite explained, and I can't just now, so you'll have to just believe me when I say it's so important. Please."

"You don't understand, Charlotte. I'm guessing you've not heard the news."

"Well, not for a few hours."

"It's …" Iris stopped. "It's nothing. I was, erm, going up to a friend's in the mountains for a few days. How about you come with me?" Something in Iris's manner made Luke catch his breath. She was up to something.

"What's going on, Iris?"

"What do you mean?"

"There's something you're not telling us."

"You're a fine one to talk!"

"Look, there's no time for you and me to get into an argument. We both want Charlotte to be safe, so how about you tell me what's really going on?" He could see Iris knew he had caught her in a lie.

"There's no time for all this chatter. Charlotte, you come with me, please dear." She eyed Luke. He felt her antipathy for him pouring forth. "I'm sorry, Luke. It's best for Charlotte if you don't come. You can take my truck and anything else you need from the house, but I can't help you any more than that. And so we're clear, I'm only offering that because of Charlotte."

"But Grannie, can't he …?"

When the Universe Called

"Charlotte, it's okay." Luke walked over and hugged his daughter. It was the first time. She froze at first, then softened, hugging him back. "Charlotte, it's for the best. I don't want you to get hurt. It's safer if you go with Ir ... your grandmother. I'll text you when I'm settled somewhere." He looked across at Iris and nodded grimly. Luke watched as Charlotte hesitated.

"I'm going to get some things together. It's up to you, dear." Iris waited for Luke to move out of the doorway and went upstairs.

Eagle Cove, Sunday, March 16, 2014

Brina heard the door of the Kavama tinkle, and she came out from behind the curtain, ready for the next customers. Two elderly women in golfing gear were peering around, as though they'd stepped in something unpleasant. One of the women went to take a seat, carefully taking out a linen hanky from her Gucci bag and dusting the chair over before slowly edging down as though she were about to sit on sharp glass. The other sidled up to the counter, squinting at the menu above, too vain to put on her reading glasses, it would seem. Brina was about to continue puttering around when she stopped. There was something familiar about this woman that she couldn't place.

"I'll have a latte to go." Her voice was curt, perfunctory, a woman not used to offering pleasantries. She was thin in a dry, could-snap-any-moment kind of way that not even expensive designer clothing could camouflage. She turned to her companion.

"Dolly, have you decided?"

Dolly cringed, wrinkling the fake orange tan of her face even further so that she looked like a withered nectarine. "Latte too. I suppose it's hard to get *that* wrong." She smoothed her white linen shorts.

"That's two lattes to go. Large."

Brina felt her heart constrict. She knew that voice, that demeanor. She dared to look closely into the woman's eyes. It was her, it had to be. The years had made their mark to be sure, but the likeness was still there, a shadow of who she used to be.

"Oh, and Bailey, perhaps something sweet. You choose."

247

Maggie Denhearn

"Tulia, will you serve please?" Brina was unable to hide the tremor in her voice. She quickly drew back and went to hide behind the curtain, but it was too late. In a split second Bailey's expression changed from irritation to dismay as she caught sight of Brina's hand and the diamond-shaped birthmark. They exchanged a look of mutual recognition.

CHAPTER 19

Mid-morning Thursday, April 17, 2014

Kali started turning the mixture over in the bowl, carefully following Brina's instructions.

"What are we making now exactly?"

"Applesauce muffins."

Kali pondered this for a moment. While the others were off, potentially putting their lives in danger, she was baking muffins.

"Why?"

"Because it'll soon be Beltane." Kali looked at Brina, nonplused. "Beltane is one of the Sabbats, or seasonal Gaelic celebrations. It's usually celebrated May first, or with a bonfire the evening before, to mark the beginning of summer. It's a time to think of abundance and growth. Apples represent our immortality. They are a reminder that we are constantly creating and that we need to be mindful of what we think about, as each thought is an act of invention. It seems apt to make them. And we need something to raise the positive energy between us, to lift our spirits to get through the next few days."

Kali paused. "Chocolate. I've been hankering after chocolate, but there isn't any here. That would cheer me up, raise my energy."

"Did you ask any of the others to get you any?"

"No, I didn't think of it until after they'd left."

"Good. So try this. Imagine the kind of chocolate you like, not just any old chocolate, something special. Close your eyes. Imagine the look of the

Maggie Denhearn

wrapper ... the feel of the foil as you peel it back ... the velvety touch as you pop a piece into your mouth ... the creamy texture and sweet rapture as it melts in your mouth ..." Kali started to salivate.

"If you can describe the experience of eating chocolate so well, how come you didn't bring any?"

"Because I know that when I want some, it'll be around. Keep at it. Imagine you're already eating it."

"Why?"

"Because it's the feelings that are attached to what you want to manifest that are so powerful, so if you want to manifest it, you need to imagine how you feel when you eat it."

Kali considered this for a few moments as she continued folding over the muffin mixture. It would be easier just to call Vanna or Maria and ask them to pick some up for her, but she was intrigued; it was worth having a go.

Brina dipped her finger into the bowl. "Hmm, good. The muffin cases are all ready."

Kali was glad to have something else to focus on. The morning was dragging. She knew she should have called Andy, but couldn't face having a conversation with him so opted to send him a text instead, pretending she'd decided to go shopping in Victoria for a couple of days. She was in no hurry to find out what Andy might be involved in or to experience the kind of revelations Maria was going through. The sun was streaming through the window and she heard the birds singing. It was so blissfully quiet here. Kali poured the raw muffin mixture into the cases and put them in the oven, setting the timer, then went out onto the deck. Breathing in the scent of the fresh spring air and closing her eyes, she imagined she could smell chocolate.

*　　*　　*　　*

Brina wondered how Iris was getting on at home. She wasn't sure exactly why she had felt Iris needed to go back there, only that she did. She lifted the lid on her laptop and typed in her password. Clicking on her email account, she scanned through her inbox. There was a message from Darcy, finally. The Consortium was definitely moving forward with the bill. A report had

When the Universe Called

been tabled yesterday. They were ready for the third reading. After that only Senate approval was needed, and given that most of the Senate either belonged to the Consortium or were being bribed or blackmailed by it, that part of the process was a mere formality. FPH would have the documentation ready for Torporo in the next few days. The only person who had a hope of stopping this now was Brina.

Brina read the message quickly a couple of times and then deleted it from her inbox and also from the trash box. She hoped Darcy was taking the same precautions. With each message or communication to Brina, Darcy was putting her own life on the line. She stood up and began pacing back and forth, leaning heavily on her cane. She needed to stretch, the pain in her hip ever present. She rummaged in an amethyst-colored velvet bag and pulled out a stone. She held the stone in her hand, contemplating the symbol on its smooth surface: journey. Kali came back into the kitchen.

"Not interrupting you, am I?"

"No, no. Just catching up on a few bits and pieces." She saw the look on Kali's face.

"I know I'm old, but I do know how to use the Internet." Kali reddened.

"I think I'll lie down. I'm feeling a bit odd still. How long do the effects of Rohypnol last again?"

"I thought you would be over them by now, but you've had a lot to deal with. I'll make you another tonic. I need your help soon, though. We need to talk about how you're going to hack into the FPH computers up at Gold River. I need to know how long it'll take you."

"That depends on their security system and a number of other factors. I won't be able to tell until we get there, unless you have remote access."

"I don't. Go lie down; we can talk in a bit. You'll need your energy for later."

* * * *

Luke stopped talking as soon as he heard Iris come downstairs. He hoped Charlotte would go with her, but he wasn't about to force the issue. She was a grown woman and capable of making her own decisions. He only hoped for all their sakes that she started making better ones, particularly

Maggie Denhearn

since he'd spent part of the night telling her what Bailey and the Consortium were involved with.

"I'm leaving." Iris was speaking to Charlotte, avoiding looking at Luke.

Charlotte glanced across at him. "I'm coming too, Grannie." Luke nodded. There was nothing else to say.

"Maria is picking me up." Luke stiffened. Maria had been leaving him message after message, but he had not yet responded. He wasn't sure how he could even begin to have a conversation with her. This wasn't how he'd planned her finding out that he had a daughter. He only hoped Charlotte would be able to keep her mouth shut about the Consortium and that Iris would keep her promise not to mention she'd seen him. He'd managed to cover up so much over the last twenty years. It was like he'd spent all that time pedaling backward, and now someone was asking him to go in the opposite direction. His mind and his body were locked, and he wasn't entirely sure how to change, or even if he could.

The conversation he had been avoiding with Maria was looming, and he would have to tell the truth eventually. He closed the door behind Iris and Charlotte as he saw Maria's car pull up. Better that she didn't see him right now. He needed to text Brina again to see what was going on, though it seemed a lost cause now, trying to stop the bill going through. One more victory for the Consortium. He felt his stomach sink, standing at the side of the window behind the curtain to watch Charlotte and Iris leave. Charlotte turned, like she was searching for him. He ducked back behind the curtain. It wouldn't be fair to make her doubt her decision to leave him behind. Or for his wife to see him.

* * * *

Charlotte saw Maria's eyebrows shoot up her forehead when she spotted her coming toward the car with Iris. She turned back toward the house to check if her father was waving, but he was nowhere to be seen. As she got into the car, the tension hit her as though she'd slammed into a brick wall. Maria said nothing, but her expression spoke volumes. Whatever Maria was thinking, it was evident that she did not like Charlotte. She had sensed this a few days ago, but not nearly to this degree. Charlotte squirmed as she put

When the Universe Called

on her seatbelt and settled into the plastic seats. The words *frying pan* and *fire* came to mind. Already she was regretting her decision to come with her grandmother.

"Maria, we need to go. Sorry, I'd forgotten … you two haven't met, have you?" Iris looked from Maria to Charlotte.

"We have, actually. Charlotte works with Luke," Maria said sharply. She turned to Charlotte. "Not working today? I thought you'd be in Vancouver, with Luke on his so-called 'business trip.'" Her grandmother must have picked up on the air quotes.

"You mean you know?" Iris sounded incredulous. "I was just fretting how I was going to tell you."

Charlotte felt heat rising up her neck and face, stifling anything vaguely coherent she might have been able to utter.

"I er …"

"Hang on … know what?" Maria faltered. "Iris, what are we talking about here?"

Iris glanced nervously from Maria to Charlotte. "Oh my! You don't know, either, do you?" Charlotte put her hand on her grandmother's arm, as she appeared she might swoon.

"What? Iris, tell me, what are you saying?" Maria was turning redder and redder.

Charlotte wasn't sure whether she should be offended that Iris and Maria were discussing her as though she were invisible, or grateful that she wasn't directly involved in the conversation. She should have stayed with Luke. Reenacting some kind of Bonnie and Clyde escapade, albeit the father–daughter version, suddenly seemed preferable to being part of some Jerry Springer-like talk show extravaganza.

Her life seemed to be turning into a full-on Greek tragedy. When she came looking for her birth family, this wasn't quite what she had been hoping for. Corporate fraud and crazy middle-aged women wasn't what she'd had in mind. Nor was being accused of some kind of reverse Oedipal relationship with her father. She rather hoped they could save this conversation for another time, as Maria's driving was already frighteningly erratic.

"Grannie, can we talk about this later?"

"Grannie? *Grannie?* Charlotte's your granddaughter?"

Maggie Denhearn

"Yes. Don't you remember me telling you about my daughter and the child she put up for adoption?"

"Yes, but I thought you had a grandson for some reason."

"No, it's Charlotte. I do call her Charlie, so perhaps that's why. Anyway, I didn't know you knew each other. I didn't know she worked with Luke either, or that he's her father. Not until just now, that is."

"What? Charlotte is Luke's daughter? My husband Luke?" Maria swerved, almost letting go of the steering wheel.

"Grannie! I really think we need to let Maria concentrate on driving, don't you? I'm sure we can all discuss this later." She glared at her grandmother. Iris put her hand to her mouth and said nothing further. "Maria, for what it's worth, I did keep asking him to tell you ... By the way, where exactly are we going?"

"To pick up Vanna." Maria spoke through gritted teeth, as though trying to hold in some kind of explosive force that any minute now would erupt.

Charlotte sighed and stared out of the window. That wasn't helpful. She had no idea who this Vanna was. It was going to be another long day. She really wished she'd had time for a shower and to change her clothes. She felt grungy. And hungry. She closed her eyes and tried not to watch the road as Maria weaved in and out like she was trying to avoid something that only she could see.

*   *   *   *

Brina put a pot of water on the stove to boil and started adding some dried blueberry leaves, all the while contemplating what they needed to do in the next few hours. Letting the leaves infuse for several minutes and using a pestle to crush them into the water, she strained the liquid into a cup, added a large teaspoon of honey, and handed it to Kali, who was still dozing on the sofa.

"Drink this. It'll do you good."

"What is it?"

"Blueberry tea with honey. Drink as much as you can."

She watched as Kali sniffed the concoction suspiciously, then finding that it smelt pleasant, took a small sip.

When the Universe Called

"Don't worry, it's sweet. Get some rest. The others will be back soon."

Brina returned to her laptop and began reading the latest news on FPH's website. What she knew of the company and what was written on the website made it seem like there were two completely different companies. She bit her lip, trying to breathe and to stay calm. Now was not the time to give in to her anger.

Leaning back in her chair, she began flicking through the memories in her head as though she were fingering the pages of a catalogue. Connection after connection had brought her closer to the Consortium as she had planned, as she had manifested—and closer to Frost. He would be nearly eighty-eight now. As long as he drew breath he was dangerous.

As for Alexis Bailey, she had done well for herself. The years had not diminished her; she had always been a powerful woman. Her political sway was self-evident. It didn't take much to figure out that she was angling to take over from Frost. It was just a matter of time.

It would take more than getting rid of Frost to bring down the Consortium. Brina's feelings were bittersweet. On the one hand, she felt exhilarated at the thought their battle could soon be over, at least the first one. On the other hand, she felt fearful. Despite her encouragement of everyone last night, she was not convinced they were ready. Their manifestation skills were haphazard at best. There were dangers with such powers if you didn't know how to channel them properly. Iris and Trevor were a case in point. Brina had hoped, counted on more time to train them, but circumstances were taking over.

A few months ago she had started having premonitions again. She had not exactly been surprised to see Bailey come into the coffee shop last month, but the foresight was still too new for her to have been able to avoid the meeting. And although she did not know how it would happen, she had come to terms with the fact that soon she and Frost would also meet again. There was an inevitability to it she couldn't explain.

She had said nothing of this to the others, not even Luke. She couldn't explain how her ability to intuit seemed to be changing. There was no logical pattern to it. It was merely that she had started "seeing" or "dreaming" things, just as she had as a child when she realized someone was going to

Maggie Denhearn

murder her father. Her powers were moving beyond reading others, beyond manifestation, but she was still unable to control them.

She wished she'd foreseen Noah's accident. She wished she could have stopped Iris from hurting her husband. Some events are set in karmic stone. She couldn't tell what would happen with the Consortium. And for months now, Frost had been passing in and out of her thoughts. For the last twenty-four hours it was like he wouldn't leave her. His gray, translucent apparition was standing over her, watching her every move.

*　　*　　*　　*

Charlotte tensed up and held on to the headrest in front of her as the car wheels screeched and the hood bore down on a woman standing on the sidewalk with a small white dog.

"What on earth do you think you're doing?" Letting go of the leash, the woman in the road was yelling at Maria, who threw open the car door and jumped out.

"Vanna, I'm *so* sorry!"

"You nearly ran over Morris!"

"And you, not just your stupid dog."

"He's not a stupid dog!"

"Ladies, ladies, can we keep things calm, please!" Iris got out after Maria and was picking up what Charlotte assumed to be this woman Vanna's things, now strewn all over the ground.

"Come on, there's no time for this. We have to go."

Vanna glared at Maria.

"I'm sorry. I am. I got distracted." Maria looked flushed and shaken.

"Distracted?"

"Vanna, Vanna!" Iris tugged on Vanna's sleeve and pointed in the direction of her dog, who was scurrying off.

"Oh crap." Vanna ran after him, shouting something Charlotte couldn't quite make out.

Charlotte sighed. This would have been funny if the situation weren't so serious. Heeley was still after her, of that she had no doubt. She could only hope that this place her grandmother was taking her to was sufficiently out

When the Universe Called

of the way that she could have some breathing space to figure out what she was going to do.

Pulling her phone out of her pocket, she checked it for messages. Nothing. Charlotte stared out of the window again. Vanna was now dragging her dog, which seemed less than willing to come along. Smart dog. Vanna appeared to hesitate, then grabbed the dog and finally got in the back of the car beside her. Charlotte considered introducing herself but thought better of it. The less she said about herself the better for the moment. She yawned as they set off again. The Oceanside highway rolled gently past. There was a bewitching charm to the Island that Charlotte felt to be almost magical at times. Today the words *twilight zone* came to mind. She wished she were a thousand miles away—on her own. She knew how to be alone.

*   *   *   *

Kali poked the embers and put a couple more logs on the fire, then closed the stove door. She felt chilled and hot at the same time. The blueberry infusion had made her feel somewhat better, but her head continued to feel heavy, and she still couldn't seem to shake the grogginess that she'd been wearing ever since she'd woken up after her kidnapping. Or rather, since Noah had smashed his head against that rock. She desperately needed to find relief from the brain fog if she was going to be any use at all later on.

Her mind was doing the action replays of the last few days, and although they were slightly less frequent, they remained equally vivid. She should try to focus on chocolate. That's what she should do. This whole manifestation thing was most likely the musings of a dear but peculiar elderly lady, but it couldn't hurt to try. Musing on mint chocolate or almond and raisin was more appealing than hearing that crack and seeing the look in Noah's eyes after he crumpled to the forest floor.

She wished it were possible to go back in time. Given the choice, she'd scroll back to the day before her mother had walked out on her and her father when she was eleven years old. Even if she couldn't stop her mother leaving, knowing she was about to would have somehow made a difference. Everything in her life led back to that single point in time. She wasn't entirely sure how, but the backward glance she'd seen her mother give as

Maggie Denhearn

she walked out of the house—that was the pivotal moment when everything had changed for Kali, and not for the better. That was the last time she'd ever seen her, and the moment her father had stopped living, even though his heart continued to beat for another six years. If that moment had been different, somehow the whole Noah thing would never have happened, she was sure. And quite possibly she wouldn't have married Andy, either. She'd have made better choices. She'd have listened to her heart rather than to her fears.

"Life is how it's supposed to be." Brina's voice broke into her thoughts. Kali turned to look at her but didn't know what to say. She didn't understand.

"We're here to learn certain lessons. It's not about what other people in our lives do. It's about how we react to what life brings us. It's about the choices we make." Kali felt tears rising up again. Brina continued.

"Emotions are fine. It's okay to be happy, sad, and angry. Don't try to hold them in. It's the holding them in that causes energy to be stuck inside you, and that's when we get sick."

"I have to confess, Brina, I find it hard to know what you're talking about a lot of the time. I'm much better with computers."

"I know, dear. And right now I'm very glad of your gift. The others will be back any minute, so we must get ready. ... We need to do some smudging."

"Smudging?"

"Sort of like spiritual housecleaning. We'll do that when the others get back. We need to get rid of all this negative energy that's been accumulating."

"Of course we do," Kali muttered. Brina was behaving more and more weirdly.

"They're back." Brina opened the door and went out onto the deck. Kali went out to join her. Straining her eyes across the gray horizon, a film of gray mist drifting down upon them, she couldn't see or hear anyone coming along the dirt road. "Where?"

"They'll be here in a few minutes. They're on their way."

* * * *

When the Universe Called

No one had spoken for a long while by the time Maria pulled to a stop in front of an old, run-down cabin. They had been driving for about an hour, moving higher and higher up into the mountains and bumping along increasingly remote roads. The last had been nothing more than a dirt track, lined by huge balsam and maple trees on either side. As Maria began to drive slower and slower, the narrower the road, the more ominous everything felt. It was barely mid-afternoon, but dark enough to need headlights. It was one of those dismal April days that throw you back to the fall and leave you wondering whether some being in the heavens has thrown a shroud over the sun.

Charlotte kept looking at her phone, still hoping for a message from Luke. Nothing. An elderly woman, leaning heavily on a cane, robes flowing and long silver hair flying behind her in the breeze, came out to greet them, giving each a hug in turn, including Charlotte. She stifled the urge to push her away.

"Nice to meet you, Charlotte. I'm Brina." Charlotte smiled and said nothing. How come she knew who she was? Iris must have sent her a text. More old ladies; just what she didn't need. It would have been safer if she'd stayed with Luke. Regret filled her stomach like concrete being poured into a foundation. Feeling incredibly heavy, she could barely move her legs up the few steps into the cabin.

"I know we're not much to look at, dear, but you'll be fine with us, I promise."

Charlotte stared at Brina in surprise.

"That's Brina's party piece," remarked Maria. "She has an uncanny knack for knowing what people are thinking if your guard is down, so be careful with those thoughts of yours."

"I ... er ..." Charlotte stopped, a shiver running through her. Speechless, she followed her grandmother into the cabin, who introduced her to Kali, a young blonde woman with an anxious expression, only a few years older than Charlotte herself. Brina's granddaughter perhaps?

"This is Kali. How are you feeling?" Iris rested her hand affectionately on Kali's arm. Charlotte was reminded that she barely knew her grandmother, knew nothing much of her life. It dawned on her that they had met only a

259

Maggie Denhearn

handful of times. Charlotte had felt the need to keep her distance. Sadness spilled over the regret.

"A little peculiar still. By the way, I don't suppose you brought back any chocolate with you, did you?" Kali looked sickly.

"No, sorry."

"I did." Maria walked through the door and dumped a huge black duffle bag by the woodstove. "Mint chocolate and some almond raisin I had in the fridge. Thought there was no point in leaving it behind." She pulled out a small plastic bag out of her purse. The dull look in Kali's pale blue eyes switched to one of astonishment. Charlotte had never seen such a curious reaction to the sight of chocolate.

*   *   *   *

Judge Rawley had managed to stall signing the search warrants for Luke's and Noah's houses, but he couldn't stall much longer. It would look suspicious. Hopefully Knox, his main contact in the Vancouver Police Department, would have found everything they needed before the local police arrived. Knox had not yet been in touch, and this lapse was frustrating. At least with Bailey in charge, this aspect of their operations would improve. Frost had already let too much slip. As much as he held the utmost contempt for her, he realized the Consortium and everyone's interests would fare much safer in her hands. The judge glanced over at the grandfather clock, standing like a sentry next to his office door. He shouted out to Darcy to come into his office. He hated using the intercom.

"Sir?"

"Let Petturi know the warrants have been signed for both the Morgans' residences."

"Very good, sir. Anything else?"

The judge paused, tapping a pencil on the desk.

"Yes, and get me Frost on the phone."

Darcy nodded and went back to her desk.

It had to be done. The judge had been dreading calling him but could delay it no longer. He knew the proverbial excrement was about to hit the

When the Universe Called

fan and had already started to plan how he would avoid it. Darcy came back into his office.

"No luck getting hold of Frost. No one's picking up at his home. Should I keep calling?"

The judge sighed, continuing to tap the pencil. "Erm, no, no. I'll try myself later."

He coughed. His chest felt tight, and he had a pain in his arm. He needed a vacation. In a couple more weeks, when the bill was passed, he'd take some time off, maybe a long weekend down in Mexico. It had seemed like a long gray winter. He needed more sun than British Columbia could offer. Hopefully, a few days in the warmth would help him shake this enduring weariness he had been feeling of late.

* * * *

They all devoured the soup and bannock that Brina and Kali had prepared as though they'd not eaten for days. Maria was feeling dazed, numb. Thoughts of Luke crowded her mind as she stared across at Charlotte. Daughter? She was confused. She had been so convinced Luke was having an affair. Why had he not told her he had a daughter?

She couldn't look Iris in the eye. The little anyone knew about her and Ena was enough to know that it was too painful a topic to broach. How could she ask? A seismic shift was taking place inside her that was too much to bear. Any minute now a magnetic force would suck her into the catacombs of the earth. She wished it would hurry up and get on with it.

She glanced across at Vanna, who was cuddling Morris and every now and then feeding him a morsel from her plate when she thought no one was looking. It was cute and pathetic at the same time.

Brina broke the silence. "When you're all done eating, there's something else I need to say." The others stared at her.

"That doesn't sound good." Iris echoed the apprehension they all felt at Brina's words.

"There have been some developments since you left this morning." Iris groaned. "I knew it."

261

Maggie Denhearn

Right at that moment they heard a vehicle pull up outside. Maria turned to the door, trying to focus through a vague mist enveloping her senses.

"What the …? I mean, what the …? I thought you said no one knew about this place?" Maria stared accusingly at Brina. Morris, alert to the sound of an apparent intruder, got up and headed towards the door, a low growl brewing in his throat.

Getting up to follow her dog, Vanna peered round the curtains. "It's a truck. I think it's a man getting out." She moved back away from the window and turned to look at the door.

It seemed to Maria that they were all stuck in suspended animation as they heard footsteps crunch the gravel up to the cabin steps. The door creaked open.

* * * *

Bailey sat in Judge Rawley's office, waiting for him to come back from court—some aggravated assault case, according to Darcy. Cases like these would become few and far between once Bill 267 was passed. A drugged population would be much more compliant. She smiled to herself. She had waited a long time for this moment, put up with nonsense from an awful lot of arrogant men who somehow thought they could get one over her, but she had bided her time. Her patience was now being rewarded. According to Darcy, Frost was in a coma. Mary had called her. It was only a matter of time now. With him truly out of the picture, there was no one else to stop her.

A door opened at the back of the office and the judge walked through, black silk court robes fluttering around him. He stopped, staring at Bailey, then slumped down into his chair.

"Can't keep away?"

"It's your powerful charisma. You know how intoxicating I find it."

"Quite." The judge didn't seem in the mood for her sarcasm, though it amused her. "I'm busy. What do you want?" He cleared his throat and poured himself some water from a jug on his desk.

She feigned a look of concern. "Apparently Frost has been in a coma for some hours now. It doesn't look good. The doctors aren't sure he'll come out of it. I guess the shock of hearing about Luke sent him over the edge."

When the Universe Called

"Interesting how that happened." The judge narrowed his eyes and scrutinized her. She didn't flinch.

"Heeley messed up. We can address that later. At least that's one of the brothers out of the way. Right now we have more important issues at hand. I hear the bill is all set to be passed."

"It's in the bag. Parliament will come together after the Easter break. Most people won't have even looked at it, I'm sure."

"Good." There was a pause.

"So why are you here?" Bailey knew the judge trusted her as far as he could throw her, and these days that wouldn't be very far. He was so desperately out of shape. She knew he found her oddly and disturbingly attractive, and she was quite prepared to use that.

"I just wanted to check you were 'on side,' so to speak. I noticed your hesitation at the executive committee meeting. It's important that there be a smooth transition to the new leadership, don't you think? Particularly given how close we are to the bill being finalized—for the good of the Consortium, obviously. If there are any issues between us, I do hope you'll speak freely."

"Obviously," he said curtly. Bailey knew there was not a chance that he would or that she actually meant that. They regarded each other closely. The judge was the first to look away.

"Yes indeed. And if you're asking whether you have my support? Of course. Now if you'll excuse me ..." He turned to his computer and flicked the switch. It was her turn to hesitate. She wasn't used to being dismissed in such a manner, but she would let it go this one time.

*   *   *   *

"Luke! Are you for real?" Maria nearly fell off her chair. "What are *you* doing here? Oh, don't tell me. I don't want to know." She slammed her glass down on the table, so close to the edge that she almost dropped it on the floor. Iris moved it out of reach of her hand before she had a chance to pick it up and hurl it at him.

"There's still too much to be done ... and I couldn't leave you," said Luke meekly.

263

Maggie Denhearn

Maria scowled at him venomously as the others alternated between staring at Luke and looking at her. "In that order? And did you mean leave *me*? Or perhaps your daughter?"

Brina addressed the others, "I think we should give them a few moments."

Maria didn't miss the look that her husband and Brina exchanged before she limped into the back bedroom. Kali, Charlotte, Iris, and Vanna followed her, leaving Maria and Luke standing in the middle of the living room, an island stranded in the middle of the cabin.

"Maria."

"Luke."

"Drink?" Maria reached over for the brandy bottle left on the table from last night, that she had so far carefully avoided.

"How about we go outside for some fresh air?"

"Let's." Maria lurched toward the door, disequilibrium taking hold of her limbs as though they now belonged to someone else. Luke grabbed her arm, guiding her gently through the door. They sat down on the sofa on the deck. Both stared out into the half-light, neither one daring to look at the other. Gray clouds scudded across the somber skyline, moving swiftly as though late for an appointment. The weather on the Island could change in minutes. Realizing there was no time for a long, drawn-out heart-to-heart, Maria finally broke the silence between them. Better to rip off the Band-Aid quickly than to prolong the agony.

"You have some explaining to do."

"I know. I'm sorry." She glanced across at him, seeing the pleading in his eyes.

"Sorry for what?"

"Everything, I suppose."

"Well, that's okay, then." Her tone was deliberately cutting.

"Maria, please, I'm doing my best here."

"Really? Well, so am I. Do you think it's easy suddenly finding all this stuff out, and from my friends too? It's humiliating."

"You mean ..." He hesitated, having no idea how much she now knew or whether there were more surprises to be revealed.

"That your father isn't in fact dead and is actually a millionaire criminal. And that you're caught up in some saving the world crap. Oh yes, and

264

When the Universe Called

that you have a daughter you've elected to not tell me about, yet saw fit to bring her to *our* home. Can you imagine how stupid I feel?" She couldn't be bothered to try and keep her voice down. The sounds of her anger reverberated across the treetops.

"I didn't want to hurt you. I was trying to protect you."

"How exactly was not telling me protecting me?"

"Look, the Consortium is dangerous; you have no idea. If you didn't know what I was up to, there seemed little chance they'd come after you if anything went wrong. And as for Charlotte, well, I just didn't know *how* to tell you about her. You and I planned to have kids. It just seemed very unfair when it didn't work out. Then Charlotte just turned up out of the blue, and I was shocked, and …"

"It *is* unfair." Maria knew she sounded whiny but couldn't stop herself. More than anything she was angry with herself for realizing she still loved him when she actually wanted to despise him. This seemed like a weakness, a betrayal of herself.

"My father … he's a bad man, a very bad man. He desecrates anything he touches. I didn't want him to do that to you. I guess I was scared I'd got that from him too. Keeping you at a distance felt like the best way of showing I care about you."

Turning away from Luke, Maria wiped away the tears now streaming down her cheeks.

"So not telling me you have a child, that was protecting me? Lying about your father, that was protecting me? Who are you? Do you seriously think I'm that fragile? I'm not made of bone china, for God's sake, and this isn't the eighteenth century. I won't break!"

Luke grabbed her hand and pulled her toward him so she had no choice but to look at him. Even in the fading light of the day his eyes sparkled.

"Look at me Maria, please. Maria, I love you." He tried to hug her but she resisted

"There, I've said it. I know I don't say it often enough. But I do, truly. I wrote you a letter. It's hidden in the house. If anything would have happened to me, I wanted you to know the truth."

She tried to pull away but he held on to her hand. His words felt stiff, awkward. His grip was strong; he wouldn't let go of her. Finally she relaxed

Maggie Denhearn

into his grasp and let herself be enfolded in his arms. The feel of his embrace hurt; it had been too long.

"I know. I just found it today. I've not dared read it yet, though."

"I'm sorry, I really am. I thought I was doing what was best."

"Well, for now I'll have to take your word for that. We have to help Brina"

"That's true. I don't expect you to understand, but ... I just hope you can one day."

"I don't know. I'm mad at you."

"I know. And I hope we can work this out. But in the meantime there's bigger stuff at play."

"I know. I know." Maria let him hold her for a few moments and then made to get up.

"We should go in. The others are waiting for us." They held hands as they went back inside. The world was swirling around Maria, and any minute now she knew she would wake up, would be lying in her bed, and this would just have been a dream. She glanced up to see if there was a piano about to fall.

Back inside the cabin, the others were still busy cleaning up in a "we weren't really trying to listen in on your conversation" kind of way. Brina signaled that she needed them all to sit down. She handed Maria a glass.

"Drink this. It'll calm your nerves." Maria did as she was told. Her head was spinning in a nausea-inducing way that was truly unpleasant.

"This morning I got an email from Darcy. Everything is set for the bill to go through. And Bailey knows I'm on to them. Her people are definitely after me. It's only a question of time before she and the Consortium find this place."

"Then we have to act." Luke's voice had a resonance that Maria didn't recognize. She looked across at her husband as they all sat around, looking at Brina for direction.

"After we break into the laboratory in Gold River tomorrow, we'll have to find somewhere else for a while to lie low."

"The lab? What are you planning?" Luke asked.

"We need to get all the information we can about Torporo directly from the computers up there, then send it out on the Internet. It's the only thing I can think of that will at least stop the bill going through, if nothing else.

When the Universe Called

What do you think, Luke?" To hear Brina ask advice from someone else sounded odd to Maria.

Luke paused, rubbing his chin and biting his lip.

"It could work," he said thoughtfully.

Brina smiled.

"Charlotte." He turned to his daughter, "do you have that pen you had earlier? And some paper? I need to make some notes." Charlotte nodded and took out a gold pen and a small notepad from her pocket. It struck Maria as somewhat odd that someone Charlotte's age would have a pen like that. It looked like the kind of pen that was given as a retirement present: heavy and expensive. Luke examined it, almost like he'd never seen a pen before. A faint smile crossed his face.

Maria glanced across at Charlotte. Was there some secret passing between them? A tinge of jealously caught her off guard. Charlotte seemed engrossed in hunting around for something else in her pocket until she finally brought out a stick of lip salve and applied it absentmindedly to her lips, her mind seemingly elsewhere.

"So the plan is we're going to break in tomorrow and hack the computers?" Luke seemed to be talking into the pen.

"That's it." Brina nodded.

Luke got up and headed outside, and reappeared a few moments later with a bag. Vanna came out of the bedroom carrying a printer that Brina had directed her to find under the bed.

"Let's give it a go then," said Luke.

Maria watched Luke as he opened his laptop and began to tap the keyboard, his hands deftly flying over the keys. As he wasn't the boring tax lawyer he had claimed to be all these years, she wondered who he really was. A lock of hair fell across his forehead. She resisted the urge to brush it out of his eyes and closed her eyes, unable to fight a sudden urgent need to sleep.

*   *   *   *

Bailey and the judge stood by Frost's bed. His breathing was strained, but he had managed to breathe on his own without the oxygen mask for the

Maggie Denhearn

last twenty minutes. Mary stood in the shadows, quite obviously pretending to be busy arranging clothes, and trying to listen in on their conversation.

"Do you think he's going to make it?" Bailey glanced away from Mary to look at the heart monitor, hoping for it to stop beeping.

"I'm not sure that's quite the conversation we should be having here." The judge shifted awkwardly in his chair.

"What, afraid he's going to get up and shout at you? Rawley, you are quite spineless sometimes."

"It's called sensitivity, but I'd not expect you to recognize the difference. You should try it some time."

"Highly overrated from what I hear. Mary, dear, could you fetch us some coffee?" Bailey raised her voice, pretending she didn't know Mary could already hear every word they were saying.

"I don't ..."

Bailey interrupted him, waving her hand at Mary, who nodded and left the room.

"I don't care if you don't want coffee. She was eavesdropping. I've never liked how watchful she is."

"Mary's fine. Frost would be lost without her."

"Exactly what we should be afraid of. It's never good for one person to have so much power over another. And if Frost could just hurry up and depart this mortal coil, it would be an awful lot easier."

"Are you sure about that? Just because that'll mean he can't contest your taking over being head of the Consortium, doesn't make you head of FPH."

"I know that. What are you getting at?"

"Think about it. If he dies, FPH still goes to Noah. He's still alive."

"He'll shortly be in our care, so that's not a problem. And if something untoward should happen to Noah, as far as I know, ownership of FPH reverts to the shareholders if there is no apparent heir. I'm sure Frost just assumed it be would one of his sons. I checked with his solicitor; he hasn't changed his will recently. In which case, the majority share belongs to the Consortium. Oh, and I'm the head."

"You've thought of everything."

"Someone has to. Ah, thank you Mary." Mary placed a silver tray laden with a coffee jug, two cups, cream, sugar, and a plate of cookies on a

When the Universe Called

side table next to Bailey and went back to sorting clothes. Bailey poured them both coffee and sat down, not taking her gaze off Frost. She could see his eyelids flickering, his sagging skin almost transparent, a web of veins showing through. *Dreaming or listening?* she wondered. She didn't care whether he had heard their conversation. His time was over, regardless of whether he came out of this alive. After a few sips of coffee, she got up.

"Leaving already? I thought vultures stayed to circle their carrion."

"He's still breathing, my dear Rawley, so there's time enough for that."

CHAPTER 20

Friday morning, April 18, 2014

B rina sat outside on the deck, watching as dawn tentatively crept over the horizon with a stealth that made the change in light almost indiscernible to the naked eye until suddenly it was light. The smell of pine wafted through the air that was crisp and clean. She pulled the duvet she had brought out with her tightly around her, trying to keep the warmth of her bed around her. She let the others sleep. Hers had been a fitful slumber, a dreamtime that only increased her anxiety. More premonitions. Her senses were expanding. She had known who Charlotte was and what she was thinking the moment she got out of Maria's car, and it was their first meeting.

Frost would not leave her. She knew he was sick, very sick. It was as though she could feel the chill of his dying skin near hers, and the sensation left her struggling for air. None of this made sense and only served as a distraction from what she should actually be focusing on. The cabin door opened, and Luke came out, two cups of coffee in hand.

"I thought you might need another cup."

She took it from him and smiled. "Thank you."

"I'm sorry I wasn't in touch more the last couple of days. I thought it would be safer."

"I knew I'd finally hear from you. You're here now, that's what counts. Nothing much is safe at the moment. ... Luke, have you talked with your father at all?"

When the Universe Called

"Tuesday morning was the last time. He wanted to see Noah and me. He's not been in touch since, and after finding out about Noah ... Why do you ask?"

"We didn't' get chance to talk about your brother last night. I'm so sorry." She stared across at him. Other than his frustration, he was adept at hiding his emotions. His eyes were those of a lost little boy. He looked lonely.

"I still can't believe it. It doesn't seem real."

"It really wasn't Kali's fault."

"I know. She and I did talk briefly. She's a mess. At least Heeley didn't get to him. That's the only consolation."

Silence fell between them as they drank their coffee.

The door creaked, and Maria peeked her head around, her hair falling in front of her eyes. Brina was pleased to see she seemed less distracted, had the flush of someone who had slept well. If this plan was to work, they needed Maria to be totally on the ball.

"Morning. We're all wondering what time you want to set off. We're mostly packed up. I am, anyway, and the others seem to be busy."

"We'd better set off soon. We don't want to run the risk of Bailey's people catching us here."

"How could they find this place?"

"I don't know. All I know is that she's capable of anything." Brina sighed and got up, following Luke back inside.

*　　*　　*　　*

The sun was high in the sky as they wound their way along the old island highway. Brina watched the glint of the ocean as rays of sun bounced off the water. This was her favorite time of year. She looked over at Iris, who was driving the truck, deep in thought. She had a different aura about her today: stronger, undaunted. Looking over her shoulder, she saw Maria's car behind. They had had to bring two vehicles, but it was probably just as well. They all knew the deal. If anything went wrong, whoever was able was to would get away as fast as possible, all for the greater good.

Brina wasn't kidding herself that this was the end of the war. It was the first of several battles. As they drove through small communities, she

Maggie Denhearn

wondered whether these were sights she would ever see again. Her growing second sight had its limits. She couldn't tell yet whether she would come out of this alive.

* * * *

It was later than they'd planned when they reached the outskirts of Gold River. By the time they'd sorted out everything they thought they might need; packed Iris's truck and Maria's car; and then run around trying to catch Morris, who had dashed out of the cabin in a bid to be allowed to come along too, it was early afternoon. Maria couldn't help thinking that the FPH laboratory would have been easy to mistake for a country lodge, as its wooden framework blended in with the stunning backdrop of Strathcona Park, mountains forming a giant curtain around an emerald lake.

Maria had wanted to throw up several times on the way there. She had never been very good with winding roads, and the road past Gold River snaked this way and that in a way that left her leaning her head out of the car window and wondering if their journey would ever end. Fortunately, Luke was driving.

The rolling beauty of the mountains, majestic lakes at their feet, worshipping the great kings and queens of rock towering above them, were an awe-inspiring sight, none of which Maria felt fully able to appreciate. The peaks maintained their frosted tops, like whipped cream among the green of the treetops.

This place was good camouflage for the FPH laboratory. No one would ever consider that such graceful scenery could be home to a perfidious institution like FPH. It was only when you got within fifty meters that the electrified fencing and the security cameras strategically placed among various trees became evident.

The lab lay at the end of a dirt road, set back amidst stately Douglas firs, a quarter of a mile off the main highway, which itself was barely wide enough for a car to travel in each direction. Both vehicles stopped in a cloud of dust just after pulling off the highway.

Maria got out of the car as quickly as she could and stood by the side of the road, breathing in the clean, cold air. A wave of relief washed over her.

When the Universe Called

She should have asked Brina for some kind of concoction before they'd left, but she'd forgotten how travel sick she could get. Iris took out a basket with a couple of thermos flasks of coffee and the muffins that Kali had baked the day before. To a casual observer, they were tourists stopping for a comfort break.

The papers that Luke and Kali were pawing over, spread out on the hood of the truck, included details of the security systems of the FPH facility. Maria leaned over Luke, holding on to his shoulders. It seemed such a long time since she had felt such affection for him. She didn't want to think about what it would be like to lose him in all of this. The loss of Noah had yet to sink in for her, but she could see it was taking its toll already on her husband. He looked burned out.

"So tell me again how come you've got all this?"

Luke touched Maria's hand gently. "I managed to convince the manager of the facility that I needed an intimate knowledge of the security systems to ensure that FPH was covered from a legal and insurance point of view, should there be any break-ins and ensuing legal wrangle with the insurance company. I saved the information into my Dropbox account. I was hoping it might come in handy one day."

"That was forward thinking."

"As it happens, yes, it was. The information is about a year old, but I'm pretty sure nothing has changed. I guess we'll find out."

"How are you doing, Kali; think you can remember it all?"

"Already memorized. Did it last night: each and every camera location, setting, timing, and angle. It's not hard. … Well, I guess having a photographic memory helps. I'm pretty sure that if we manage to get into the building, I can disable the entire system within about ten minutes; probably five, but let's say ten."

"Are you all sure about this?" Maria, along with the others, turned to look at Brina.

Brina replied, "Don't forget to breathe, and focus. Concentrate on how you'll feel when this is done. Remember, where your attention goes through all of this is where your energy will go, so make sure it's in a positive direction. Do you all know what you have to do?"

"Yes, yes." Maria couldn't hide her impatience to get on with things. It wasn't exactly nervousness that she was feeling. She wasn't entirely sure

Maggie Denhearn

what the emotion was. At least it was no longer nausea. There was a softness between her and Luke now that she didn't recognize. They were in uncharted territory. She needed to keep moving. The thought of stopping and facing the maelstrom whirling around inside her was far more terrifying than the thought of getting caught breaking and entering.

Maria turned to Kali. "Once you've got us access to the information we need, I'll log on to YouTube and we'll start shooting. I'll take it from there." She wasn't entirely sure exactly what that would look like. She was trusting she would know when the time came.

"I've got the security system figured out. And I'm sure I can hack into the computers." This was a Kali Maria didn't recognize: strong, self-assured.

"Once we have more information about the drug, I'll see what I can do." Vanna sounded the least confident of them all.

"Iris, are you ready?"

"I am."

"Let's do it." Brina strode forward, Iris quickly behind her. Maria was impressed at the speed Brina could muster with her cane. She and the others hung back at a distance.

* * * *

When the two women arrived at the security gate, a couple of men were sitting in the gatehouse, staring intently at the monitors in front of them, one guard facing outward toward the direction Brina and Iris were coming, the other guard facing the facility. Iris looked over, trying not to look as though she was prying, and noticed that instead of showing various images of inside and outside the laboratory, the guard who had his back to them was concentrating on the hockey playoffs.

She coughed. A short, squat man, balding, with an expansive girth, glanced up at them but didn't get up. His spindly partner watching the hockey game didn't even acknowledge their presence. Iris glanced down and could just make out a beer bottle tucked at his feet.

"Yes?"

When the Universe Called

"So sorry to bother you. We've broken down a kilometer or so away, and wouldn't you know it, we can't get cell reception. Could we use your phone to call for help?"

"Sure, go ahead." The short, squat guard turned back to his monitor.

"Yes!" He punched the air triumphantly to the roar of the crowd. Obviously, he was watching the hockey game too. Brina and Iris hovered, but neither man seemed in a hurry to let them get at the phone on the desk right by the open door of the gatehouse. Iris waited a few moments and then cleared her throat. Finally the short, squat guard beckoned them over. As he did so, Iris walked forward. Brina snuck behind her, lunged forward, and grabbed the neck of the skinny guard. Within seconds he was slumped across the console. Like a quick-draw gunslinger, Iris pulled a tiny spray bottle from her pocket and spritzed the face of the other guard. Wrinkling up his eyes, he started coughing and spluttering. Brina grabbed him and squeezed his neck. Within seconds he too was slumped over, unconscious. Iris looked at her dumbfounded.

"I thought we were just going to distract them. What did you just do?"

"Acupressure. If you apply it to certain points it renders someone unconscious, assuming you get the point right and don't accidentally kill them. But not for long, though."

"What's in the spray?" Iris sniffed. The scent was familiar, but she couldn't place it.

"Water and bee pollen. A lot of people find it makes their throat itchy. And chloroform, just to give us more time."

"That's quite the move you do there."

"We should get them tied up. How long will they be unconscious?"

"With that dose of chloroform, about three hours. I'm hoping that'll be enough."

Pulling ropes out of their bags, they set about binding and gagging the guards. The others had now caught up to the gatehouse. Iris gaped as Kali began tapping away on one of the computer keyboards, every now and then giving Vanna instructions to type something on the other console. Luke, Maria, and Charlotte were poised, ready for the signal to move.

"Iris and I will head back to the vehicles and bring them back up to the gate so we can get away quickly if we need to." Brina started walking away.

275

Maggie Denhearn

Iris hurried after her, their part in the plan over for the moment. Iris gazed over at Brina. She looked worn out, her limp now more pronounced than usual.

"Are you okay?"

Brina sighed wearily. "I am, just tired. And my hip is throbbing. I'm glad we have time to sit for a bit while the others work their magic."

"You seem ... preoccupied."

Brina stared at her and smiled tiredly. "It's going to be a long day."

*   *   *   *

Kali continued to tap away on the computer and Vanna followed her instructions.

"Yes! Done it!"

"Wow, six minutes and twenty-seven seconds. You're fast."

"I would have been faster if the computers weren't so slow. I thought this system was supposed to be state of the art?"

"It is."

"Well, whoever sold them the system has ripped them off. It's child's play to get into it. Okay, let's get going." She pressed the button to open the gates in the perimeter fence and they ran in. At the first door, they stopped.

"Damn it!" Kali sighed impatiently and began punching various buttons on a keypad next to the door.

"I don't like this." Vanna stared around, then glanced up at a camera peering down at them. "There's a camera. We're being watched."

"I deactivated those. I just didn't know about the lock on this door. Damn it!" She slammed her hand against the wall in frustration and took a few steps away.

"Take your time," said Luke. "Breathe, center yourself. You won't do this any quicker by getting frustrated."

"I know, Luke, I know. Just ... There, got it!" The door slid open.

"Aren't there any other guards?"

"I don't know. But stop looking for problems, Vanna." Kali strode forward. It had been a long time since she'd had anything to challenge her. She didn't want to admit to the others how much she was enjoying this.

276

When the Universe Called

"It can't be this easy."

"Why not?" The words were barely out of Kali's mouth when a siren sounded. She scowled across at Vanna. "Don't you dare say I told you so!" They started running—Kali first, followed by Vanna, Maria, Charlotte, and Luke.

"Quick, in here!" Kali signaled, and they darted after her into a small side room. She peered out of the tiny window in the door, then ducked down as a couple of men in security uniforms came running past. They waited for the sound of their footsteps to die away.

Kali turned to Luke. "I think your information is out of date."

"It was the best I could get. Sorry."

"No matter. The cameras are disabled. That'll buy us some time."

Cautiously, they edged out of the room and back along the corridor in the direction of where they were originally headed, the siren still blaring. The door with the panel seemed to be jammed open. Kali winced at the screeching as she played with the buttons on the panel and the alarm stopped.

"Finally!"

Walking quickly through the corridors, left, then right, straight, then right again, they all followed Kali through a stark white labyrinth, so clean and bright that Kali wished she'd brought her sunglasses. Conjuring up a picture in her head of the layout of the building that Luke had managed to get hold of, she managed to navigate them to lab 46, home of Torporo. It was a large, open room on the ground floor, the mountains outside looming beyond a wall of windows. Several benches were lined with state-of-the-art equipment that looked like something out of a futuristic horror movie. Kali glanced around for the nearest computer terminal, and only then did she see a gaunt, well-dressed woman sitting on a stool casually sipping from a bottle of mineral water. She was wearing a cerise Armani jacket and black Jimmy Choo stilettos.

Kali stopped in her tracks. Vanna and Charlotte, who were close behind, nearly ran into her. They gawped at the woman who looked more like she should be in a Chanel store shopping for the latest designer clothes.

"What took you so long?" The woman smiled coldly.

"Who is she? It's like she's expecting us." Vanna turned to Luke.

277

Maggie Denhearn

"It's rather rude to talk about someone in their direct presence, don't you think?" Bailey coolly took another sip of water and set the bottle down on the counter next to her, then stood up, extending her arm to Luke.

"Noah, how marvelous to see you. Or is it Luke? You're devilishly hard to tell apart sometimes. Heeley clearly couldn't, so I'm not entirely sure who you are. No matter." She went to shake his hand but his arms remained by his side.

"Bailey." His gaze was steely.

"Oh, call me Alexis, please. Such formality hardly seems necessary." She turned a withering smile on Charlotte. A look of horror was etched across her young features. Kali thought she caught a flash of recognition, and looked between Luke, Charlotte, and the woman, trying to figure out what could be going on.

"My dear, you're looking a little peaky. Your father really ought to take better care of you." She laughed sharply.

"Who *is* this woman?" Vanna was glancing around uneasily.

"This is Alexis Bailey. Former police commissioner, second in command of the Consortium." With his teeth gritted, Kali could barely make out what Luke was saying. His face was flushed with anger, and he held his fists as though any minute he was about to hit someone. Charlotte gulped loudly. Kali suddenly understood why Luke had told only herself and Maria that they would meet Bailey here. Charlotte looked more than a little alarmed at seeing her.

"*Head* of the Consortium. *Head*," Bailey corrected him. Luke seemed to falter.

Bailey continued. "Oh, you've not heard about your dearest daddy? In a coma, poor thing, not expected to last the weekend. Perhaps you ought to be by his side rather than breaking and entering. Do excuse me while I call the police and ask them to come and arrest you. Whoops, that would mean you wouldn't get to see Daddy. Oh dear, such is life." She stood up and pulled out her cell phone from her designer jacket.

"I wouldn't bother." Maria moved forward as though she was trying to protect Luke. When she continued trying to dial, Maria added, "We've blocked the signal. You can't call anyone, or they you for that matter. These jamming devices are very clever." Bailey's face darkened. "No matter. If my

When the Universe Called

people don't hear from me very soon, they'll be in here looking for me in no time. You may as well just admit defeat."

"Well, here's the thing. They won't. You actually sent out an email to everyone saying the operation was off—the one to catch us, I mean. You've sent out a message saying you've already caught us. So your backup won't be coming."

Bailey glared at Maria, still holding her phone, seemingly not sure she believed her.

"Kali hacked into your computer and sent it for you. You really should talk to your computer security people. It only took her a few minutes this afternoon to get into it. And just to make sure, the message went out again an hour ago, but this time from your phone, to all your 'people' as you call them, just in case they're lax in checking their emails."

Kali waved a hand at Bailey to get her attention.

"Hi, I'm Kali. Maria's right. You really do need to do something about your Internet security. It's not all it could be."

Bailey stumbled backward and slumped back down onto the stool, almost missing it and landing on the floor. Kali tried not to snigger. "So, this is the Alexis Bailey who betrayed Brina."

"I, I ..."

Luke smiled triumphantly. "Oh, you're wondering how we knew? That's easy. The pen you slipped into Charlotte's pocket when she met up with you. She found it. And after the evening we spent at Charlotte's parents' house, it was obvious to me that more than the house and the car were being bugged. It didn't take much to figure out it must be that. It's hardly the kind of pen a young woman would buy. I figured the only way to get you off our backs was to draw you in, so I let you hear exactly what you wanted to hear."

Maria added, "No, don't speak. Best not say too much right now. Luke and I are going to tie you up—we won the coin toss—while Kali and Vanna finish what we came here to do."

Her face drained of all color, Bailey went limp as Luke and Maria gagged and bound her, leaving her on the floor in the corner, looking less than elegant.

"Shouldn't be too long," Kali said over her shoulder as she began tapping away on a computer, every now and then giving instructions to Vanna, sitting at another console.

Maggie Denhearn

Kali worked steadily, scrolling through screens, searching the databases, and collating as much information as she could find. Every now and then she glanced around at the others. Maria was staring uneasily at the door through which they'd come, and Luke and Charlotte were having some kind of discussion in low whispers.

"I don't like it," said Maria. "Those guards. Surely they'll come back or raise the alarm." Luke looked up.

"I'll go check."

"I'm coming too." Charlotte went to follow him.

"Me too, then," said Maria. The three of them left, leaving Kali and Vanna tapping away.

The knot in Kali's stomach was tightening. She wasn't sure how much time they had. It wasn't that she couldn't hack quite easily into the system. It was more that it was time-consuming. Her breathing quickened as the sound of footsteps running and shouting suddenly broke the quiet of their work. Vanna stopped and got up, but Kali carried on furiously. She had to do this; she *had* to.

"Vanna, go see if you can close the door. Type in 679484356."

"What? Surely they would use something like retinal scan or fingerprints, not numbers? I can't remember all …"

"They use both, but I overrode the system earlier. It's a series of codes. Quickly, type in 6 … 7 … 9 … 4 … 8 … 4 … 3 … 5 … 6. … Did it work?"

The door to the lab slid shut.

"But what about the others?" asked Vanna, panic evident in her voice. Kali glanced up to see Vanna standing before her, shaking.

"We have to get this information. You know that—whatever it takes."

"I guess, I just …" At that moment there was pounding on the door. Both women turned round. It was Luke. They could just barely hear him.

"It's okay, it's okay, let us in." Through the glass of the door they could see Maria and Charlotte coming running up behind him. Kali repeated the sequence of numbers backward so that Vanna could let them back into the lab.

"What happened?" Vanna sounded out of breath, even though she wasn't the one who had been running.

280

When the Universe Called

"We found the guards. We pretended to let them take us and then Charlotte whipped out one of those spray concoctions that Brina put together and sprayed them. They're out cold. And tied up."

"Oh, thank goodness!" Vanna slumped down on the chair next to Kali. "Please tell me this is working."

Maria, Luke, and Charlotte looked equally exhausted and drained. Kali looked over at Bailey. Her eyes were shut and Kali couldn't tell whether she was sleeping or merely pretending not to pay any attention.

Kali smiled. "Done!"

It had felt like an age that Kali had been working away, but it was only about twenty minutes. Vanna had no idea what she was doing. She was typing in some foreign language that Kali was speaking to her. Information was now flashing up on the screen in front of her. She pored over the first few pages, scrolling down quickly, nodding her head as she made sense of what she was reading. Various chemical symbols and ratios of compounds were listed. She felt herself blanch as she got to the end of the second page. If this was what they were putting into Torporo, no wonder people had died taking it. She glanced up to find the others all staring at her expectantly.

"It's bad," she said quietly, "very bad."

"Are we ready to do the broadcast?"

Vanna nodded at Maria in reply. "Almost. I'll just copy and paste the main bits of information onto one document and print it off so you've got something to read from." She got up and headed in the direction of the sound of a printer, spewing forth paper.

Vanna handed Maria the first three pages of what she'd printed. "Just read that. It's got the main dates of the drug trials, how many people took part, how many survived, and the chemical composition of the various iterations of the drug. Kali's done a great job of pulling off exactly the right information we need from the system."

Kali blushed. "Are you ready, Maria? I've got things set up all ready for you to broadcast straight to YouTube. Once you've done that, I'll copy the information straight onto the Internet for people to read for themselves."

Vanna saw Maria hesitate, then smooth her hair and adjust her blouse. "I'm ready. Let's do it." Her hands didn't shake as she held up the pages Vanna had given her and began reading.

Maggie Denhearn

"Good afternoon from Vancouver Island. This is an important announcement regarding Frost Pharma Health. It's important that anyone who sees this broadcast pass it on. Share it across the globe. We need your help to stop FPH. Over the last five decades, this pharmaceutical company has been dedicated to testing drugs on people ..."

Calmly and with a poise Vanna could not have imagined after seeing Maria so shaken the last few days, they quietly sat back while Maria read to the world the darkest secrets of FPH.

"And all of this has been made possible by the Consortium. The people who we trust in our community have betrayed us: John Frost, owner of FPH; Alexis Bailey, former police commissioner; Judge Argus Rawley ... and many more. ... Stop Bill 267. Say no to forced genetic testing. Don't believe those who say we are defined by our DNA. Read the new research for yourself."

Vanna glanced over at Bailey, still bound and helpless in the corner of the lab. Her eyes were closed, and her body seemed shrunken, like she was slowly dissolving in the corner.

"Our health depends on all of us taking action. Our freedom depends on all of us asking questions of those in authority. ... Don't let FPH get away with this. Thank you."

Maria stopped talking and nodded to Kali, who clicked a button. A huge sigh rose up from everyone.

"We'd better get going. Brina and Iris will be wondering if we're alright." There was silent agreement as they all followed Maria quickly out of the lab.

*   *   *   *

In the light of the YouTube and Internet broadcast by the Vancouver Island women, social activists have been quick to call for the proposed Bill 267 to be scrapped as an infringement of human rights. The prime minister has declined to speak publicly about this, but issued a statement saying that a thorough investigation is now underway. Turning to local news, two deaths in Eagle Cove on Tuesday that were initially thought to be suspicious in nature, have

When the Universe Called

now been confirmed as accidental. An as yet unidentified body and a local lawyer, Noah Morgan, not his twin brother Luke as originally believed, fell victim to a random bolt of dry lightning that then started a forest fire, the first of the season. And now to sports.

Maria switched off the radio. Huddled round the wood stove in a small cabin in Tahsis, hugging mugs of tea and coffee, and eating the last of the apple muffins, Maria sensed the communal feeling of relief. She was studiously ensuring she had as little to do with Charlotte as she could. She wasn't quite ready to face the reality that she had a stepdaughter. She needed more time. Iris, on the other hand, couldn't stop smiling.

"I can't believe it! Can we really be off the hook that easily because of the fire? Am I really off the hook too for … you know?" Iris whispered. Maria saw Iris glance sideways at Charlotte. Apparently she'd still not mentioned to her what she'd done. Charlotte seemed to be hanging off Brina's every word and thankfully not paying much attention to her grandmother. Ever since they'd left Gold River and headed here, Charlotte and Brina had been engrossed in one conversation or another. Maria could understand why Iris was avoiding certain topics with Charlotte.

"Who's place is this again?" Brina didn't seem to hear Maria, so Vanna spoke up.

"Brina's technically, but it was left to her by a family friend or something. I'm not sure where we're all going to sleep, but I guess we'll figure that out." Vanna was enjoying playing tug of war with Morris, who was growling happily as he pulled on an old rag that she had found lying by the hearth. It was a relief to be doing something normal.

Brina overheard her name. "Sorry, Maria. Yes, it's mine. It was left to me only recently. We should be safe here until we can figure out where to go next. I'm pretty sure no one knows about this place. The Consortium won't stop coming after me, though. Or Luke. And now you, for that matter. The rest of you … well, you should be okay."

"Hmm, I don't think they'll be particularly pleased with me either." Charlotte blushed.

283

Maggie Denhearn

"Ah, my dear, yes."

"I er ..."

"No need to explain." Before anyone else could ask why Charlotte should be worried, Brina changed the subject. "So how hard were you all hoping for a positive outcome?"

"Well none of us wanted this to end badly, obviously," said Maria.

"I know you're not convinced, but you will be soon. The power of your thoughts is real."

Brina was tired but felt oddly exhilarated. It didn't matter whether Maria truly believed in the *Law of Attraction* or not. It existed regardless of what any of them thought. Brina was patient. Maria would come around eventually; they all would. They just didn't realize the power they had. Did they really think that all this would have been so effortless without the power of their thoughts, of manifestation? She would need to teach them how to harness the energy better, but there would be time enough for that.

Vanna asked, "What about the whole breaking and entering episode, though? Aren't we still going to be in trouble for that? I'm worried I'll get my permanent residency revoked if I'm convicted of doing something criminal. I don't fancy being deported back to the UK."

"Don't worry, Vanna. I spoke to Petturi earlier." Brina touched her phone lightly as she said this. It had been a while since she and Petturi had spoken. After all this time, he was still watching over her.

"He can get us off the breaking and entering charge on a technicality. He can't do much about the Consortium at this point, though, since he's due to retire in the next couple of months. Some guy named Knox is taking over. I've no idea if he's trustworthy or not. Neither has Petturi. We've made a start, though. After all these years, we've finally made a start."

Brina sipped her tea and leaned back in her chair. Her hip was starting to ache again. She pushed the thought to the back of her mind. She was tired, that was all.

"What's the technicality?" Concern was still evident in Vanna's voice.

"Well, as Frost remains in a coma, according to his will, his next of kin and heir is considered to be the owner of FPH for as long as he is either incapacitated or, when he finally passes. The police finally realized it was Noah who died in the forest fire, which leaves Luke. And Luke can't be

When the Universe Called

charged for breaking into his own company. If he says we were with him, we're all in the clear."

Luke replied, "I'd completely forgotten he'd put us back in his will. I guess he never got a chance to change it. Bailey won't be happy about that."

"I still don't get why they don't know the other body is … who the other body is," Iris corrected herself quickly, glancing nervously over at Charlotte.

Brina hesitated, holding Iris's gaze. "According to Petturi, the lightning struck that body directly. There was nothing left and no teeth to use to check the dental records. I guess whoever it was had taken his false teeth out." Iris put her hand to her mouth, then glanced over at Charlotte again. Brina caught her look and cautioned her with her eyes to say nothing.

"Where is Bailey, by the way?" asked Maria. She had picked up on Brina's signals to Iris. "I didn't like the look of her. There's something about her that makes my skin itchy, and it wasn't just the way she talked as though she had a bad taste in her mouth." She was scratching her arm as she said this.

Brina couldn't help smiling as she replied. "The police found her. Apparently she was more than a little furious by the time they got to the facility. I guess we did take a while before leaving that anonymous tip. She could try to press charges for assault, but it's doubtful she'll try anything, for now anyway. Given what's going viral, she'll be trying to keep a low profile for a little while. This is just the kind of publicity the Consortium is desperate to avoid."

"I'm impressed she got in the building and before we did, too" said Vanna.

Luke laughed tiredly. "When I knew she was listening to us through the bugged pen, I made sure she'd know to get there long before we would. I knew she'd have no trouble getting let in by security. Everyone knows her and is afraid of her. Was, anyway." He sighed.

Brina touched her hip again, wincing. She got up and moved over to the sink, trying to stretch out her leg as she did so. She poured herself some more coffee and remained standing for a while, staring out of the window into the dusk. Cherry blossoms were in full bloom on the trees just outside the front door, raining down scented petals and leaving a soft pink blanket on the ground.

*   *   *   *

Maggie Denhearn

Maria looked over at her husband. "Hang on a second, Luke. If you're head of FPH, doesn't that also make you technically the next head of the Consortium?"

Luke hesitated, then glanced up at her, suddenly aware that she was looking at him. He hadn't been paying much attention to the conversation. Now that they were safe, for the time being anyway, his body was relaxing, and he could no longer avoid thinking about Noah. It was hard to fathom that he wouldn't see his brother ever again. There was a dark space inside him, a void he was afraid of falling into. He ached from the inside out. Luke hadn't even been thinking about his father, or FPH, or about who would head up the Consortium.

"Bailey said she'd taken over already, didn't she? So I guess she's the head now. Be careful what you wish for. I bet she wishes she hadn't taken over from my father. Talk about bad timing." He paused. "I guess I should call Darcy and see what's happening with him."

"If the Consortium is still going strong, doesn't that mean they'll just try again with the bill or something else?"

No one replied to Kali, as the implications of the work still to do slowly started to sink in. Luke knew this was just the first battle. He picked up his phone and got up, hoping the signal would be better outside. There was just enough light for him to make out the outline of the tops of the mountains as he stepped out into the evening. For the first time in a long while, he felt safe, the mountains offering a ring of protection from the rest of the world.

* * * *

Brina closed her eyes wearily and lay back in the armchair. She felt herself being dragged into her unconscious. The air in the cabin was becoming stale. As she slipped into a dream state, she watched herself in her mind's eye get up and follow Luke outside. It was a peculiar experience, being both inside and outside her body at the same time. As her outside self glanced over at Luke, she saw that his phone was pressed against his ear, and that the sound of a car breaking the silence made him look up. It was a dark car—the car that Luke had told Brina had been watching him and Maria for months.

When the Universe Called

Luke froze, and her outside self followed his gaze. A man in a black suit and shiny shoes stepped out of the car and went to open the trunk, pulling out a collapsible wheelchair like it weighed nothing at all. He placed it near the now open back passenger door, then lifted a frail figure out and into the chair. It was as though a saggy suit was slumped in the seat, the skeletal frame inside barely registering, the head covered in an oxygen mask held up to a face by a bony hand. Brina watched herself limp as quickly as she could over to Luke and grab his arm, almost pulling him down as she fell, gasping. Luke caught her in his arms and held her up. Her voice was barely able to whisper.

"John ..." Brina woke with a start, panting, holding her chest, and opening her eyes to find Maria and Luke peering anxiously down at her.

"Are you okay?" Luke took her wrist, trying to feel her pulse. It took a few moments for Brina to recognize her surroundings, to take in that she was in Jakob's cabin.

"We have to leave." She knew it was she who had spoken, yet it felt as though her outside self was still talking from far away. "We have to leave. Now."

"What? You're not well, Brina. It's been a long day, and you need to rest." Maria was pulling a musty brown blanket over her and trying to get her to drink some water. It was a long time since Brina had felt the concern of another human being, the care. She was so used to ministering to others.

"I mean it." Her throat was dry and scratchy. "Trust me. Frost, John, your father ..." She turned to Luke, hoping he would see the pleading in her eyes if not in her voice. "Frost's coming. He knows where we are."

"What? That can't be. How could he?"

She sighed, wishing she could just close her eyes and fall back asleep, yet afraid to do so, scared of what other premonitions her dreams would bring. "I don't know. All I know is that he does and that we have to leave."

"Now?" Vanna's voice came to her at a distance, and she looked across the room trying to focus her eyes. Iris, Kali, Charlotte, and Vanna were all staring at her with looks of confusion.

"Yes ... Now."

ABOUT THE AUTHOR

Born in England, Maggie Denhearn fled back to Canada (for the second time) after an alarming adventure in "love." Bolstered by her view of the Salish Sea, supported by her family and small dog, Maggie has boldly embarked upon her dream of becoming a writer.

Printed in the United States
By Bookmasters